"*The Fisherman* is an epic, yet intimate, horror novel. Langan channels M. R. James, Robert E. Howard, and Norman Maclean. What you get is *A River Runs Through It*...Straight to hell."

—Laird Barron, author of *X's for Eyes*

"Stories within stories, folk tales becoming modern legends, all spinning into a fisherman's tale about the one he *wishes* had gotten away. Langan's latest is at turns epic and personal, dense yet compulsively readable, frightening but endearing. Already among the year's very best dark fiction releases."

—Adam Cesare, author of *The Con Season* and *Zero Lives Remaining*

"In this painful, intimate portrait of loss, two damaged men take steps toward redemption, until the discovery of an obscure legend suggests a dangerous alternative. Can men so broken resist the temptation to veer away into strange, unfamiliar geographies? *The Fisherman* is a masterful, chilling tale, aching with desire and longing for the impossible."

—Michael Griffin, author of *The Lure of Devouring Light*

"Reading this, your mouth fills with worms. Just let them wriggle and crawl as they will, though—don't swallow. John Langan is fishing for your sleep, for your soul. I fear he's already got mine."

—Stephen Graham Jones, author of *Mongrels*

"John Langan's *The Fisherman* isn't about fishing at all. Yes, there's fishing in it, but it's really about friendship, loss, and bone-deep horror. What starts as a slow, melancholy tale gains momentum and drops you head first into a churning nightmare from which you might escape, but you'll never forget, and the memory of what you saw will change you forever."

—Richard Kadrey, author of *The Everything Box*

"Whenever John Langan publishes a book I am going to devour that book. That's because he's one of the finest practitioners of the moody tale working today. *The Fisherman* is a treasure, the kind of book you just want to snuggle up and shiver through. I can't say enough good things about the confidence, the patience, the satisfying cumulative power of this book. It was a pleasure to read from the first page to the last."

—Victor LaValle, author of *The Ballad of Black Tom*

"A haunting novel about loss and friendship, *The Fisherman* is a monstrous catch in the sea of weird fiction."

—Cameron Pierce, author of *Our Love Will Go the Way of the Salmon*

"For some fishing is a therapeutic, a way to clear one's head, to chase away the noise of a busy world and focus on one single thing. On good days it can heal the worst pains, even help develop a sense of solace. John Langan's *The Fisherman* isn't about the good day fishing, it isn't even about a bad day fishing, it's about the day that you shouldn't have even left the house, let alone waded chest deep into a swollen stream of churning water. Langan tells you that up front, warns you this isn't going to be that story, but you ignore the signs, lured in by the faint smell of masculine adventure, hooked by tragedy and the chance of redemption, and reeled in by a nesting tale of ever growing horrors. By the time you realize what has happened it's already too late, you're caught in an unavoidable net of terror that can end in only one way. It doesn't matter how strong you are or how prepared, John Langan has you hook, line and sinker, and he doesn't let go until the very last page."

—Pete Rawlik, author of *Reanimatrix*

"John Langan's *The Fisherman* is literary horror at its sharpest and most imaginative. It's at turns a quiet and powerfully melancholy story about loss and grief; the impossibility of going on in the same manner as you had before. It's also a rollicking, kick-ass, white-knuckle charge into the winding, wild, raging river of redemption. Illusory, frightening, and deeply moving, *The Fisherman* is a modern horror epic. And it's simply a must read."

—Paul Tremblay, author of *A Head Full of Ghosts*
and *Disappearance at Devil's Rock*

CHILDREN
OF THE
FANG
AND OTHER GENEALOGIES

Other Books by John Langan

Novels
The Fisherman
House of Windows

Collections
Sefira and Other Betrayals
The Wide, Carnivorous Sky and Other Monstrous Geographies
Mr. Gaunt and Other Uneasy Encounters

CHILDREN
OF THE
FANG
AND OTHER GENEALOGIES

JOHN LANGAN

WORD HORDE

PETALUMA, CA

ISBN: 978-1-939905-60-4

A Word Horde Book
http://www.WordHorde.com

TABLE OF CONTENTS

For Fiona

INTRODUCTION

STEPHEN GRAHAM JONES

You know *The Monster at the End of this Book*? A lot of horror's built more or less like that. The story goes to great and meticulous pains to make its world real and palpable and delicately balanced, then it takes some more time to get the character deep enough we can engage her not as a puppet on word strings, but as a person, one who's kind of, for these pages, *us*, our secret self, the version we don't show anyone but can't deny. Once all that front-work's done, then the story springs its monster on you—the bad place, the ghost, the toothed slobbering thing just past the light, the hidden face of the one you never thought to suspect. It's a good build, is the default setting for good reason.

With John Langan, though, what you need to understand is that if it's horror, he's not just read it, he's sat with it long after closing the book. He's considered it from every angle, then rolled his eyes back into his head to study the *experience* of reading it, and the strangeness of thinking about it now.

The result of that, I have to think, is a kind of . . . not 'intolerance' of the monster being at the end of all these books, followed by some chase-and-run, turn-and-fight action, but a keen awareness that there must be another way to inflect the story, right? If you just push it over a little this way? If you nudge it a touch more that direction?

That's what this collection feels like to me: John Langan, both delivering us some compelling horror but at the same time interrogating the basic form of horror. His monsters, I'm saying, they're not the jack-in-the-box clown that springs up after you've been turning on that crank. Not always. Sometimes Langan *leads* with his monsters, and then turns his gaze back inward, to the readers-who-are us, and waits for the truth to spring up from our chests, from our mouths, from our eyes.

Reading this collection is a horror rollercoaster, yes—spectral dinosaurs and cosmic slugs, gooey fathers and interdimensional travelers, a voice or two from the grave, maybe even a kaiju—but it's also a sort of . . . either education or induction, I'm not sure yet. And there's a third possibility: infection.

The best horror, it provokes a thrill from our imagination, yes—just to *see* this horrifying stuff, right?—but it also rides our shoulders into the small hours, the dark hours, the lonely places we didn't even realize were that lonely. Not until John Langan whispered to us that they maybe are. Even with people all around.

These stories, you start reading them for the same reason you engage any horror: you want the rush, the release. You want to touch something dark, and then study the pad of your finger, maybe bring it to your nose, your tongue. Basically, it's poor self-preservation, or, at the very least, it's not practicing the preparatory part of good sleep hygiene. But—and this, to me, is the magic of reading John Langan—a few steps into the clammy dark space of this story, you hesitate. You ask yourself if this is really what you wanted, if this is going to be too sticky in your head, if it's going to rewire you in a way you hadn't bargained for, if it's going to reveal something about existence that you were maybe better off not knowing.

So, you start reading these stories for the ride, the ride you think you know, but then about halfway through a sensation creeps in that's both crushing and falling, and you realize that this isn't a ride anymore, and all you're really waiting for now, it's a pinhole of light at the end of this tunnel, please.

This is when John Langan, at his writing desk, chuckles, I'm pretty sure.

INTRODUCTION

I can even see him dialing his words-per-minute back, to draw this out all around us, really dilate the dread, just pack that darkness with whispers and staring, with the rancid bite in the air of scales.

It's what we asked for, picking up this collection, isn't it?

The monster isn't at the end of the book, the monster is at the keyboard. And I wouldn't have it any other way.

SWEETUMS

I

"Feeney?" Keira said.

The cell phone reception here was terrible; her agent's voice cracked and snapped. "Yeah," Ralph was saying, "I know, but it's the only thing I could come up with. Times are tough in Tinseltown, same as everywhere else. If Feeney hadn't pissed off everybody and his uncle with his shit, there's no way I'd be able to get this for you. Fortunately, the guy's an *auteur*, which is to say, a fucking asshole. Not to mention, his last three films've done shit box office."

"I heard," Keira said. "Honestly, I'm amazed any studio would bankroll him."

"Any studio won't," Ralph said. "Guy's toxic; no one'll touch him. Apparently, he's put together a group of private backers."

"Really?"

"Really. I did a little asking around."

"Who's cutting his checks?"

"Buncha guys from eastern Europe. Probably the Russian mob, looking to launder money."

5

"Jesus."

"Nah, I'm just fucking with you. The backers are from Hungary or Romania or some shit. From what I hear, they're on the up and up. Bastions of culture and all that."

"Huh," Keira said. "What's the film about?"

"I couldn't tell you. I wouldn't be surprised if Feeney doesn't know, himself. You see his last one? The one he made by intuition?"

"How long is the gig for?"

"Three weeks, with an option to extend for another three. Because you're so busy."

She wasn't. The restaurant where she waited tables had cut her to Sunday night, which had become the last stop on its employees' ways out the door. She said, "Where is it?"

"Feeney's rented a warehouse on the waterfront. I'll e-mail you the address. First day of shooting's Monday. Bright and early: five a.m."

"Ouch."

"Again—because you're so busy."

"All right, all right."

"So…?"

"I'll take it. Of course I'll take it."

II

Keira pulled into the warehouse parking lot almost twenty minutes late. She was not as late as she could have been, considering how hung over she was—how much alcohol was doubtless still coursing through her veins. Last night had brought her firing from the restaurant, after which, her (former) co-workers had insisted on taking her out to the bar across the street—though she had suspected they were as much celebrating their own continued employment as they were commiserating her termination. She had intended to tell them about her gig with Feeney, had felt the news washing closer to the tip of her tongue with each rum-and-Coke, but had been unable to consume enough liquor to release it into speech. It wasn't embarrassment at working with such a well-known flake—an acting job was an acting job, and though this one didn't sound like a leading role, even a few minutes on screen put her one step closer to the day when it would be her name over the title. She hadn't let anyone know her good news, not her father, who kept track of how many weeks had passed since her walk-on part in the shampoo commercial, or her mother, who guaranteed her a position teaching drama at her prep school if she would move back east, or even her roommate, who met her anxieties about losing her job at the restaurant by asking her when she was planning on moving out. She wasn't especially superstitious—well, no more than any other actor—but she had been seized, possessed by the conviction that, were she to reveal her change in fortune to her companions, her parents, her roommate, she would arrive early Monday morning to a deserted address.

So she had swallowed rum-and-Coke after rum-and-Coke, watching the interior of the bar lose focus, starting at the edges of her vision and moving steadily inwards, until the faces of her friends dissolved like pieces of butter sliding around a hot pan. With every drunk-driving PSA she'd ever heard overlapping in her ears, she'd driven home crouched over the wheel of her GEO Metro, which was also the position she'd maintained during her slightly-more-sober race back down I-710 a few hours later. Ahead, the moon was a doubloon balanced on the horizon. When she looked at the road, the satellite elongated, stretching into a pair of gold circles connected by a narrow bridge, an enormous, cartoon barbell. She did her best to ignore it.

The warehouse at which Feeney was shooting was somewhere on the outskirts of the Port of Los Angeles proper, heading in the direction of Long Beach. Within minutes of leaving the highway, Keira was hopelessly lost, unable to recognize or in some cases read the names on street signs. Then, a right turn, and there it was: a wrought-iron gate wide as the street it ended, the word VERDIGRIS suspended between a pair of parallel arches overhead. The left side was open; taped to the right was a piece of canary paper with "Actors Park In Lot 3" written on it in black marker. The doom that Keira had felt pressing her into the steering wheel was pushed up by a wave of euphoria. She sped through the opening. Lot 3 was located to the left side of the warehouse. What were the chances that anything was underway, yet? It was a Monday morning, for Christ's sake. She locked the car and half-ran towards the warehouse.

The place was enormous. If you had told her they docked the container ships inside it and loaded them there, she could have believed it. Eight, ten storeys high, hundreds of yards long, it seemed less of a building and more of a wall, a great barrier built to keep out something vast. The nearer she drew, the smaller she felt. It was like the wall in *King Kong*, except the beast this was to restrain was no overgrown ape, but a creature whose slimy bulk would blot out the sun. *I guess that makes me Fay Wray.*

The entrance to this part of the warehouse was surprisingly modest, a single door above which a bare bulb cast jaundiced light. A piece of legal paper reading "Actors" was thumbtacked to it. Keira was almost at the door when a pair of shapes detached from the surrounding shadows, one to her right, one to her left. Men, they were men. There was time for her to think, *Oh my God I'm going to be mugged*, for her heart to lurch, her arms to tense, and they were on her. The one to the right circled behind her; the one to the left circled in front. She snapped her head back and forth, the sudden motion making her stomach boil. The men moved with a long, leg-over-leg stride, more like dancers preparing to execute a leap than criminals preparing to beat and rob her. Their hands were up, not in a boxer's guard, but higher, at their eyes. They were holding something to their eyes—cameras, small, rounded video cameras. She could see the red Record light lit on both. "Wait," she said. "Wait." The men continued their circling. "Shit." She grinned, shaking her head more slowly. "Okay, okay. I get it." She held up her hands. "I'm Keira Lessingham. I'm part of the cast." The men continued filming. They appeared to be dressed the same: black, tight-fitting turtlenecks, brown corduroys, and black Doc Martens. She could not see their faces, though one was wearing a black beret. "I'm, uh, I guess I'll just go in, then." The men continued circling. Keira walked through them to the door and opened it.

III

A narrow corridor receded into the warehouse. Heart still knocking against her ribs, Keira walked up it. The passageway was lit by a series of round, blotchy bulbs hanging in space, a row of poisoned suns leading her into blackness, to a gap in the wall to her right. She stepped through, and found herself on a city street. The set was not the most elaborate she'd been on, but taking into account Feeney's limited resources, it was not unimpressive. Across a wide, cobblestoned street, the brick façade of a low row of apartments was pierced by an archway large enough for a small car to drive through. Stationed along the sidewalk in front of the apartments, one to a doorway, black lampposts whose crowns curved into question marks cradled frosted glass globes that coated the scene with thick, creamy light. Above the apartments, the spire of what was probably a cathedral occupied the near distance; a fairly convincing night sky filled the background. She might have been in some small, middle-European city, one of the places her parents had dragged her to when she was younger and they were trying to inoculate her with culture, a settlement against whose stone walls the tides of invasion, religion, and nationalism had risen and fallen for millennia.

"Finally."

Keira turned to her left, and there was Feeney with a pair of camera men—possibly the same two who had swept down on her outside the warehouse: it was difficult to be certain, because this pair also began circling her, and she was trying to focus on the director.

He was not shorter than Keira had expected—wasn't that the impression most people reported on meeting a celebrity? Keira had never had a sense of Feeney being anything other than average height, even short. His hair stood up in a pompadour that made his forehead seem exposed, his eyes surprised. He was wearing a long wool coat that was either navy blue or black. Around a cigarette that had been smoked almost to the filter, he said, "Great. You can stay where you are. Actually, come forward a couple of steps. Now take half a step to your right. Good." He looked to the camera men, who had stopped their movement. "One of you over there," he said, pointing to the archway, "and the other…here." He gestured to a spot ten feet to Keira's left. "Right. You—"

Feeney was talking to her. "Uh, Keira Less—"

"Right, Keira. Let's see if you're up for this. You start here. You're on this street in—well, it doesn't really matter where. Someplace far from home. The natives don't speak English. You're in pretty rough shape. Actually, you're not that bad, but you feel like you are, okay? Put your hands in your pockets."

Keira jammed her hands into her jeans.

"All right. Roll your shoulders forward—hunch over. Not too much. Good. Okay. When I say, 'Action,' you're looking at that place." He pointed to the apartment row. "Something is going to happen. Something. I won't tell you what; I just want you to react to it."

Keira nodded. "Improvise."

"React," Feeney said. "Got it? Good." He clapped his hands. "Okay! Ready?"

"Yes," Keira said. The camera men held up their free hands in OK signs.

Feeney retreated a half-dozen steps in the direction Keira had come. "And…action."

Four doors down from the archway, almost parallel with the spot where Feeney had positioned her, one of the apartment doors swung inward. *Guess he can't afford to waste any time*, Keira thought. Light the color of dark honey filled the doorway. Somewhere inside that space, that light, a dark shape moved forward—pushed forward, as if struggling through the light. If it was a man—and how could it be anything else?—he was huge, so broad it was hard to believe he would be able to squeeze out onto the front stoop. The silhouette of his head was round, what was visible of his shoulders rough, as if he were wearing a fur coat, or covered in a heavy pelt, himself. Keira could hear the floorboards the man was crossing shrieking with the burden. Without being aware of it, she had withdrawn her hands from her pockets and raised one to her mouth, the other in front of her. Something about the man's movement was off, out of kilter in a fundamental way Keira could recognize but not articulate. It was curiously *soft*, as if the man were nothing but a heaping of flesh, the near end of a monstrous worm. The response it evoked in her was immediate, profound: Keira was more afraid than she could remember ever having been; her arms and legs trembled with it. It was intolerable that she should see any more of the figure in the doorway. She looked back the way she had entered the set, but could not find the opening in the wall, only the façade of another apartment row. Feeney was nowhere to be found. When Keira turned back to the street, she saw the man occluding the doorway. Almost before she knew it, she was running, her feet carrying her across the street and into the archway through the apartment building.

The camera man stationed to the right of the arch tracked her passage smoothly.

IV

For a moment, her footsteps chased one another around the tunnel. Then she was in a large courtyard, the empty center of a square whose sides were further blocks of apartments. In the far right corner of the square, an alley offered the only egress she could see from the space. Keira ran towards it. It seemed to take twice as long to cross the distance as it should have. All the while, she was aware of the archway gaping behind her, the naked space surrounding her.

By the time she reached the mouth of the alley, her chest was heaving, her blouse sodden. Though crowded with metal trashcans, the alley appeared passable. Feet sliding on rotten peels and soggy papers, Keira ran along the alley, narrowly avoiding a collision with an overflowing trashcan whose crash would have directed her pursuer straight to her. Above, on the walls to either side, fire escapes held their ladders just out of reach, taunting her. Ahead, the alley ended in a brick wall. The panic that flared in her was as quickly extinguished by her realization that this alley t-junctioned another. She turned right, saw an opening in the wall now to her left, and ducked through it.

Except for a large, bright rectangle glowing to her left, the long room she had entered was dark. The carbon reek of charcoal threaded the air, as if a fire had scoured the place in the recent past. In between where she was standing and the block of light, dark lines formed rectangles and squares of varying dimensions. As she moved closer to them, she saw that they were the frames of uncompleted walls, their timbers blackened and notched. A motor whirred softly somewhere in front of her. In the center of the bright space, a shape loomed.

Blood surged in Keira's ears. How had the man found her so quickly? She was already half-turned the way she had come when her brain caught up with what her eyes had seen. The figure in the light was Feeney, his head and shoulders, anyway. The steady whir was the sound of a blocky projector resting on a camp table, casting the director's image onto a burnt wall. The footage was rough, the timecode running in the lower right corner.

Keira approached the projector. Feeney had been shot facing right, in three-quarter profile. He was holding a bulky phone to his left ear, a freshly-lit cigarette between his teeth. With a pop that made her jump, the audio thundered on, catching Feeney mid-sentence.

"—sweetums," he was saying. "My little turd." He paused. "It's the Sign." Another pause. "No. Not about the Sign, it is the Sign." Pause. "How can—" Pause, during which he removed the cigarette from his mouth, considered its white length, and returned it to its place. "What does any of that have to do with me?" Pause. "No." Pause. "No." Pause. "Don't be ridiculous, sweetums. Don't be stupid." Pause. "Yes you are being stupid. Why are you being so Goddamned stupid?" Pause. "Because it isn't like anything. It's not a metaphor, my little turd." Pause. "You are my little turd. My little piece of shit." Pause. "Sweetums. How I'm going to enjoy fucking you, you little turd. How I'm going to enjoy fucking the shit out of you, you little piece of shit. Oh yes I am." Pause. "I am."

A shoe scraped the floor. Keira spun, and found herself facing one of the camera men, the red Record light shining on his camera. "Jesus." The man offered no response. Keira's cheeks flushed. Of course all of this was part of the movie. What had she thought it was? No doubt, there had been camera men stationed along the route she'd run. She hoped Feeney would be happy with the mix of relief and shame reddening her face.

Behind the camera man, a doorway led out of the room into another. Keira considered leaving this place in favor of a return to the alley that had brought her to it; however, the prospect of encountering the man (it had to be a man) whose presence had produced such a dramatic response from her was sufficiently unwelcome to send her around the camera man and into the adjoining room.

V

Heavy, mustard-colored curtains blocked her way. Keira pushed them to the left, searching for a part. The fabric was grimy against her fingertips. Dust and mildew rose in clouds around her. She sneezed once, twice. She found the end of the curtain, pulled it up, and passed under it.

She was standing in a small, dimly-lit space whose walls consisted of the mustard curtains. In front of her, a man sat behind a typewriter supported by a card table that quivered as his thick fingers stabbed its keys. The man's longish hair was more brown than red, unlike the beard that flared from his cheeks, which was practically orange. His broad face was pink, puffy, the blood vessels broken across it mapping a route signposted with empty siblings of the bottle of Jack Daniel's stationed at the typewriter's left. At the same time, there was a certain open, even unguarded quality to his eyes that made him appear oddly innocent. As Keira watched, the man tugged the page on which he'd been working free of the typewriter and held it up for scrutiny. His brow lowered, his lips moving soundlessly. Maybe halfway through his reading of it, he smashed the paper between his hands, crushed it into a ball and dropped it to the wood floor, where it joined a host of similar casualties. The man took a measured pull from the bottle of liquor, then selected a fresh sheet from the stack of paper to the typewriter's right side and spun it onto the roller. His fingers resumed their assault on the keys.

Was this guy an actor? It was hard to think what else he might be. Keira surveyed the folds of the curtains. Almost immediately, she saw a red Record light shining in one of the recesses to the right. So the guy was part of the movie. Keira wasn't sure how to proceed. Feeney hadn't covered what to do when she encountered another cast member. Unless his instruction to "react" had been intended to cover everything that was to follow that initial command of "action." The man appeared to be talking to himself. Keira approached him.

It was difficult to hear the man above the clattering of the keys. His voice was sanded smooth by a Southern drawl whose precise origins Keira could not place. He was saying, "Not dreaming, but in Carcosa. Not dead, but in Carcosa. Not in Hell, but in Carcosa. Why then I'll fit you. A true son of Tennessee. Jesus, what an asshole. Come, let us go, and make thy father blind. This was the creature that was once Celia Blassenville. Thus the devil candies all sins over. Excellent hyena! I would have you meet this bartered blood. What creature ever fed worse, than hoping Tantalus? Welcome, dread Fury, to my woeful house. The evil of the stars is not as the evil of earth. 'Tis true, 'tis true; witness my knife's sharp point. Why, this is hell, nor am I out of it. And touched a cold and unyielding surface of polished glass. Rhubarb,

O, for rhubarb to purge this choler! There sits Death, keeping his circuit by the slicing edge. *Solomon miseris socias habuisse doloris.* I'll find scorpions to string my whips. Vergama leaned forward from his chair, and turned the page. I account this world a tedious theater. And while Grom howled and beat his hairy breast, death came to me in the Valley of the Worm. Nothing but fear and fatal steel, my lord. Continually, we carry about us a rotten and dead body. No mask? This banquet, which I wish may prove more stern and bloody than the Centaurs' feast. You have seen the King…? Man stands amaz'd to see his deformity in any other creature but himself. Where flap the tatters of the King. It is a fearful thing to fall into the hands of the living God. In dim Carcosa. In lost Carcosa. In dead Carcosa."

The man reached forward and pulled the page from the typewriter. This time, he sampled the bottle while he was scanning it. As before, he had not completed reading it when he crumpled the page and let it fall to the floor. While he rolled a clean sheet into the typewriter, Keira knelt and picked up the closest ball of paper. On one knee, she eased the mass apart and smoothed it over her other knee.

The paper was blank. Keira looked at the man, who had resumed his typing and was repeating his monologue. "When then I'll fit you." Strictly speaking, there was no reason for there to be anything typed on the sheet, but given the ferocity with which the man was punching the keys, she had expected to find something on the page, even random combinations of letters and numbers. "Thus the devil candies all sins over." She had wondered if the guy might be transcribing his weird monologue, which was what she would have done. "Welcome, dread Fury, to my woeful house."

A burst of hammering made Keira leap to her feet. From the other side of at least one of the curtains, sounds of rapid construction—hammers pounding nails; saws chewing wood; lumber clattering together—drowned out the typewriter's chatter. The man did not appear to notice them, nor did the camera man filming him. Was the noise coming from the left? She was reasonably sure it was. There seemed little point in remaining here. She supposed she could attempt to speak to the man, but she was reluctant to break into whatever state the guy was in. React, right? She would react by investigating the source of the building sounds. Keeping near to the curtains, she passed around the man at the typewriter. There was a part in the curtains she could slip through. As she did, a glance back showed the

14

view over the man's shoulder. Though his fingers drove the typewriter's keys down in steady rhythm, none of the corresponding typebars rose to imprint the paper with its symbol.

VI

Keira emerged on the right side of a shallow stage facing an empty auditorium. Center stage, half a dozen men were busy with a wooden box whose proportions suggested a coffin stood on one end; albeit, a coffin for a man a good foot and a half taller than Keira. Dressed in the same black turtlenecks, brown corduroys, and black boots as the other camera men she had encountered, these men had traded in their cameras for an assortment of tools. Without the cameras obscuring their faces, Keira could see that the men resembled one another to a degree that was unusual, even artificial. Bald, their protuberant eyes stretching heavy lids, mouths wide, lips thin, their skin rendered sallow by the bank of lights shining overhead, the men might have been brothers from an almost comically large family. Undoubtedly, they had been made up after the same model; although why Feeney should have cared for his camera men's appearances, Keira couldn't say. Maybe they had parts in the film, too; maybe she would be required to record some of the day's performances.

She had drawn near enough to the activity for one of the men to turn to her and say, "Beautiful, innit?" He spoke with an approximation of a lower-class English accent, Dick Van Dyke playing the cockney in *Mary Poppins*. Keira nodded and said, "What is it?"

The man stared at her as if amazed. "What is it? Did you seriously just ask what this is?"

"I'm sorry. I'm new, here—this is my first day on set, and—"

"This is—come over here," the man said, waving her closer. "Come on, don't be shy."

From the front, Keira saw that the box was at least twice as wide as a coffin. A door that slid to the left disclosed a narrow compartment on the right. She thought of a photo booth, especially when she saw the row of green buttons set in the compartment's left-hand panel. A pair of slots had been cut in the wood above the buttons, the topmost level with a person's face, the one below set approximately throat-high. Below the green buttons, a pair of holes had been drilled in the panel, the upper level with a person's waist, the lower set approximately thigh-high. "This," the man said, "is the King's Beneficence."

"The King's...?"

The man sighed. "You're not from around these parts, are you?"

"No," Keira said. "I mean, I am now, but I'm from New York. Originally."

"You don't say?" the man said. "If you're a denizen of the Old Imperial, then you should be well-acquainted with the Lethal Chamber."

"I, uh, no, I'm afraid I'm not."

"Catlicks, your people?"

Her parents? "Episcopalians," Keira said. When the man frowned, she said, "Anglicans."

"Ah," the man said. "Say no more. This," he gestured at the box, "is the means by which a man—or a woman—with a mind to might make his—or her—own quietus, to quote old Will-I-Am of Avalon. Only, instead of a bare bodkin, you've got your choice of these four buttons."

Her arm stretched out, Keira leaned toward the compartment, only to have the man catch her other arm and haul her back, shouting, "Are you out of your bleedin mind?" At the expression on Keira's face, the man said, "Right, right, you don't know." Releasing her from his grip, the man bent over and picked up a slender piece of wood the length of a yardstick. "'Bout time for a test, anyway," the man said, and tapped the closest button with the wood.

Something bright and metal shot out of the top slot and hung quivering in the air. A broad, flat tongue of steel, its razor edge shone. "The King's Philosophy," the man explained, "with which he relieves us of the burden of our thoughts." He moved the tip of his improvised pointer to the next button and pushed.

From the next slot down, something flashed out and around. Wider than the blade above, this one curved in a crescent inlaid with fine filigree. "The King's Counsel," the man continued, "with which he relieves us of the burden of our words." He shifted the sword to the third button and triggered it.

A pointed length of steel thrust out of the upper hole. When it reached its limit, a dozen blades sprang into a corona around its head. The man said, "The King's Sup, with which he relieves us of the burden of our appetites." He pushed the fourth and final button.

From the lower hole, a bundle of needles sprang forward, twisting first to the left, then to the right. "The King's Chastity," the man concluded, "with which he relieves us of the burden of our desires." He dropped the piece of wood. "Well, that's all right, then. Oi!" he shouted. "One of you lot reset the Beneficence." No one replied. "You see?" he said to Keira.

"But," she said, "I mean, I know things can get bad, believe me, but even if they do, would you—I mean—you could take some pills, or—"

"Don't you worry about it," the man said.

Stage left, there was a commotion on the other side of the curtains: someone shouting, the scuff of boots on wood, the curtain swelling. A trio of camera men shoved through to the stage. Their arms were linked, as if they were the world's shortest chorus line. Not to mention, least-coordinated: the man in the middle was badly out of step with his fellows. This, Keira saw, was because he was struggling against his companions.

"Well well well," the man beside Keira called. "The prodigal son makes his entrance."

At his declaration, the man in the middle glanced up from his contest and, seeing the King's Beneficence, began to scream, "No! No! Not now! Not now!" He succeeded in tearing his left arm free of his fellow's grasp, only to have the man on his right pivot in to him and drive his fist into his gut. The captive man folded at the waist like a marionette whose strings have been scissored. The other two took him under the arms and dragged him towards the box.

The remaining camera men had retrieved their cameras and were filming their companions' progress. As the trio passed in front of her, the captive man turned his face to Keira and, in the wheeze of a man whose lungs have been emptied of air, said, "Do you know what this means? Do you?"

"It means what it means, old son," the man beside Keira said. "It's the Sign, is what it is."

While his fellows were preparing to force him into the compartment—from which all deadly accessories had been retracted—the captive man made one final attempt at escape. But the others were ready for him, and the one punched him in the head, the other splayed his hand on the captive man's chest and shoved. Hands covering his head, the man stumbled backwards through the opening in the box. His companions wasted no time in sliding the door closed over it. Keira's last glimpse of the man was of his hands dropping from his face, his features a mix of terror and profound sadness. Once the door was shut, the men secured it with a trio of brass locks.

"Wait—" Keira said, but already, the camera men had begun to chant, "Choose. Choose. Choose," one word repeated in steadily-escalating volume. "Hang on," she said to the man beside her. He ignored her in favor of the chant. "Choose. Choose. Choose."

From within the King's Beneficence, the captive man shouted, "You can go fuck yourselves!"

In answer, the camera men raised their voices another notch. "Choose! Choose! Choose!"

"Do you think I'm going to do this? Just because it happened before, do you think it's going to happen now?"

"Choose! Choose! Choose!"

"Stop it! Stop this right fucking now!"

"Choose! Choose! Choose!"

"Don't you understand what's happening?"

If any of the camera men did, he did not share it. Instead, the group roared, "CHOOSE! CHOOSE! CHOOSE!"

"God damn you! God damn you all to hell!"

"CHOOSE! CHOOSE! CHOOSE!"

Keira had had enough. Eyes straight ahead, she walked off the stage, exiting the direction the captive man and his fellows had entered, stage left.

VII

The other side of the mustard curtain was a short hallway at the end of which a fire door opened on a cul-de-sac. To the left, an alley cornered to the right. Across from her, a metal staircase climbed a brick wall to a doorway. To her right, a camera man stood amidst a herd of trash cans, recording Keira as she considered what might lie around the alley's turn before opting to cross to the stairs and hurry up them.

At the top, she hesitated. A hallway like the one that had brought her into the warehouse stretched in front of her, a similar procession of mottled lights keeping utter darkness at bay. It occurred to her that she was, if not completely lost, uncomfortably close to being so. Should she retrace her steps, try to find her way back to the entrance? It would mean returning to the camera men and the bizarre scenario they were enacting, which she had no desire to do. Okay, the King's Beneficence was some kind of special effect—it had to be; she couldn't imagine Feeney presiding over a snuff film—but she had little taste for torture porn. Were she to step onto that stage again, no doubt she'd be met by a pool of stage blood, seeping out from under the box's door, or, worse, a wash of pig or cow blood, splashed for maximum realism.

Straight ahead it is, then. Besides, there were camera men all over the place. When she needed to find her way out of here, she could ask directions from one of them.

Her footsteps were loud, as if the space beneath the floor were hollow. Echoes of her passage lagged behind, raced ahead of her. Were the lights growing farther apart? She looked over her shoulder. They were: at least twice as much space separated the nearest globes as did those by the doorway. The next bulb was more distant still. Nor could she detect the red light of any of the camera men.

To the right, someone was walking beside her. With a gasp, Keira turned and, for a moment, did not recognize the dimly-lit woman staring back at her in equal surprise. Then she realized she was seeing herself, reflected in a large, rectangular window. "Shit." She approached the window. Through her ghostly image, she saw a bare room in which a desk lamp cast canary-colored light onto a plain table. There were chairs on either side of the table, the one on Keira's left pushed in to the table, the one on her right slid back several feet out of the light by the man seated on it. She couldn't distinguish much of him, mostly a long black or navy-blue coat and a haze of cigarette smoke floating around his head. *Feeney?* What was he doing here? Behind him, a camera man kept record of the scene.

A door in the wall on the other side of the table opened, and a woman entered the room. Tall, thin, wearing a black pantsuit, white blouse, and a necklace of black beads, her long hair dyed platinum blond (badly), she could have passed for Keira's mother—for herself in another dozen years, if time were unkind to her. She thought of the camera men. Was this why Feeney had hired her, because she resembled one—or more—of the actors he already had cast for the film?

The woman tugged the chair away from the table, reversed it, and straddled it, folding her arms on its back. "Well," she said, and Keira heard her, her voice carried by a speaker set above the window. The quality was poor; she sounded flat, tinny.

The man in the chair said, "Kay." Keira couldn't tell if it was Feeney, speaking.

"Don't," Kay said.

"Just talk," the man said. "Say something."

Without pause, Kay said, "I heard about Laceration Parties when I was still pretty new to this place. There was this girl from Vancouver I used to hang out with once in a while. Kirsten or Karen—I think it was Karen. She used to say, 'It's Vancouver, Seward, not the Vancouver in Canada.' Maybe it was Kirsten. Big girl. There was a tavern near one of the more popular King's boxes, The Debt Owed, where we'd stand at the bar and let failed businessmen and despondent troubadours buy us rounds of Pernod while they worked themselves up for the Beneficence. Anyway, it was during a particularly slow night that Karen, I'm pretty sure her name was, told me about these parties, these soirees, a friend had been invited to. In the hills, somewhere near the Observatory. It was just the A list at it, it was the A+ list, the A++ list. Supposedly, the King, himself, had put in an appearance; although Kirsten's friend hadn't seen him, personally. At the door, the guests had been met by a butler who presented them with a ceramic bowl full of razor blades. Everybody picked one for later. The friend had been a little vague as to exactly what had happened later, but her left hand and forearm were heavily bandaged, and she claimed she couldn't move a couple of her fingers, anymore.

"I'd been in this place long enough not to doubt the story. I didn't think I'd ever attend one, though. Not because of any moral reservations; I just couldn't see myself being allowed to mingle with the upper crust—with the powdered sugar sprinkled on top of the upper crust.

"That was before René. If you'd told me I would let a corpse-driver set foot on the same street as me, let alone lay his hand on me...I knew he was, I guess 'interested' is as good a word as any. He would drive past the booth I was working twice a day, once on his way to the morgue, the second time on his way to Potter's Field. They never repeat a route unless something's caught their attention. I knew the risks of acknowledging, let alone encouraging, his notice. Several of the girls I'd met when I came here decided to find out what lay on the other side of the mortuary doors, and I never saw any of them again. I also knew that, without my consent, the corpse-driver's designs would remain hypothetical. Despite the rumors, they adhere to the Compact religiously. It took years before I granted him recognition. It wasn't that he won me over; it wasn't that I had a death-wish, either. There was nothing else left for me: every other avenue had dead-ended. So I made eye contact, raised my left hand with the palm out, and let what would come next, come.

"There was no romance, no spark, no magic moment I realized he was the same as me. To be honest, I'm not one hundred percent sure why he kept me around. It was months until I could stand to have him touch me, and that was only under the influence of a good bottle of Pernod. I've never gotten used to the way his flesh feels; I still jump anytime he puts his hands on me. The smell of formaldehyde makes me ill, and I have zero interest in what he does with the bodies in the back chambers.

"But there are consolations to the role of corpse-driver's companion. The money's not bad, and even better, there's the prestige, this weird, oblique status that allows you access pretty much everywhere. I hadn't understood this the day I recognized him, that eventually, he would be my passport to a Laceration Party. It was in the hills, near the sign. What a sight we must have made, him in that tiny bowler hat and the fur coat, me in a feathered dress and boa. Not to mention, him five times the size of me—of pretty much everyone there.

"At the front door, a kid in a tuxedo held up a wooden bowl layered with razor blades for us to choose from. I took one; René didn't, which should've kept him out of the Party, but really, who was going to refuse him? The house was full of celebrities and people too powerful to be celebrities. The deeper into it you moved, the higher the profile of your company climbed, until you were in a room whose original purpose you couldn't guess with people whose names you didn't know. That was where the razors were put to use. More or less in the center of the room, there was a stainless steel table with a woman lying on it, nude. I'm not sure what process had led to her being there. One by one, the people in the room walked up to her, surveyed the length of her body, and chose a spot on which to employ their razors. The only rule seemed to be that you were not allowed to slice an artery or vein. After you were finished, you cast your blade into a plastic bucket under the table.

"By the time my turn came around, the floor around the table was slick with blood. I stood beside the woman, whose body was a patchwork of exposed muscle and nerve. I had avoided looking at her face, which had remained untouched. I'm not sure why. But I could feel it, dragging my eyes up the bloody reach of her toward it. The second I saw her, I knew her: Karen, or Kirsten, my old crony from The Debt Owed. She remembered me, too; I'm positive of it. There wasn't any fear or anger in her gaze, just a kind of blank fascination. I pressed the razor to her right eyelid, and drew it across.

"When I was done, I straightened, and there was the King, leaning over the other side of the table from me. They say only one person at a time ever sees him, and I guess that's true, because around me, the partiers carried on as if nothing were happening. For a long, long time, while Karen's eyes filled up with blood that spilled onto the table, the King considered me, and I him. He reached out his right hand, and I saw that he was wearing a white cotton glove. He touched the tip of his index finger to Kirsten's eye, and the blood climbed the thirsty fibers, dyeing the lower half of his finger scarlet. He nodded, drew back a step, and the crowd kind of closed around him. I didn't tell René what had happened, but I did hold onto that razor blade.

"So I've seen the King and lived to tell the tale. Everyone always makes a big deal about his face; you know, 'No mask? No mask!' As if he's any different from the rest of us. As if all of us aren't naked for the world to see."

This time, Keira was not surprised by the camera man to her left; she supposed she must have heard him approach. Beyond him, she could distinguish a doorway through which amber light reached into the hallway. She stepped around the man, and headed for the doorway.

VIII

The room she entered reminded Keira of nothing so much as the living room of her parents' brownstone. In front of a round of bay windows, an old television whose blocky dimensions suggested an altar broadcast footage of Feeney to an abbreviated couch and a recliner. Some error in the TV's settings tinted the screen goldenrod. The director had been shot in three-quarter profile, facing right. He was holding a bulky phone to his left ear, a freshly-lit cigarette between his teeth. Keira knelt and twisted the volume knob clockwise. The soundtrack was playing whomever he was talking to. Their voice was flat, tinny; they were in mid-sentence.

"—about the sign?" There was a pause, as the voice waited for a reply Feeney did not deliver. "What does that even mean? It's a movie." Pause. "You know what? Forget about it," the voice continued, as Feeney removed the cigarette from his mouth, considered its white length, and returned it to its place, "it's not important. What is is that I'm here, in this fucking... I'm here, and everything is wrong. I don't know where to start. The God-damned sky, for Christ's sake." Pause. "You're the one who brought me here, asshole." Pause. "Yes, you did." Pause. "Yes, you fucking did." Pause. "I'm not being stupid." Pause. "It's like—" Pause. "Fuck you. You do not talk to me like that." Pause. "Fuck you. You're the piece of shit." Pause. "You try to lay a finger on me, and I'll cut it off." Pause. "Fuck you."

Keira stood. Framed by the archway that led to the front hall, a camera man filmed her crossing the room. Passing in front of him, and unlocking the front door.

IX

She emerged into a wide, flat space—a parking lot—the parking lot outside the warehouse. It was dark, the sky full of stars. Except for her car, the lot was empty. Had she spent the entire day inside? She didn't feel as if that much time had passed, and yet, here it was night. She supposed she could return to the warehouse, but a wave of exhaustion rose over her. Just being around all of that…whatever you wanted to call it had left her legs weak, her head light. Missing lunch and, from the looks of it, dinner probably hadn't helped, either. Behind her, the door she had exited clicked shut. That settled the matter. Within a minute, she was behind the wheel of the Metro, driving out the gate to the place.

The highway was quiet. Good. She would be home sooner rather than later. It was unlikely she'd manage enough sleep, but she'd take what she could get. Call time tomorrow was 5:00 a.m., again. *Ugh*. Ahead, the full moon hung golden over the hills. She could not remember it ever having been so near, so enormous, the vague face suggested by its topography so apparent. For a moment she had the impression that something enormous had inclined its attention towards her.

Tires ringing on the road, a convoy of eighteen-wheelers swept around her. The windows of their cabs were tinted; rather dangerous for traveling at night, she judged. The trailers were flatbeds, each festooned with a holiday's worth of blazing colored lights, as was the cargo lashed to it. Such was the glare that Keira could not distinguish what the trucks were transporting until they pulled away from her, when she saw that the squared frames ribboned in crimson, mauve, and lemon lights belonged to gallows, their nooses dancing in the rushing air.

As quickly as they had surrounded her, the trucks were gone, their tail-lights red points in the distance. Keira's eyes were sufficiently dazzled that, at first, she mistook the second moon rising into the sky for an illusion.

HYPHAE

The house was in worse shape than he'd anticipated, the roof warped, the siding faded, the window frames clearly rotten. The yard was a mess, too, grass grown hay-high and yellowed, the ornamental bushes either gone or overgrown. The driveway had never been the best—his father had refused to blacktop it, insisting it was perfectly passable—and the rain and snow of the last fifteen years had only deepened its ruts. The bottom of his Subaru scraped an exposed rock, and James winced.

Who knew if his key would fit the front lock, anymore? He rolled to where he remembered the driveway ending and shut off the engine. His father had not taken his mother's departure especially well; it would not be a surprise for him to have swapped out the locks. He stepped out of the car. If he couldn't enter the house, then that was his obligation fulfilled, right? He could imagine what his sister, housebound following her C-Section, would say to that.

His key slid home easily; the lock released without struggle. With a sigh, he pushed open the front door.

The smell that rushed out made him step back. "God…" It was the rotten milk and mold stench of strong cheese left to liquefy in the sun. He leaned towards it, recoiled, tried again. "Dad?" The smell flooded his sinuses. He breathed through his mouth. "Hello? Dad? It's James." "Your gay son," he

25

almost added, but decided to forego the hostilities for the moment. Was his father even here? Cupping his hand over the lower half of his face, he entered the house.

He expected to find the living room littered with months of dirty dishes, the putrefying remains of their half-eaten meals the source of the odor his hand did nothing to shield him from. It was clean, as were the dining room and the kitchen, his father's room and the bathroom. His and Patricia's old rooms had been repurposed to TV room and sewing room, respectively, but neither held anything worse than mild clutter.

"Dad?"

He opened the refrigerator. Except for the water jug, it was empty, as were the oven, the toaster oven, and the microwave. Did he need any more proof that his father was not here—had been gone, from the looks of it, for some time? But, but…he ducked his head into the bathroom. His father's toiletries were ranged around the sink. Not out of the question for him to have purchased new ones, of course, if it weren't out of keeping with a lifetime's parsimony. A rummage through the closet in his father's room revealed no gaps in its shirts, slacks, and jackets, no ties missing from his accumulated father's day and birthday presents—which appeared to lend weight to his father's having stayed put.

"In a house with no food," he said, returning to the kitchen. The basement door was closed, but he supposed he should check downstairs, too. His father's workbench was there, behind the furnace, the home to a collection of power tools that had frightened James when he was younger, in no small part due to the lurid cautions his father had given him about each one. This'll slice your hand clean off. This'll burn the eyes out of your head. This'll take the flesh from your arm before you know what's happened. Strange to think James had wound up living with a carpenter.

At the basement door, he paused. Downstairs had been his father's retreat. After a bad day at IBM or especially after an argument with James's mother, he would throw open the door, tromp down the stairs, and clatter about his workbench. Sometimes, James would hear the power tools screaming, smell sawdust burning, as his father threw himself into one project or another, cutting wood for the new mailbox he was always on the verge of building, or fashioning a new trellis for the front porch. He had spent ever more time down there in the couple of years prior to James's departure for Cornell and, from what Patricia had told him, before their mother had walked out, he had practically been living in the basement.

The conflict that had come to define his parents' marriage had had a single subject, his father's health, specifically, the horrible state of his feet. It was beyond funny, it was absurd to think that such a topic could have undone twenty-five years together but, in all fairness to his mother, there had been something seriously wrong with his father's feet. The toenails had been thick, jaundice-yellow, like bits of horn sprouting from the ends of his toes. The toes, the sides of his feet, had been fish-belly pale, the heels gray and traversed by cracks from which thin, almost ghostly fibers projected. Nor had their appearance been the worst of it: their smell, an odor of stale sweat mixed with the muddy reek of mildew, had made sitting next to him when his feet were uncovered an act of endurance. Mention the condition of his feet to him, and he would flare with anger. James had not understood how the man who insisted on taking him to the doctor for the slightest sniffle could not tend to a part of himself so obviously unwell, and the sight of his father's bare feet had stirred in him an obscure shame. As he had grown older, adolescence had curdled his shame to contempt, as it had dawned on him that his father was afraid of what a visit to the doctor would tell him about his feet. In the last few years, contempt had mellowed to something like pity, though it was difficult not to feel a modicum of anger at his father's inertia.

He opened the basement door and was pushed back several steps by the fresh wave of reek that rushed over him. Gagging, his eyes watering, he threw his hand back over his mouth, his nose. "Jesus," he coughed. This was too much. He stumbled into the dining room, to the back door. He fumbled with the locks and flung the door wide, pushing the screen door out of the way and stepping onto the back porch and fresh air.

Wiping his eyes, his nose, he crossed to the other side of the porch. The smell clung to him. He inhaled deeply. Something caught in his throat and bent him double coughing. He straightened, only for a second round of coughing to convulse him. His mouth filled with phlegm. He spat, and what spattered on the porch was gray. "Shit." He remained hunched over until his lungs had calmed. His chest felt bruised, his throat raw. He stood, gingerly, and something in the tall grass behind the porch drew his notice.

It was a car, his father's car, the same red Saturn he'd been driving when

James had left for college. Descending the porch's steps, James approached the car. The thick layer of pollen lying yellow on it, obscuring its windows, testified to its having been parked here for some time. James felt a momentary surge of panic that his father might be seated in the car, dead of a heart attack or stroke. Heart pounding, he opened the driver's side door, bracing for the sight of his father's desiccated corpse. The car was empty. He sagged against it.

He dug his cell phone out of his jeans, flipped it open. No bars. He held it up, rotating slowly. Nothing. Terrific. Was the phone in the house still working? And what was he planning on saying to his sister if it was and he reached her? "Dad isn't here and there's a weird smell coming from the basement"? He folded the phone and returned it to his pocket.

Maybe his shirt…he unbuttoned, untucked, and removed it, then folded it into a rough scarf that he tied over his nose and mouth. Already, the faint odor of rotten milk and mold had attached to the fabric. It was bearable. James climbed to the porch and returned inside.

At least the basement light was working. He descended the stairs slowly, on the lookout for…what? Whatever was producing that smell. He'd never dealt with black mold; maybe that was the culprit. The odor pressed on his improvised mask. He concentrated on breathing through his mouth.

At the foot of the stairs, the water heater stood in its recess, closeted from the rest of the basement by a dark brown door whose upper half was laddered with slats that allowed you to see the off-white cylinder and not much else. As a child, James had felt a prickle of unease at the base of his neck every time he'd passed in front of that door. Perhaps due to the design of the slats, each of which was set at a forty-five degree tilt, light didn't reach very far into the alcove, leaving the walls of the recess invisible and giving the impression that the water heater stood at the near end of a large, dark space. When he was fourteen, he'd helped his father replace the tank, and although the closet had been well-lit by a pair of worklights his father had hung on the walls, James still had judged it unusually spacious for its purpose.

He was almost past the recess when his eye caught something through the slats, a wooden pole resting on the water heater. He slid his fingers under the lowest slat and eased the door open. It was the handle of a shovel, its blade rusted except for the edge, which was bright from use. On the floor beside it, a pickaxe had fallen over. The points of its head shone. Bracing his hands on either side of the doorway, James leaned into the alcove.

To his left, a sizable hole had been chopped into the wall. Three feet wide by four and a half, five feet high, its margin ragged, it appeared to extend into the earth behind the wall. James released the doorway and stepped around the water heater, in front of the hole. It was too dark for him to see into. He fished his cell from his jeans, unfolded it, and turned the screen toward the blackness. Its pale light revealed a rough, narrow tunnel receding to an uncertain destination.

"Dad?"

Was that a reply? He called to his father a second time, stood listening for a response. None came. Holding his cell out before him, he ducked his head and advanced into the tunnel. It was a bit of a tight fit—his father was smaller than James by a good six inches and thirty pounds—but passable. The floor slanted down, while the walls curved gradually to the left. He looked over his shoulder. Already, the water heater was almost out of view. The passage appeared to have been hacked out of solid rock. He didn't know what type lay beneath the house, but his father had cut his way through it.

Where had he been going? Had he been building some kind of underground shelter? From what? His father had always been a man to follow his own impulses, to a fault and to extremes. Of course, there was the example of his feet, which James's mother had told him had become infected from something he'd picked up while on a business trip to Paris. A French colleague had taken him on a tour of the catacombs, during which he'd stepped into a deep puddle of foul water. His socks and shoes had been soaked. Who knew what had been swimming around in there and decided to hitch a ride on his father's skin? No doubt a treatment for athlete's foot would have taken care of it, but the most his father would do for his feet was soak them in a basin of warm water. James could remember the expression on his father's face as he lowered his feet into their bath, agony that dissolved into something like pleasure.

Beyond his feet, and what he called his thriftiness, James his stinginess, there was his father's refusal to leave this house, despite what must have been a decade-and-a-half campaign by James's mother to have them move. While James and Patricia had lived home, their mother had argued that the house was too small, the school district substandard. After they'd left, she had insisted that the house was too much trouble to maintain, its location too remote. No matter her line of attack, his father's defense had been the same: this was their home, the emphasis he placed on the word substituting for hours of reasoning. From his mother, James knew that his father's early life had been rootless. Only son of a master sergeant in the Army, James's father and his mother had moved from New Jersey to what was then West Germany, from West Germany to Washington State, from Washington State to Kansas, from Kansas to Japan, from Japan to New York, where his grandfather had been killed in a car accident when James's father was thirteen. Afterwards, James's father and his mother had continued to wander, living with this relative or that until James's grandmother fell out with them and went in search of a new place for them to stay. Even knowing the little he did about his father's early life—because the man refused to discuss it in any detail with him—James could appreciate what must have been a profound longing, a need, to have a home of his own. To insist on remaining in that spot at the expense of your marriage, however, went beyond need to pathology, a layman's diagnosis that appeared confirmed by the tunnel down which James was moving.

How far did this thing go? The air had grown noticeably cooler and damper. How deep did you have to dig for that to happen? The spoiled milk and mold odor had grown strong enough to force its way through the fabric of his mask. Were the walls growing narrower? What would happen if he couldn't turn around in here? Dread pooled below his stomach, started to rise. Relax. Relax. He stopped, concentrated on breathing slowly and deeply. You're fine. Relax. The fear subsided.

He swept the cell phone up and around the stretch of tunnel he was standing in. Its blue-tinged glow showed only rock, nothing to account for the smell. Could it be some species of microorganism residing within the rock? Holding the cell phone in front of him, he continued forward.

Maybe fifteen feet ahead, the tunnel ended in darkness. Some kind of rock? Coal? Was there coal in these parts? It wasn't stone, he saw as he drew nearer. The light went out into it, as if he were looking into space, which, he realized, he was. His father's tunnel had broken into a cave.

At the end of the passage, James halted, shining the cell phone back and forth. The light revealed a low ceiling arcing over something shining—water, a subterranean lake whose margins lay beyond his light's reach. Directly before him and to his right, a rock shelf gave the lake a shore. James set a tentative foot onto it. The rock held. He brought his other foot down beside it and, when the shelf did not crack and spill him into the water, began moving along it.

This must be part of the aquifer that supplied the house's well. Had his father been trying to reach this? How had he known about it?

To his right, a white rectangle lay on the floor. Bags—large bags made of heavy white plastic, a dozen or more flattened and stacked neatly. There was green lettering on the top one: Ammonium Nitrate, under the words a percentage, 34.40% N, under that a measurement, Weight 500kg, and finally, under that, Produced in Ukraine. He knelt to check the other bags. More of the same. Wasn't this what the Oklahoma City Bomber had used as the active ingredient for his homemade bomb? Was that what his father was doing, planning to blow up the house from below?

No, that was ridiculous. One thing was certain: whatever his purpose, his father had been here. James stood and continued along the shore, keeping close to the wall. Who knew how deep that water was? There couldn't be anything living in it, could there? An image of an eyeless fish, its skin translucent, flashed across his mind's eye. Thanks, *National Geographic*.

When he came upon his father, it was almost anticlimactic. Back braced against the wall, he was standing with his hands in his trouser pockets, the casual pose of a man passing the time. Were it not for the detail that his pants were rolled above the knee, presumably to avoid dirtying them on the white fertilizer heaped most of the way up his shins, he might have been acting the punchline to an elaborate and overlong joke: *Oh, hi, son, what brings you here?*

"Dad!"

His father's eyes were closed, his lips parted. He did not respond to James's shout. James drew to the edge of the pile of fertilizer and stretched his free hand to his father's chest. Through his shirt, his skin was distressingly soft. James waited. The rotten milk and dirt smell was overwhelming; he could feel it filming the surface of his eyes. Under his fingertips, his father's chest stirred, barely enough to register. A thrill ran up James's arm. "Hang on, Daddy," he said. "I'm getting you out of this."

Dementia: that was the only answer that made any sense of…this. No doubt, his father had been sliding into it for far longer than any of them had realized. His refusal to depart the house suddenly seemed less stubbornness and more anxiety. A surge of pity swept over James. Placing the cell phone on the floor with its screen angled towards his father, he stepped into the fertilizer. He slid his hands between his father's arms and sides, bringing them up and around his back, hugging his father to him. God—there was nothing to him. How long had he been standing here? "Hold on, Dad," he said, lifting and stepping back. His arms sank into his father's back. His father's chest flattened against his. He tilted towards James, but did not come loose from the fertilizer. Grunting, James strained upwards. Between his arms and his chest, his father's trunk shifted, as if his bones had grown not just brittle, but spongy. The reek of bad milk and mold clouded the air around them. He leaned back, pulling as hard as he could. Sweat tickled the sides of his face.

There was a sound like wet cardboard tearing, and his father was free. Overbalanced, James fell, pulling him on top of him. The base of his skull cracked on the stone shelf, detonating fireworks in front of his eyes. A host of sighs escaped his father. Taking him by the shoulders, James gently rolled him onto his back. "Hold on," he said as he struggled to his feet, swaying with dizziness. Pressing the back of his head with one hand, he retrieved the cell phone with the other. He turned the screen to his father.

He did not scream at what the light disclosed. For a long time, his brain simply refused to register the gaps below his father's knees, insisting that he must be confusing the fertilizer caked on his father's skin with blankness, absence. In the same way, his brain would not acknowledge the long rents in his father's neck, the top of his chest, as anything more than shadows. The pale fronds pushed out of the ends of his legs, the vents in his neck and chest, the front of his shirt, were hair, dust, cobwebs. Not until his father's eyelids raised and revealed a pair of orbs speckled with rust-colored patches did James make a sound, and that was a loan moan, the utterance of an animal when it understands that the jaws of the trap have bitten deep into its leg and will not release it.

His father's mouth opened. The tip of his tongue appeared, trying to moisten his lips. His voice was a thin wheeze forced out. "Who?" he said.

James did not answer.

"Light," his father said, his eyelids lowering.

James did not move the cell phone.

Hyphae

With the weak, tentative motions of something very old or very sick, his father twisted from side to side. He was trying to flip over onto his stomach, which he could have accomplished more easily had he removed his hands from his pockets or if his legs had extended below the knees. Instead, he relied on his elbows and hips. It required several attempts. Once he had succeeded, he raised his head as if scenting the air and started a half-crawl towards the mound of fertilizer. His body scraped on the rock floor.

What sent James running from the cave and what had become of his father was seeing the things he was leaving in his wake and identifying them as pieces of himself, chunks of flesh that more resembled the pale meat of a large mushroom. That, and the white threads that rose out of the place where his father's legs had been immersed in the fertilizer, and that inclined towards him as he worked his way back towards them. When what had been his father shoved itself up onto the pile of fertilizer, it exhaled, the sound of something come home.

Cell phone in hand, James fled up the tunnel to the basement, roughing his hands, his head, on the rock, not caring, concerned only with escaping what he had witnessed. The knot of emotion in his chest was indescribable. He scaled the basement stairs three at a time, emerging into the kitchen and daylight that stung his eyes. He stumbled across the living room, out the front door to his car. As he was reversing up the driveway, he realized he was still wearing his improvised mask and breathing in the odor that had saturated it. He clawed it from his face, rolled down the window, and flung it into the tall grass beside the driveway.

When he was almost home, James pulled to the side of the road, shifted the car into Park, and screamed until the cords on his neck stood out, slamming his hands against the steering wheel until it cracked on one side. When he could scream no more, he picked his cell phone up from where he'd flung it on the passenger's seat and dialed his sister's number. Her answering machine picked up. Voice hoarse, he told her he had changed his mind: he wasn't going to visit Dad, after all.

MUSE

Hey Paul,

Thanks very much for the invitation to write the intro for Stephen Graham Jones's gig at Milehicon, which I'm afraid I'm going to have to decline. Mostly—and this is what you can tell Stephen—it's because the new semester's upon me, and I'm already behind with my class prep; not to mention, there are about a half-dozen writing projects, including my next novel, that I have to try to find a way to complete in the next month or so. Otherwise, I'd be more than happy to use up five hundred words talking about my profound admiration for Stephen's work. It's funny: he's one of those writers whose first story I can still remember reading. It was that one he published in *Cemetery Dance*, "Raphael." I think it was Laird who told me I had to check it out; although I have this half-memory of him recommending that I read it and me telling him I already had. Either way, the story was one of those pieces whose first sentence announces its writer's mastery; there was that same compelling storytelling you associate with a writer like Stephen King—as well as the dead-on take on adolescence. I thought I knew what he was up to—the figure we're being led to think is a monster becomes the victim of the real monsters—and then he whipped the rug out from underneath me. No, the monster is the monster, and that reveal remains one of the genuinely creepiest moments in recent fiction I've encountered—as well as a nod to the figure of the girl in the "Ring" movies. That ability to be both the storyteller around the campfire, urging you to draw in closer, this next one's pretty scary, and the metafictionist, crafting a story that's fully aware of its tradition and exploits it in all kinds of subtle ways, is something I admire intensely in Stephen's writing.

Actually, you could pass on all of the previous paragraph to Stephen, along with my regrets. Maybe the people who run the con could cut and paste some of it into a blurb for the program. Whatever you do, please do NOT, under any circumstances, pass along what comes next. You may have noticed that, this past Readercon, I kept my distance from Stephen. Maybe you didn't think anything of it: after all, at any con, there are only so many people you're going to be able to spend time with, and if you find yourself in a series of intense conversations, as I did with the ChiZine crew, well, that's just the nature of the beast. I know you thought my reaction to finding out that you'd left Stephen alone with Lisa and the kids was a little on the odd side, but I'd had a generous sampling of Nathan's single malts, and it wasn't hard to pass off my response as so much alcohol-fueled nonsense.

The thing is, though, it wasn't nonsense; nor was my avoiding him an accident. To tell you the truth, I have a hard time remaining in the same room as the guy without screaming. I know: What the fuck, right? Look: when we were all in Austin for World Horror last year, I spent a fair amount of time with Stephen. With the crutches, he wasn't very mobile, and he didn't seem especially interested in tying one on at any of the room parties, so we hung out in and around the hotel lobby and shot the breeze the way you do at these kinds of events. The guy's knowledge of crap-tastic horror cinema far outshines mine, but he still seemed pleased to chat with someone who'd seen a couple of his personal favorites. I really wanted to talk with him about writing, but he seemed kind of evasive, which I blamed on the pain meds he was taking for his foot, and which didn't stop me from gradually steering the conversation back to writing. Each time the subject came up, he grew more and more agitated, until finally, after my third attempt at asking him about his process, he leapt up off the couch, grabbed his crutches, and said, "Come on."

I didn't know where we were going, but I followed him to the elevators. "What is it?" I said as we stood in front of the closed doors. He wouldn't look at me; instead, he stared at the lit call button and said, "You'll see.

Oh, you'll see." Of course, I thought his behavior was a little strange, but I chalked it up to the meds. He kept saying, "You'll see," as we rode to the elevator to the fourth floor, and when we left the car and turned right—towards his room, I'd figured out—he started to laugh. I guessed he was setting me up for some kind of prank, but that laugh—that laugh was not a happy sound. It was the high-pitched giggle of someone whose sanity has just bowed under the pressure of something he's spent the day not admitting to himself but can no longer be avoided. His room was at the far end of the hall; by the time we reached it, he was howling, tears streaming down his cheeks. He fumbled the key card out of his short pocket and unlocked the door. He pushed it open, then drew back. "Go ahead," he said, nodding at the doorway.

"What?" I said. "What is it?"

"You'll see, man. You'll see. Go ahead."

I did. Not a proverbial bone in my body thought this was a good idea, but I walked into the space I expected to find dark. It wasn't: the small lamp over the desk was on, and by its creamy light, I could see the pair of double beds, the covers rumpled on one of them, an open suitcase on the other, and the easy chair draped with clothes. The drapes were drawn, the air-conditioner on high. There was a faint, foul odor, like spoiled milk, but that was the only detail that caught my notice—until what I had mistaken for the shadow of the drapes scrambled higher up the wall, into the far corner at the ceiling. It was a person, or it looked like a person. There were pale arms and legs poking out of a ragged kind of shift, and a long veil of thick, black hair that hung down well past its face. It wedged itself into the corner, and that was the most awful thing, the way it moved, as if belonged up off the ground, scouring the walls, the ceiling. Its head jerked from side to side, swinging the hair like a pendulum, and I knew with absolute certainty that it was about to leap straight at me. I turned, and although I was sure I was going to collide with the dresser, one of the beds, threw myself towards the doorway. Three lunging steps, and I was in the hall, slamming the door shut behind me and holding it closed, fully expecting whatever I had seen to try to claw its way through it.

Stephen was leaning against the wall, still laughing. "Well," he said. "What do you think?"

"What," I said, "what."

"That's my muse, man."

It was like the punchline to some ridiculous shaggy-dog story, except that there was whatever that was scuttling across the walls of his room. A thousand questions were begging for me to ask them; instead, I released the door lever and, even though there was a fire door on the other side of Stephen, and stairs back down to the lobby, I ran for the elevator, half-certain I could hear something racing along the ceiling behind me. In the elevator, I kept expecting a pale hand to punch down into the car and start grabbing for me. I spent the night dozing on the couch in the lobby where I'd been talking to Stephen, where I couldn't leave well enough alone. I had an early flight the next morning, and I swear, I've never been so glad to see 5:00 a.m. come around.

Funnily enough, a couple of weeks after I'd returned home, Stephen e-mailed me a copy of a story he wanted my opinion on. I replied with one of my own—not that I wanted anything to do with him, but I wanted even less to have him upset with me. Thankfully, he hasn't sent me anything else.

Yeah, I know how all of this—I know. You can think whatever you like about it, but for Christ's sake, don't show it to Stephen. Please.

Best,

John

ZOMBIES IN MARYSVILLE

Some of you know that my older son, Nick, is currently undergoing his field training as a member of the Baltimore city police department. (Please save the concerned references to *The Wire*; believe me, I know.) He's been calling me every couple of days to share the latest amusing anecdotes about life in the part of the city to which he's been assigned, a neighborhood known as Marysville. Much of what he's related has consisted of relatively low-level interactions between him and his training officer and the general populace. Yesterday and today, however, the stories he's had to tell have been of a different order altogether, and given some of what I've noticed on the web this weekend, have me more concerned—more worried than I like to admit.

The first incident occurred around dinner time, yesterday, when he and his training officer responded to a call for backup to a domestic disturbance. They arrived at a modest house whose front door had been broken open by a large stone planter, which partially blocked the doorway. Inside the house, a middle-aged man was brandishing a baseball bat at the much younger, and bigger, man who was standing on the front step. Apparently, the young man was responsible for the baby swelling the belly of the middle-aged man's daughter—who was somewhere inside the house—and was also involved with one of the local gangs, the White Rhinos, who, despite their name, are not to be trifled with. When the homeowner had seen the younger man walking up the sidewalk, he had locked the door and called the police. He did not answer the young man's knocking, after which, the young man stepped back, noticed the stone planters flanking the front step, and wrestled one of them up and over his head. He threw it into the door, which burst inwards. By that time, the first police officers had reached the scene, and were putting out the call for backup that Nick and his training officer would answer. They had seen the young man heft and throw the planter, so had their hands on their guns as they shouted for him to back away from the door. When Nick stepped out of the car, these officers had drawn their guns and were pointing them at the young man, who had not yet answered their calls to step back from the house. Complicating matters, the homeowner was brandishing his Louisville slugger at the young man, daring him to come one step closer, and from her place somewhere behind him, his daughter was screaming and crying.

Nick drew his own gun as the young man finally stepped back from the doorway and bent to pick up the other stone planter. It was quite the sight: each one was easily a couple of hundred pounds, yet this young man wrapped his arms around it and hefted it off the stoop as if it were a quarter of that weight. The cops, Nick included, were screaming at him to drop it, to put the planter down, which, even at the time, sounded absurd. Yet when the guy heaved it at them, and it struck the windshield of the first cruiser, it smashed a hole through it. That was enough for one of the cops: he shot the guy once, through the chest. The young man staggered back, but remained on his feet. At first, Nick thought that maybe the round hadn't struck the young man dead center, but no, the hole in the guy's sweatshirt was clearly visible. It wasn't bleeding, which made him wonder if the guy were wearing some kind of body armor under his sweatshirt. All the cops were still shouting, telling the young man to lie down, but not only did he remain standing, he started to walk towards them. Because of where they were positioned, neither Nick nor his training officer could get a clear shot at the young man without endangering the homeowner behind him, but Nick was fully expecting the young man to collapse as his wound caught up with him. He did not, and the same officer who'd fired the first shot did so a second and a third time, tracking his shots up the young man's torso as he went. His fourth bullet struck the young man in the face, under the right eye, and all at once, the guy dropped where he was. Things after that were fairly chaotic: once Nick and his colleagues had swarmed forward to check on the young man, who was indeed dead, there were calls to be made for an ambulance, for additional officers to support the investigation that was now required. It was, as you might imagine, a fairly intense experience for an officer still in training, and we spent a good deal of last night discussing it. It was strange, Nick said, but he couldn't get over the lack of blood. He'd checked: that first shot looked to have gone clean through the guy's heart. He should have bled all over the place, but even after he was down, there was no blood to speak of.

This was on my mind throughout the day, today, as I skimmed what seemed to me some of the more…extravagant stories making the news, popping up on the web. When Nick called tonight, those reports were the first thing he mentioned. Once I told him that yes, I'd seen them, but didn't really give them much credit, he asked me if I were sure. I wasn't, but didn't a virus that could reanimate the recently deceased seem to be pushing the limits of believability, just a little? It did, Nick said, but the guy from yesterday? The M.E. wasn't done with his examination, yet, but the word was, the young man he'd seen walking around, who'd thrown a stone planter forty feet at him and his fellow officers, had been dead for between twelve and fifteen hours when he'd done so. Nor was that all. Something had gone down last night—some kind of big operation involving the guys on the night shift and a group of feds who weren't wearing any identifying logos on their body armor but whose orders command had told the night shift crew were to be followed without question. No one would say anything very definite, but apparently, they'd conducted a raid on a building that had been under surveillance as one of the way stations the White Rhinos used in their human trafficking operations. There was some kind of huge basement under the place where things had gotten pretty hairy. Today, everyone on Nick's shift was given a handout detailing a set of behaviors to be on the lookout for ranging from aimless wandering to extreme, bath-salt-style acts of violence. The streets had been quiet, but there were rumors of things happening elsewhere, in D.C., Philly.

"You know," he said before we hung up, "I know you're not really into guns and all that, but maybe you should think about getting a shotgun or something. Just in case."

41

"I'll think about it," I told him. To be honest, I already was. And I was wondering if it was already too late for that.

WITH MAX BARRY IN THE
NEARER PRECINCTS

N one of us should have been surprised: if anyone could have been expected to find his way back, it was Max Barry. Hadn't he spent the last three-quarters of a century investigating the murky terrain just the other side of this life? Hadn't one of the three of us accompanied him for the last two decades, as he roamed the country searching out and interviewing those who had ventured the margins of existence? Hadn't we entered those accounts into Barry's massive archive (properly cross-referenced, of course), and helped him coordinate the information he retrieved, to arrange it into practically a map of the undiscovered country's nearer precincts? With almost the final breath his failing lungs could muster, Barry promised us at least a sign—not so original a pledge, perhaps, but one weighted by the accumulated years of his research.

And yet, when myself, Torres, and Schaefer were the recipients of not just a sign, but the presence of the man, himself, our combined reactions might have been lifted from the most formulaic horror film. We had gathered around the oak table in the study as we did every Thursday evening. With Barry a fortnight in the family mausoleum behind the house, there was little reason for the three of us to be there, for while we had been more than diligent in the work we performed for him, the quality of our efforts owed itself less to any shared passion for the subject and more to the generous paychecks he signed every other week—that, and the force of his personality, which had the effect of a powerful magnet on a scattering of iron filings, snapping them into alignment with itself. While his will appointed us trustees of his estate at salaries every bit as comfortable as those we had drawn as his assistants, and while that document allowed and encouraged us to use a substantial portion of the Barry fortune to extend his research, absent Max's presence, the offer held scant interest for us.

Although we had spent the first meeting after his death in reminiscences of Max, and half the second in gossip, we continued to gather in the study with its thick green carpet and heavy black curtains from an obscure sense of loyalty, a desire not to allow the project of a man's life to end mid-sentence, but to bring the paragraph to a full and complete stop. We hadn't any notion how this was to be done, whether the archive, for example, might find a home at a sympathetic university; or whether one or the other of us might write the account of our experiences in Barry's employ; or even whether we might hire a new, younger group to continue the task of exploring the other side by proxy—but I believe we felt that, if we carried on our meetings, eventually, the solution to our dilemma would present itself.

There were two empty chairs at the table that night: the one usually occupied by Barry and the one which frequently went unoccupied but occasionally sat a guest Barry had invited. It was in this second, typically-vacant chair that Max Barry suddenly sat.

If I were to attempt to justify the screams that erupted from Torres, Schaefer's string of oaths, my start up from my seat, it would be through an appeal to Barry's appearance. Anyone who has been in the presence of a corpse knows the fundamental *difference* of the dead, their utter stillness, the lack of barely-perceptible motions through which life percolates out of us. Although it wore his favorite black suit, white shirt, and black tie, the figure that sat in our midst was as motionless as it had been in its coffin. Because of its slackness, the face was at first unrecognizable to me; it was the work of some seconds to identify the large, round nose, the long forehead, the lips that always seemed too thin for the wide mouth. Had the eyes been open, I might have fitted the pieces of the puzzle more quickly, but they were—and remained throughout his visitation—closed.

Once I assembled its components into Barry's large, plain face, however, and understood who it was beside me, a rush of pure terror caused me to shove my chair back and retreat to the couch, which I almost fell over. Torres found her voice before the rest of us. "Max—Mr. Barry?"

The figure's mouth dropped open like that of a ventriloquist's dummy. The voice that issued from it was unmistakably Barry's broad, pleasant one, but it sounded off, as if it had been poorly-recorded, then played on a stereo with a shorted speaker. "Ms. Torres," it said. "Mr. Schaefer. Mr. Anderson."

"Mr. Barry," Schaefer and I said.

"You've returned," Torres said.

"Yes," the figure said. "Did I not say I would?"

Torres stuttered an answer. The figure—Barry—said, "It is all right, Ms. Torres. You were right to be skeptical. It has ever been your role in our little group."

"How are you?" Schaefer said.

"I still *am*, Mr. Schaefer. What about you, Mr. Anderson? Do you have no words for your old employer?"

The note of familiarity in that strange voice made my bowels clench. My mouth was dry. I licked my lips and said, "What can you tell us?"

"Very good," Barry said. "Very good. I am not sure how much time I will have with you, so I'll try to be direct. From the beginning, then—or the end:

The passage was about what we had anticipated. As my vision grew dark at the edges, it brightened at the center. From a point, the brightness swelled to a circle, which opened into a tunnel. I rose out of my body toward it. The process was as easy as the reports led me to expect. If I had to compare it to anything, it would be to swimming, to pulling your arms and kicking your feet and feeling the water move around you. My astral body was a fairly exact copy of my corporeal form, with the exception that its senses appeared sharper for the transition. That, and I wore, not my hospital gown, but my suit. The sensation—the white tunnel seemed to be tugging me to it as much as I was floating to meet it. I looked down, and saw the three of you around my bed, the doctor turning away. I saw my body, the final breath leaving it. I felt more buoyant. Ahead, the white tunnel reached to an end incredibly distant and blindingly brilliant, the heart of a star. The nearer I drew to the opening, the stronger its pull became.

I had the impression that, were I to exert myself, I might resist the tunnel's attraction. There was some interest to me in this. Having investigated so many reports of ghosts, what an opportunity, to assume the role, myself. This temptation paled, however, in comparison to that of venturing the white tunnel. Now, I could see figures within it, detaching themselves from the wall. There were three of them. Each appeared dressed in white robes. Their faces were too far away to distinguish yet, together, they produced a feeling of profound calm, almost familiarity. I thought they might be members of my family, come to welcome me to the next stage, my mother and father, perhaps, one of my sisters. I gave myself up to the tunnel.

There was the impression of traveling without movement. Whiteness sped by; otherwise, I might have been standing still. The trio of white forms swept around me. Their faces were no clearer; each remained a bright blur. I saw that what I had taken for their robes was in fact their substance. They brushed against me, and the calm this produced was almost soporific—even hypnotic. Ahead, the tunnel's brilliant destination was larger, closer. It seemed I could glimpse something beyond that opening, a landscape of rolling hills through which wound a shining river. Beyond the hills, a city like an arrangement of great white crystals rose into a blue sky.

On all sides, the white trio pressed against me. Despite the tranquility they radiated and the impression of familiarity, I was uneasy; indeed, it was that overwhelming calm that disturbed me. Rather than the Heavenly peace I at first took it for, it verged on the anesthetic. Through the blur, I perceived one of the trio's faces, and it was empty, as an open mouth is empty. I was more shocked by this than made afraid, but a profound fear gripped me when I concentrated on the end of the tunnel—nearer and brighter still—and saw, not the slopes of paradise, but a vast, shining emptiness. Dulled as my senses had become, I felt what lay at the terminus of the white tunnel alive, a living void. It was hungry, primordially so, and it was that appetite that drew me up from my failing body along the white tunnel. I had a vision of an aardvark searching for ants. This was not the God-as-blank of negative theology; it was the open maw of the Behemoth.

Although wrapped in lethargy, I knew at once I must escape my escorts. This was no easy task. The closer we approached that great mouth, the more the white figures crowded me. One kept directly in front, the other two behind and to either side. There was no time. Summoning what little energy remained, I threw myself to the left. One of the figures behind grabbed me, but surprise gave me the advantage and I pulled free. The wall of the white tunnel rushed toward me. I struck and plunged into it—I would compare the sensation to diving into a pool or lake, except the medium that enveloped me was thicker than water, more viscous, though not so much as to immobilize me. Brightness blinded me. Kicking and pushing, I struggled through the material of the tunnel wall. For a long moment, that I might remain trapped in this place seemed an awful possibility, a fate only slightly less worse than being swallowed by that enormous gullet. The medium thickened around me, my movement became difficult. Frantic, I pushed forward. In response, the wall stretched. Mustering my strength, I pressed against it a second time. At the tips of my fingers, I felt the substance part.

All at once, I was free, tumbling through darkness. Behind me was a brilliant glare, a river of light filling the near horizon, flowing out of the distance, into the distance. Beyond it, I could discern other, similar streams, as I could when I turned my attention to what lay before me. From their appearance—narrow brooks in comparison with the flood next to me—I guessed each must lay at a considerable remove from its fellows. As I slowed, I perceived more of the lines of light, so that the entire, I suppose I should call it the sky, above me resembled a tremendous net.

Pieces of the white trio had adhered to my arms, my chest. When I tried to work my fingers under one of them, my eyes filled with the sight of the celestial landscape I had thought I'd seen at the end of the white tunnel. Nausea climbed my throat. In a kind of frenzy, I ripped and tore at the fragments attached to me, flinging each a different direction once it was loose.

Somewhat more calm, I decided I must move. While the white trio had not appeared in pursuit, I was reluctant to venture any direction that would bring me too close to the blazing tunnels. This precluded all courses save one, down, into the darkness below. In the collective glow of the tunnels, I picked out dim, shadowy forms an uncertain distance away. The nearest of them did not appear unduly far. By kicking my legs, pulling my arms—in effect, "swimming" as I had in the tunnel wall—I was able to propel myself toward it.

I descended I am not certain how much, but when I looked up, the tunnel I escaped was a good three-quarters diminished in width, from river to stream. Sufficient light remained for me to distinguish that the nearest shadowy form I sought was actually a structure.

It was a staircase, rising from the deeper dark. The top three or four steps were jagged, incomplete, as if it previously had climbed higher; what was visible of the remainder appeared whole. Each of the steps was wide enough to accommodate two adults at a time. Their surfaces had been grooved by the passage of countless feet. I circled the staircase warily. There were no individual bricks or slabs I could see; the entire thing appeared to have been carved from a single piece of material. I swam closer. I thought the staircase might have been struck from a great block of stone, cut free from a mountain, or chiseled from a tree of Redwood proportions, but the texture of the material was wrong for either. I reached out and touched the nearest step. It was warm, and though apparently firm enough to support the combined weight of countless people, oddly spongy. I eased myself over until I was directly above the stair, then rested on it, ready to spring off should the staircase threaten to give way. When it did not, I decided I would follow these steps down for as long as was safe.

As I descended step to step, I reflected on my experience. Obviously, the map of the next life I had charted was, to say the least, incomplete. When the tunnel of light had opened for me, I assumed myself *en route* to some version of paradise. Instead, I had been lured into what was, for all intents and purposes, a trap. Try as I might, I could not reconcile this with the details of any religions I knew, living or dead. The white void I saw might be hell or a similar place, but if such were the case, then why employ not only the bright tunnel, but the white trio to lure me there? Surely, a deity powerful enough to create such a place would have no need to resort to trickery to deposit souls there; surely, there were more direct means available. Not to mention, if eternal damnation were my fate, you would not expect me to have evaded it with such relative ease. Nor did my impression of that great emptiness as living fit with the descriptions of hell I knew; though, I will admit, it put me in mind of those medieval paintings in which the gates of hell are represented as the mouth of an enormous scarlet head.

From the moment I started down them, I kept track of the number of stairs I descended. By the time I reached four hundred, I could distinguish more clearly the other shapes I had seen from above. In what looked the middle distance to my right, a slender spire stood alone. Several smaller beams angled from its base, but the light was too dim, the spire too far, for me to tell whether these were supports, or bridges, or smaller towers that had collapsed against this one. Conceivably, they might have been pieces of the spire, itself, upper reaches broken by the same cataclysm that had sundered the top of the staircase.

To my left was a trio of squat towers that gained definition as I passed the five hundredth step. The nearest of these was no more than fifteen or twenty feet away, the next-closest just the other side of it, and the third not much further beyond. They were constructed of small bricks, each approximately the size of my hand, of a style so basic as to be universal. A long gash split the nearest tower's near wall; its companions showed similar damage. What was visible of the tower's interior showed plain, undecorated rooms full of shattered furniture, chairs, and tables broken to kindling.

Far ahead, an elaborate archway marked one edge of the dark plane to which the staircase led. To either side and beyond, the archway was joined by low, box-like structures that reminded me of rows of apartments. It was in one of these, past the archway, that I saw a light shining in a rectangular opening I realized was a window. This was not the brilliance of the white tunnel and its minions; this was the homely glow of an oil lamp, a fireplace. The sight of it hurried my feet past the six-hundredth step.

Another forty-three stairs and I reached the foot of the great staircase. In front of me stretched a broad, flat space. At about the level of my thigh, a thick, black fog rolled slowly over the plane. So dense was the stuff that I could not see through it. I eased one leg into it. The fog eddied around my flesh. Under my foot, the plane was sandy, but not uncomfortable. I was reluctant to wade through it, but the gravity of this place seemed to have me in its grip. I could not float across; there was no choice but to walk through. Eyes fixed on the distant glow, I set off.

Overhead, lines of light sliced the sky into narrow strips of black. Although I still could identify the tunnel from which I fled, the remainder of my trip down the staircase had reduced its width further, to the point it was barely larger than its neighbors. While I am not much of a physical scientist, I felt fairly certain I had not crossed a sufficient distance to result in so dramatic a change in the tunnel's size. It was as if the stairs bridged more territory than they showed. I was unsure what this implied, beyond the suggestion that space did not appear to follow quite the same rules as it had the other side of death. I looked back at the staircase, the towers beside it, yet though diminished slightly, nothing seemed as out of proportion as the white lines to which my eyes once more strayed. I saw them bending slightly at either end: so far to the right it was barely visible, they disappeared into a pale yellow glow that suffused the horizon; equally far to the left, they were swallowed by what might have been a wall of heavy gray clouds.

I reached the midpoint of my trek across the dark plane. So intrigued was I by that yellow light, that surface of roiling gray, I stopped in my tracks in order to study both more attentively. As I stood gazing at the sky, something bumped into me.

The collision occurred at about the level of my knee, and while not violent, so startled me that I leapt back. In so doing, I struck a second object, which sent me lurching into something else. All at once, it seemed, I could not move without encountering whatever was about me. My way forward had been blocked by whatever my leg had met, which seemed to have closed off the space behind me, as well. Around me, the dark fog shifted. That I had blundered into a fate equal to or worse than the one I escaped at the end of the white tunnel loomed before me as a distinct possibility.

Beyond the arch, the window dimmed, then brightened, its glow eclipsed by a shape whose outlines appeared distinctly human. Of course, the white trio had looked human enough, at first, but something about this silhouette—the particularity of its form—spoke of the human in a way those gauzy shapes had not. The sight heartened me. If I were to reach that window, I would have to find my way off this plane, which meant I must ascertain the nature of the objects that hemmed me in. I lowered myself into a crouch.

Even this close, the fog was tar-thick. Nonetheless, I distinguished an outline within it. In front and to the right, suspended horizontally in darkness as if in a bath or pool, was a man. He was naked, eyes closed, face calm, hands at his sides, legs together. I should place his age at thirty-five. I looked behind me and saw a woman, likewise suspended, naked, her face also blank. She appeared the same age as the man. Floating in the shadows beyond was another, somewhat older, man, and a child, a girl of perhaps twelve years of age, and another woman. As far as I could determine, the fog overlaying this plane was full of bodies. I stretched out my hand and touched the man in front of me. His skin was dry, papery; it crackled under my fingers. He seemed curiously light, not only from whatever quality of the fog kept him suspended, but as if he, himself, were hollow. Gently, I pushed his arm, and he swung away from me as if he were an oversized balloon. He bumped the person behind him, an old woman, who in turn jostled a younger woman beyond her, and so on. About half a dozen bodies away, one of them released a sound, a sort of high-pitched gasp. I straightened. At the spot from which the gasp emanated, the fog belled up. A man stood up through it. He was tall, and within a decade or two of my age. His features were difficult to discern, because of what I took for wisps of fog clinging to his face. With a lurching gait, he staggered toward me. As he did, I saw that the black fog about his face spilled out of it, streaming from his eyes, his nostrils, his mouth, his ears. He raised his arms, and the motion unbalanced him, forcing him to half-run at me. When his hands found me, they gripped my shoulders with surprising strength. I caught his wrists and attempted to steady him, but he continued to push forward, thrusting his head at me, his mouth open.

I attempted to speak to him. "My dear fellow," I said, but his fingers dug into my shoulders, his neck stretching, lengthening, bringing his gaping jaw near. Black vapor poured down his face, into the fog below. The sound of crackling filled my ears. I said, "Please, I am not—" but did not know how to conclude. I *wasn't*, not the same as he was. I released his left wrist, clenched my hand, and struck what I hoped would be a solid blow to his sternum.

With the noise of a heavy paper bag tearing, my fist punched through his chest. A black cloud burst out of the wound. Horrified, I jerked my hand out of the man, whose hands let go of me. Black vapor venting from his chest, the man leaned back, as if trying to draw away from the hurt I caused him. His left arm drooped. He swayed to that side, and toppled under the fog, which leapt up where he splashed into it.

A mix of revulsion and confusion swept over me. The sight of a handful of men and women standing from the fog at various spots around me did nothing to help. I looked for the gateway, located it, and ran with all the speed my fear would lend. Black fog churned about me. My legs struck hidden bodies, sent them crashing into their neighbors. From points across the plane, other gasps sounded. Additional figures raised themselves out of the fog. I was reasonably certain they were moving in my direction, but was not inclined to stop to be absolutely sure. The gateway was close enough for me to see that, like the staircase that conveyed me here, it had been carved from a single block of material into the scene of an enormous battle. Dozens, if not hundreds, of men and women, dressed in armor and employing weapons whose style suggested ancient Greece, struggled against a quartet of huge, fantastic creatures. I was too concerned with reaching and passing through the gate to devote any more scrutiny to it. I was positive that, at any moment, a hand would seize my ankle and pull me down into the fog; either that, or I would find the clumsiness which had bedeviled my earthly existence had accompanied me to this place, and I would trip over my own feet and plunge myself beneath the fog.

Such, fortunately, was not the case. I ran through the huge gate, and among the buildings beyond. A backward glance showed a score, perhaps more, of men and women walking on the plane, none with any speed, and all a comfortable distance away. I slowed my pace, but did not stop running.

The space in which I found myself was wide, flat. The ground was the same sandy texture as it had been under the black fog. At random intervals, the stumps of what must have been modest trees raised edges broken and jagged. Long, low structures bordered the place. Each was two stories tall, constructed of the same, hand-sized bricks as the towers I had seen from the staircase. Their ground floors were punctuated by between fifteen and twenty plain wooden doors, their second stories by a pair of windows. All of the buildings showed damage of a kind consistent with that I had observed done to the towers, tears and rents through their walls that revealed the wreckage of their interiors. An entire corner of a building to my left had collapsed; while a building to my right had been practically bisected.

The light that had set me on this course lay ahead, splashed over the interior of a window set to the right of a wooden door. To either side of this window and its door, the building in which they were set bore enormous holes. This close, I had a better view of the rooms that had been exposed by the damage; though their contents were a jumble, I noted a mirror in a gilt frame, a polished chest of drawers, and a large bookcase full of fat volumes. As I drew nearer my destination, my run slowed, until it was a brisk walk. I strode up to the door, one hand raised to knock on it, and it swung open.

Framed in the doorway was a devil.

Or, rather, framed in the doorway was a man dressed as a devil. His costume consisted of a red, satiny bodysuit that rose to a tight-fitting hood from the front of which sprang a pair of fabric horns. His face was ornamented with a Van Dyke no doubt intended to accentuate his infernal appearance. His hands were fitted with black gloves, his feet with black boots, and over the bodysuit, he wore a pair of black shorts from the left leg of which dangled a fabric tail, complete with barb.

The sight of him halted me where I was. With a wave of his hand, the man urged me inside, saying, "Come on, come on!" I hurried past him into a narrow hallway. He shut the door and secured it with a quartet of heavy locks and bolts. "It's too much," he said, "for the Hungry Men, and not nearly enough for a Child of Nun. But then, what is enough for one of the Children? You can't call it peace of mind, but you can call it the illusion of peace of mind, which, oddly, *provides* a certain peace of mind." The man walked by me to the end of the hall, where three doors opened right, center, and left, respectively. He pushed the door to the right, and gestured for me to follow him.

I did, and entered a high-ceilinged room whose red wallpaper, oriental carpet, and fire snapping in a marble fireplace suggested the drawing room of a Victorian gentleman, an impression bolstered by the pair of high-backed leather chairs positioned before the fire. Under the room's window, an arts-and-crafts-style desk was stacked with papers and books, as was the abbreviated table to its left. The room was warm, even cozy. The man in the devil costume closed the door behind me and crossed to a small stand holding a crystal decanter and a collection of tumblers. He said, "Can I offer you a drink?"

If the question was absurd, it was no less so than anything else I had experienced thus far. I said, "I take it that isn't ambrosia."

"It is very good Scotch," the man said.

With something like good humor, I said, "Perhaps this is paradise, after all."

The man's face fell. "Oh no," he said. "In days gone by, it was—it was something, but not now, no."

He poured liberal portions into two of the glasses, and held one to me. With thanks, I took it. The dense odor of peat and brine, leavened with honey, hovered over the liquor. I said, "What shall we toast?"

"There is nothing to toast," the man answered.

"For me, there is," I said. "I shall drink to your offering me shelter in this—in this place."

The man did not reply, though he took an ample sip from his glass. The Scotch burned down my throat like the water of life its creators had christened it. I said, "Permit me to introduce myself. I am Maxwell James Barry, late of the city of Wiltwyck, New York," and extended my hand.

"I am pleased to make your acquaintance," the man said, taking my hand in his. "When I walked amongst the living, I was called Herbert Herne."

"And now," I said, "are you known as Mephistopheles?"

For a moment, my host did not appear to understand my joke, then understanding lit his face and he said, "The costume, yes—even here, it must look odd. Call it a bit of self-mockery, and something of an act of self-censure, the scarlet without the A, if you see what I mean."

"What use is such a gesture, here?" I asked. "I admit, I wondered whether this might be hell; in which case, your action might be appropriate. However, I strongly suspect this is not hell, and so must question the need for your penance."

"Not penance," Herbert Herne said. He drank the rest of his liquor. "I do not repent anything I did. Anything. At the same time, I recognize its cost. I know how I would be judged, were there any left here to judge me. It is out of deference to those absent intentions that I bear this sign in place of the one with which they would have branded me."

"I don't understand," I said. "Can you tell me where we are, what this place is called?"

"I can." Herne refilled his glass, held out the decanter to me. I shook my head. He replaced the container and said, "We are in what remains of First Heaven, sometimes known as Šamû. It was here that the first men and women to depart the lands of the living found their way."

"Who is its creator?" I said.

Herne shrugged. "Some say it appeared when the chaos that preceded everything grew chaotic to itself and birthed form and order. Others say it is a remnant of the paradise of another cosmos. It was here long before our universe burst into existence. It was a rough, rude place, an island floating in a Sea of Chaos from which creatures vast and terrifying emerged, giants with a hundred arms, dragons whose fire melted rock, chimeras whose hooves sundered the ground. The first inhabitants were confused, afraid. They built what shelter they could from the raw material at hand and huddled together for comfort. For decades, centuries, longer, as the island's population grew, little changed. The shelters became more elaborate, but the beasts of the surrounding deep, the Children of Nun, as they were later called, continued to climb onto the island and rampage through the buildings in their paths, carrying off what inhabitants they could to a fate none of their companions wanted to guess.

"Not until the arrival of a young man to whom posterity would give the name amar-Utu did the islanders' situation improve. While alive—somewhere in Mesopotamia, the stories say—this amar-Utu had not been held of much account, because of a right leg that was noticeably shorter than the left. No such affliction troubled his spirit form—what the residents of these parts call the ka. Once arrived and apprised of the state of affairs, he set about improving them. Such efforts had been made before, of course, over and over, but none who attempted them possessed amar-Utu's combination of charm and brilliance. The inhabitants had established a watch along the island's shores, but its staffing was irregular. amar-Utu convinced the islanders to maintain a more consistent schedule, and to set up a network of runners to pass the sentries' alarms more efficiently. In the same way, he improved and extended the shelters that had been built. His chief accomplishment, though, was in devising a strategy for confronting, defeating, and binding the Children of Nun.

"It was a labor to be measured in centuries. amar-Utu fashioned weapons to be used against the beasts. He organized the islanders into an army. He led this army against the beasts and, when it was defeated, forged new and better weapons. In the end, he and his forces dismembered several of the worst monsters, and pursued the rest to their lairs in the deep, where they chained them fast."

I said, "What became of this amar-Utu?"

Herne said, "He left. Once Šamû was secure, and its people could turn their attention to building it into something more grand—a heaven worthy of the name—amar-Utu took his leave. In his campaigns about the island, he discovered it was not, in fact, an island, but the tip of a much larger land mass to which it was joined by a slender bridge of rock. Accompanied by Mušḫuššu, one of the Children of Nun he won over to his side, he set out to explore that other place. As the population of First Heaven grew, some of its more adventurous inhabitants followed him to what would be called Second Heaven. amar-Utu was no longer there, though he left signs indicating he had traveled further still into the unknown, moving through what those to come after him named Third, Fourth, and Fifth Heavens. By the time I arrived here, there were a full dozen heavens. amar-Utu's whereabouts were long-unknown; if asked, most inhabitants said he had 'gone to deeper heaven.'"

"What happened here, then?" I asked. "Did amar-Utu return and find the place not to his liking?"

"Oh no," Herne said. "amar-Utu has remained unseen despite the catastrophe. There were, naturally, some who looked to his return in their hour of need, but they were...disappointed." Before I could repeat my question, he continued, "As for what befell this and the other heavens: I did."

"You?"

"In life, I worked in insurance," Herne said. "I resided in Hartford, Connecticut, during the first decades of the twentieth century. I was something of a prodigy at puzzles, games, figures, and this talent served me well. Upon graduation from high school, I obtained a position at a medium-sized insurance company, where my abilities allowed me to achieve ten years' promotions in three. It occasioned no small jealousy in those I vaulted over, but I was otherwise well-liked. I performed in a community theater—*Faustus*, yes, among our productions, though I was cast as Wagner—and regularly attended the local Methodist church. When the United States entered the Great War, I was not enthusiastic to enlist; indeed, it required all my acting skills to convince my fellow workers that only my sense of responsibility to the company restrained me from joining the mad dash to bayonet a Hun in the name of liberty. With the war's end, I judged myself safe from foreign peril. I did not reckon on the influenza epidemic of 1918, which conveyed me, and so many others, here.

"The possibilities for me in this place—once I adjusted to the revelation that it was not the destination Reverend MacGonagle had assured me was awaiting—the possibilities were as large as was it. I opted to work in one of the libraries, the better to learn about my new home. It was amidst the bookcases that I read the history of this place, the story of amar-Utu, which, as I'm sure you can imagine, is considerably more elaborate than the summary I provided you. I was fascinated with what the historians named the *Titanes Theoi*, the Straining Gods, the Children of Nun that amar-Utu and his forces had conquered and bound. Even here, on the other side of the grave, it was hard to credit that such fantastic things could exist. I made inquiries and found that, if I so desired, a guide would lead me to the Straining Gods. I should not have been so amazed: when eternity is the measure of your days, you realize all things are possible, and make plans for them.

"An older woman, a member of the army—largely a ceremonial force— met me on the far side of First Heaven, in sight of the rock bridge to Second Heaven. We were on the shore, where the Sea of Chaos does not look much different from any other sea. My guide, whose name was Cosette, walked toward the sea, at the very edge of which a stone slab had been sunk into the ground. She stepped onto it, and down onto another below it, and so on. I followed her, and we descended a staircase that skirted the very edge of the Sea of Chaos, but did not touch it. It was as if a wall of glass held the sea back, though I could not see any such glass present. Most of the way was dark, lit by lamps placed every hundred steps. I made what conversation I could with Cosette, but she was not talkative—odd, for a guide. There were ten thousand steps between First Heaven and the Straining Gods. We took them at a steady pace. At the bottom, we arrived at a flat, square space bordered by darkness. I walked to one side of the square and said, 'Where are they?'

"'Look,' Cosette said, and it was as if her command adjusted my vision. There, in front of me, no further away than the reach of my arm, was a nightmare. It was immense as a mountain is immense, a rounded bulk whose mouth was wide enough to swallow a battleship. Teeth—fangs tall as sequoias jutted from its lower jaw. Its three eyes were dim moons set high above. It appeared to be lying on its belly, its head propped toward me. In the distance beyond it, other forms, larger still, loomed in the darkness.

"I screamed," Herne said. "I am not ashamed to admit it. Making matters worse, I could see no chains encircling the beast. I said as much to Cosette when she ran to my side. My guide pointed out a slender rope strung around the creature. Similar bonds, she said, held all the creatures. You can appreciate the skepticism with which I met this information. I wondered if this were an elaborate joke, an entertainment for bored immortals, but Cosette was earnest. In front of us, the ends of the rope met in an elaborate knot that had callused the great beast's warty hide. Cosette took my hand and pressed it to the knot. I thought she wanted to make a point about the pattern into which the rope had been tied. When my palm brushed the rope, though, an electric jolt shot through me. With that shock came understanding.

"You will remember I mentioned those islanders the Children of Nun had carried off with them. One of amar-Utu's pledges to the inhabitants of Šamû had been that he would learn their fate and, if possible, rescue them. He fulfilled the first half of his pledge. After he and his army pursued the monsters to their lairs at the bottom of the Sea of Chaos, he discovered those who had been taken for provender. I am not sure if you've discovered this, yet, but we ka are difficult to destroy outright. It is not utterly impossible, but it is beyond the power even of the Children of Nun. What the creatures could do was feed on their captives, suck and scrape every last vestige of everything that made those men and women who they were out of them, until all that remained was a husk, too tough for digestion. Emptied, the husks wandered the lairs, hungry for what they had lost. They attacked amar-Utu and his forces, who defeated them handily. Once the soldiers realized what the Hungry Men were, they were aghast.

"I do not know what led amar-Utu to recognize that the stuff of the Hungry Men could be fashioned into bonds that would hold the Children of Nun. His words on the subject are vague. It would have been an awful scene. The end result was that, when amar-Utu and his forces subdued each of the remaining beasts, they had a means with which to restrain it. Various writers to come after amar-Utu sought to rationalize his decision, but it seemed clear to me that he did not depart Šamû to search out what was ahead, but to escape what lay behind.

"I could have viewed the remaining beasts—there were another three—but that one was enough. The return from my excursion left me with much to consider. Not least amongst it was the knot securing the monster's bonds. As we mounted the stairs, I asked Cosette if she did not fear that the knot might loosen. Of course she assumed I was foisting my anxiety onto her, and told me there was no need to worry. amar-Utu, himself, had devised and tied the knot that held this and all of the Children of Nun. She did not know how much attention I had given the knot, but its complexity was such that none who studied it since could work out how to undo it. Tug at one part of it, and you tightened another. Solving the Gordian knot would have been simpler. I reminded my guide that Alexander had answered that riddle with the edge of his sword. Such a reply, she assured me, would be useless in this case, as no blade in anyone's possession could sever the ka rope in which this knot and its brethren had been tied. Even were someone to own so fine a sword, who would use it to that end?"

I interrupted Herne, "You would. You did."

Herne said, "You must understand, from the instant my eyes fell upon that knot, its solution was obvious to me. This was part of the reason I became as agitated as I had at Cosette's assertion that this slim rope was sufficient to the task of holding a Straining God in check. With a quick pull of the correct loop, the design that was responsible for keeping this unlikely prison in place could be undone, which seemed the clearest madness. Twice, I was on the verge of speaking to Cosette about it, the first time when she pointed out the knot to me, the second while we climbed the stairs."

"Why didn't you?" I asked.

"I doubted myself," Herne said. "In the face of Cosette's expression of utter faith in the knot, I assumed I was mistaken. After all, how many men and women must have viewed that knot before me? Was it likely that, after none of them had been able to untie it, I should understand the means to do so the moment I saw it? And yet, and yet...I had apprehended its undoing. I was as sure of it as I had ever been of anything. Fearing embarrassment, I kept silent. Back in my quarters, however, I immediately found a length of rope and set about first tying the knot, which took me several tries, and then untying it, which I managed on my first attempt. My success did nothing to reassure me. I was certain I must have missed something in the fashioning of the knot, some detail that would render my solution of it null and void. At the same time, I knew that nothing had escaped my notice. I searched the library's holdings for images of amar-Utu's knot, and every last one of them I found matched the copies I had made."

"Then why not share your knowledge?" I said. "Surely, the powers who oversaw this place would have appreciated your discovery."

"Perhaps they would have," Herne said. "Or perhaps they would have imprisoned the man in possession of such information, fearful of the use to which he might put it."

"Would they have been wrong?"

"It was all I thought about," Herne said. "If there was a piece of thread lying about, I tied it into amar-Utu's knot and untied it. If there was a pen or pencil and a sheet of paper, I drew the steps to constructing the knot. If my hands were empty, they went through the motions of looping this end of the rope through that. If I were to say I was outraged by the use to which the ka of those long-ago captives had been put, that I burned for vengeance on their behalf, I expect my motivations would sound more compelling. But if I were disturbed by the material from which the Children of Nun's bindings had been drawn, I understood and accepted the necessity for it. No, what led me to return to that staircase on my own, to descend the ten thousand stairs, to stand once more in front of that Straining God, was nothing so grand. It was more a case of the knot's solution pushing its way out of my fingertips."

"Obviously," I said, "you were correct."

Herne said, "I had not anticipated the speed with which the beast would seize the opportunity I presented it. Despite millennia of imprisonment, during which it was fed nothing, it heaved itself up with the suddenness of an earthquake. Beyond it, the other beasts groaned and thrashed. I fled for the staircase, sure that I was going to be the morsel with which the monster would break its fast. It rose past me, larger even than I had appreciated. I was afraid it would smash the staircase on its way, which, despite my terrified state, I realized would constitute a kind of poetic justice, but though its bulk veered close, it completed its ascent without destroying my means of escape.

"I returned to war in the heavens. The great beast hung in the air. Its canyon mouth yawed, swallowing flaming missiles like so many fireflies. Its three tails raked the ground, toppling buildings as if they were children's blocks. Up and down its armored flanks, bombs and rockets burst in flashes of white, yellow, and orange. Behind its blunt head, an enormous mane dangled its ends above the forces gathered below. As I watched, one of the strands snaked into the ranks and jerked up, carrying a man with it. Other strands followed, plucking the defenders from their positions. The mane was composed not of hair, but of tentacles, each one terminating in a mouth. Once it wrapped around a man or woman, the tentacle's mouth sought his or her chest, clamped onto it, and fed. When the defender was drained, emptied, in the process of a minute, less, the tentacle dropped the remains and went in search of new prey. It was as if I watched a grotesque resident of the Pacific's depths, a fish half-dinosaur, feasting on a shoal of hapless fry. To be sure, there were those who remembered their last battle against this beast, but surprise gave it an advantage that the panic and confusion of the other inhabitants cemented. Vast as it was, it swelled with the lives on which it gorged, moving through the heavens with the slow, steady pace of a fire devouring a forest. In the end, it settled its bulk on the remnants of Seventh Heaven. From there, its tentacles rose into the sky, arcing toward the line of light that marks the boundary between this place and the world of the living."

"The bright tunnel," I said.

"Yes," Herne said. "The beast's limbs have enlarged over time."

"The figures within?"

"Parasites, I believe," Herne said. "They live off what they can siphon from the ka on its way to the beast. The tranquilizing effect they produce facilitates the process of consumption, so the creature tolerates them."

"Does no one escape?"

"Some," Herne said. "Enormous as the beast's appetite and reach are, it has its limits. Some elude its clutches; others, it never gets around to."

"What becomes of them?"

"Most find their way to what remains of the heavens. A few wander the dark. If those who arrive here can evade the Hungry Men, they usually wind up at my front door."

"I see no one else," I said.

"Come," Herne said, walking to the door. "Bring your drink, if you like."

I had forgotten I held it. I would rather have set it down, the taste for alcohol having left me, but already, Herne was through the doorway, so I carried the tumbler with me. He opened the door to the right of this one—the door at the end of the front hall—and started down a flight of wooden stairs. I hurried after him.

We entered a considerable basement, one which must have served for the entire building. Its walls were several feet higher than those of the room in which Herne had entertained me and, together with its breadth and width, gave the feel of having served as a market place, a common where the residents of the building could have gathered for conversation and commerce. The use to which Herne had put it, however, was anything but benign. From the wreckage of the rooms above, the surrounding buildings, he had scavenged material to construct the devices of a torture chamber. A pair of crude racks leaned against the opposite wall. A handful of heavy wooden tables, from whose corners thick chains dangled, occupied the center of the floor. Beside each, a smaller table held an assortment of knives, a sheaf of paper, and a mug filled with pens. A Catherine Wheel stood at the far end of the space. At points across the ceiling, coarse ropes draped sturdy pulleys. Herne was talking, explaining all of this, but while I heard his voice, his words did not register. Chained to the wall between the racks, a slender man with large eyes and ears regarded our entrance with terror. On either side of each rack, one of the creatures from which I had fled on the plane—the Hungry Men—had been bound.

Herne was counting on my shock at the sight of the room and its inmates to paralyze me. It very nearly did, which would have allowed him to strike me with the truncheon he had slipped from a hook on the wall at the top of the stairs. As it was, he caught my left wrist with his left hand and was in the process of pulling me into the blow he started with his right hand when I smashed the glass in my right hand into his face. Scotch misted the air. One of the shards drove into his left eye. He screamed, releasing my arm and dropping the club. Splinters of glass stuck up from my fingers, but I ignored them, driving my left fist into Herne's mouth. Dazed, he retreated, backing up a step. I took advantage of his movement, shoving him toward the nearest large table. He did not comprehend what I was doing until I pushed him half-onto the table and cuffed one of his wrists. He struggled, but my blood was up, and I struck his face again. I believe he expected me to turn his instruments on him, to seize one of the knives arrayed to my right and set its edge to his skin, but my chief concern was my safety, not his punishment—however deserved such might be.

My next thought was for the man fettered to the wall. There were assorted tools propped against the tables; I selected a sledge hammer and used it to break the plaster which anchored the chains to the wall. Free to move, the man walked to the nearest of the small tables and removed a set of keys hung under it. From these, he chose the key that unlocked his manacles.

Next, we began the laborious process of introductions and explanations.

I say laborious because the man, whose name was Franz, spoke German, a language with which I have only a passing acquaintance. He knew a smattering of English, so we muddled through as best we could. He had died relatively young, and arrived in the heavens in the last stages of the war against the great beast. He joined a rocket brigade in time to witness it torn asunder by the monster's limbs. After evading its tentacles, he roamed the ruined heavens, encountering the occasional fellow-survivor, shocked and despondent. Among these remnants, there was a move to leave this place, to set out for deeper heaven—"to follow amar-Utu," as the phrase went. In the end, each of Franz's companions elected to undertake this journey. Theirs was a choice he could not embrace; though he could not say why. In time, this led him here, to Herbert Herne, who captured and tortured him.

Have no doubt, I demanded answers from Herne, who, surprisingly, was happy to give them. Left alone, he had become fascinated, then obsessed, with the material of the ka, with the uses to which it might be put. After all, it sufficed to restrain the Children of Nun, a single one of whom was sufficient to wreck the twelve heavens. What, Herne wondered, might a man who had the crafting of such stuff do? What might he become? He ransacked the remains of the library, and while no one would admit to having carried out experiments in this direction, a few authors had speculated—sometimes in considerable detail—on the potential applications of the ka and the means by which those ends might be wrought. An abundance of raw materials lay at his disposal, including the remnants of those who had been drained by the beast, the Hungry Men. His laboratory complete, Herne succeeded in luring the creatures in ones and twos from the black fog in which they resided and trapping them. His testing of them had not been without success, but those very successes prompted him to wonder how much more he might accomplish with a soul not emptied of its essence. Herne observed the occasional survivor of the great beast's devastation picking his or her way through the rubble, and though he worried they might be wary of him, it proved laughably easy to coax them into his dwelling and subdue them. What Franz described as torture had been no more than the process by which he prepared the ka for its new role, breaking it down to a state in which it might be fashioned into any number of…devices. To be candid, it was both a lengthy and an unpleasant affair for the subject of his attentions, but there was no malice behind it, only the disinterest of the craftsman preparing the material upon which he would work.

I feared the man mad, unhinged by the ruination he had precipitated. Yet Herne described his endeavors with a level of detail that gave the appearance of rationality, diseased though it might be. At the end of his account, I expressed my skepticism, to which Herne responded by directing me upstairs, to the one door I had not opened. Naturally, I suspected a trap, but my curiosity was piqued, and I ascended the stairs. I took what precautions I could, and opened the final door.

The room I entered was of the same dimensions as the study into which Herne first led me. Its wallpaper was white, its floor bare wood, its marble fireplace dark. In the center of the floor, a round table supported three objects. I approached it cautiously. Arranged in a triangle were a lens, a wand, and a coil of rope. The lens was approximately the size of a dinner plate, its upturned side convex. A slender gold ring enclosed its circumference, and seemed to lend its shine to the depths of the glass. The wand was long as a man's forearm, its surface pale and smooth. It was bowed in the middle, tapered at the ends. The coil of rope was small enough to rest in my palm. It did not appear braided; rather, it was a single, golden strand. That these could be props in an extended joke occurred to me: the man who had sent me to them was dressed in costume, and not just any costume, at that. But the air above them quivered, vivid with energy. I could almost see the suggestion of a face in the glass of the lens, the outline of a bone in the shape of the wand, the texture of a length of hair in the rope. Knowing what they were—what they had been—I could not bring myself to handle them. Not then...

The lens allows its holder to focus himself into another location, no matter how distant. It permitted me to join you here, tonight. The wand is a tool, something like a pen, and something like a sword. The use of the rope, Herne has not taught to me, yet. Yes, I have had to continue my dealings with the man. In the end, his store of knowledge was too great for me to forego. Franz has not been happy with my decision, but he understands my reasoning. I charged him with the task of guarding Herne, whom I was compelled to release from the rack. Franz watches Herne closely; all the same, I am careful in his company. I believe—

Barry's next words were interrupted by his image faltering. As if he were a television channel whose signal had ebbed, his outline blurred, his color dulled. His voice disappeared. For long seconds, Torres, Schaefer, and myself stared at the place in his chair where the shadowy outline that had been our late friend flickered. It regained its definition just long enough for Max Barry to deliver his final words to us: "My time with you is almost done. When I have progressed in my study of the lens, I shall contact you again. In the meantime, I am in the company of the devil and a man who assures me he was an agnostic. The heavens lie in ruins. Perhaps we may repair them. Perhaps, if amar-Utu will not return to us, we may seek him out, win his aid. If he will not, we may subdue the great beast, ourselves. I am in possession of Herne's inventions, and they are mighty. Every day, I learn more about them. It may be that they will prove sufficient to rout the monster. It may be that others will be required.

"Tell those who are nearing the end of their time in this world to beware the light, the bright tunnel and its denizens. In the light lies annihilation. Tell them to seek the broken staircase. But fly, fly the hungry light."

INTO THE DARKNESS, FEARLESSLY

I

The morning after the police found the final piece of Linus Price, Wrighton Smythe, his frequent editor and occasional friend, opened the front door of his apartment and saw a manila folder lying on his doormat. With a sigh, Smythe bent to pick it up. It appeared his morning paper and cruller were going to have to be delayed. He made no effort to conceal his address, and it was not unheard of for aspiring writers to locate it and mail him their efforts; although a good few years had passed since anyone had gone so far as to hand-deliver their work. This manuscript was novel-thick, the folder bound to it with a pair of heavy pink rubber bands. There was no writing on either the front of the folder or the back. Smythe carried the delivery into his apartment, to the round table in his undersized living room upon which he placed the manuscripts awaiting his review. A modest pile of stories from writers well-established rose on the right side of the table; a pair of considerably-taller stacks from writers unknown loomed on the left. In between was a space, temporarily empty, where Smythe set whatever work was currently under his review. A pair of Pilot Precise V7 pens—blue ink—and a pad of yellow Post-It notes marked the top of what Smythe referred to as the operating theater. He dropped the new manuscript onto the table. Was it worth unwrapping? The odds were against it; though it was in exactly this way that Smythe had encountered Linus Price's first collection of stories, in a rectangular box wound about with packing tape. A spasm of grief and nostalgia pushed his fingers under the rubber bands, which he attempted to slide up and off the folder, but which resisted his efforts as if clinging to it. He had to pull the manuscript one way and the rubber bands the other before they slithered off, snapping his fingers as they released. "Shit!" Smythe waved his hand, dropping the rubber bands, which twisted on the carpet. He opened the folder, and on the top sheet of paper, read

A GRAMMAR OF DREAD, A CATECHISM OF TERROR
BY
LINUS PRICE

Smythe's vision contracted to a dark tunnel at the other end of which the name, LINUS PRICE, appeared to float above the page. His ears filled with buzzing, the din of a field of locusts. His legs shook; he gripped the edge of the table to steady himself. The towered manuscripts to his left shifted.

Even as he was thinking, *There's no way*, the thought laying the track for the train of anger, of fury, that was lurching into motion in response to this outrage, this fucking *travesty*, his hands were lifting the cover sheet, feeling the flimsy onionskin that Linus had favored. His fingers traced the letters of the title, the name, incised in the paper by the strike of an electric typewriter's keys. The title's religious reference fit Linus, whose passion for esoteric metaphysical traditions had led to some of his best work. The page beneath bore an epigraph, unattributed: "And as God, turning within Himself, found a world to bring forth, so might man, turning within himself, find a world to bring forth." He had encountered the sentiment in other of Linus's stories. Smythe let the page drop, took up the next one. Single-spaced, one space after the periods, quarter-inch margins, prose an unbroken block. He scanned the middle of the text. "The lines of its roof, its sides broken by ornaments that would have been more appropriate to a Medieval castle—gargoyles resting their pointed chins on taloned hands, faces too-broad, vines that coiled like serpents—the house had been stuffed between its neighbors in a manner that suggested a bundle of papers shoved between two sturdy volumes of an encyclopedia." It certainly read like Linus. Cars clashing together, the train of Smythe's anger shrieked to a halt. He replaced the page on the manuscript.

How? He hadn't noticed anyone walking away from his front door, let alone, lingering to one side or the other as he picked up the manuscript. And by anyone, he meant Dominika, Linus's wife—widow. While technically separated (a rupture Smythe had forecast years earlier) Linus's failure to amend his abbreviated will (despite Smythe's urging that he do so) had left her executor of his meager estate. In the days since the e-mail that had brought the first word of Linus's murder, Smythe had contemplated the fate of his writing. In several interviews, Linus had claimed to have file cabinets full of stories in various stages of completion; though in other interviews, he also had declared writing an almost intolerable agony, so there was reason to take those brimming cabinets with a helping of salt. From having worked with him, Smythe knew that the man was a relentless, meticulous reviser, submitting additional changes to his stories even after the volumes containing them had gone to print. Yet every time he had asked him for a submission to an anthology, Linus had responded with two and sometimes three stories, each of them eight to ten thousand words long. His writing absorbed him, Linus had said, an ambiguous enough statement, but Smythe judged it likely he had left at least some work behind. Assuming it was publishable—and Smythe was confident that some if not most of it would be—there might be enough for one, even two posthumous collections. There wasn't much money to be made from such a project—at its most accessible, Linus's fiction had been an acquired taste, with much of it so hermetic as to be opaque to all save a small company of devoted readers. But while it was a principle difficult to keep in clear view in this era of diminishing book sales and The End Of Publishing As We Know It, there was more to the industry than the bottom line. There was the pursuit of art. If Linus's work had reached that goal for a relative few, cross that finish line it had, and Smythe thought such an accomplishment ought not to be forgotten.

For this reason, he had been unhappy to learn that Dominika had remained in charge of Linus's estate. In Smythe's experience, the amicable divorce was a fairy tale concocted by lawyers to encourage couples to begin a process that had more in common with a bare-knuckle boxing match. Even by that standard, Linus and Dominika's split had been brutal, an exchange of dirty blows that had continued long beyond the usual time limit, leaving the combatants bloody, broken, and bitter. Dominika had blamed Linus for misrepresenting himself as a famous writer during the course of their (mostly online) courtship, leading her to abandon her budding career as a model in Warsaw for a job waiting tables at a local diner. Linus had accused Dominika of feigning affection for him in order to gain her green card. The separation proceedings had achieved a low level of notoriety in the local press, the consequence of a bored reporter wandering into the courtroom and being struck by the contrast between the tall, statuesque woman with the head of shining blond hair and the short, dumpy man with the stubbled head and protruding eyes. To be frank, there was a beauty-and-the-beast quality to their relationship, but the papers had exaggerated it, recasting Dominika as the beautiful, hapless immigrant ensnared by the unsavory, cunning writer—a writer of horror stories, to boot. She had emerged from the courtroom with a position as the weather-person for a local cable news channel, whose owner she was rumored to be dating. Linus gained nothing but the confirmation of the conviction he had long nurtured that the world was actively hostile to him. Smythe had little trouble believing that Dominika would be happy to let whatever manuscripts Linus had left behind molder in their filing cabinets unpublished; if she didn't consign them to the dumpster, or tip them into a metal drum and add gasoline and a match.

He had debated contacting her about the matter, but the situation was complicated by the fact that, a few years earlier, he had made a protracted and sloppy pass at Dominika. It was at the annual Weirdcon, which he'd convinced Linus to attend because it was being held in Albany, just up the river. Smythe had spent most of the weekend parked on a stool at the hotel bar, measuring his hours in shots of Johnnie Walker Red, neat. It was, in his experience, the preferred method for enduring these events, whose attendance had long since moved from pleasure to duty. For every writer of merit who stopped to exchange a few words with him, a dozen, more, of varying degrees of inconsequence lowered themselves beside him and

Into the Darkness, Fearlessly

attempted to engage him in a protracted conversation, usually on the merits of their work. If he was lucky, they at least stood him a round. This weekend, he had not been especially lucky. By the time he realized Dominika was standing beside him, waiting for the bartender to deliver her white wine, Linus nowhere to be seen, the drunk Smythe had maintained at a steady level just this side of belligerence had tipped over into naked hostility. The sight of Dominika leaning over the bar, her arms crossed over her full breasts, her round ass thrust out behind her in a tight denim skirt, and Linus still absent—Smythe had glanced about the bar—had filled him with a sour rage. He wasn't sure exactly what he had said to her—it had begun as a question about whether she wouldn't prefer to join him in his room, away from all of *this*, and escalated to an extended description of the things he would do to her that had stretched from the sadistic to the masochistic. Throughout, she had watched him impassively, the fingers of her right hand tracing the stem of her wineglass. By the time Smythe had finished, his face was flushed, and he was panting. He had been certain that Dominika was going to dash her wine at him; either that, or grab his hand and take him up on his proposition. *Nothing ventured...*

Instead, she had burst out laughing, laughter spraying from her lips as if Smythe had related the single funniest joke she ever had heard. Nor had she stopped: she had thrown her head back and continued to fill the bar with the sound of her mirth. It wasn't an explosion of good humor; it was harsh, mocking. His cheeks burning, Smythe had sat where he was, trying to compress himself into the smallest possible space he could. When he could stand her laughter no longer, he had swallowed the remainder of his drink, pushed himself up from his seat, and delivered a long string of invective to that grinning mouth, those pearled teeth. Though he liked to consider himself well-practiced and -skilled at insult, Smythe's second outburst had evoked the same response from Dominika as the first, that braying laughter. Even through the Scotch mixed with his blood, Smythe had felt himself lessened in ways he didn't like to contemplate. He had flipped her the bird, and stalked out of the bar, the assembled eyes of the writers gathered there on him.

Afterwards, Linus did not confront him about the episode, which Smythe was anticipating and which he was preparing to deflect through an appeal to his inebriation and possibly Dominika's uncertain grasp of English.

71

When nothing was said via phone, e-mail, or at their next meeting, Smythe started to tell mutual acquaintances that, in his view, Linus and Dominika's marriage was doomed. Smythe had not seen her since that weekend, for which he considered himself generally grateful but which made contacting her following her estranged husband's death seem more complicated.

It appeared, however, that his worrying had been over naught. Smythe supposed he couldn't blame Dominika if she wasn't inclined to deal with him face to face, right now. As long as she had delivered this manuscript to him, he could excuse much. There wasn't much point in pretending he was going to accomplish anything with Linus's manuscript sitting here, was there? He lifted the heap of paper from the table and carried it to the couch, under the living room's picture window, where he settled down to read. A book written by a dead man: it was like the plot to one of Linus's stories.

II

Three (?) hours later, something flapping past the window caused Smythe to start. It hadn't been a bird, had it? Not one that big, not in the middle of the city. It must have been a trick of the light, a reflection from a passing car thrown on the glass. No matter—he needed a break, anyway.

Smythe lowered the manuscript. Had he been asked what he expected from Linus Price's latest work, his answer would have been, More of the same. More disaffected characters whose dead-end existences admitted them to scenarios in which the futility and hostility of life was made manifest through some cryptic supernatural agency. In one of his college classes, Smythe had encountered the argument that every writer rewrites the same story over and over again. While the statement was as reductive as most critical generalizations typically were, he had recognized a grain of truth to it which three decades as an editor had confirmed. Writers were obsessives. The trick was to return to your obsessions in a way that made them seem fresh each time. From the beginning, Linus had achieved this feat. His new work was no exception. What was different—unprecedented—about it was the element of undisguised autobiography. Specifically, the manuscript dealt with the six months leading up to his murder.

Linus's death. Christ, there was a subject for a horror story, and not of

Linus's stripe. This was no collection of hints and allusions wound in labyrinthine prose; this was brute blood and gore delivered in blunt, declarative sentences, the very kind of narrative against which he and Smythe had railed in print and online, the sensational, lowest-common-denominator type. Well, God was supposed to be a lousy writer, wasn't He?

It had started with a woman. Scratch that: it had started with whatever confluence of inclination and experience had caused the teenaged Linus Price to haul his mother's old typewriter out of storage, balance it atop a card table, and begin composing the ancestors of the stories he one day would deliver to Smythe's doorstep. That joining of talent and memory had tangled a host of emotions with itself, chief among them arrogance, jealousy, and insecurity. There was nothing particularly noteworthy about a writer displaying these feelings; in Smythe's experience, it would have been remarkable for Linus not to have demonstrated them. Linus's problem lay in his inability to maintain any kind of balance of or perspective on his feelings. When he received a positive review, it was proof that he was the best writer of his generation. When someone else earned a six-figure advance for their trilogy of vampire novels, it was symptomatic of the fundamental idiocy of the publishing industry. And when his stories and collections were passed over for the field's short list of awards, Linus plunged into black moods which released themselves online, in extended screeds on his blog or on those of the writers who had claimed the awards he deemed his. This last tendency had escalated over the last several years, immediately before, during, and in the aftermath of his marriage's collapse. Smythe had gone so far as to write him a brief, bluff e-mail suggesting that maybe it was time to stop confronting every billy-goat that trip-trapped across his bridge, but his caution had gone unheeded. Linus liked playing the troll; he appeared to take a perverse pleasure in living down to everyone's worst expectations. Smythe had been concerned, but Linus was far from the first writer to play the part of the obnoxious gadfly, and his irritation at Linus's refusal to heed his advice had kept him from repeating it.

If you had to select a more recent starting point for the chain of events that had resulted in Linus's murder, Smythe supposed it had to be last year's Blackwood Awards. Linus's most recent book, *Epistles to the Damned*, had garnered a nomination in the single-author collection category, along with work by a few, perennial favorites and *Medusa's Fruit*, a collection from a newcomer, Suzanne Kowalczyk. His friendship with Linus aside, there was no doubt in Smythe's mind that *Epistles to the Damned* merited and would win that year's award. All the reviews agreed that it was far and away Linus's best collection of stories, and since the Blackwood was decided by the votes of those attending that year's Weirdcon—held in Columbus—Smythe assumed Linus had the category sewn up—as did Linus. What neither Smythe nor Linus had counted on was Suzy Kowalczyk making electronic copies of her collection free to whichever members of the convention requested it, with the result that more of them would read and cast their votes for her book than Linus's. So sure had Linus been that the award was his that, as the title of Suzy's book was being read out, he was already halfway to his feet. Once the name of the actual winner registered, he stood where he was, in the fourth row of a crowded room, while Suzy Kowalczyk rushed to the front of the room to accept her plaque and offer tearful thanks. After the ceremony had concluded, Smythe had pushed through the groups of people milling around to where Linus was sitting, slumped. Smythe had not won his category (original anthology) either, but though the loss piqued him, as they always did, Linus was stunned by the upset to his expectations. Putting aside his own disappointment, Smythe had squired Linus to the hotel bar, where over a couple of ludicrously-expensive double-martinis, he had done his best to cheer up Linus, reminding him of all the great works of art that had gone similarly unrecognized. Where was *The Sound and the Fury*'s Pulitzer? Where was *Vertigo*'s Oscar? Where was *Let It Bleed*'s Grammy? Not such a bad club to be a member of, Smythe had told him. Linus had nodded, but said little. Eventually, Smythe had had to leave him in order to catch his ride to the airport.

That Linus's disappointment would spur him to action, and that said action would consist of a minimum of one, lengthy blog post on the woeful deficiencies of *Medusa's Fruit* was for Smythe a foregone conclusion. It was hardly the most gracious response, but neither was it unprecedented in the world of letters. In his, somewhat-less-invested estimate, Suzanne Kowalczyk's stories were decently-written efforts, one or two of which gave evidence that she might develop in genuinely-interesting directions. There was enough in her present volume, though, in terms of technique and theme, for someone inclined to do so to find fault with.

What Smythe was unprepared for was Linus's decision to ignore Suzy's writing and to focus instead on her appearance. Suzanne Kowalczyk was a tall, striking woman who wore her blond hair up and whose crisp skirt-and-jacket combinations lent her the appearance of a mid-level executive on the rise. She was also similar enough to Dominika for the two to have passed as cousins, if not sisters, Irish twins. To his subsequent astonishment, Smythe failed to pick up on the resemblance until after Linus accused her of having used her "charms" to bamboozle an electorate unaccustomed to the attention—and manipulation—of so attractive an individual. During the resulting firestorm that swept their corner of the internet, another of Smythe's writer-friends e-mailed him, "Wasn't it enough for Linus to get his ass handed to him by Dominika once?" and the scales had dropped from his eyes. He had wanted to write to Linus, to try to make him see what he was doing, but Linus had always resisted any effort at analyzing his behavior that put it in doubt. There was nothing to do except let the conflagration burn itself out, which it had started to do when Linus unleashed his second round of accusations. These focused on the brief afterword Suzy had written for her collection, in which she discussed writing its stories in the aftermath of the loss of her daughter, aged seven, to leukemia. This, Linus had opined, was an obvious attempt at playing on her readers' emotions, which the attendees of Weirdcon had fallen for like so many rubes.

Smythe had thought the reaction to Linus's first rant pronounced—Suzy Kowalczyk was well-liked and the internet tended to fan what fires broke out on it—but that was nothing compared to the response to his follow-up remarks. There were no actual death-threats as such, but there were offers from an assortment of men and women from around the globe to inflict bodily harm on Linus the next time they encountered him. Linus's reaction was to announce that he was reporting them all to the police and then to do so. Especially once the facts in the case were made clear to them, though, the police were less than sympathetic. All that saved Linus from the debacle he had created was a new controversy that sprang up a few days later and sucked all the oxygen away from his. For a short while, Linus did his best to keep the argument alive, but by the time he decided to level his scorn at Suzy's writing, no one was interested, anymore.

Smythe had hoped the lack of interest in his dissection of *Medusa's Fruit*'s shortcomings would communicate to Linus that it was time to move on. Since everyone else had left the fight before he did, Smythe imagined he could count that as a kind of victory. A few weeks later, when the World Fantasy Award nominations were announced and both Linus and Suzy's names were absent from the ballot, Smythe figured that would provide Linus something new to stew over.

Not until Linus's next stories appeared, six months later, did it become clear to Smythe that, rather than easing it, the passage of time had only deepened his outrage. He hadn't spoken much about it to Smythe, but then, he hadn't spoken much to Smythe, at all. Almost no one had seen or heard from Linus since his post-Blackwood meltdown. Every now and again, Smythe had considered dropping him an e-mail, just to touch base, but he had been occupied with a number of unanticipated projects whose short deadlines left him scant room for anything else. If he were telling the truth, he didn't mind the excuse to maintain his distance from Linus for a little while. Smythe had witnessed Linus go off the rails before, usually at a slight real or perceived from a writer he admired, but this last incident had seemed to carry him further away that in the past. Linus could contact him when he felt ready.

As the stories debuted, however, two at small online 'zines and one in *Lovecraft's*, Smythe found himself unable to imagine what, if anything, he would say to Linus were he to answer the phone and hear his sometime friend's voice. It was the story in *Lovecraft's* that was the real problem, a piece about a beautiful émigré from an unnamed former-Eastern-Bloc-country whose picturesque house concealed a hideous secret: the child she kept bound and tortured in the attic, whose agonies were channeled through occult means to feed its mother's success as a painter. The actual details of the story were executed with as much tact, as much artistry, as anything Linus had written, but its significance was clear. This time around, Linus played coy, greeting the anger that sprung up virtually overnight with the insistence that he didn't know what anyone was talking about. He had written a work of fiction: that was all. His protests had sounded perfunctory, as if written to forestall any legal action from Suzanne Kowalczyk, who was, unsurprisingly, livid. Claiming to have contacted a lawyer, she did indeed threaten to sue Linus for libel. It was so much bluster—libel was next to impossible to prove in the U.S.—but Smythe could picture Linus blanching at the prospect of having to put yet another lawyer in his employ.

The second phase of Linus's feud with Suzy should have been the last, especially after she announced that she'd decided not to seek redress through the courts. But Smythe had had a queasy feeling the matter had yet to be settled, and this past week, that nausea had been justified. Suzy's neighbors had reported a man loitering outside her house, checking her mail, investigating her garbage, whose description matched Linus. Each time the police arrived, though, he was nowhere to be found. Suzy, herself, did not complain of a stalker, but that appeared to be because she had her own plans for him. Through means of which no one was certain, she had lured Linus into her house. Once the front door was closed, she had subdued him, possibly with a taser, stripped, bound and gagged him, and dragged him into her large kitchen. There, she had used her collection of very sharp, restaurant-grade cleavers and knives to joint him like a chicken. In the coroner's estimate, he had remained alive much further into the process than Smythe would have guessed possible. Suzy Kowalczyk had scattered his body throughout her house and fled for parts unknown; as yet, she had not been captured. During the initial investigation, the police had been afraid that she had taken Linus's head with her, since it was the only part of him they had been unable to locate. Only when an enterprising young cadet decided to unload the freezer was Linus's head discovered, wedged in a corner behind the rounded bulk of a frozen turkey.

What Linus had been doing at Suzy's house had not been discovered. Speculation had been voiced in some quarters that he had been staking out her place preliminary to assaulting her, which sounded plausible unless you had seen Linus. Suzy's motivations were considered self-evident: at the sight of the man who had bedeviled her this past year, she finally had snapped—which also sounded as if it made more sense than it did. There was nothing in her history to indicate that she would lose her mind, or that she would do so in so spectacular a fashion. Yes, that was the point to saying she had snapped, but Smythe judged such reasoning flimsy, weak.

And now, here was Linus's manuscript, which further muddied the waters. Smythe supposed you would have to call it a collection; although Linus had attempted to knit the stories within it (which included the *Lovecraft's* piece) into something approaching a larger narrative. The result was a study in resentment and paranoia, threaded through with gnostic mysticism. Punishingly candid, beautifully-written sections about the breakup of his marriage, his descent into self-loathing and depression, his envy of and anger at Suzanne Kowalczyk's success, alternated with shorter, more elliptical and ornate sections concerning a fragment of gnostic writing on which Linus had become fixated. Supposedly discovered as part of the Nag Hammadi manuscripts, this sheet of papyrus had been included with the *Gospel of Thomas*, until certain inconsistencies of grammar and syntax had caused other differences of content to become apparent. Debate continued as to whether the text to which the selection belonged had been part of the original library of early Christian texts, or if its origins lay with another sect. What was known as the demiurgic fragment began with the maxim Linus had chosen for the epigraph to his book: "And as God, turning within Himself, found a world to bring forth, so might man, turning within himself, find a world to bring forth." It moved on to a discussion of the word through which the Deity had accomplished His act of creation, a sample of the divine speech that was represented pictographically, as a pair of ovals, one contained within the other, the outer oval open on the left side, the inner on the right. With this word, the passage concluded, a man might give rise to that which was within him.

The conceit of this ancient text formed the basis for a brief parable about a man who came to the court of the great caliph, Haroun al-Rashid, before whose assembled courtiers the man declared he would replace the ruler this very night. When the court guards went to slay the man, the caliph stayed their hands and asked him what cause he had to speak so boldly. He had learned, the man replied, the word that is known as the egg, against whose power the messengers of paradise dared not contend. Ah, the caliph said, truly, that was a powerful weapon to have at one's disposal. But, he went on, it seemed to him that its possession was like gripping a sword by the blade, of no less danger to the one holding it than to those he faces. For who could say all that a man might find in himself? What man but he who was utterly at peace with himself would dare to grant exit to the residents of his soul? Nonetheless, the man said—albeit, with a tremor in his voice that had not been there, before—this night is your last upon this earth. If it be God's will, the caliph said, then so be it, and he gestured for his guards to allow the man to depart the court unmolested. Nor did Haroun al-Rashid speak of the matter again. However, a number of the caliph's most trusted advisors, disturbed by so blatant a threat to their ruler, gave orders that the man should be followed. This proved more difficult than those advisors anticipated, with the result that the man's lodgings in one of the poorer quarters of the city were not discovered until early the next morning. The guards who broke open the door were greeted by a scene of horror, the man torn to shreds as if by a pack of wild dogs. What had done so crouched in the middle of the room, licking the blood pooled on the floor. None of the guards would describe it, but when they slew it with their swords, the neighbors heard the sound of an infant shrieking. Those advisors who were summoned to view the thing ordered it burnt and its ashes scattered. To no man who was part of these events did sleep ever come easily, again.

In turn, this parable was succeeded by the *Lovecraft's* story, which Linus had positioned between a pair of lengthy expository paragraphs in which he did his best to explain his fiction as a means of representing the truth behind Suzanne Kowalczyk's lies. The second paragraph led into a kind of prose-poem in which Linus portrayed himself meditating ceaselessly on the double-ovals, what the man in his story had called the egg. If this was the avenue by which creation had come to be, then might there not be some trace of it remaining in that creation? For a long time, he searched for such a trace. And then, one day, while he was sitting at his local diner prolonging a cup of coffee and a slice of apple pie, the accidental flash of sunlight on a serving platter had caught his eye, and like Jacob Böhme, he had seen through to the center of things. Before he understood what his lips and tongue were doing, they were uttering that word, the egg, whose sound was almost silent. He looked down, and found his mug filed to the steaming brim with fine, strong coffee, not the watery mix he'd been sipping for the last half-hour. On the plate next to it sat a thick slice of apple pie, the buttery taste of whose flaky crust blended perfectly with the crisp sweetness of its filling. Unable to believe fully what had happened—what he had made happen—Linus had left the diner and went straight home. There, he had locked the door, drawn the blinds, and commenced experimenting with the word. He was somewhat vague as to exactly what uses he had put his discovery to; although he mentioned causing a tank full of half a dozen white and orange goldfish to appear on his kitchen counter. At the end of his session, Linus had been convinced of the authenticity of his breakthrough. Granted such an ability, Linus wrote, it would have been easy enough to indulge in more venal pursuits, to make himself rich, to surround himself with women beside whom Dominika would appear the slattern he had found her to be. To do so, as he saw it, would be to admit a kind of defeat. His life's goal had been nothing more and nothing less than to earn a modest living through his writing, and he still deemed it a worthy ambition. What the word could give him was a means to make the world see the truth in what he had been saying about Suzanne Kowalczyk, namely, that she was a manipulative, talentless fraud.

How like Linus, Smythe thought. *He writes a fantasy in which he grants himself ultimate power, and the best use he can think of putting it to is settling a score.* The section concluded with Linus turning off all the lights in his apartment, seating himself cross-legged on the living room floor, and commencing the process of opening the door to what was inside him. The manuscript ended with a narrative written in the form of a journal. Its style, Smythe judged, was Poe filtered through Beckett, terse paranoia. There were no proper names, only pronouns and generic descriptions. Its action was disjointed. Its narrator received a visit from a beautiful woman with whom he had immediate and ferocious sex. Later, he wandered streets whose names were familiar but whose houses were strange. He felt feverish. He found a park and sat on one of its benches. The woman reappeared beside him. They had some kind of sex on the bench. When they were done, he saw a figure watching them across the park. It was short, dressed in a winter coat with the hood up. He could not see its face. Later, he saw the figure at the end of a street he could not remember walking to. It ran down an alley between two houses. The way it moved made him feel sick. He approached the end of the street. The door of the second-to-last house on the left was open. The woman was standing in it. She was naked. The small figure in its coat slouched behind her. He turned up the walk towards them. That was the end of the manuscript.

Jesus. Smythe pushed himself up off the couch. As a rule, he was leery of psychoanalytic readings of a writer's work, but in this case… He shook his head, deposited Linus's manuscript on the work table. No doubt, the thing was publishable—the sensation value would probably move more copies of it than anything else Linus had written. But as a last book, a summation of his career, it cast a light over his body of work that was, to put it mildly, less than flattering. Perhaps there was something else, another collection of stories that might better serve as Linus's final publication. He would have to ask Dominika about it when he saw her tonight, at Linus's wake.

III

Smythe had expected Linus's sendoff to be a somber affair, but he was unprepared for the full, depressing extent of it. For one thing, both the funeral parlor Dominika had selected and the neighborhood in which it was located had, to put it mildly, seen better days. *Which one of us hasn't?* Smythe thought as he steered up the potholed street to the tall old house. *Especially Linus.* Aside from a wire garbage can whose side bore a long, jagged gouge, the curb before the funeral parlor was empty. Smythe parked his Metro directly in front of the place, and before he left the car, locked all its doors. He could not conceive of even the most desperate of criminals finding anything of value in or inside his vehicle, but the prospect of being proved wrong and having to walk the blocks to the nearest bus stop was sufficiently unpleasant for him to secure the car. A scrape on the pavement behind him jerked his head around. A scrap of newspaper was being hustled along the sidewalk by a breeze too slight for him to notice. There was nothing in the shape of the paper to remind him of a large, pale crab scuttling over the concrete. He hurried up wooden stairs that announced his climb in a series of dull booms, into the funeral parlor.

Inside, the air was clotted with yellow light that made the narrow hallway more, rather than less, difficult to distinguish. A podium whose carver had doubtless intended its sinuous leg as a vine, and not the tentacle it actually resembled, held aloft a marble composition book whose repurposing as a Book of Remembrance was announced by the spiky handwriting on its cover. Opening the book, Smythe was more surprised than he would have expected to find the first page empty. Perhaps the entries began further in…? No: the rest of the pages were equally blank. Granted, Linus had made his fair share of enemies, but surely, at a moment such as this, a flag of truce could be raised over old battlefields, the scars of old wounds covered over? Apparently not, if the pristine pages, the silent hallway, were to be believed. A surge of emotion that was equal parts pity and outrage rose in his throat. He seized the Bic lying beside the notebook and wrote his name in large, jagged letters that crossed a half-dozen of the page's pale blue lines. Beside it, he wrote, "Into the Darkness, Fearlessly!" It was the phrase with which he had titled his laudatory review of Linus's first collection of stories, and if it did not quite fit the manner of Linus's death, Smythe intended it to evoke that earlier, happier time.

Spurred by indignation, he strode down the hall to the viewing room. A piece of paper with the word, "Prise," magic-markered on it had been taped to the wall to the right of the doorway. Smythe paused at the threshold, confronted by one end of Linus's coffin, which crowded most of the doorway. Its lid closed, the coffin was plain, unvarnished wood, no railing along its side for pall-bearers to grip. A small, potted cactus rested on its opposite end. There was no point to the sour taste that filled Smythe's mouth. Linus had been possessed of, at most, minimal resources; what he was looking at was what Linus's bank account would cover. In fact, it was probably more than he would have expected Linus to afford. The cactus was a bit much, even if he could imagine Linus snorting at it. He squeezed around the coffin, noting as he did that there was no kneeler in front of it. Already, he had seen Dominika at the other end of the small room, seated in one of the folding chairs lining the back wall, something on the chairs to either side of her. He ran his hand over the coffin's smooth surface, wishing he could think of a remark that didn't reek of sentimentalism. He had attended the wakes of a number of writers, most of them figures he had grown up reading, met, and occasionally published at the ends of their careers. A few had been his contemporaries, the victims of accidents or aggressive cancers. Linus was the only writer—the only person—Smythe had known who had been murdered, and so horribly, at that. A weight seemed to pull down the center of his chest. He supposed he should speak to Dominika, offer his condolences, maybe discuss Linus's manuscript with her. He turned towards her, and what he saw made him jump back into Linus's coffin, which gave a muffled thud and rocked on its supports. On the chair to his widow's left sat Linus's head, resting on its truncated neck. The eyes were closed, the mouth was closed, the expression slack. Smythe struggled for breath. "You," he managed. "You."

Dominika laughed, that same bray she'd visited upon him years ago, coarsened by the wine she'd consumed from the bottles open on the chair to her right. "Oh, Smythe," she said. "You think—?" She nodded at Linus's head. "This—?" More laughter. She rested her hand on top of Linus's head in a gesture almost tender. "It's a model," she said in a stage whisper.

"Wha—a what?" Smythe said.

"A model," Dominika said, "you know, like a mannequin. I had it made when the police could not find the real thing. Actually, it was after they looked and looked, and it was still missing. I waited to have the funeral, because I wanted to bury all of him, you know? Who wants to be buried without his head? But then the detective says to me, 'I don't know if we are going to find your late husband's head.' He thought the woman ran away with it. So, I decided not to wait, anymore. I went on the internet, found a man who could do this, and here it is." She slapped the head. "It was not cheap, either. Of course, the minute, the second after I hung up the phone with the man telling me the thing is done, who calls but the police? I couldn't tell them I didn't need their head, I had one of my own, so I decided this one would keep me company while I sit here. Linus would approve, I think."

No doubt he would have; though I'm not so sure about your outfit. Dominika's clothes were mourning-black, but her high-necked blouse, short skirt, and thigh-high boots lent her the appearance of a dominatrix. *Scratch that—he would have loved it.* Smythe seated himself on the other side of the wine bottles. A scattering of plastic cups surrounded them. Smythe selected a cup. "Do you mind?"

Dominika waved the hand holding her own cup. "Go ahead."

The bottle was tall, heavy, the label one Smythe did not recognize. A vineyard in Bulgaria, apparently. The liquid that poured out of it was thick, ruby bordering black. Its nose was the grape of children's fruit juice. Smythe raised his cup and said, "To Linus." He waited for Dominika to join his toast; when she did not, he put his cup to his lips. The wine was cloyingly sweet, more like cough syrup than alcohol. Nonetheless, he served himself a second cup of it. If he was going to be sitting here with Dominika, he fancied he would need all the assistance he could get. After he consumed that cup, and set himself up with a third, he said, "Before, you mentioned the police. Has there been any more news—"

"Nothing." Dominika shook her head. "The woman is gone, vanished."

"I assume they told you—"

"Oh yes, I know everything. They were fucking, and this is what happened."

"They were—what?" Smythe thought of Linus's book, that final story.

"But Linus was Linus, and you know…"

"Wait—who said they were—the police told you this?"

"No," Dominika said. "It's obvious, isn't it?"

"Certainly not," Smythe said. "Linus hated that woman. He detested her. He thought she was a fraud."

"And such things don't make sparks?" Dominika said. "What we detest, we also desire. I thought you would know that."

Smythe ignored the implications of her axiom. Instead, he refilled his cup. "Linus was not involved with that woman."

"He told you this?"

"He didn't have to," Smythe said. "I read the manuscript."

Dominika frowned. "The manuscript?"

"The book—Linus's book."

"Ah. What did it say?"

"That he despised Suzanne Kowalczyk."

"Which would have made the fucking better."

"Linus was not having sex with her."

"Why is this so upsetting to you?"

"Because it isn't true," Smythe said. "This isn't some relationship gone horribly wrong. This is murder."

"You don't have to worry about me," Dominika said. "It does not bother me to think that Linus was fucking another woman. Good for him, you know? Except when it wasn't."

"I'm not worried about you. I'm concerned with my friend."

Dominika patted the head. "Your friend doesn't need your concern." She listed towards Smythe. "Actually, his cock wasn't bad. I'm sure she enjoyed it."

Was the bottle empty, already? Smythe hardly felt the effects of the wine at all. He replaced the empty, selected one mostly full.

Dominika continued. "That was why I turned you down all those years ago, my husband's cock."

Smythe's cheeks flushed. "This is hardly the place—"

"Linus doesn't care," Dominika said. "He wouldn't care if I fucked you right now. Would you?" she asked the head, whose features seemed to have taken on an appearance of distaste. "You see," she said, "nothing."

"I was wondering if I could speak to you about Linus's book," Smythe said.

"His book?"

"The manuscript—what was it? *A Grammar of Dread, A Catechism of Terror.*"

"What a title!" Dominika said, slapping her leg. "He was very good with titles."

"He was. I'm not sure if you've read the collection—"

"None of it. I never read any of Linus's things."

"You never—"

Dominika shrugged. "Linus's stories were difficult. He told me so, himself. He was proud of it. 'Not just anyone can understand my stories:' that was what he said. I said it was more like, 'Not anyone can understand any of your stories.' He didn't think that was so funny. But come on! You read them. You know what I'm talking about. The long sentences. The strange words. The people in them no one could like. Sometimes, he would tell me his stories—that only made me glad I hadn't read them."

For an instant—less—Smythe was possessed by the absolute, unshakable conviction that the woman he was speaking with was not Dominika Price. She might be Suzanne Kowalczyk—no, she was someone else, altogether. Quickly as it had come, the feeling passed, and Smythe swallowed another (his eighth? ninth?) cup of wine. "Linus Price," he said, "was a great writer."

"So you say," Dominika said. "Who knows? Maybe he was. But he was not a very good writer, I think."

"What is your position, then, on publishing his final work? If," Smythe added, "it is his final work."

"How should I know?"

"Haven't you gone through his things?"

"Why should I?"

"Because you're his executor—executrix." Smythe struggled with the word, his tongue suddenly full of the alcohol he'd consumed. "It's your responsibility."

"To who?" Dominika said. "Linus is dead."

"To posterity," Smythe said, a still-trickier word. "To his readers."

"What? Ten people? That was something else he used to say, when he was depressed: 'I'm lucky if ten people buy my books.'"

"If you feel this way, then why did you give me his manuscript?"

"What manuscript?"

"The book, Linus's last book. *A Grammar of Terror*—no, *A Grammar of Dread, A Catechism of Terror*."

"I didn't."

"What do you mean, you didn't?"

"What I said. I didn't give you Linus's book."

"But I found it at my front door this morning."

"So?"

"Did you give it to someone to give to me?"

"Smythe," Dominika said, "I haven't seen the fucking book, okay? Maybe Linus's wife gave it to you."

"His wife?"

"Her—the woman who killed him. Whatever."

"She was hardly his Goddamned wife."

"Yes, yes. It doesn't matter. Whatever you want to do with Linus's book, you do."

Smythe choked down his anger. "Of course, I would ensure you received the proceeds from such a project."

"With nothing for you?"

"I—"

"It's okay," Dominika said. "I don't need this money. You can have it."

"I wouldn't—"

Dominika waved her free hand. "Shhh. We'll drink to it."

"All right," Smythe said. He lifted the bottle from which he'd been serving himself, found it, too, empty. He set it down, chose a third. "To the beginning," he said over his brimming cup, "of a beautiful friendship."

"Don't get crazy," Dominika said.

"It's—never mind."

Another portion of the syrupy wine, and a wave of intoxication rolled over him, as if that last amount had tipped an internal scale, plunging him into a full drunk. His head seemed to rise above his body, which felt simultaneously hot, heavy, and hollow, as if he were no more than the suit and shirt he was wearing, held in place solely by its purpose. Linus's coffin appeared mere feet away, the cactus at its head large as a bush. Smythe stretched out his right hand and slid his fingers over the coffin's side. He turned his head to Dominika to remark on this—the room swaying lazily as he did—and saw that her neck had grown, carrying her head a good foot, two, past the edge of her high-necked blouse. Her lids were lowered, her lips parted. She had set her cup down, and was playing with the top button of her blouse with her left hand, while her right flopped in her lap.

Despite the wine, Smythe was instantly, painfully erect, his cock tenting his trousers, throbbing in time with the pulse pounding at his temples, his throat. His mouth was dry, his hands trembling. When Dominika's hand made the jump to his lap, the shock it produced did nothing to stop his hands from unbuckling his belt, unbuttoning and unzipping his pants. *For Christ's sake, you're in a fucking funeral home!* It didn't matter: Dominika's fingers had made their way under the waistband of his briefs and encircled his cock. His fingers had pushed up her skirt, and found her pantiless, shaved, soaking. He half-fell off his chair, angling towards her. Without losing hold of him, she scooted her ass to the edge of the chair, then pulled him into her. Enclosed in her wet heat, he gasped. He grabbed the edges of her blouse, tore it open. A black, lace bra supported her creamy breasts. His fingers worked underneath the underwire, pulled the bra up and over, revealing her large, rosy nipples. His mouth descended on them. Somewhere above, Dominika groaned and uttered words in a language Smythe didn't know. Her hips ground against his. He took her nipple between his lips, sucked hard on it. Dominika yelped, pushed him backwards, riding him off the chair into a kind of half-crouch on the floor. She leaned into him, her right hand slapping Linus's coffin. He thought she was keeping time with his thrusts, but she pressed forward more, threatening to overbalance him. He flung his hands to the sides and braced himself against the coffin. His knees were screaming with pressure, his cock dulling. With her left hand, Dominika caught his collar and pulled him over and to the side. They landed hard, Smythe on top, Dominika already moving under him. His cock stiffened, the pressure at its base returning. Dominika's words had fallen into a rhythmic pattern. She pushed her right hand between them, around and under Smythe's balls. Something scraped along the flesh behind them; her fingernails, he thought, his cock close to bursting with the touch. A pinprick, several, tickled his skin, and he remembered the cactus ornamenting Linus's coffin just as Dominika drove the needles she'd freed from it into him. The pain was astonishing, and seemed to combine with the orgasm that convulsed him. He threw his head back, and from the corner of his eye, saw the model of Linus's head, its eyes open, yellow fluid streaming from them. He recoiled in horror, striking his head on the coffin. Supernovae flared behind his eyes, and were replaced by darkness.

IV

Smythe woke the next morning with a splitting headache, a consequence of the four double-scotches he'd sent following the wine once he'd arrived home. (However that had been; his memory of that particular detail was a blank. Please, Christ, someone at the funeral home had called a cab for him.) The buzz had been wearing off, and he'd justified the additional alcohol as a salute to the man he'd once christened the great hope of horror fiction. Not to mention, as a salve for the pain behind his balls, whose sharpness made him draw his breath in sharply every time he moved. No doubt, Linus would have had a sharp remark to offer his pain. (Not that he would have delivered it to his face, of course: he would have passed it to some mutual acquaintance he could be sure would transmit it to Smythe.) Smythe considered a swallow of the hair of the dog, but opted instead for a trio of aspirin crunched between his teeth, their bitterness welcome after the taste he'd awakened with. The aspirin seemed to help, loosening the vise around his forehead, blunting the pain between his legs. His stomach was too scorched for anything other than a glass of lukewarm tapwater. Nothing would have pleased him more than to return to bed, write this day off as a loss, but a host of deadlines were bearing down on him, and he could not afford another lost day. Well, he'd worked through the aftermaths of worse binges than this one, hadn't he? He shuffled towards his computer.

Once he'd (gingerly) seated himself, though, the first e-mails of the day brought news that made his vision blur. One of the writers he'd solicited for a reprint for the latest volume of *Fatal Frights* had sent a reply declining his offer. Mixed in with the pain, Smythe felt a certain astonishment: had any writer ever refused his invitation to be part of *Fatal*? He could not recall one. As a rule, writers—horror writers especially—were vain, insecure creatures, only too eager to accept whatever crumbs of approval were doled out to them by whoever set him- or herself up as arbiter of value. It was hard to imagine this fellow could be any different. Smythe wondered if he'd done something to offend the man, some (drunken) display at one convention or another. He couldn't remember. *Well, fuck.* This was going to leave a ten-plus-thousand-word hole in his book, which was due in little over a month. It wasn't as if there was a surplus of other stories from which to choose; he'd only selected this one because the year's pickings were so slender.

Of course, there was Linus's manuscript. Perhaps one of its stories might be carved into a shape that would plug the gap. Leaning on his desk, he pushed himself to his feet. For once, he was glad of his modest apartment: moving from the computer to the work table was an exercise in agony; he shuddered to think what a trip from one room to another in a larger place, let alone a house, would feel like. By the time he reached table, his groin was singing with pain. Sweat spilled down his face; his breathing was labored. He placed his hands to either side of Linus's manuscript and leaned over it, waiting for his nerves to cool. When they had, he focused on the top page of Linus's collection, dotted with his sweat.

It was blank. *Must have set it back upside-down.* He turned the sheet over, and found the other side blank, too. As were both sides of the page underneath, and the one under that—as were all the pages of what had been Linus's manuscript. Sure he was suffering a momentary occlusion of his vision, Smythe flipped through the book a second, then a third time. The pages remained blank. "What the fuck?" he said. "What the fuck? What the FUCK!" He flung the book across the table. It struck the nearer tower of un-read stories and sent it toppling into its companion, spilling their collected manuscripts onto the floor in an avalanche of paper. "GodDAMN it!" Before he could stop himself, Smythe had swept the pile of stories from established writers off the table, as well.

Dominika. That was the answer. During their conversation last night, she had realized the mistake she'd made in giving him Linus's final collection. Hadn't he thought she seemed different, everything about her more studied (even her accent, which had verged on a parody of itself)? No doubt, the stress of her act leaking through. So once she was confident that he was sufficiently impaired, she'd driven him home, thus allowing herself entry to his apartment, where she had retrieved the manuscript. To delay his dis-covering her duplicity, she'd replaced Linus's book with one of the reams of paper Smythe kept under his printer. No doubt, she already had contacted a number of high-powered agents to discuss what money might be made from the collection. In the meantime, he had lost the opportunity to bring Linus's last book out in a fashion befitting it, and he was up shit creek, very possibly without a paddle, on the next *Fatal Frights*. What a perfect fucking disaster.

Someone spoke. Smythe turned, his injury flaring. There was no one with him—as of course there wouldn't have been. The voice spoke again, whatever it was saying muffled, diffuse. Was it something on the computer? He checked, but only his e-mail was open. The TV was off, yet the voice continued. His neighbors to either side were elderly, quiet, and anyway, the words didn't sound as if they were carrying through the walls. They seemed closer.

Surely it couldn't be coming from the kitchen, from the freezer. That would be too much, more of a breach of good taste than anyone could tolerate. Yet when he pulled back the freezer door, the ice inside crackling, there was the mannequin head of Linus. Despite himself, Smythe retreated a step. "Fucking..." At least the voice had stopped (some kind of tape recorder, set to a timer?). The eyes, he was oddly relieved to see, were closed. What the hell was he supposed to do with this?

When the model's mouth fell open, Smythe assumed it was a consequence of the sudden change in temperature caused by his holding the door open—which he also assumed was responsible for the thick, yellow liquid that dribbled over its lower lip onto the freezer's floor. *Great—probably some kind of toxic chemical.* When the tongue spasmed, however, and the lower jaw twitched upward, Smythe stumbled backwards. *There's no way*, he thought, and it was true, there wasn't, this had to be a prank, a hoax. But by Christ, it did look real, the lips trembling madly as they tried to frame a word there was no way they could speak. Even with his heart hammering, Smythe could appreciate the level of craftsmanship that had gone into this thing.

The sound that uttered from Linus's mouth was not a word. Nor was it mere noise. Smythe felt himself pressed upon from all directions at once, as if the very air had tightened against his skin. His ears filled with a syllable rang like a cathedral bell, the way the very first word must have troubled the infinite silence that had preceded it. Phosphorous-white light bleached the room around him. He squinted, but it did no good. It was as if the light was inside him. The sensation of fullness in his ears increased from dull to sharp, stabbing pain. He cupped his hands to his head as something gave first in his left, then his right ear. Crying out, he doubled over. He couldn't hear himself. His hands were wet. He held the right up in front of him, saw blood streaking his palm.

Into the Darkness, Fearlessly

Whether the sound was continuing to issue from Linus's mouth, or Smythe's brain was stuck replaying the noise that had exceeded it, he didn't know. But, especially now that that the brilliance was ebbing from the air around him, he was possessed by the urge to flee not just the kitchen, but his apartment, the building that contained it. He didn't worry about locking the door behind him; he wasn't sure he'd shut it. He didn't bother waiting for the elevator; the pain that raged between his legs as he descended the five flights of stairs did not seem too large a price to pay for exiting this place.

Smythe emerged from the front lobby into a gray day. Already, he was starting to trace a line of reasoning whose starting point was Dominika spiking his wine with some variety of long-lasting hallucinogen. The chalk skidded off the board, however, at the sight across the street that greeted him.

It was a house, one that had not been there when he left the building to attend Linus's wake last night, or on any of the roughly five thousand other days he'd walked out the front door. *It's a gingerbread house*, he thought, which was not quite accurate but which encapsulated the emotion its appearance evoked in him, mingled wonder and terror at having confronted a dwelling from one of the Grimm brothers' darker stories. The lines of its roof, its sides broken by ornaments that would have been more appropriate to a Medieval castle—gargoyles resting their pointed chins on taloned hands, faces too-broad, vines that coiled like serpents—the house had been stuffed between its neighbors in a manner that suggested a bundle of papers shoved between two sturdy volumes of an encyclopedia. Open wide, its front door framed a tall, naked woman with long, blond hair who was neither Dominika nor Suzanne Kowalczyk. The knives she held at her sides were large, curved.

What sent Smythe running across the street, up the front walk, and into her terrible embrace was not some spontaneous *liebestod*. It was the figure he met as he turned to go back into his building. Small as a young child, it was wearing a heavy winter coat whose hood had been pulled up far enough to obscure its face. Smythe was about to tell it to get out of the way when it raised its gray hands to either side of the hood and drew it back. That couldn't be—surely, that wasn't—

It was. Oh, it was.

CHILDREN OF THE FANG

1. In the Basement (Now): Secret Doors and Mole-Men

The smells of the basement: dust, mildew, and the faint, plastic stink of the synthetic rug Grandpa had spread down here two decades ago. The round, astringent odor of mothballs stuffed in the pockets of the clothes hung in the closet. A distant, damp earthiness, the soil on the other side of the cinderblock walls. The barest trace of cinnamon, mixed with vanilla; underneath them, brine.

The sounds of the basement: the furnace, first humming expectantly then switching on with a dull roar. The rug scraping under her sneakers. What Rachel insisted was the ring of water in the water tank, though her father swore there was no way she could be hearing that. The house above, its timbers creaking as the air in its rooms warmed.

The feel of the basement: openness, as if the space that she knew was not as large as the house overhead was somehow bigger than it. When they were kids, Josh had convinced her that there were secret doors concealed in the walls, through which she might stumble while making her way along one of them. If she did, she would find herself in a huge, black, underground cavern full of mole-men. The prospect of utter darkness had not troubled her as much as her younger brother had intended, but the mole-men and the endless caves to which he promised they would drag her had more than

93

made up for that. Even now, at what she liked to think of as a self-possessed twenty-five, the sensation of spaciousness raised the skin of her arms in gooseflesh.

The look of the basement: the same dark blur that occulted all but the farthest edges of her visual field. Out of habit, she switched her cane from right hand to left and flipped the light switch at the bottom of the stairs. The resulting glow registered as only the slightest lightening in her vision. It didn't matter: she hardly needed the cane to navigate the boxed toys and clothes stacked around the basement floor, to where Grandpa's huge old freezer squatted in the corner opposite her. For what she had come to do, it was probably better that she couldn't see.

2. The Tape (1): Iram

Around her and Josh, the attic, hushed as a church. Off to one side, their grandfather's trunk, whose lack of a lock Josh, bold and nosy at sixteen as he'd ever been, had taken as an invitation to look inside it. Buried beneath old clothes, he'd found the tape recorder and cassettes. Rachel slid her index finger left over three worn, plastic buttons, pressed down on the fourth, and the tape recorder started talking. A snap and a clatter, a hiss like soda fizzing, and a voice, a man—a young man's, someone in his teens, rendered tinny and high by time and the age of the cassette: "Okay," he said, "you were saying, Dad?"

Now a second speaker, Grandpa, the nasal complaint of the accent that had followed him north to New York state from Kentucky accentuated by the recording. "It was Jerry had found the map and figured it showed some place in the Quarter, but it was me worked out where, exactly, we needed to head."

"That's Grandpa," Josh said, "and…Dad?"

"It isn't Dad," Rachel said.

"Then who is it?"

"I'm not sure," she said. "I think it might be Uncle Jim."

"Uncle Jim?"

"James," she said, "Dad's younger brother."

"But he ran away."

"Obviously, this was made before," she said, and shushed him.

"—the company would have been happy to have the two of you just take off," Uncle Jim was saying.

"Well," Grandpa was saying, "there was time between the end of work on one site and the beginning of work on the next. It's true, though: we couldn't wander off for a week. If we said there was a spot we wanted to investigate, the head man was willing to give us a day or two, but that was because he thought we meant something to do with oil."

"Not the Atlantis of the Sands," Jim said.

"Iram," Grandpa said. "Iram of the Pillars, *Iram ḏāt al-ʿimād*."

"Right," Jim said, "Iram. So I guess the sixty-four thousand dollar question is, Did you find it?"

Their grandfather did not answer.

"Dad?" Jim said.

"Oh, we found it, all right," Grandpa said, his voice thick.

3. The Freezer (1): Early Investigations

Enamel-smooth, the surface of the freezer was no colder than anything else in the basement. Once he understood this, at the age of nine, Josh declared it evidence that the appliance was malfunctioning. Rachel corrected him. "If it was cold," she said, "it would mean it wasn't properly insulated." She softened her tone. "I know it sounds weird, but it's supposed to feel like this." She had tested the freezer with her cane, drawing the tip along the side of it and knocking every six inches. "There's something in it," she announced. She set the cane on the floor and pressed her ear to the appliance. She could hear ice sighing and shifting. When the motor clicked to life and she placed her hands on the lid, the metal trembled under her fingertips.

Six feet long by three high by three wide, the freezer served her and Josh as a prop when they were young, and a topic of conversation as they aged. She would lie, first on top of, then beside the metal box with one ear against it, trying to decipher the sounds within, while Josh ran his fingers along the rubber seam that marked the meeting of lid and container. Both of them studied the trio of padlocked latches that guaranteed Grandpa's insistence that the freezer's contents were off-limits. Josh inspected the bolts which fastened the locks to the freezer, the makes of the padlocks, their keyholes; she felt for gaps between the heads of bolts and the latches, between the latches and the freezer, tugged on the padlocks to test the strength of their hold. After speculating about diamonds, or some kind of rare artifact, or a meteor, she and Josh had decided the freezer most likely housed something connected to their grandfather's old job. Grandpa had made his money helping to establish the oil fields in Saudi Arabia, in what was known as the Empty Quarter. As he never tired of reminding them, it was among the most inhospitable places on the planet. It was, however, a desert, whose daily temperature regularly crossed the three-digit mark. What he could have brought back from such a land that would require an industrial freezer remained a mystery.

Interlude: Grandpa (1): The Hippie Wars

The house in which Rachel and her brother were raised was among the largest in Wiltwyck. However, its second storey belonged entirely to their grandfather. Within the house, it was accessed by a staircase which rose from the front hall to a door at which you were required to knock for entry; outside the house, a set of stairs that clung to the southern wall brought you to a small platform and another door on which you were obliged to rap your knuckles. There was no guarantee of entry at either door; even if she and Josh had heard Grandpa clomping across his floor in the heavy workshoes he favored, he might and frequently did choose to ignore their request for admission.

When he opened the door to them, they confronted a gallery of closed rooms against whose doors her cane knocked. Should either of them touch one of the cut-glass doorknobs, Grandpa's, "You let that alone," was swift and sharp. To her, Josh complained that Grandpa's part of the house smelled funny, a description with which Rachel did not disagree. It was the odor that weighted the air after their father performed his weekly scrub of the bathroom, the chlorine slap of bleach. Heaviest in the hallways, it was slightly better in the sitting room to which Grandpa led them. There, the couch on which she and Josh positioned themselves was saturated with a sweet scent spiced with traces of nutmeg, residue of the smoke that had spilled from the bowl of Grandpa's pipe for who knew how long. Once he had settled himself opposite them, in a wooden chair whose sharp creaks seemed to give warning of its imminent collapse, he conducted what amounted to a brief interview with each of them. How was school? What had they learned today? What was one thing they'd learned this past week they could explain to him? In general, she and her brother were happy to submit to the process, because it ended with a reward of hard candy, usually lemon-drops that made her cheeks pucker, but sometimes cherry Life Savers or atomic fireballs.

Once in a while, the questioning did not go as smoothly. As time passed, Rachel would understand that this was due to her grandfather's moods—generally neutral if not pleasant—which could take sudden swings in a hostile, and nasty, direction. Should she and Josh find themselves in front of him during one of these shifts, the hard candies would be replaced by a lecture on how the two of them were squandering the opportunities they hadn't deserved in the first place, and were going to end up as nothing but hippies. That last word, he charged with such venom that Rachel assumed it must be among the words she was not permitted to say. If Josh had done something particularly annoying, she might use it on him, and vice-versa. Long after her parents had clarified the term's meaning, it retained something of the opprobrium with which Grandpa had infused it—so much so that, when Josh, aged twelve, answered the old man's use of it by declaring that he didn't get what the big deal about hippies was, Rachel flinched, as if her brother had shouted, "Motherfucker!" at him.

Given Grandpa's reaction, he might as well have. Already sour, his voice chilled. "Oh you don't, do you?" he said.

Josh maintained his position. "No," he said. "I mean, they were kind of weird looking, I guess, but the hippies were into peace and love. Isn't that what everyone's always telling us is important, peace and love? So," he concluded, a lawyer finishing his closing argument, "hippies don't sound all that bad, to me."

"I see," Grandpa said, his phrasing given a slight slur as he bit down on the stem of his pipe. "I take it you are an expert on the Hippie Wars."

The name was so ridiculous she almost burst out laughing. Josh managed to channel his amusement into a question. "The Hippie Wars?"

"Didn't think so," Grandpa said. "Happened back in 1968. Damned country was tearing itself apart. Group of hippies decided to leave civilization behind and live off the land, return to the nation's agrarian roots. Bunch of college drop-outs, from New Jersey, New York City. Place they selected for this enterprise was a stretch of back woods belonged to a man named Josiah Sparks. He and his family had shared a fence with our people for nigh on fifty years. Good man, who didn't mind these strangers had settled themselves on his land without so much as a by-your-leave. 'Soil's poor,' he said. 'Snakes in the leaves, bear in the caves. If they can make a go of it, might be they can teach me something.' All through the spring and summer after they arrived, he left them to their own devices. But once fall started to pave the way for winter, Josiah began to speak about his guests. 'Kids'll never make a winter out there,' he said. Good, folks said, it'll send them back where they came from. Josiah, though—it was as if he wanted them to succeed. Not what you would've expected from a marine who'd survived the Chosin Reservoir. One especially cold day, Josiah decided it was past-time he went up and introduced himself to his tenants, found out what assistance he could offer them.

"Turned out, they didn't need his help. Could be, they had in the weeks right after they'd arrived. In the time since, they'd figured out a crop they could tend that would keep them in money: marijuana. When Josiah went walking into their camp, that was what he found, row upon row of the plants, set amongst the trees to conceal them. He hadn't spoken two words to them before one fellow ran up from behind and brought a shovel down on Josiah's head. Killed him straight away. Hippies panicked, decided they had to get rid of his body. They had a couple of axes to hand, so they set to chopping Josiah to pieces. Once their butchery was finished, they dumped his remains into a metal barrel along with some kindling, doused the lot with gasoline, and dropped a match on it. Their plan was to mix the ashes in with their fertilizer and spread them over their plants. Anything the fire didn't take, they'd bury.

"Could be their scheme would've worked, but a couple of Josiah's nephews decided their uncle had been gone long enough and went searching for him. They arrived to what smelled like a pork roast. Hippies ambushed them, too, but one of the brothers saw the fellow coming and laid him out. After that, the rest of the camp went for them. They fought their way clear, but it cost an ear and a few fingers between them.

"By the time Josiah's nephews returned with the rest of their menfolk and what friends they could muster, the camp had improved its armament to firearms, mostly pistols, a few shotguns. I figure they were supplied by whoever had partnered in their little enterprise. For the next week, your peace and love crew proved they could put a bullet in a man with the best of them. They favored sneak-attacks—sent a handful of men to the hospital.

"So you'll appreciate why I do not share your view of the hippie, and you'll understand my views, unlike yours, are based in fact."

Neither Rachel nor Josh questioned that their visit was over. She picked up her cane. As they stood to leave, however, Josh said, "Grandpa?"

"Hmm?"

"Weren't you already living up here with Grandma in 1968?"

"I was."

"Then how did you know about the Hippie Wars?"

Grandpa's chair creaked as he leaned forward. "You think I'm telling stories?"

"No sir," Josh said. "I was just wondering who told you."

"My cousin, Samuel, called me."

"Oh, okay, thank you," Josh said. "Did you go to Kentucky to help them?"

Grandpa paused. "I did," he said. His voice almost light, he added, "Brought those hippies a surprise."

"What?" Josh said. "What was it?"

But their grandfather would say no more.

4. The Tape (2): Down the Well

"—the shore of a dried-up lake," Grandpa was saying. "Looked like an old well, but if you'd dropped a bucket into it, you'd have come up empty. Ventilation shaft, though Jerry thought it might've helped light the place, too. He lowered me down, on account of he was a foot taller and a hundred pounds heavier than I was. Played football at Harvard, was strong as any of the roughnecks. The shaft sunk about fifty feet, then opened out. I switched on my light, and found myself dangling near the roof of a huge cavern. It was another seventy-five feet to the floor, and I couldn't tell how far away the walls were. The rock looked volcanic, which set me to wondering if this wasn't an old volcano, or at least, a series of lava tubes."

"Was it?" Uncle Jim asked.

"Don't know," Grandpa said. "I was so concerned with what we found in that place, I never managed a proper geological survey of it. I'd stake money, though, that it was the remains of a small volcano."

"Okay," Jim said. "Can you talk about what you found there?"

"It was a city," Grandpa said, "or a sizable settlement, anyway. Maybe two-thirds of the cavern had collapsed, but you could see from what was left how the ceiling swept up to openings like the one I'd been lowered through, which gave the impression of enormous tents, rising to their tent poles. Huge pillars that joined ceiling to floor added to the sensation of being under a great, black tent. Iram had also been called the city of the tent poles, and standing there shining my light around it, I could see why."

"But how did you know it was a city, and not just a cave?"

"For one thing, the entrance I'd used. We took that as a pretty clear indication that someone had known about the place and used it for something. Could've been a garbage dump, though—right? We found proof. Around the perimeter of the cavern, smaller caves had been turned into dwelling-places. There were clay jars, metal pots, folded pieces of cloth that fell apart when we touched them. A few of the caves led to even smaller caves, like bedrooms. There was evidence of fires having been kept in all of them. Plus, most of the walls had been written on. I didn't know enough about such things to identify it, but Jerry said it resembled some of what he'd seen on digs down in Dhofar."

"You must have been pretty excited," Jim said. "I mean, this was a historic find."

"It was," Grandpa said, "but we weren't thinking about that. Well, maybe a little bit. May have been some talk about an endowed chair at Columbia for Jerry, a big promotion for me. Mostly, we were interested in the tunnels we saw leading out of the cavern."

5. Family History

Officially, Grandpa had been retired from the oil company since shortly before Rachel's birth, when a series of shrewd investments had vaulted him several rungs up the economic ladder. His money had covered whatever portion of Rachel's appointments with a succession of retinal specialists her father's teacher's insurance did not, and he had paid for all of the specialized schooling and instruction she had required to navigate life with minimal vision. To Rachel's mother, in particular, her grandfather was a benefactor of whose largesse she was in constant need of reminding. To Rachel, he was a sharp voice which had retained most of the accent it had acquired growing up among the eastern Kentucky knobs, when a talent for math and science had allowed him to escape first to the university, then to the world beyond, working as a geologist for the American oil companies opening the oil fields of Saudi Arabia. The edge with which he spoke matched what he said, which consisted in almost equal parts of complaint and criticism—a rare compliment thrown in, as her father put it, to keep them on their toes.

According to Dad, his father had tended to the dour as far back as he could remember, but the tendency had been locked into place after Uncle Jim had run away from home at the end of his junior year in high school. Jim had been the brains of the brothers, a prodigy in math and science like his father before him. He tried not to show it, Dad said, but Grandpa favored his younger son, seemed genuinely excited by Jim, by his abilities, kept saying that, once Jim was old enough, there were things he was going to show him... When they realized that Jim had left home, and without a note or anything, the family was devastated. The police had conducted a lengthy investigation, which had included multiple interviews with each member of the family, but which had led nowhere. Grandma was heart-broken. Dad had no doubt the pain of Jim's departure lay at the root of the heart attack that killed her the following year. Grandpa was overtaken by bitterness, which his wife's death only deepened. Dad had already been away at college, and so had missed a lot of the day-to-day pain his parents had suffered, but for a long time, he said, he had been angry at his miss-ing brother. Jim had given no hint of anything in his life so wrong as to require him abandoning it, and them, entirely. Later, especially after he'd met Mom, Dad's anger had softened. Who knew what Jim had been going through? Still waters run deep and all that.

Jim's disappearance, combined with Grandma's death—not to mention, the blossoming of his stock portfolio—had set Grandpa on the path to retirement, a destination he had reached in the months before his first grandchild appeared. As far as Dad could tell, it had been years since the old man had been happy with his job. Every other week, it seemed, he was complaining about the idiots he worked with, their failure to recognize the need for bold action. Dad had never been much interested in his father's problems at work, and while Jim had been more (and genuinely) sympathetic, Grandpa had said that he couldn't explain it to his second son, he was too young. Dad supposed it was a wonder his father had stayed at his job as long as he had, but the pay was good, and he had responsibilities. After his principal obligation shrank from three members to one, however, he was free to play out the scenario he'd probably imagined a thousand times, and tender his resignation.

Grandpa's retirement had been an unusually active one. Several times a year, sometimes as often as once a month, he hired a car to take him and several large cases down to one of the metropolitan airports, JFK or LaGuardia or Newark, from which he boarded flights whose destinations were a survey of global geography: Argentina, China, Iceland, Morocco, Vietnam. Asked the purpose of his latest trip by either of his grandchildren, he would answer that he'd been called on to do a little consulting work, and if they were good while he was gone, he'd bring them back something nice. Any attempts at further questions were met by him shooing them out of whatever room they were in, telling them to go play. He was usually away for a week to ten days; although once, he was gone for a month, on a trip to Antarctica. While he was abroad, Rachel missed his presence in the house, but her missing him had more to do with her sense of a familiar element absent than any strong emotion. Neither her father nor her brother seemed much affected by his absence, and her mother was clearly relieved.

6. The Tape (3): The Tunnels

"—two kinds," Grandpa was saying. "There were four tunnels leading out of the main chamber. Big enough for one, maybe two folks to walk along side-by-side. They led off to smaller caves, from which further tunnels branched to more caves. Jerry was for investigating these, trying to map out as much of the place as time would allow."

"But you wanted to look at the other tunnels?" Uncle Jim said.

"There were two of them," Grandpa said, "one next to the other. Each about half as tall as the first set: three and a half, four feet. Much wider: eight, maybe nine feet. More smoothly-cut. The walls of the taller tunnels were rough, covered in tool marks. The walls of the shorter tunnels were polished, smooth as glass. To me, that made them all sorts of interesting. While Jerry sketched the layout of the main cavern, I got down on my hands and knees and checked the opening of the short tunnel on my right. Straight away, when I passed my light over it, I saw it was covered in writing. That brought Jerry running. The characters were like nothing either of us had seen before, and Jerry, in particular, had seen a lot. Had the tunnel's surface not been so even, you might have mistaken the writing for the after-effect of a natural process, one of those times Mother Nature tries to fool you into believing there's intent where there isn't. The figures were composed of individual curved lines, each one like a comma, but slightly longer. These curves were put together in combinations that looked halfway between pictures and equations. We checked the tunnel on the left, and it was full of writing, too, the same script—though whatever it spelled out seemed to differ from tunnel to tunnel.

"Thing was," Grandpa went on, "while the shorter tunnels had the appearance of more recent construction, they had the feel of being much older than their counterparts. Sounds strange, I guess, but you do enough of this work, you develop a sense for these things. To Jerry and me, it was obvious that some amount of time had passed between the carving of the two sets of tunnels, and whichever came first, we were sure a long time separated it from the second. What we had was a site that had been occupied by two different—two very different groups of people. We crept into each of the shorter tunnels about ten feet, and right away, felt the floor sloping downwards. The tunnel on the right veered off to the right; the tunnel on the left headed left. I think it was that decided us on exploring these tunnels, first. The taller tunnels appeared to be carved on approximately the same level. The shorter ones promised a whole new layer, maybe more. We flipped a coin, and decided to start with the one on the right.

"We didn't get very far. No more than fifty feet in, the tunnel had collapsed. If it had been our only option, we might have searched for a way around it. As it was, we had another tunnel to try, so we crawled out the way we'd come and entered the tunnel on the left.

"Our luck with this one was better. We followed the passage down and to the left for a good couple of hundred feet. Wasn't the most pleasant trip either of us had taken. The rock was hard on our hands and knees, and it had been a spell since we'd done much in the way of crawling. We had our lights, but they didn't seem that much in the face of the darkness before and behind us, the rock hanging above us. I'm not usually one for the jitters, but I was happy enough to see the end of the tunnel ahead. Jerry was, too. "The room we emerged into was round, shaped like a giant cylinder. From one side to the other, it was easily a hundred feet. Dome ceiling, twenty feet overhead. Across from where we'd entered was another tunnel, same dimensions as the one that had brought us here. I was all for finding out where that led, but Jerry stopped to linger a moment. He wanted to have a look at the walls, at the carvings on them."

Interlude: Grandpa (2): Cousin Julius and the Charolais

As a rule, Grandpa did not interfere with their parents' disciplining of them. Any decision with which he disagreed would be addressed via an incident from his own experience which he would narrate to Rachel and Josh the next time he had them upstairs. For Rachel, the most dramatic instance of this occurred when she was twelve. Seemingly overnight, a trio of neighborhood girls her age, previously friendly to her, decided that her lack of vision merited near-constant mockery. While she had been able to conceal the upset their teasing caused her from her parents, Josh had witnessed an instance of it in front of their house and immediately decided upon revenge. Rather than attacking the girls then and there, he had waited a few days, until he could catch one of them on her own. He had leapt from the bushes in which he'd been concealed and swung his heavy bookbag at the side of her head. The girl had not seen him, which had allowed him to escape and attempt the same tactic with another of the girls the following day. After what had happened to her friend, though, this girl was prepared for Josh. She raised her shoulder to take the brunt of his swing, then pivoted into a punch that dropped him to the sidewalk. As black spots were dancing in front of his vision, the girl seized him by the hair and dragged him into her house, where she turned him over to her shocked mother. During the ensuing rounds of phone calls and parental meetings, the girls' cruelty to Rachel was acknowledged and reprimanded, but the heaviest punishment descended upon Josh, who was grounded for an entire month.

In the aftermath of this incident, the mixture of embarrassment, anger, and gratitude that suffused Rachel received a generous addition of anxiety the next afternoon, when Grandpa descended to the first floor to request her and Josh's presence in his sitting room. The two of them expected a continuation of the lectures they had been on the receiving end of for the last twenty-four hours—as, Rachel guessed, did their parents, who released them into their grandfather's care with grim satisfaction. Despite her belief that Josh hadn't done anything that bad—and that there was no reason at all for her to be involved in any of this—the prospect of a reprimand from Grandpa, who had a talent for finding the words that would wound most acutely, made her stomach hurt. If only she could leave Josh to face the old man himself—but her brother, stupid as he was, had acted on her behalf, and she owed him, however grudgingly, her solidarity. Swinging her cane side-to-side, she followed Josh up the stairs to the second floor and passed along the halls with their faint smell of bleach to Grandpa's sitting room and the smoky couch. She collapsed her cane and sat beside Josh. Maybe Grandpa would finish what he had to say and turn them loose quickly.

She recognized the tinkle of glass on glass that came from one of the six-packs of old-fashioned root beer that their grandfather sometimes shared with them. The pop and sigh of a cap twisting loose confirmed her intuition that he was going to sit in front of them and drink one of the sodas as he lectured. The second pop and sigh, and the third, confused her. Was he planning to consume all three of their root beers? The floor creaked, and cold glass pressed against the fingertips of her right hand. She took the bottle, its treacly sweetness bubbling up to her nostrils, but did not lift it to her mouth, in case this was some sort of test.

Grandpa seated himself, and said, "The two of you are in a heap of trouble. It's your parents' right to raise you as they see fit, and there's naught anyone can say or do about it. It's how I was with my boys, and I won't grant your Dad any less with you. Joshua, they don't take too kindly to you walloping this one girl and trying for the other, and Rachel, they're tarring you with some of the same brush in case you had anything to do with putting your brother up to it. These days, folks tend to take a dim view of one youngster raising his hand against another. Especially if it's a girl—your Dad would say I'm wrong, times've changed, but rest assured: if those had been two boys you'd gone after, the tone of the recent discussions you've been in-volved in would have been different.

"I can't intervene with your parents, but there's nothing that says I can't have a few words with you. So. When I was a tad older than the two of you, I went everywhere and did everything with my cousin, Julius Augustus.

Some name, I know. It was the smartest thing about him. I expect your folks would call him 'developmentally delayed' or somesuch. We said he was slow. He was four years older, but he sat through ninth grade with me. It was his third time, after two tries at the grade before. He'd wanted to quit school and find a job, maybe on his uncle's farm, but Julius's dad fancied himself an educated man—which I guess you might have guessed from the names he loaded on his son—and he could not believe a child of his would not possess the same aptitude for learning as himself. Once I'd moved on to tenth grade and Julius had been invited to give ninth another try, his father relented, and allowed him to ask his uncle about that job.

"Julius's dad, Roy, was my uncle by marriage. His family owned a farm a couple of miles up the road from where I lived. Had a big house set atop a knob, from which they looked down on the rest of us. They'd been fairly scandalized when Roy took a liking to Aunt Allison, who was my Mom's middle sister, but Roy had proved more stubborn than the rest of his family, and in the end, his father had granted Roy and Allison a piece of land which ran along one bank of the stream that swung around the foot of the hill. Julius Augustus was their only child who lived, and if folks judged it ironic that a man of Roy's intellectual pretensions found himself with a boy who had trouble with the Sunday funnies, none of them denied the sweetness of Julius's temperament. You could say or do nigh-on anything to him, and the most it would provoke was a frown.

"It let him get along at his uncle's, which had been his grandfather's until the old man's heart had burst. The grandfather hadn't been what you'd call kind to his laborers, but he had been fair. His elder son, Roy's brother, Rick, was less consistent. Not long after his father's death, Rick had sunk a fair portion of the farm's money into a project he'd been talking up for years. He bought a small herd of French cattle—Charolais, the breed was called. He'd seen them while he was serving in France, in what we still called the Great War. Bigger cattle, heavier, more meat on them. Cream-colored. Rick had a notion that they would give him an advantage over the local competition, so he returned to France, found some animals he liked and a farmer willing to sell them, and arranged to have his white cattle shipped across the Atlantic. This was no easy task, not least because the Great Depression still had the country in its claws. More than few palms wanted crossing with silver, and then a couple of the cows sickened and died on the journey. The

Charolais that arrived took to the farm well enough, but Rick had imagined that, as soon as they were grazing his fields, everything was going to happen overnight, which, of course, it didn't. The great sea of white cattle he pictured needed time to establish itself. I guess some folks, including Roy, tried telling him this, but Rick would not, maybe could not, accept it. After another pair of the Charolais died their first summer, Rick decided it was because they hadn't been eating the best grass. Anyone could see that the grass all over the farm, and all around the farm, was pretty much the same. But Rick got it in his head that the grazing would make his herd prosper lay on the far side of the stream that snaked around the base of their family's hill—where Roy, Allison, and Julius had their home. Had he asked Roy to allow the cattle to feed on his land, his brother might've agreed. Rick demanded, though, said it was his right as elder son and heir to the farm to do what was best for it. Roy didn't argue his authority over what happened on the farm. But, he said, his property was his property, granted him fair and square by their father, and the first one of those white cows he caught on his side of the stream was going to get shot, as were any subsequent trespassers. As you might expect, this did not go down so well with Rick.

"Despite the bad blood between his father and uncle, Julius was offered and accepted a job on the farm. Consisted mostly of helping with whatever labor needed done, from repairing a fence to painting the barn to baling hay. I suppose I found it unusual that Uncle Roy would permit his son to cross the stream to the farm, but there wasn't much else I could picture Julius doing, except digging coal, which was a prospect none of our parents was eager for us to explore. Anyway, Julius let me tell him how to spend what portion of his wages his parents allowed him to keep. Usually, this was on candy or soda pop; though sometimes, I'd promise him that, if he bought me a certain funnybook I especially wanted, I'd read to him from it. I would, too, at least until I was tired of explaining what all the big words meant. I reckon I wasn't always as kind to my big cousin as I should've been, and I reckon I knew it at the time, too. He was a great, strapping fellow, taller, stronger than me. Long as he was near, the boys who teased and occasionally pushed and tripped me kept their distance. Julius never let on that he didn't like spending time with me, so I didn't worry about the rest of it too much.

"Did I mention that Rick had a daughter? He had three of them, and a pair of sons, besides, but the one I'm speaking of was the second youngest, a girl name of Eileen. Plain, quiet. Don't know that anyone paid her much mind until her daddy showed up at Roy's house with her on one side of him and the Sheriff on the other. Eileen, Rick said, was going to have a baby. Julius, he also said, was the baby's father. I don't know what-all your folks have told you about such matters, but a man can force a baby on a woman. This was what Rick said Julius had done to his Eileen. Julius denied the accusation, but it was Eileen's word against his, and given he wasn't the sharpest knife in the drawer, her yes carried more weight than his no. The charge was a serious one, enough to have brought the Sheriff to the door; though you can be sure Rick's house on top of that knob helped guarantee his presence. The way the Sheriff told it, he already possessed sufficient evidence to put Julius under lock and key, at least until a trial. And, Rick chimed in, did his younger brother know what would happen to Julius once the other prisoners learned what he was awaiting trial for? Messing around with a young girl—it would not go well for him. Julius might not reach his day in court, and that wasn't even mentioning the cost of hiring a lawyer to defend him…

"In a matter of ten, fifteen minutes, Rick and the Sheriff maneuvered Roy and Allison into believing that all they held dear was about to be taken from them. They were frantic. You can be sure Roy had some notion that there was more going on here than his brother was letting on, but he couldn't ignore the situation at hand, either. Rick let Roy and Allison sweat just long enough, then sprung his trap. Of course, he said, there might be another way out of this for all of them. He wasn't saying there was, mind you, only that there might be. Everyone knew that Julius wasn't equipped with the same faculties as those around him. There were places which would take care of such folk, ensure they would not be a danger to anyone else. In fact, there was a fine one outside of Harrodsburg, small, private, where Julius could expect to be well-looked-after. Wasn't cheap, no, though Rick supposed it was less than they might lay out for a decent lawyer, especially if the trial dragged out, or if Julius was convicted and they needed to appeal. Not to mention, it would avoid the talk about Julius that was sure to spread as a result of his imprisonment. Thing about that kind of talk was, it got folks riled up, thinking they needed to get together and take matters into their own hands. There wasn't much the Sheriff and his boys would be able to do if a mob of angry men marched up to the jail and demanded his prisoner, was there?

"By the end of an hour, Rick had everything he needed. To pay for the asylum to which their son was to be shipped in lieu of criminal charges and time in jail, Roy and Allison agreed to sign over their property to him. Within a couple of days, Julius's bags were packed and he was on his way to Harrodsburg. I saw him before he left, and he wasn't upset—mostly, he seemed confused by everything. Soon after he left, his parents went, too, to be closer to him. A school hired Roy as a janitor, and Allison took in washing.

"I saw Julius once, not long after he'd entered the asylum. Nice enough place, I guess, an old mansion that'd seen better days. But Julius was different. Among the conditions of his entering this place was that he not pose a danger to any of the women who worked or were patients there. Shortly after he arrived, he was given an operation to prevent him forcing babies on anyone else. When I called on him, he hadn't fully healed. They'd dressed him in a white shirt and pants, to make him easy to track down in case he went to leave. There was a patch of damp blood down one leg of his trousers. He couldn't understand what had been done to him, and they had him on some kind of pain medicine that made things worse. He kept asking me to explain what had happened to him, and when I couldn't, tried to show me his wound to help. I don't imagine my visit made things any clearer for him.

"All the ride home, I kept thinking about those white cattle. Our family had talked about the situation. Wasn't anyone doubted it had been a way for Rick to get where he wanted to go. Question was, had the road presented itself to him, or had he paved it, himself? No one could credit the charge that had been brought against Julius. On the other hand, whatever his intelligence, his body was a man's, subject to all a man's urges. With only a boy's understanding to guide him, who could say what he might have done, had his blood been up? The women, in particular, would have liked a word with Eileen, but she was gone, sent off to a cousin in Memphis the day after her daddy had reached his agreement with her uncle.

"I knew. I knew that my cousin was innocent and that a terrible crime had been committed against him and his family. Sitting with him in the asylum had made me certain. For a brief time, I hoped the other members of my family might take action, avenge the wrong done Julius, but the furthest they would go was talking about it. One of my uncles proposed shooting Rick's special cattle, but the rest of the family rejected the plan. Rick would guess who'd done it right away, they said, and he'd already proved beyond any doubt he had the law snug in his pocket. God would take care of Rick in His time, my Aunt Sharon said. We had to be patient.

"While I didn't put much stock in Divine Justice overtaking Rick, I saw that my aunt was right about the necessity of waiting. Such a man as Rick couldn't help making enemies. He collected them the way a long-haired dog does ticks. The secret was to wait until he had gathered so many enemies as to move our name well down a list of potential suspects. This meant another six years, till I was halfway done with the university. Julius was dead—had died not many months after I'd seen him. The wound from his operation had never closed properly. Infection set in, and though he fought it for a good long time, this was in the days before penicillin. I was at his funeral. Rick insisted he have a place in the family plot. As much as anything, what he intended as a magnanimous gesture settled me against him. If a man had done to your daughter what Rick had accused Julius of, there was no way you'd make room for him alongside the rest of your kin. Had he been your patsy, you might try to soothe any twinges of conscience by permitting him the privilege of a burial amongst the elect of your line. I swear to you, it was all I could do not to walk over to where Rick and his wife stood beside Roy and Allison and spit in his face. Not then, though, not then. Years had to pass, Julius's grave receive a fancy headstone, the grass grow thick over it. Roy and Allison had to leave for a fresh start in Chicago, where the family lost touch with them.

"At last, the time came around. It was a rainy night, the tail end of storm that had hung about for a couple of days. I wanted it raining so no one would think twice of my wearing a raincoat and hat, gloves and boots. There was a fellow at the university who owed me a considerable favor. He owned a car. I proposed to him that, should he drive me a couple of hours to a location with which I would provide him, wait there no more than an hour, and return me to campus, we would be square. He agreed. I had him take me to a crossroads a mile or so up the road from Rick's farm, where the stream that circled the bottom of his hill swerved close to the road. The stream was swollen with the rain, but not so much that I couldn't wade it to the spot where Roy and Allison's house had stood. Rick had torn it down, had a kind of lean-to built for his cattle to shelter under. This was where I found the lot of them, crowded in together. Their huge white bodies glowed in what little light there was. I dug around in my coat pocket, and came out with my buck knife. I didn't know if the cattle would spook, so I opened it slowly. The ones on the open side of the lean-to shifted their feet, but made no move to run. Speaking softly, smoothly, the kind of nonsense you coo to a baby, I approached. I put my free hand on the cow to my right, to steady her. Then I leaned behind and drew my knife across the backs of her knees. She didn't scream, just gave a little grunt as her hamstrings split and her back end collapsed. That knife was sharp as a smile. I doubt she felt much of anything. I did the same to her forelegs, and moved on to the cow in front of her. Once I had the cattle on the open side done, and the way out of the lean-to blocked, I relaxed. The rest of Rick's Charolais put up no more resistance, though a couple called in protest. I was quick and I was thorough, and when I was done, I retraced my steps to the stream and walked it to where my friend sat waiting for me. The rain and the stream had washed most of the blood and mud from me. All the same, he kept his eyes fixed straight ahead. I told him we could go, and we did.

"You can be sure, I spent the next few days wondering what had been reported by the local press. It was all I could do not to rush out and buy them. Problem was, as a rule, I didn't pay much attention to newspapers; plus, I was in the middle of exams. I wasn't sure at what stage the investigation into what I'd done to Rick's cattle was. I didn't want to do anything, however trivial, that might cast suspicion on me, later. I didn't really need to read a reporter's account of what had taken place after I'd left. I could picture it well enough. Early the next morning, whoever Rick had put in charge of tending the cattle would've wandered over to check on them. He'd have discovered the herd under the lean-to, unable to move, blood watering the mud. He'd have run for Rick, who might've sent someone to fetch the veterinarian. The precise details weren't important. What was, was there was nothing could be done for the animals. To a one, they would have to be destroyed, the meat sold for whatever Rick could get for it. I couldn't decide if he'd have what it took to load the rifle and do what had to be done, himself, or if he'd direct a couple of his men to it. I preferred the former scenario, but either possibility would suffice, because whoever's finger was on the trigger, he'd hear the gunshots, each and every one of them.

"For a couple of months afterwards, I half-expected a visit from one law-man or another. Over the Christmas holidays, I kept a low profile. Rumor was, Rick's suspicion had lighted on a fellow out towards Springfield with whom he'd had a dispute about money the man claimed Rick owed him. Naturally, everyone in my family had an opinion as to who was responsible, but none of them so much as glanced in my direction. I was at the university; I was the last person who would commit such an act, and jeopardize his future. The exception was Aunt Sharon, who, as she decreed that God's wrath had descended on His enemy, let her eyes fall on me long enough for me to know it.

"Obviously, what I did on behalf of Julius, I got away with. Even if I hadn't, though—even if the police had broken down my door and dragged me off to prison—it was the right thing to do. Family comes before every-thing. Someone wrongs one of yours, you do not let that go unanswered. You may have to bide your time, but you always redress an injury to your own. And when you do, you make certain it's in a way that will bring misery to whoever offended. That's what your blood demands of you.

"So anybody who stood up for his big sister to a trio of girls who deserve to have their lips sewn shut, I'd not only give him a bottle of pop, I'd hoist mine in salute to him."

Rachel followed her grandfather's direction and lifted her soda in Josh's direction. The time it had spent in her hand had taken the chill from it, but it was still sweet, and she drank it down eagerly.

7. The Freezer (2): Opened

One time that Grandpa was away, he left the freezer unlocked. As they always did after he was safely gone from the house, Rachel and Josh de-scended the basement stairs; although she, for one, had done so without much enthusiasm, as if she were going through the motions of a ritual grown stale and meaningless. At least in part, that was due to her being seventeen, and more concerned with college applications and the senior prom than with a riddle whose solution never came any closer, and was probably not all that exciting, anyway. But Josh had insisted she come, the moodiness that had erupted with his fifteenth birthday temporarily calmed by the reappearance of their familiar game. He had been working on his lock-picking skills, he said—for reasons she did not wish to consider—and was eager to exercise them on the freezer's locks. Rachel couldn't remember the last time she'd spared any thought for the freezer, but the change in Josh was welcome and substantial enough for her to want to prolong it, so she had accompanied him.

As it turned out, her brother would have to find another test for his burgeoning criminal skills. For a moment, she thought the trickling she heard as she swept her cane from basement stair to basement stair was water running through the brass pipes concealed by the basement's ceiling tiles. Except no, there was none of the metallic echo that passage made. This was water chuckling into open air. At almost the same time, the smells mixing in the basement reached her. The typically faint odors of cinnamon and vanilla, with the barest trace of brine, flooded her nostrils, the cinnamon filling the end of her nose with its powdery fragrance, the vanilla pushing that aside with its almost oily sweetness, the brine suddenly higher in her nose. There was another smell, too, stale water. In comparison, the basement's usual odors of synthetic carpet, dust, and damp were hardly noticeable.

Josh's, "Holy shit," was not a surprise; nor, really, were his next words: "It's open. Grandpa left the fucking thing wide open." The sound, the smells, had told her as much. She said, "He's defrosting it."

He was. He had pushed the freezer a couple of feet to the left, until the spigot that projected from its lower left side was hanging over the edge of the drywell. He unplugged and unlocked the freezer, turned the lever on the spigot, and who knew how many years' worth of ice was trickling down into the ground. Late-afternoon sunlight was warming the basement, but Josh flipped on the light. Rachel would have predicted her brother would run across to inspect the freezer, but he hesitated, and she swatted his leg with her cane. "Hey," she said.

"Sorry," he said.

"What?"

"This is kind of weird."

"No weirder than having the Goddamned thing here in the first place."

"Do you think he knows—you know?"

"That we've been fixated on it since we were kids?" she said. "Yeah, I'm pretty sure he's figured that one out by now."

"Could it be some kind of, I don't know, like a trap or something?"

"A trap? What the fuck are you talking about? This is Grandpa."

"Right," Josh said, "it is. Are you telling me he'd pass up a chance to teach us a lesson, especially about minding our own business?"

"You're being paranoid." She shoved past him and made her way across the basement. Her cane clacked against the freezer. When her hand had closed on the edge of it, she said, "You want to come over here and tell me what's in front of me?"

With the exasperated sigh that had become the trademark of his adolescence, he did. "Move over," he said, pushing her with his hip. She shuffled to her left. Standing over the open freezer, she found the cinnamon-vanilla-brine combination strong enough to make her cough. "I know," Josh said, "pretty intense, huh?"

"What do you see?"

"Ice, mostly. I mean, there's a lot of ice in here, a shitload of it. I'd say that Grandpa had this thing about two-thirds full of ice."

"Well, it is a freezer."

"Ha-fucking-ha."

"The question is, what has he been using it for?"

"Storage."

"Obviously. Any sign of what, exactly, was being stored?"

"I—wait."

She felt him lean forward, heard ice shifting. "What the fuck?" he breathed.

"What is it?"

"I don't know. It's like, paper or something."

"Let me—" she held out her hand.

"Here." He placed a piece of what might have been heavy tissue paper in her palm. She leaned her cane against the freezer and ran her other hand over the substance. Its texture was almost pebbled. It crinkled and bunched under her fingertips. Josh said, "It's translucent—has a kind of greenish tint. At one edge, it's brown—light brown."

"It's skin," she said. "It could be from a plant, I guess, but I think it's a piece of skin." She brought it to her face. The cinnamon-vanilla-brine mix made her temples throb.

"Skin?" Josh said.

"Like from a snake," she said, "or a lizard."

"What the fuck?" Josh said.

Rachel had no answer.

8. The Tape (4): The Carvings

"—ten disks," Grandpa was saying, "evenly-spaced around the room. Each was a good six feet or so across. They were hung low, only about a foot off the floor. I'm not one for art, but I reckon I could find my way around a museum. The style of these things wasn't like anything I'd run across before. What was pictured tended more in the direction of abstract shapes—cylinders, spheres, cubes, blocks—than of specific details. The scenes had been carved in something like bas-relief, and incised with the same writing we'd found at the tunnel mouths. I couldn't decide if it was vandalism, or part of the original design. The letters seemed too regular, too evenly-placed to be graffiti, but I'm hardly the expert in such things.

"Jerry had brought his camera. He'd used up most of his film shooting the main cavern, but had enough left for the disks, so he photographed them."

"What did they show?" Uncle Jim asked.

"Half of them, I couldn't make heads nor tails of. Maybe if I'd had another few hours to study them, I might've been able to decipher them. The hands on our watches were moving on, though, and there was that other tunnel to consider."

"How about the ones you could figure out?"

"There was a picture of a city," Grandpa said, "although no such city as I'd ever seen, in or out of a book. Great buildings that curved to points, nary a straight line amongst them, like fangs of all different sizes. Another showed that same city—I'm pretty sure it was—destroyed, shattered by an enormous sphere crashing down into it. Third was of a long line of what I took for people, crossing a wide plain full of bones. There was one of another catastrophe, a large group of whoever this had been being trampled by a herd of animals—actually, this disk was a bit confusing, too. The animals were at the lead edge of a mass of triangular shapes that I took to be waves, but whether the animals were supposed to represent a flood, or vice-versa, wasn't clear to me.

"The picture that was most interesting was the one set over the tunnel out of the room. At its center, there was a person—or, what was supposed to be a person—and, at all four points of the compass surrounding him, there was another, smaller person, maybe half his size. Seemed to me there was more writing on this disk than the others, concentrated between the fellow in the middle and his four satellites. Jerry said it might be a representation of their gods, or their ancestors, or their caste system—which was to say, just about anything."

"Did you explore the other tunnel?" Jim said. "Of course you did. Did you find anything?"

Grandpa laughed. "I guess you know your old man, don't you? Jerry would've been happy to return, said we'd already found plenty. We had, and I wasn't too sure of our lights, but by God did I want to find out what lay at the end of that other tunnel. Told Jerry I'd go, myself, which I would've; though I was betting on him not wanting to be left alone. He didn't, but he made me promise we'd turn around the second our lights started to go.

"The tunnel out of the chamber was the exact copy of the one that brought us to it. For another couple hundred feet, it slanted down and to the left. The darkness wasn't any darker here than it had been at any point since we'd started our descent, but I found myself estimating how far below the surface we'd come, and that number seemed to make the blackness thicker.

"We issued into a room that was pretty much identical in size and shape to the one we'd left. Only difference was the tombs along the walls."

9. A Familiar Debate

"Suppose everything Grandpa told Uncle Jim on that tape—suppose it's true."

"What?" Rachel said. Her bed shifted and complained as Josh lowered himself onto it. She closed the textbook her fingers had been trailing across. "Are you high again? Because if you are, I have the LSAT to prepare for."

"No," Josh said, the pungent, leafy odor he'd brought with him a clear contradiction of his denial. "I mean, I might've had a little grass to chill me out, but this is serious. What if he was telling the truth?"

With a sigh, Rachel placed her book on the bed. "Do I have to do this? Are you really going to make me run through all the problems with what's on that tape?"

"They were in the Empty Quarter," Josh said, "the *Rub' al Khali*. There's all kinds of crazy shit's supposed to be out there."

"Actually," she said, "that point, I can almost believe. Apparently, there are some famous caves not too far from where they were, so why couldn't they have discovered another? And why couldn't it have been inhabited? If there was a cave-in, and the desert came pouring through the ceiling, there's your Atlantis of the sands legend."

"So—"

"But. This would have been an archaeological find of historic significance. It would have made his friend Jerry's career. He would have been famous, too. You don't think two young guys wouldn't have publicized the shit out of something like this?"

"Ah," Josh said, "but you're thinking in twenty-first century terms. They couldn't snap a picture with their phones and upload it to Facebook, while verifying their coordinates with their personal GPS's. They had to do things the old-fashioned way, which meant returning for additional photos and a survey of the location."

"By which time," she said, "there had been not one, but two week-long sandstorms, and the terrain had been entirely changed."

"It's the desert. There are sandstorms all the time."

"I'm sure there are, which begs the question: how did they find a map to guide them there, in the first place?"

"Maybe it was a star map."

"Then why couldn't they find their way back?"

"Okay, so it was dumb luck they found the place. There's still the pictures they did take."

"Most of which," she said, "were ruined by some kind of mysterious radiation they're supposed to have encountered underground. What could be developed is—apparently—so generic it could be anyplace."

Josh paused. "What about the egg?"

"Seriously?"

"Why not?"

"Why—because extraordinary claims require extraordinary proof."

"There's the freezer," Josh said, "and its locks."

"That's hardly—"

"Remember the piece of skin we found in it?"

"You don't think that was Grandpa fucking with us?"

"We hadn't found Jim's tape in the attic, then. What would have been the point?"

"I said: to fuck with us."

"I don't know," Josh said.

"I do," Rachel said. "Our grandfather is not keeping a pet monster in the freezer in the basement."

"Not a monster," Josh said, "a new species."

"An intelligent dinosaur?"

"It's not—that's like calling us thinking monkeys. It's what the dinosaurs developed into."

"Again—and this is ignoring a ton of other problems with your scenario—what you're describing would have been—I mean, can you imagine? A living example of another, completely different, rational creature? Grandpa and Jerry would have been beyond famous. Yet we're supposed to believe Grandpa raised it, himself?"

"They wanted to study it. They thought it would be better for them to observe and document its development."

"Which neither of them had any training for," Rachel said. "And, once more, where's the data they're supposed to have accumulated?"

"Presumably, Jerry lost it, sometime before his heart attack."

"How incredibly convenient, on both counts."

"Anyway, from what I can figure, it isn't as if the thing is all that smart."

"Does it matter? You do not keep an earth-shaking scientific find on ice in the cellar of your house in upstate New York. Shit," she added, "why are we even having this conversation?"

"It's Uncle Jim," Josh said.

"What about him?"

"I've been thinking about him running away—the timing of it. Near as I can tell, he and Grandpa sat down to record that tape about a month before Jim split."

"And?"

"Well—do they sound like they aren't getting along?"

"No," Rachel said, "but that doesn't mean anything. This could have been the calm before the storm."

"Not according to Dad. The way he tells it, everything was fine between

Uncle Jim and Grandpa and Grandma right until he left."

"You have to take what Dad says about Uncle Jim with a chunk of salt. It's safe to say he was a little jealous of his baby brother."

"What I'm getting at," Josh said, "is maybe Uncle Jim saw what was in the freezer. And maybe he didn't like it. Maybe he freaked out."

"So he ran away?"

"Could be. Could also be, he never left the house."

"What—the thing ate him?"

"Maybe it was an accident," Josh said. "He figured out how to unlock the freezer while Grandpa wasn't there. Or Grandpa was there, but Jim got too close. Or—what about this?—Grandpa turned the thing loose on Jim because he was threatening to tell people about it, go public."

"That's pretty fucked-up," Rachel said. "Grandpa's an asshole who's committed some acts that are, to put it mildly, of questionable morality, but that doesn't mean he'd sic his pet monster on his child."

"It would explain why Jim disappeared so completely, why he's never been found."

"As would a less-elaborate—and -ridiculous—narrative. Not to mention, weren't you sitting beside me during his family-comes-first lectures? Remember cousin Julius Augustus, the terrible things you do for your kin?"

"Family loyalty cuts both ways. If Jim set himself against the family, then he'd be liable for the consequences."

"Seriously? Are you sure this paranoid fantasy isn't about Grandpa and you?"

"Don't laugh. You honestly believe that, if Grandpa thought I was harming the family, he wouldn't take action?"

"'Take action:' will you listen to yourself? He's an old man."

"With a very powerful weapon at his command. You don't need to be too strong to fire a gun."

"Jesus—okay, this conversation is over. I have to get back to studying." As Josh raised himself from the bed, Rachel added, "Occam's razor, Josh: the simplest answer is generally the right one."

"If I'm right about what's in that freezer," he said, "then this is the simplest answer."

Interlude: Dad and Mom

Neither of Rachel's parents cared to discuss her grandfather at any length. In her father's case, this was the residue of an adolescence complicated by the loss of his brother and mother, and an adulthood spent in a career for which his father showed a bemused tolerance, at best. In her mother's case, it was due to her father-in-law's decades-long refusal to be won over by her efforts to achieve anything more than a tepid formality. Mom had been enough of a hippie in her youth for Rachel to have a sense of the root of Grandpa's coldness to her; on a couple of occasions, however, she had hinted to Rachel that her uneasiness around her husband's father had to do with more than his disdain for her lifestyle. There was something she thought she had seen—but it was probably all her imagination. Rachel wasn't to say anything to her grandfather, or he'd accuse Mom of having had a flashback, or worse, of having been tripping. Rachel tried to coax her mother into describing what she had seen, but she refused to be drawn.

10. The Tape (5): Visions of the Lost World

"—eight sarcophagi," Grandpa was saying. "That was what it looked like, at first. Huge stone boxes, ten feet long by four high by four deep. Cut from the same stone as the tunnels and the chambers. Six of them set around one side of the room, the remaining two opposite. It appeared the tombs had been turned over, because the front of each was open. Full of what we took for rocks, smooth, oblong stones the length of a man's hand, all a speckled material I didn't recognize. We circled the room, and it seemed every last one of the stones was cracked, most from end to end. I picked up one to inspect. Lighter than its size, almost delicate. Surface was tacky. I aimed my light into the crack, and saw it was hollow. I replaced it, and chose another one. It was empty, too, as were the others I checked. I moved onto the next stone box, and the one after that, and all the stones I examined were the same, fragile shells that stuck to my fingers. Not until I lifted a rock which hadn't split all the way—and which was heavier than the others—and shone my light into it did the penny finally drop. These weren't stones. They were eggs. The stone containers weren't sarcophagi. They were incubators. This wasn't a mausoleum. It was a nursery."

"What?" Uncle Jim said. "What was in there? What did you see?"

"Broke the shell, myself," Grandpa said. "Shouldn't have, wasn't anything like proper procedure, but what was inside that egg…"

"What?" Jim said. "What was it?"

"Conditions in the chamber had preserved the creature it contained well enough for me to make out the pattern on its skin. It was dried out, more like paper than flesh and bone. Guess you could say I found a mummy, after all. Curled up in the half-shell I was holding, it put me in mind of an alligator, or a crocodile. The body and tail did, anyway. Head was something else. For the size of the skull, the eye was huge, round, like what you find in some species of gecko. Its brow, snout, flowed together into a thick horn that jutted beyond the end of its lower jaw. Damnedest looking thing, and when I studied its forelimbs more closely, I noticed the paws were closer to hands, the toes fingers."

"No way," Jim said.

"Boy, have you ever known me to lie to you?" A warning edge sharpened Grandpa's question.

"No sir," Jim said. "So what was it? Some kind of pet lizard?"

"Not by a long shot," Grandpa said. "I was holding in my palm the withered remains of one of the beings who had carved out the very room in which we were standing." During the pause that followed Grandpa's revelation, Rachel could feel her vanished uncle's distant desire to call her grandfather on his bullshit vibrating the silence; apparently, however, Uncle Jim had decided to water his valor with discretion. Grandpa went on, "Of course, I didn't know this at the time. I assumed the thing I'd found was another lizard, if a strange one. There were a couple more mummified creatures in amongst the eggs in this box, and something even more important: a single, unopened egg, its outside sticky with a coat of the gel that had been left on the others. I wrapped the unbroken egg with the utmost care, and placed it in the bottom of the rucksack I'd worn. Beside it, I packed the three dried-out creatures, along with a sampling of a half-dozen empty eggs. Wasn't anything else we could take as proof we'd been here, but I figured this was better than nothing.

"The trip back to the main cavern, then to the surface, then to the camp, was uneventful. Jerry and I talked about what we'd found, what it might portend for us. We agreed not to say anything to anyone until he'd developed the pictures he'd taken and we'd found someone we could trust to examine the things in my rucksack. Neither seemed as if it would take long—a week or two at the outside—and once we were in possession of evidence we could show someone, we didn't think we'd have any difficulty locating a sponsor who would reward us generously for leading a second, larger and better-equipped, expedition to Iram.

"What we didn't count on was the rolls of film Jerry had shot being almost completely ruined, most likely by some variety of radiation we encountered underground. The couple of photos you could distinguish in any detail showed cave structures that could've been anywhere. On top of that, within twelve hours of our return, I developed a rash on my hands that raced up my arms to my chest and head, bringing with it a raging fever and a coma. Camp doctor'd never seen the like, said it was as if I'd had an allergic reaction to some kind of animal bite."

"The eggs," Jim said, "the stuff that was on them. Was it poisonous?"

"Delivery system," Grandpa said, "for a virus—several, each hitched to a cartload of information. Imagine if you could infect someone with knowledge, deliver whatever he needed to know directly to the brain. Was what was supposed to happen to the creatures when they hatched. On the way out of their eggs, they'd contract what learning they required to assume their role in their civilization. I assume the process was more benign than what I, the descendant of a different evolutionary branch, went through. Prior to this, had you asked me what I thought a coma was like, I would have predicted a deep sleep. It's what the word means, right? Not once did it occur to me such a sleep might be filled with dreams—nightmares. Now, I understand what I saw while unconscious as my brain's effort to reckon with the foreign data being inserted into it. At the time, I felt as if I was losing my mind. Even after I came out of the coma, it was weeks till I could manage a day without some pretty strong medicine, or a night in anything close to peace."

"What did you see?" Jim said.

"Lot of it was in fragments," Grandpa said, "whether because the viruses had decayed over time, or my brain chemistry was too different, I'm not sure. Maybe both. I saw a city standing on the shore of a long, low sea. Made up of tall, triangular structures that curved to one side or another, like the teeth of a vast, buried beast. Their surfaces were ridged, like the bark of a plane tree, and I understood this was because they hadn't been built so much as grown. They were of a piece with the forest that surrounded the place. Herds of what looked like a cross between a bird and a lizard, their feet armed with a single, outsized claw, patrolled the forest lanes, chasing off the larger animals that wandered into them from time to time. These bird-lizards had been grown much the same way as the city, what was already there shaped to the ends of the place's inhabitants. That was what the creatures had raised it did, took what the world around them gave and altered it to fit their purposes. They'd done so for an unimaginable length of years, while the stars rearranged into dozens of sets of constellations. They did it to themselves, steering their biology down certain paths, until they'd split into four...you might call them castes, I suppose. They were distinct enough from one another to be almost separate species. Soldier class was at the bottom; next came the farmers, then the scientists, and finally the leaders. They'd fixed it so they developed from infant to adult in about three years.

"Some kind of disaster brought the whole thing tumbling down. I couldn't tell exactly what. I glimpsed a wall of fire reaching all the way to the sky, but that was it. There weren't many of the creatures to begin with. Their civilization had been in decline for tens of thousands of years, pulling back to the location I'd seen, the original city. Had it not been for some of them working underground, the things would've been burned away, entirely. As it was, there were only a few thousand survivors, left with a landscape that had been charcoaled, bunched up like a blanket. Overhead, the sky was black clouds. A few of the creatures proposed throwing in the towel, joining their brethren in oblivion, but they were outvoted by the rest of the survivors, who decided to search for a new spot to call home. Dissenters didn't have much choice in the matter: their leaders had the ability to force their actions with their minds. So the lot of them left on a journey which would consume decades. Everywhere they went, things were the same, the earth and pretty much everything that had lived on it seared to ash. Once, they came to an ocean, and it was choked with carcasses out to the horizon. The air chilled. Clouds churned above, spilling dirty snow by the foot. Half the creatures died over the course of their travels. In the end, the leaders decided their best hope was hibernation. There were places—the sites of cities long-abandoned—where they could find sufficient facilities left to put themselves into a long, deep sleep, from which they might awaken when the planet had recovered itself. They found one such location in the far south, on the other side of what would be called Antarctica. As best they could, they secured the site, and settled down to sleep.

"And sleep they did, for fifty thousand, a hundred thousand years at a stretch. The world's wounds scarred over. New plants and trees appeared, spread across the land, were joined by new and strange animals. The creatures had lived during the great age of the dinosaurs—were its crowning achievement. They'd witnessed families of beasts like small mountains ambling across the grasslands; they'd fought feathered monsters with teeth like knives in the forests. Now, when they sent scouts to inspect their surroundings, they heard tales of smaller animals, covered in hair. As they woke from rests that lasted millennia, those animals grew larger, until it was if the wildlife they'd known in their former existence was being recast in other flesh. Nor was the rise of these beasts the only change in their environment. The continents were shifting, sliding towards the positions we know. Antarctica was cooling, ice and snow spreading across it. Never ones to act in haste when they didn't have to, the creatures chose to wait. Eventually, they did abandon that location. I can't say when, or why.

"The rest was even more fractured. They left Antarctica in search of a spot closer to the equator. That might have been what we called Iram, or it might have been another spot before it. For a little while, they did all right. Population increased, to the point a group set out west, to find another of the old sites. The two settlements kept up contact with one another. After more time than you or I could comprehend, it appeared the creatures might be on the rebound.

"There was one problem for them, one fly doing the backstroke in the ointment: us, humans. They'd been aware of us as we'd risen from four legs to two and started our long climb up the evolutionary staircase, but it was only as another instance of the weird fauna that had overtaken the world. In what must have seemed the blink of an eye, we were on our way to becoming the dominant life-form on the planet. To make matters worse, we were hostile to them from the get-go, aggressively so. If a human encountered one of them, he fled screaming in the other direction. If a group of humans ran into one of them, they would do their level best to kill it. The creatures had the advantage in terms of firepower. Each of their soldiers had been crafted to be all the weapon it would need against foes much worse than a handful of hairless apes. We had the advantage in terms of numbers—not to mention, we had an ability to make leaps in our reasoning that was completely alien to them. We could surprise the creatures in ways they couldn't us. So began a war which spanned a good deal of man's prehistory. By and large, it was fought by small groups from either side, sometimes individual warriors. There was a point when the creatures who'd settled in the west came out in force against the human kingdom that had arisen near them. Fought all the way into its capital city, to have it swept by a mighty wave that drowned both sides alike. Creatures never recovered from that. They ceded more and more of what territory they'd held to humans. In the end, they opted for the only route left open them: another long sleep. As they had before, they fortified their retreat as best they could, and let slumber take them."

There was a moment's pause, Uncle Jim allowing his father to pick up the thread of his narrative. When it was clear that was not about to happen, Jim said, "Then what?"

"That was it," Grandpa said. "Wasn't anything else. Believe you me, what had been stuffed between my ears was more than enough. You know how full your brain feels after you've pulled an all-nighter prepping for a big test? This was like all the cramming you'd ever done for every test you've ever taken, present at the same time. After I'd climbed out of the coma, the doctor and nurses thought I was delirious. Wasn't that. It was a library's worth of new information trying to squeeze itself into my neurons. Gradually, over a span of weeks, I came to terms with the knowledge I'd gained. By the time I was walking out of that room, though, there was more for me to reckon with. For one thing, after sweating whether anyone would blame him for the sickness that had overwhelmed me, Jerry had gone off in search of Iram, alone. But the entire region had been swept by sandstorms that had reconfigured the landscape beyond his ability to accommodate. For another thing, our team had been moved to a new site, fifty miles east of where we'd been. Fortunately, Jerry had kept my rucksack close and unopened. Absent his photographs and unable to retrace the path to Iram, he doubted anyone would credit him with finding anything but a cache of lizard eggs.

"They were more than that—much, much more. I'd an idea we might locate a scientist to show the eggs to. Wasn't sure if we'd be better with a paleontologist, or a zoologist. I also figured a biochemist might be interested in the substance that had coated the eggs, what it contained. Hadn't paid much mind to the single unhatched egg I'd found; guess I assumed its contents would be useful for purposes of comparison. I certainly was not expecting it to hatch."

11. Thanksgiving

Thanksgiving was the kitchen summer-hot, humid with dishes simmering and steaming on the stove. It was the tomato-smell of the ketchup and soy-sauce glaze her mother had applied to the turkey in the oven; the rough skins of the potatoes Mom had set at one end of the table for Rachel to peel, a tradition that reached back seventeen years, to when her seven-year-old self had insisted on being involved in the preparation of the meal, and her mother had sat her down with a peeler and a handful of potatoes and allowed her to feel her way through removing the tubers' skins. Mom usually bought potatoes whose surfaces were covered in ridges and bumps, and there had been moments Rachel fancied she could almost pick out letters and parts of words encoded on them. She had advanced well beyond those first four potatoes; now, she was responsible for peeling and chopping all the necessary vegetables. For a brief time in his late teens, Josh had insisted on helping her; mostly, she had thought, to improve his standing with their parents. The last few years, he had abandoned the kitchen in favor of the living room, where their father and grandfather passed the hours prior to dinner watching whatever football games were on the television. Dad wasn't a big football fan, not in the same way as Grandpa, who took an almost visceral delight in the players' collisions. But he had grown up with his father's passion for the sport, and had learned enough about it to discuss the plays onscreen with the old man. It wasn't something they did that often—the Super Bowl was the only other instance she could think of—but it seemed to fulfill a need both men felt to demonstrate their bond as father and son. Rachel hadn't been surprised when Josh, despite his almost complete ignorance of anything sports-related, had wanted to join their fraternity. She judged it a demonstration of the event's ongoing importance to him that he had raised himself from the bed into which he'd collapsed at who-knew-when this morning, and, still reeking of stale cigarette smoke and watery beer, shuffled in to join them, stopping in the kitchen long enough to pour himself a glass of orange juice. Their father had greeted him with typical irony—"Hail! The conquering hero graces us with his presence!"—their grandfather with his typical grunt.

Afterwards, Rachel would think that she hadn't been expecting any trouble, today. Then she would correct herself, as she realized that she had been anticipating a disruption of the holiday, and had tied it to Josh. What she had been prepared for was her brother disappearing for ten minutes right as they were about to sit down to eat, and returning reeking of pot. Mom would say, "Josh," the tone of her voice a reproach not so much of the act—she and Dad had done (and continued to do, Rachel thought) their share of grass—as of his total lack of discretion. Grandpa wouldn't say anything, but his end of the table would practically crackle with barely-suppressed rage. Dad would hurry to ask Rachel, who would be attempting to recall a sufficiently lengthy and distracting anecdote, how Albany Law was going. Scenarios approximating this one had played out over the last several Thanksgiving and Christmas dinners, since Josh had discovered the joys of mood- and mind-altering substances. To the best of her knowledge, his proclivities hadn't interfered with his studies as an undergraduate or graduate student, which Rachel guessed was the reason their parents hadn't come down on him with more force than they had. But it angered Grandpa to no end, which, Rachel increasingly believed, constituted a good part of the reason her brother did it.

But the argument that erupted this day: no way she could have predicted it. It began with something her grandfather said to her father, something that registered as background noise because she was answering her mother's question about where she was planning on going after she passed the bar. Clear as a bell, Josh's voice rang out: "Hey, Grandpa, why don't you give Dad a break, okay?"

"Josh!" their father said.

"All I'm saying is, he should take it easy on you," Josh said.

"That's enough," Dad said. "We're watching the game."

"That were my boy," Grandpa said, "he'd speak to his elders with a bit more respect."

"Dad," their father said.

"That were my son," Josh said, "I wouldn't treat him like a piece of shit all the time, especially after what I did to his brother."

"Josh!" Dad said. "What the hell is wrong with you?"

Grandpa said nothing.

"I'm fine," Josh said. "Not like poor Uncle Jim. Right, Grandpa?"

"What the hell are you going on about?" Dad said. "Are you high?"

"No I am not," Josh said. "If I were, it wouldn't have any bearing on what we're talking about, would it, Grandpa?"

"Stop it," Dad said. "I don't know what you're talking about, but give it a rest, okay?"

"What I can't work out," Josh said, "is whether it was an accident, or deliberate. Did things slip out of control, or did you turn that thing on your son? And if you did loose it on him, what can he possibly have done to drive you to do so? Oh, and one more thing: how can you stand yourself?"

"Leave," Dad said. "Just leave. Get out of here."

"Boy," Grandpa said, "you've gone beyond the thin ice to the open water."

"Which means what? That I can expect a visit from your friend in the freezer?"

"Josh," Dad said, his easy-chair creaking as he sat forward in it, "I'm not kidding. You need to leave."

"All right," Josh said, "I'll go. If there's anything you want to show me, Grandpa, you know where to find me." The couch springs groaned as he stood. Rachel half-expected him to pause in the kitchen on his way to his room, or for her mother to call his name, but neither happened. When his footsteps had finished their tromp along the hall, their father said, "Dad, I am so sorry for that. I don't know what got into him. Are you all right?"

"Game's on," Grandpa said.

12. The Second Tape

The second tape had been damaged, to the extent that the portion of Uncle Jim's conversation with Grandpa it recorded had been reduced to a stream of garble to whose surface select words and phrases bobbed up. The majority of them ("room," "go," "space") were sufficiently generic to be of little aid in inferring the contents of Grandpa's speech; although a few ("scared," "raw meat," "soldier") seemed to point in a more specific direction. From the first listen, Josh insisted that their grandfather had been describing how the creature which crawled out of the egg had been frightened, until he had fed it the uncooked flesh of some animal or another, probably winning its trust. Later on, Grandpa had identified the creature as belonging to the soldier class he'd learned about during his coma. While she conceded that Josh's interpretation was reasonable, Rachel refused to commit to it, which Josh claimed was just her being a pain in the ass. Given what they'd already listened to, what better construction did she have to offer?

None, she was forced to admit, nor did the three longer passages they found on the tape provide any help. The first came five minutes in; the babble unsnarled and Grandpa was saying, "—like when you come down with the flu. High temperature, head swimming, every square inch of skin like a mob of angry men beat it with sticks. Maybe it would have had the same effect on the creatures, but I doubt it. Has to do with the difference in biology, is my guess. Doesn't help that the thing fights you. Especially if there's blood in the air, it's like trying to wrestle a strong man to the ground and keep him there. Sometimes, there's no choice but to let it go, a little bit. Why I use the freezer. Long as it's in there, it's dormant. After you take it out, if you're careful and don't overdo things, there's no problem keeping it under control almost the entire time. I—" and his words ran together.

Twenty-four minutes after that passage, long after they had given up hope of encountering another and left the tape playing so they could tell themselves they had listened to all of it, the garble gave way to Grandpa saying, "After that, I received a visit from a couple of fellows whose matching crew cuts, sunglasses, and black suits were as much ID as what they flashed in their wallets. I'd caught sight of such characters before. Every now and again, they would show up at the camp, ask to speak to one of the experts about something. Wasn't too strange, when you thought about it. Here we were, working in a foreign land, where we might notice a detail about the place or people that would be useful for these boys. Cold War was in full swing, and the lessons of the last big one were fresh in everyone's mind, especially the strategic advantage of a plentiful supply of fuel. Our work was tied up with national security, so it wasn't a surprise that the fellows who concerned themselves with it should keep an eye on us. Tell the truth, I was curious to find out what they'd driven all this way to ask me about. Naïve as it sounds, not once did it cross my mind that they might be here to inquire about my other activities. Not that the company would have had any remorse over what they'd had me do to the competition: I just assumed they wouldn't want me revealing such a valuable secret. Never did learn if someone had blabbed, or if the G-men had sweated it out of them. No matter. These boys cut straight to the point. Said they knew I'd been up to some extra-curricular activities, and were going to provide me the opportunity to put those activities to work for my country. Which was to say—" a paraphrase that was swallowed in a mess of sound.

Before the third and final section, the tape spat out the phrase, "children of the fang." Three minutes after that, at the very end of the second side of the second tape, the nonsense came to an end and was replaced by silence. As Rachel was running her finger across the tape recorder's buttons, Grandpa's voice said, "What we never could work out was whether the viruses floating around my blood had changed me permanently. Could I pass along my control of the creature to my child, or was it confined to me? How could we know, right? I hadn't met your ma, hadn't settled down and started a family, yet."

Uncle Jim said, "What do you think, now?"

"I think we might find out," Grandpa said, and the tape recorder snapped off.

Interlude: Grandpa (3): Knife Wants to Cut

Whether birthday, Christmas, or other celebration such as graduation, the gift Rachel or her brother could expect from Grandpa was predictable: money, a generous amount of it tucked into a card whose saccharine sentimentality it was difficult to credit their grandfather sharing. When they were younger, the bills that slid out of their cards from Grandpa had been a source of puzzlement and occasional frustration to her and Josh. Why couldn't their grandfather have given them whatever present they'd requested of him, instead of money? In a relatively short time, their complaints were replaced by gratitude, as Grandpa's beneficence enabled Rachel and Josh to afford extravagances their parents had refused them.

The exception to this practice occurred on Josh's thirteenth birthday. After he had unwrapped his gifts from his parents and Rachel, but before he had moved on to their cards, Grandpa said, "Here." A box scratched across the table's surface.

"Grandpa?" Josh said. Whatever was inside the box thwacked against its side as Josh picked it up. Something heavy, Rachel thought, probably metal. A watch? "Buck knife," Josh read. "Really?"

"Open it and find out," Grandpa said.

Rachel could feel the look her father and mother exchanged.

The cardboard made a popping sound as Josh tore into it. "Coooooooooool," he said. Plastic crinkled against his fingers.

Their father said, "Dad."

Grandpa said, "Boy your age should have a knife—a good one."

The blade snicked as Josh unfolded it into place. "Whoa," he said.

Their father said, "Josh."

Grandpa said, "It's not a toy. It's a tool. A tool's only as good as your control of it, you understand? Your control slips—you get sloppy—and you'll slice your skin wide open. Someone's next to you, you'll slice them open. That is not something you want. Knife wants to cut: it's what it's made for. You keep that in mind every time you reach for it, and you'll be fine."

Their mother said, "Josh, what do you say?"

"Thank you, Grandpa," Josh said, "thank you thank you thank you!"

Within a week, the knife would be gone, confiscated by Josh's homeroom teacher when she caught him showing it off to his friends. After a lengthy conference with Mrs. Kleinbaum, their father retrieved the knife, which he insisted on holding onto until the school year was out, his penalty for Josh's error in judgment. By the time summer arrived, Josh had pretty much forgotten about his grandfather's present, and if he remembered to mention it to their father, it was not in Rachel's hearing.

Before all of this, though, Josh let her hold the gift. The knife was heavy, dense in the way that metal was. Longer than her palm, the handle was smooth on either end, slightly rougher between. "That's where the wood panels are," Josh said. On one side of the handle, a dip near one of the ends exposed the top edge of the blade. By digging her nail into a groove in it, she could lever the blade out. As it clicked into place, a tremor ran up the handle. Rachel slid her finger along the knife's dull spine. About a third of the way from its end, the metal angled down to the tip. "Like a scimitar," Josh said. She dimpled her skin on the point. "Careful," Josh said.

"Shut up," she said, "I am being careful." Ready to part her flesh, the blade's edge passed under her touch. In her best approximation of Grandpa's voice, she said, "Knife wants to cut." She folded the knife closed, and handed it back to Josh.

He laughed. "Knife wants to cut," he said.

13. In the Basement (Now): The Thing in the Ice

Because of Grandpa's stroke Christmas Eve, neither Rachel nor her parents paid much attention to what they assumed at the time was Josh's refusal to appear for Christmas. Granted, it had been a few years since he'd last missed a family holiday, but he had spent most of his Thanksgiving visit complaining about the workload required by his doctoral classes (the stress of which their parents had diagnosed as the cause of his blowup with Grandpa). He had a trio of long papers due immediately before Christmas break—not the most work he'd ever faced, but on a couple of occasions on the day before Thanksgiving, he'd alluded to Rachel about a mid-semester affair with a guy from Maine that had crashed and burned in spectacular fashion, leaving him dramatically behind in all his classes. She had offered his backlog of assignments to her mother as the reason for his abrupt departure Saturday afternoon, while Rachel and her parents were braving the crowds at the Wiltwyck mall. His assignments were probably the reason that none of them had heard from Josh the last few weeks, either.

And if she and her parents were to be honest with one another, it was likely as well that Josh had opted to give Christmas a pass. After Mom heard the thump and crash on the front stairs and went to investigate, and found Grandpa sprawled halfway down, his breathing labored, the left side of his face slack, his left arm and leg so much dead lumber, the focus had shifted from holiday preparations (which included planning for a possible Round Two between Josh and Grandpa) to whether the old man would survive the next twenty-four hours. Even after the doctors had pronounced Grandpa's condition stable, and expressed a cautious optimism that subsequent days would bear out, he remained the center of attention, as Rachel and her parents talked through what needed doing at home to accommodate his changed condition, and set about making the necessary calls to arrange the place for him. She left a couple of messages on Josh's phone, the first telling him to call her, the second, a few days later, informing him of Grandpa's stroke, and though she was annoyed at his failure to respond, especially once he knew the situation, she didn't miss the inevitable torrent of self-reproach with which he would have greeted the news—and which certainly would have been worse had he been there with them.

By Valentine's Day, what Rachel referred to as her brother's radio-silence had become a source of worry for their mother. "Do you think he's still upset about Thanksgiving?" she asked during one of their daily calls. Rachel could not believe that Josh would sulk for this long; although there had been a couple of occasions during his undergraduate years when a particularly intense relationship had caused him to drop off the face of the earth for a couple of months. She phoned his cell, but her, "It's me. Listen: Mom's worried. Call her, okay?" betrayed more pique than she intended. But she could not credit the edge to her voice for Josh's continuing failure to phone their mother. And, despite his assurances that Josh was probably caught up in some project or another, Dad's voice when she spoke with him revealed his own anxiety. Only Grandpa, his speech slowed and distorted by the stroke, seemed untroubled by Josh's silence. Both her parents were desperate to drive up to Josh's apartment, but feared that appearing unannounced would aggravate whatever the situation with him was. Rachel bowed to their none-too-subtle hints, and offered to do so for them.

Before she could take a taxi to the other side of the city, however, one of Josh's fellow students at SUNY Albany called her to ask if everything was okay with her brother, whom, he said, he hadn't seen since he'd left for Thanksgiving vacation the previous semester. He'd left messages on Josh's cell, but had heard nothing in reply. He'd remembered Josh mentioning a sister at Albany Law, so he'd looked up her number, which he'd been meaning to call for a while, now. He didn't want to be intrusive. He just wanted to be sure Josh was okay and knew his friends were asking for him. That conversation was the first of a chain that led to several of Josh's other friends, then their parents, then the police. By the end of the day, her mother had left her father to watch Grandpa and raced up the Thruway to pick up Rachel and drive to Josh's apartment, where they were met by Detective Calasso of the Albany PD and a pair of uniform officers. Both Rachel and her mother had keys to the door. Her heart was beating so fast it was painful, not because of what she was afraid they were going to find, but because of what she was certain they were not. The moment the door swung in, the smell that rolled out, dry, cool dust, confirmed her suspicion. During their search of Josh's small living quarters, the detective and his colleagues discovered two bags of pot, a smaller one in the top drawer of the bedroom dresser, and a larger one sunk inside the toilet's cistern. Once they'd found the second bag, the tenor of the detective's questions underwent a distinct change, as Josh went from graduate student in philosophy to small-time drug-dealer. Rachel could hear the narrative Calasso's line of inquiry was assembling, one in which her brother's criminal activities had brought him into jeopardy from a client, competitor, or supplier. Best case, Josh had gone into hiding; worst, he'd never had the chance. From the detective's perspective, she could understand: it was an attractive explanation, that had the virtue of neatly accounting for all the evidence confronting him. Her and her mother's protests that this wasn't Josh were to be expected. How often, in such situations, could family members admit that their loved ones were so markedly different from what they'd known? Detective Calasso assured them that the police would do everything in their power to locate Josh, but by the time her mother was dropping her back at her apartment, she was reasonably sure that the detective deemed the case essentially solved.

That she would entertain Josh's claims about Grandpa and what he had locked away in his basement freezer was at first an index of her frustration after four weeks of regular calls to Detective Calasso, during which he never failed to insist that he and his men were working tirelessly to ascertain her brother's whereabouts. Approximately every third conversation, he would inform Rachel that they were pursuing a number of promising leads, but when she asked him what those leads were, he appealed to the sensitivity of the information. She hardly required a lifetime spent mastering the nuances of spoken expression to recognize that he was bullshitting her. She could believe that Calasso had queried what criminal informants he knew for information on her brother, as she could that his failure to turn up anything substantive would have done little to change his theory of the case. Compared to the plot in which her brother had been assassinated by a rival drug dealer and his weighted corpse dumped in the Hudson, the prospect that the accusations he'd lobbed at their grandfather at Thanksgiving had prompted the old man to some terrible act had the benefit of familiarity.

In the space of a week, however, the Grandpa's-monster-theory, as she christened it, went from absurd to slightly-less-than-absurd, which, while not a huge change, was testament to the amount of time she'd spent turning it over in her mind, playing devil's advocate with herself, arguing Josh's position for him. Her dismissal of the story Grandpa had told Uncle Jim was based in her assumption that he and his friend, Jerry, would have been sufficiently competent to take full advantage of the opportunities with which their supposed discoveries presented them. What if they hadn't been? What if they hadn't known how to exploit their findings? After all, why should they have? Especially if they couldn't trace their way back to the place? And say, for the sake of argument, that Grandpa had come into care of… something, something fantastic. Who was to say he would have turned it over to a zoo, or university? It wouldn't have been the most sensible course of action, but, as her favorite professor did not tire of reminding her, logical, self-consistent behavior was the province of bad fiction. Actual people tended to move in ways which, while in keeping with the peculiarities of their psychology, resembled more the sudden shifts in course typical of the soap opera.

Which meant, of course, that her younger brother could have had a secret life as a drug dealer. And that their grandfather could have been keeping an unimaginable creature in enforced hibernation in the basement. The impossibility of what she was considering did not stop her from making a couple of discreet inquiries among her closer friends as to the possibility of acquiring a set of lock picks and being instructed in their use. This proved remarkably easy. One of those friends had a friend who earned extra cash as a stage magician whose skill set included a facility with opening locks. For the price of a couple of dinners, the magician was happy to procure for Rachel her own set of tools and to teach her how to employ them. She wasn't certain if she was one hundred percent serious about what she appeared to be planning, or if it was a temporary obsession that had to work itself out. The entirety of the bus ride to Wiltwyck, she told herself that she was not yet positive she would descend to the basement. That her parents were away for the afternoon and Grandpa still of limited mobility meant no more than it meant. She managed to keep that train of thought running for the taxi ride from the bus station to her parents' house. But once she had let herself in the front door, hung up her coat, and slid the soft bag with the lock picks in it from her pocketbook, it seemed pointless to continue pretending there was any doubt of her intentions. She listened for Grandpa, his home health aide, and when she was satisfied there was no one else on the first floor, set off sweeping her cane from side to side down the front hall, towards the basement door.

In no time at all, she was resting the cane against the freezer. How many times had she been here, sliding her hands along the appliance's edge until they encountered each of Grandpa's locks? Always with Josh maintaining a steady stream of chatter beside her. Now, the only sound was the low hiss of her palms over the freezer's surface, the click of metal on metal as she found a lock and tilted it up. How long ago had Grandpa switched entirely to padlocks? It made what she was about to do easier. She placed the lock pick bag on top of the freezer, rolled it open, selected her tools, and set to work.

The locks unclasped so easily, it was almost anticlimactic. Half-anticipating an additional security measure she'd missed, Rachel searched the freezer lid. Nothing. She put the opened locks on the floor, returned her tools to their bag and put it beside the locks, and braced her hands against the lid. After all these years, to be…There was no point delaying. She pushed upwards, and with the pop of its rubber seal parting, the lid released.

A cloud of cinnamon, vanilla, and brine enveloped her. She choked, coughed, stepped away from the freezer. Her eyes were streaming, her nose and tongue numb. She bent forward, unable to control the coughs that shook her lungs. So much for secrecy: if Grandpa had been unaware of her presence in the house previously, she'd just advertised it. Still coughing, she returned to the freezer and plunged her hands into it.

Ice cubes heaped almost to its top rattled as her fingers parted their frozen geometry. She moved her hands back and forth, ice chattering and rattling. There was a click, and the freezer's motor whirred to life. When had Grandpa loaded all this ice in here? Funny to think that not once had she and Josh asked that question.

Her fingertips brushed something that wasn't ice. She gasped, overcome with sudden terror that she had found her brother, that Grandpa had flipped out, murdered him, and used the freezer to hide the body. Even as her heart leapt in her chest, her not-completely-numb fingers were telling her that this wasn't Josh. It was an arm, but it was shorter than her brother's, the skin weird, pebbled. She followed it to one end, and found a hand with three thick fingers and a thumb set back towards the wrist. A claw sharp as a fresh razor protruded from each of the fingers.

Nausea roiled her stomach. She withdrew her hands from the ice and sat down hard on the basement floor. Her head was pounding. She pressed her cold palms to either side of it. Somewhere in the recesses of her brain, Josh crowed, "See? I told you!" Her pulse was racing. She felt hot, feverish. The floor seemed to tilt under her, and she was lying on it. She could not draw in enough breath. Her body was light, almost hollow. She was moving away from it, into darkness that gave the sensation of movement, as if passing through a tunnel. She

14. Affiliation

opened her eyes to light. Brilliance flooded her vision. She gasped, and heard it at a distance. She jerked her hands to her face, but found her arms weighted with something that rattled and rustled as she tried to move them. Her entire body was covered in the stuff. Panic surged through her. She thrashed from side to side, up and down, the medium that held her snapping and cracking as it shifted around her. There was something wrong with her arms and legs. They were sluggish, clumsy. The brightness before her eyes resolved into shapes, triangles, diamonds, blocks, jumbling against one another. With a crash, her right arm broke free of its confinement. Her hand flailed on the rough surface of the material. She braced her forearm against it, and pushed her head and shoulders into the air.

She was in a large box, filled, she realized, with ice. That she could see this was no less remarkable than the circumstance itself. Her head had emerged near one side of the container. If she stretched her neck, she could take in more of the space around her. The figure lying beside the box startled her. She gasped again—and heard it from the woman's lips. In a rush, she took in the sweater and faded jeans, the hair in its shoulder-length cut, the round, freckled face, its eyes wide and unfocused (*and the colors, God, was this what color was?*)—

—and she was looking at a dark blur that kept all except the outermost limits of her vision from her. Above, something moved in Grandpa's freezer, shoving ice from side to side, spilling it on the carpet. She went to sit up—

—and was in the box, her head hanging over the side. Her hands clutched the metal of the box. Below her, the woman on the floor shivered. Her face was flushed, her breathing rapid. She reached a hand to her, and what already had registered peripherally—the pebbled skin, patterned with dark swirls, the three fingers, each taloned, the thumb almost too far back to be practical, armed with its own claw, longer and more curved—shouted itself at her, bringing with it a thunderclap of understanding. A fresh wave of nausea swept her, but it was the woman on the floor who coughed and vomited. For a moment, less—

—she was spitting out the remains of a partially-digested danish—

—and then she had heaved herself out of the box (*Grandpa's freezer*) and went stumbling across the basement floor, pieces of ice dropping from her on the way. Her legs were different—out of proportion in a way she couldn't assimilate. Some of the bones had been shortened, some lengthened, the angles of her joints changed. Her balance was shot. If she stood straight, she felt as if she was about to tip over onto her back. Not to mention, the sight of everything around her, which kept tugging her head this way and that, further unbalancing her. She had developed a fair estimate of the basement's appearance, but it was as if, after having encountered water a handful at a time, she had been dropped into the ocean. All of it was so *vivid*, from the swirling grain of the paneling on the walls to the spiky texture of the carpet, from the squat bulk of the freezer to the sharp edges of the cardboard boxes stacked around the floor. On top of that, the rest of her senses were dulled, practically to nonexistence. She struck the wall at the foot of the basement stairs, and realized that she hadn't felt the collision as painfully as she should. *Grandpa*, she thought, and half-pulled herself, half-climbed towards the door at the top of the stairs.

As she pushed through into the kitchen, an image burst across her mind's eye: a man, looking over his shoulder at her, his eyes widening with the shock that had stunned the rest of his face. He appeared to be wearing a gray suit jacket, but there wasn't time for her to be sure, because he was replaced by another man, this one dressed in a white robe and a white headdress, his mouth open in a shout that she heard *("Ya Allah!")*, his eyes hidden behind sunglasses in the lenses of which something awful was reflected as it bore down on him, claws outstretched. She caromed across the kitchen, slamming into the breakfast bar at its center. The tall, glass cylinders in which Mom kept the cereal toppled onto the floor, where they detonated like so many bombs, spraying glass and corn flakes across the tiles. She stepped away from the breakfast bar, and was staring down at a man whose eyes were rolling up as blood bubbled from his lips, over his scraggly beard, and the claws of her right hand slid deeper into his jaw. The next man she saw was dressed in a tuxedo, the white shirt of which was turning dark from the wave of blood spilling down from the slash to his throat. She lurched out of the kitchen, down the hallway to the stairs to the second floor. The sightless eyes of a fair-haired boy (*Jim?*) whose throat and chest were a ruin of meat and bone stared at her while a man's voice wailed somewhere out of sight (*Grandpa?*). A lab-coated man held out his hands in front of him as he retreated from her. She shouldered aside the door to her grandfather's portion of the house, and saw the terrified expression of a young man whose round, freckled face and curly hair marked him as Josh, while her grandfather's voice screamed something (*"Is this what you wanted? Is it?"*).

The door to Grandpa's bedroom had been left ajar by the home health aide. She shoved it open and crossed the threshold.

Despite the unbridled insanity in which she was caught up, a small part of her thought, *So this is what his room looks like.* It was larger than she would have anticipated, the far corner filled by a king-sized bed draped with a plaid comforter. Next to it, a nightstand held a lamp that could be bent to direct its light. On the other side of it, her grandfather sat dozing in a recliner. A coarsely-knitted blanket covered his legs and lap; under it, a thick, heavy robe wrapped his chest and arms. His face was as she'd imagined it: the flesh sparse on the bone, the mouth downturned at the corners, the nose blunt as a hatchet, the eyes sunken, shadowed by the brows. Lines like the beds of dried rivers crossed his skin, which had not lost the tan his years in the sun had burned into it. The stroke's damage was visible in the sag of the left half of his face, which lent it an almost comically-morose appearance. The ghost of her and Josh's mocking mimicry of him flitted through her memory. She leaned closer to him.

He opened his eyes, and she leapt back, thumping into a wall as she did. Although his eyelids raised ever-so-slightly, his voice remained level. Nodding, he said, "Wondered if it might be…you." His tongue slid over his lips. "Tried with…Jim." He shook his head. "Couldn't…leave remains. Beast needed…to eat…" He shrugged. "Lost…Joshua…"

Had he attempted the same experiment with Josh? Did it matter? Like a swell of lava rising over the lip of a volcano, anger rolled through her, carrying her deeper into the thing she was inhabiting. She crouched forward to steady herself. She could feel the claws jutting from her fingertips, the fangs filling her mouth. Anger swelled within her, incinerating everything in its path. She drew back her lips, and hissed, a long, sibilant vent of rage that summoned her grandfather's attention from whatever memory had distracted him.

He saw her teeth bared, her claws rising. Something like satisfaction crossed his face. "That's…my girl," he said.

"They have the power of calling snakes, and feel great pleasure in playing with and handling them. Their own bite becomes poisonous to people not inoculated in the same manner. Thus a part of the serpent's nature appears to be transfused into them."

—Nathaniel Hawthorne, *American Notebooks*

EPISODE THREE: ON THE GREAT PLAINS, IN THE SNOW

"Oh bury me not on the lone prairie"

—"The Cowboy's Lament"

"It's like I told you last night son. The earth is mostly just a bone-yard. But pretty in the sunlight," he added.

—Larry McMurtry, *Lonesome Dove*

I

The two ghosts—*impressions*, Lynch corrected himself, that was how Melinda insisted on referring to them—stood considering the wreck. It was some kind of van: Lynch didn't recognize the make; although its snub-nosed front put him in mind of the space shuttle (time was, he'd known cars as well as anyone). The vehicle had been bulled off the road onto the frozen ruts of the field beside it. It had been struck on the left side. You could see where the doors had buckled under the force of the blow. Funny that it hadn't rolled, or at least tipped, over. Probably had

141

something to do with the height at which the object that had collided with it had done so (time was, he would've known why that was, too, understood the underlying principle if not the exact equations demonstrating it). The roof had been peeled open; rudely, he thought, the way a child tore the foil off a piece of chocolate. Long gouges grooved the van's crumpled side, its hood. The windshield was a frozen explosion. Scattered around the van were shredded pieces of its seats, a white and red cooler apparently intact, half of a heavy blanket—a quilt, maybe—and assorted articles of clothing: sweatshirt, snow boot, baseball cap. Balanced on the hood, rocking slightly in the wind that whistled like a child trying to find a tune, was a squarish block of plastic. Lynch couldn't identify anything more than its geometry, wasn't sure—

"It's part of a car seat," Melinda said. She'd noticed him staring. "A child's car seat."

Ah, that was why he hadn't placed it sooner. His own children were…Anthony was twenty-four, wasn't he? He had been at some point. His memory was particularly bad, this moment, the worst it had been in the last three weeks. He tried to concentrate on his family, his children. Anthony the oldest, twenty-four. Katie was…what was she? Twenty-one? Maureen… Eighteen? Seventeen? Regardless, his children were all long past the age of car seats. (Though hadn't there been a grandson? Anthony's—Jordan, perhaps? He had a sudden vision of a little boy wearing a red sweatshirt and hugging a toy dinosaur.)

"Shall we take a closer look?"

"What for?" he said.

"I don't know. Isn't that what you're supposed to do?"

Wasn't it? "In TV shows," he said, "in TV shows about the police." He turned to her. "Were you a member of the police?"

"No."

"Then we might as well stay here until the real police arrive. Maybe we'll learn something, then."

"You just want to stand here?"

"The wind isn't bothering me."

"The wind—I'm going to check this out."

"Wait." But she was striding away from him towards the—what had been the van.

"It isn't as if I'll disturb anything," she called over her shoulder.

Not because he shared her desire to view the carnage up close, but because he didn't care to stand over here, across the road, by himself, with nothing but miles of empty field around him, Lynch hurried after her. It was strange to find himself squeamish, now, past the point of all hurt, but he was sick with dread at the prospect of seeing what might be left of the car seat's former occupant. He had been fond of violent movies, horror movies, war movies—had been watching one when Anthony was born, he remembered, something with Vincent Price, lurid Technicolor—but this: there was blood everywhere, splashes on the hood and roof, streams down the windshield and sides, puddles cupped by the frozen earth. It was as if someone had sprayed the scene with a firehose of the stuff. He had been the one to tend the kids when they injured themselves, or were vomiting-sick (he had a flash of a nail embedded in the spongy sole of a flip-flop, weeping blood), but who knew, who knew the human body had so much blood in it?

Not to mention, the things he tried to confine to the corners of his vision as he came up behind Melinda, a rope of what might have passed for sausage, a carmine slab of something, a scattering of pale chunks. Could he pass out? He wasn't sure, but this seemed like the test. He looked at Melinda, who had stopped beside the driver's door and was leaning forward, attempting to peer around the splotch of blood in the middle of the window. Voice thick, he said, "See anything?"

"Only what you do. How many do you think there were?"

"I don't know. What does a van like this hold? Four, five, six?" There had been five people in his family.

"You can squeeze eight people into one of these things," she said. "Two in the front, three in the middle, three in the rear." She glanced at him, at his expression, and added, "But I don't think there were eight people in here. Four, five tops."

"It's enough."

"Yeah."

The air was full of snowflakes, again, which, he'd noticed, was how it started snowing out here. No gradual increases, no few flakes leading the way down for more and more after that: this was like being inside a giant snowglobe you hadn't felt being shaken. The air was clear, and then it was thick with snow that didn't fall so much as swirl into existence. These flakes were small, almost freezing rain. Faintly, a siren wailed.

"Finally," Melinda said. "That guy in the Saab must've called them, after all."

"Let's stand back," Lynch said, "and let them do their job."

"Why? Don't you want to know what they find?"

"To be honest, I don't think they're going to find much. Not any more than we have."

"You never know."

"Can we please move away?"

"All right, all right, no need to raise your voice. We're all on the same side, here."

"Thank you."

Through the snow, the source of the siren appeared, a police car, its roof rack strobing red.

Lynch said, "That's it?"

"What were you expecting?"

"More than a single car. An ambulance, at least."

"He was probably closest. Besides, what good do you think an ambulance would do?"

"Suppose someone—"

"Someone isn't."

He had nothing to say to that.

They watched the police car roar up to the site, its brakes screeching at the last minute. It was a local unit, its driver so overwhelmed by what was visible to him from inside his car that he forgot to shift into Park before opening his door. The car stuttered forward, almost spilling him out of it. He lunged inside, threw the transmission into Neutral, and yanked up the parking brake. For a moment, he sat with his head on the steering wheel, no doubt telling himself that he could handle this. He raised his head and reached for his radio. Lynch could hear him reciting the string of codes that shorthanded the situation. He thought the cop sounded about sixteen. Once he had completed the call, the cop replaced the radio, reached for his hat, and stepped out into the snow. Lynch was surprised to see him wearing a baseball cap instead of the wide-brimmed quasi-cowboy hat he'd assumed was part of the general police uniform in this neck of the woods. The cop had his hand on his gun; although he hadn't drawn it. He called, "Hello?

Can anyone hear me?" as he advanced across the road towards the van, his face draining of color. He started to identify himself, then caught sight of something on the ground before him and threw up.

"Very nice," Melinda said.

"He's just a kid."

To his credit, the cop wiped his mouth with the back of his hand and continued forward on shaking legs. "Hello?" His voice so tremulous a strong gust of wind might have carried it away. "Is anyone…" Obviously, he couldn't decide how to finish the question. Alive? Here? In one piece? As he neared the van, he unholstered his gun.

"Oh, right," Melinda said. "As if the bad guy's waiting to jump out at him."

Gun in his right hand, right wrist grasped by his left hand, both hands out in front of him, down but not too low, the cop surveyed the van's interior, then began to circle it, stepping left foot across right. His eyes were cartoon-wide. Lynch guessed he was telling himself to focus on the details and finding that none too easy. By the time he had completed his circuit of the van and was backing away from it, new sirens were audible.

"The cavalry arrives," Melinda said.

There were three more police cars—two local and one state—and an ambulance. The trooper, a wide brim over his startled face, practically leapt out of his car shouting questions and commands. The first cop croaked answers, the remaining two returned to their cars and sped off up and down the road to block it. A pair of EMTs, a tall man with a beard and an even taller woman with a ponytail, emptied from the ambulance and started arguing with the trooper about whether they should approach what he was insisting was a crime scene, what they were calling an accident. The first cop told the trooper to let them have a look, then told the EMTs they weren't going to find anyone. They didn't. After they'd made their search, they retreated to the ambulance, on whose hood the woman placed her gloved hands and leaned over, while the man walked into the field on the other side of the road. He walked as if he had someplace to be, some destination in mind, and did not stop walking when the woman raised her head, caught sight of him, and called his name. She abandoned her spot at the front of the ambulance to run after him, reaching him in long strides and catching him in a bear hug that he did not return.

"I see what you mean," Melinda said. "Just look at the difference they made."

Without answering her, Lynch turned away and began walking north along the road, towards the town. The fear, horror, that had flared in him had burnt out, leaving ashy sadness. Right now, he wanted nothing more than to put as much distance between himself and the blood and ruin that had been a family on their way somewhere. Was it Christmas? Were they driving to a grandparent's house to exchange presents? He hadn't noticed anything that resembled wrapping paper, boxes...while it was snowing, he didn't think it was Christmas. He thought the snow was more because of where they were, which he couldn't quite name but which he was pretty sure was somewhere in the broad middle of the country, someplace like South Dakota or Wyoming, a state where they had snow more often than they didn't.

Melinda followed him. "Hey," she said. "Where're you going? The professionals are here. Don't you want to watch them work, see what we can learn?"

He kept walking. He had a feeling he had been the one to do the teasing in his family. He recalled Anthony, frustrated to the point of tears because the zipper on his jeans was stuck open. They were cheap jeans—K-Mart special, or maybe Marshall's—but Lynch hadn't been able to resist cracking wise about his oldest's inability to zip his pants. How old had his son been? Thirteen? Fourteen? The years of maximum self-consciousness. No surprise to find it wasn't as pleasant on the other side of the barb.

"Ah, never mind," Melinda said, falling into step beside him. "We already learned what we needed to."

He couldn't help himself. "What was that?"

"You tell me. What did you notice?"

"Notice? You mean, aside from the blood, the carnage, the parts of people I don't have names for?"

"I'm sorry. It was pretty rough, wasn't it?"

"Pretty rough, yeah."

"So what did you notice?"

"What..." He stopped. "What—all of it. I saw all of it."

"Then you saw what was missing."

"Besides whoever did this?"

"They're long gone. I told you that."

"I don't know, nothing."

"Nothing's right."

Tumblers fell into place. "They were. The family…their ghosts."

"Impressions, and they weren't. They should have been there, all of them. We shouldn't have had to speculate about how many of them there were. We should've been able to count them, ourselves. Don't know that they would have been all that much fun to talk to. Anyone who's gone through something like that—well, sometimes they never come out of it. But even if every last one of them had been standing there screaming, we should have seen them."

"What does that mean?"

"It means things just got a lot more serious."

II

The bar, whose name hadn't registered, had a plain wooden floor scattered with sawdust, onto which patrons at the dozen or so tables around it dropped the broken and empty shells of the peanuts they scooped from the bowls in front of them. Lynch was fascinated by this, didn't think he'd seen anything like it before. A jukebox whose contours were drawn in yellow and red neon finished singing in the big voice of a man who kept insisting that ladies love country boys and switched to the softer, slower sound of a woman wrapping her rich voice around her funny Valentine. Lynch sat up straighter.

"What is it?" Melinda asked.

"I know this."

"What?" She nodded at the jukebox. "Ella?"

"Yes," he said, "Ella. Ella Fitzgerald."

"Funny, I didn't tag you as a jazz fan."

"Yes."

"Not that I figured a jukebox in here would have Ella Fitzgerald on its play list."

Lynch supposed she meant the men with their cowboy hats and boots, the women in their flannel shirts and jeans, but the contrast that impressed

Melinda skated over him. His wife had given him an Ella Fitzgerald CD for Valentine's Day, a compilation. He could see the picture of Ella on its front, a sepia photograph that showed her from the waist up, wearing an off-the-shoulder gown, her generous mouth open to utter the lyrics of some song or another, the members of a big band out of focus on the risers behind her. Had he freed it from its plastic wrapping? He couldn't recall, didn't think so. He was going to wait until he was home from the hospital, wasn't he?

Melinda remained silent for the rest of the song, while Lynch drank in Ella's almost-girlish voice, the saxophone tracing her words, the steady whisper of the brushes across the drums. How long ago…he had been standing in a friend's basement den; the friend's name was a blank but his almost comically-broad face, broad forehead, curly hair, square jaw, and square glasses were vivid in his memory. The two of them—three, Anthony had been there, too—the three of them had stood in the dim den in the late afternoon light while Lynch's friend, who seemed like an old friend, someone he'd known for decades, eased a record from its sleeve, positioned it on his turntable, and lowered the needle into place. The hiss of the needle tracing the vinyl had given way to a brash, bright trumpet, which had yielded to a man's voice, deep as a well, rough as gravel, which had been succeeded by Ella's (*I got plenty a nuttin*)—Armstrong, Louis Armstrong, Louis and Ella. Anthony had surprised him by turning to show a huge grin. "This is great," he had said, and Lynch had felt suddenly, unexpectedly close to his son.

With a shimmer of cymbals and a flourish of notes from the saxophone, the song on the jukebox ended and was replaced by the vibrating twang of a guitar set to Country complaint. Lynch looked at Melinda, who was surveying the rest of the bar, and said, "Thank you."

"It's important to do stuff like that when you can. It helps you stay… coherent longer."

"Maybe I should wait for it to come on again."

"Some do," Melinda said. "Not that they hang around jukeboxes for that special song, but they attach to places that, you know, had meaning for them."

"But you didn't."

"No, I didn't. For that matter, neither did you."

"No."

"You sound less than happy. Is that what you would've wanted, hovering over their shoulders, watching them grieve?"

"I…"

"Worse, watching them stop grieving, get on with their lives."

"It would have been something."

"It would have been nothing. You would have drifted off to the basement, attic, some corner of the house or another, and sat there moping. Every now and again, when everyone was asleep, you'd have gone for a walk, wandered from room to room feeling miserable, spooking the cat."

"We didn't have an attic. Just a crawl space."

"Oh. How about a cat?"

"Yes. A white cat, with a black mark on her forehead. The kids named her—"

"Spot?"

"Ashley. For Ash Wednesday, you know."

"Not really. Anyway, the point is, it wouldn't have been long until you'd faded to next to nothing, just a tissue of a couple of unconnected memories. A year, two at the outside. And not long after that, you wouldn't have been anything more than a cold spot, a disturbance in the atmosphere. Your wife, kids, would've walked through the space that was you and shivered, rubbed the goosebumps on their arms and wondered if they'd left a window open. You can't honestly tell me you would've wanted any of that."

"I would have been with them."

"No, you wouldn't. You think you would have, but trust me, that kind of situation—the inertia—it sticks to you. I've seen it, seen guys who had the same idea as you reduced to a single word they keep whispering as they melt into the wall. Not pretty. Believe me—this is better, way better."

"This?" Lynch raised a hand to the room. "This place? I can't even remember its name."

"It's not much on the ambiance, I'll give you that. But they do have Ella on the jukebox."

Despite himself, Lynch smiled. "Yeah."

"Hey—remember when you got here and you thought it was heaven? I guess it kind of made sense, what with all the white around, but still."

"Well, I revised my assessment the minute I met you."

"What are you talking about?" She sounded almost aggrieved. "You count yourself damned lucky if I'm the angel waiting at the end of your tunnel of light. Just see how well you do on your own. Five minutes, and you'd be roaming the streets, scaring people half to death with your moaning."

"'Half to death:' very funny."

"Whatever."

The jukebox exchanged one Country song for another that Lynch knew, Kenny Rogers rasping "The Gambler." After a moment, he said, "So what about this van?"

"What about it?"

"What happened to it?"

"That's what we're trying to figure out."

"That's what I'm trying to figure out. I'm the new one, remember? I think you know exactly who did this."

"You're wrong."

"Then you have a very good idea."

"No, nothing that would count as very good."

"Stop playing word games."

"I'm not. The most I've got is a couple of facts I don't like very much."

"There was no one, no *impression*, at the accident scene. We already said that."

"Yeah," Melinda said, "but what it means…the thing that did this—you figure it has to be some kind of animal, right?"

"I don't know about that," Lynch said.

"Have you ever seen a collision between two cars that looked like that?"

"I haven't seen many—any accidents at all, if that's your reference point. Bad as it was, though, if another car had been involved, I can't imagine it would have been in any kind of shape to drive away."

"Yes, exactly."

Lynch held up his hand. "But there's no animal that could have done that to a van. Maybe a bunch of tigers, or polar bears, only those things don't hunt in groups, do they? Not to mention, they're pretty scarce in these parts. No, I think what happened to that family was the fault of people, some kind of gang, or a cult, maybe."

"How do you explain the damage to the van? You saw the shape that thing was in, like a bag of potato chips that'd been torn open. Not to mention the family—their physical remains. I saw you trying not to look too closely, but you know what I'm talking about. There's a gang of super-strong cannibals on the loose, waylaying hapless motorists?"

"It's better than rabid polar bears."

"Not by much."

"What, then?"

"Something that makes me uber-nervous. Something strong enough to push a decent-sized van that must have been going a decent speed off the road, get into it, and devour the passengers, body and soul."

"I thought we weren't souls."

"Figure of speech. Something that can consume their flesh and their impression on the quantum subjectile—their ghosts. Better?"

"What can do that? You're describing a monster."

Melinda nodded. "I am."

"And you're serious."

"It's what fits the facts."

"A monster?"

"For all intents and purposes, yes."

"And this is better than the super-strong cannibals how?"

"Would it help if I called it a self-precipitating and -perpetuating anomaly that's accumulated sufficient energy to allow it to pierce the ontological membrane?"

"Monster it is, then."

"Don't look so offended. You can't tell me you never saw this kind of thing on the way here. It hasn't been that long since I made the Walk; I know what it's like. There's that long, blank time when you don't know anything. Then you realize you're moving, shuffling along a road, which looks an awful lot like one of the main roads you live near, except that it's colorless, not white or gray so much as *faint*, a pencil drawing done on cheap paper. Whatever lies to either side of you is too vague for you to make out, but you don't worry about that very much, if at all. You're surrounded by people all around you, some heading in your direction, the rest bound for God-knows-where. Just about everyone's dressed in one version or another of normal clothing; although maybe you see an old woman over there who's in her nightgown and slippers, a guy over here who's too old and fat for the baseball uniform he's squeezed into. To your right, there's a kid—you thought he was a kid, sixteen or seventeen, but when you turn your head again, you see he's fifty if he's a day. That's a little strange, but it isn't as bad as the woman ahead who keeps *flickering*. While you watch her, she goes from being stick-legged twelve to broad-hipped thirty, like a jump-cut in a movie. You look down, and maybe the hand you hold up looks a little rough at the edges. A few folks try to walk together—could be you're one of them—but it doesn't last long. For one thing, you can't hear each other too well. It's as if your ears are clogged. Even your own voice sounds as if it's coming more from inside your head than your mouth. For another thing, you can't stay focused on what anyone else is saying long enough for a meaningful exchange. Your mind keeps returning to this question, to the Question: What happened to me?

"But it's a question that isn't really a question. It's a placeholder for an image. You, stomping the brake and steering hard to the right as the truck backs out of the alley directly ahead of you. Or you, lying in a hospital bed wired to a host of machines, a ridge of bandages rising over the fresh scar up the center of your chest. Or you, stepping backwards as the kid holding the gun sweeps it in your direction, this lavish gesture that he probably picked up in a movie he watched in re-run on channel 9. You see his index finger tightening on the trigger, and then—

"That's just it, though: there isn't any *then*. There's that moment, then this moment, this place that looks vaguely familiar, but it's like looking through a lens smeared with Vaseline. The only thing that seems one hundred percent, undeniably real is the compulsion that's drawing you forward, step-by-step, east west north south. You don't have a way to describe it. It's like nothing you've felt before, as if you're an iron filing and the biggest magnet in creation is saying, *Come to me*. What can you do? So you walk.

"And on the way to wherever it is you're bound, there are these people. A man wearing a black suit fifty years out of date, the collar of his shirt open, the ends of an actual bow tie flapping out from under the collar in the wind that blows up as the guy approaches you. From his thin hair, the lines of his face, you take him for an old man, until he draws near enough for you to tell that he isn't, he's maybe the same age as you, he just has one of those old faces, and probably has since he was in his twenties. It's the kind of face he would've spent all his life trying to catch up to. There's about two days' worth of blond stubble on his chin, his long cheeks, which is odd—not that you've made a survey or anything, but the other men you've noticed so far have been by and large clean-shaven. Even the couple of guys with beards you've run across have been pretty well-groomed.

"The man comes closer to you—he staggers, lurches, as if his legs don't work properly, the knees stiff, the hips locked. It's like when you're a kid and you play at being Frankenstein's monster, those same exaggerated motions. All he needs is both arms held out in front of him. They aren't, though. His arms weave and windmill to either side of him, trying to help his balance. He draws closer to you, bringing with him this smell, a thick stink like milk well on its way to becoming cheese. You would think the wind that surrounds him would clear the air, but it's as if the smell is threaded through it. Right before this guy reaches you, clamps one hand on your shoulder, leans toward you, so that you can see his eyes are the same blank color as the road—right then, you realize that this is the first thing you've smelled since—since the scorched rubber of your tires scraping over the blacktop; or the flat, antiseptic hand-sanitizer that your family has to rub over their hands when they enter your cubicle in the ICU, and that clings to their fingers as they slide chips of ice between your lips; or the thick grease the man pointing the gun at you applied to it before he left his apartment to walk to the little bodega you like to stop at for a glass bottle of Mexican Coke.

"When the man, this old-young man in the black suit that has a vest, too, speaks, his voice is a distant shriek, as if the wind around him is carrying it from a long distance. You can't understand everything he's saying, but you hear words like, 'Over here,' and, 'Please,' and, 'Salvation.' The man is gesturing for you to follow him, to leave the road for a place off to one side. The terrain in that direction does seem to be a little more distinct. There are other people there, a surprising number of them. They're standing around a huge bonfire—it's orange, the brightest color you've seen since you started walking. You can't believe how good it feels to see something that vivid. It's almost enough to send you off the road into this…pocket.

"What stops you is the figure on the opposite side of the fire from you. You have a hard time seeing it clearly, because the fire's giving off a lot of heavy, black smoke, but it looks enormous, far taller than anyone you've met, and wider, too. Its proportions are wrong, the arms too long, over-developed, the chest massive. Its head is narrow, rising almost to a point, as if it's wearing some kind of helmet, and you have the absurd thought that this is no person: it's an ape, a gorilla; although it's nothing like the animals you've stared at in zoos or watched in nature documentaries. This

153

is something that pulls itself up skyscrapers with one hand while swatting airplanes with the other. You're afraid, because how could you not be? but you're fascinated, too, by the sight of something so fantastic. There's still a chance you'll go with the man in the black suit, follow his distant scream, until, trying to peer through the smoke, you see that what the fire's burning are bodies, men and women who continue to move as the flames roar over them. You have the impression that the smoke is being inhaled by the thing on the other side of it—that maybe the smoke *is* it—but you're already moving away from the place, running along the road, in terror that whatever you've witnessed is going to abandon its spot and come after you.

"You wonder what all of this is. It's a question you'll have the chance to ask yourself several more times on your way to whatever your destination is. If you're lucky, you'll be pulled in the direction of one of the major currents, and once you enter it, you'll be whipped along at what feels like a thousand miles an hour. If you're less fortunate, there's more walking in your future; maybe a lot. Either way, in the course of your journey, you'll see a number of other pockets, some of them pretty elaborate, all of them presided over by huge figures that seem as if they were dreamed-up for a Hollywood soundstage."

As ever, Melinda told a good story. It shared enough details with Lynch's actual experience to have him nodding. "Yes," he said, "but I thought you told me the creatures in those pockets were confined to them. Also, that they were made up of the people in the fires, that the men and women in the pockets surrendered themselves to the flames to keep the creatures going."

"That's not the point," Melinda said. "The fact is, there's a whole lot of weird shit out there, so don't be too surprised that we're dealing with some more of it."

Lynch's reply was swallowed in the wave of sound that swept through the bar. It came from his right, where the wall behind the jukebox burst inwards in a spray of wood and drywall. Dust swirled across the floor, blown by the freezing air that rushed into the room. For an instant, the jukebox gave voice to a man insisting that he was so much cooler online, and then a second wave of sound surged through the room. It was a roar, though such a roar as Lynch could not remember ever having heard. Half freight-whistle and half avalanche, it shook the glasses on the tables, clattered the liquor bottles against one another. At the bar, someone screamed, and that solo noise swelled to a chorus when the author of the roar thrust its great head through the breach it had forced.

What Lynch saw reminded him of an alligator, if that alligator's head had been as long as a tall man. Jaws lined with fangs like carving knives thundered together as the head swung right and left, chasing after the women and men who scrambled out of its way. An eye the size of a saucer rolled in its socket. Lynch could see the thing, its pebbled flesh, which appeared feathered in a few places, but he could also see through it, to a bleached skull that would have been at home in a museum display. *Tyrannosaurus Rex*, he heard Anthony's voice say. *King tyrant-lizard*. He shook his head. The beast sucked in a mighty breath, and unleashed a fresh bellow. Lynch backed into the booth. A busboy who had dropped to the floor when the wall exploded slipped as he scurried to his feet, and the monster darted its head to catch him as he fell. Its teeth scissored him in half with a wet crunch that vented blood into the wind. Droplets spattered Lynch, who cried out and rinsed his arms against them.

Melinda seized his hand. "Come on," she said, "while it's occupied."

Lynch didn't argue. Still holding her hand, he bolted for the door, past the enormous head jerking towards the ceiling as it gulped the busboy down.

Outside, the early evening was full of snow and screaming and the distant whine of sirens. Melinda steered them to the extended porch of the second building up the street from the bar. Lynch flattened against the space between a pair of windows. Melinda remained at the edge of the porch.

"Come back!" Lynch hissed. "It'll see you."

"Hear that?" Melinda said. Through the screams and the approaching sirens, Lynch heard the crack of timbers snapping, the rattle of debris on the ground. "That's it leaving."

"Leaving? Where's it going?"

"Back out there," Melinda said, nodding towards the plains. "It's moving fast. I figured we'd have at least a few days before it tried the town. Then again, who knows how long it's been on the loose, already?"

"Okay," Lynch said. "Okay." If he acted as if he were calm, maybe he would be calm. "What now?"

Melinda had no answer.

155

III

On what Lynch thought was the north side of town, a solitary black mailbox stood on the street side of a large, vacant lot. Lynch was reasonably sure there had been a house and barn here at some point; on a couple of his and Melinda's previous stops at the mailbox, he'd had the impression of a pair of large, boxlike structures, one closer to the road, the other further back, neither quite visible, both more like the smudges left after an eraser has cleared the blackboard. Each time, he had intended to ask Melinda about the phenomenon, but the message she'd read on the letter she withdrew from the mailbox had pre-empted his question. This morning, nothing was visible in the lot except a few tufts of scrub grass poking through the crusted snow. Lynch supposed this was for the best. He hadn't appreciated how exposed this location was: only one more street of small warehouses separated the mailbox from the expanse of the plains, dazzling white under the early sun. He didn't need any distractions from the vigil he was doing his best to maintain. Had he been a soldier, once? He thought so; though it was more of the obligatory-duty variety, not the active-wartime type. Hard to imagine that combat experiences, however intense, would have prepared him for the beast that had thrown the jukebox crashing over.

After a restless night spent within the bland confines of a modest Protestant church, Melinda had set out for the mailbox. Lynch had started to protest the recklessness of her decision, but she had cut him off, asking, "What makes you think we're any safer inside? That thing didn't seem to have any trouble breaking down the wall to that bar." All the same, Lynch wanted to say, there was a difference between the beast coming looking for you and you putting yourself out where it could find you. But already, Melinda was out of earshot.

Lynch didn't understand the black mailbox. Aside from the two of them, he doubted anyone could see or touch it, but with its chipped black paint and flag broken at the base, it had a strangely substantial feel, as if whoever had leveled the house and barn it served had intended to remove it, as well, but failed to complete the job. Once a day, he accompanied Melinda to it so that she could lower its front door and check its oblong interior. There was almost always something inside, usually a letter in a denim-blue envelope whose flap Melinda split with her thumb. She would read the letter twice, return it to its envelope, and replace the envelope within the mailbox, which she shut. As yet, she had not shared any of the messages with Lynch.

Instead, presumably following directions she'd received, Melinda led them to a different part of the town or its surroundings. There, they performed a task whose significance was generally lost on Lynch. A day or two after he arrived here, they ventured to the dirt alley separating a pair of houses, where Melinda handed him a shovel he hadn't noticed her carrying and directed him to dig at a spot a foot and half away from one of the houses. Lynch, who would never be sure of the exact relationship between his present form and the world he continued to inhabit, took the shovel and sank it into the ground. About two feet down, the blade rang on metal. Working more slowly, Lynch cleared the dirt from a bronze disk the diameter of a dinner plate. Its surface was incised with tiny symbols that Lynch didn't recognize. He pried the disk loose and raised it on the shovel to Melinda, who took it with heavy gloves he hadn't seen her tug on. After he refilled the hole, and leaned the shovel against the house where she told him to, Lynch returned with Melinda to the mailbox. He guessed its opening would be too small to fit the bronze plate, but Melinda angled the disk and the mailbox accepted it without difficulty.

On another occasion, they passed unhindered and unchallenged into the recesses of the town jail. On the wall of one of its cells was an elaborate graffiti that Melinda copied onto a slip of paper whose destination was the mailbox. A third time, they made their way into the large rest home on the west side of town in order for Melinda to stare at an old woman whose face had so many lines, it was difficult to pick out her eyes and mouth closed among them. Of course, Lynch had asked what the purpose of their actions was, but Melinda had deflected his questions with one of her own: "You had plans?" If he persisted, she told him that what he was asking was above his pay grade, and refused to be drawn any further. Her answer was the same when he asked who, exactly, was sending the messages.

Today, the mailbox yielded a padded envelope whose contents jingled as Melinda tore it open. She removed a letter and a pair of keys from it. Lynch watched her face as she read and re-read the letter, but could discern nothing from her features. She replaced the letter in the mailbox, and held onto the keys. "This way," she said to Lynch, and started in the direction of the next street and its warehouses and, beyond, the open plains. Lynch had no desire to walk any distance out of town; in retrospect, their trip to survey the remains of the van the previous day seemed to him the height of recklessness. Neither did he want to abandon Melinda; in the time that he'd been here, she had been essential to him adjusting to…everything, to all of it. He wasn't sure she was an irresistible force, but he was no immovable object. Following arguments with his wife, hadn't he apologized first? After confrontations with the kids over infractions of the house rules, hadn't he sought them out in their rooms, mock-bullying them into reconciliation? Nonetheless, the white expanse sparkling in the distance made his throat constrict with dread.

Melinda led them into the shadowed space between a pair of darkened warehouses. Some kind of car sat in the middle of the passageway. Eyes dazzled by the sun, Lynch did not register the vehicle as anything more than smallish, low to the ground. Melinda stopped beside the driver's door. Bending at the waist, she slotted one of the keys she'd received from the mailbox into the lock. She swung the door wide and surveyed the car's interior. "You drive?" she said.

"Yes."

"Stick?"

"Uh-huh."

"Okay, then." Straightening, she snapped her wrist. The keys arced through the air. Lynch lunged at, caught them. He said, "Hang on. We have cars?"

"Car," Melinda said. She was circling to the passenger's door. "Chop chop."

A two-seater, the car's age was apparent in the rips in its bucket seats, the roughing of the steering wheel and dashboard. Surprisingly for this location, it was a convertible. Lynch leaned over to unlock Melinda's door, then slid the key into the ignition and turned it. The engine came to life with a coughing growl. Something about the deep rumble felt achingly familiar. Lynch put in the clutch, pushed the gearshift into first, and let the clutch out slowly. The car eased along the passageway into daylight. As it did, Lynch saw that its hood was white, its fenders a burnt-orange that might have faded from red. He jerked his foot off the clutch. The car lurched and stalled.

"Is there a problem?" Melinda said.

"This car," Lynch said. "I know this car."

"Okay."

"No, you don't…it's an MG—I can't remember the model, has a V8 engine. It was my, my fantasy car, you know? For when I won the lottery. One summer—we were on vacation—we used to vacation at a little lake somewhere north—the Adirondacks, I think. We rented a cottage just up from the beach. The couple who owned the place had a son who was the same age as my boy. Their youngest. Most days, the boys hung around together, building sandcastles, catching bullfrogs, going on hikes around the lake. The mother and father were nice enough. I can't recall their names. I talked cars with him a couple of times each trip. Nothing too involved, but he knew I liked the MG. One afternoon, he came down to the cottage and asked my wife if he could borrow me for a little while. She said, Sure, take him.

"I couldn't figure out what he wanted me for. He was big into his beer, too—thought of himself as a connoisseur. I wasn't, not really, but I'd traveled for work, places like Germany and Belgium, where I'd tasted some decent beer, so this man liked to share whatever beers he'd discovered with me. It wasn't beer, though: it was this." Lynch spread his hands to take in the car. "Somehow, he had found an MG for sale at a price he was willing to afford. He knew I'd appreciate the purchase. The car looked a little worse for wear, but the engine ran fine. We popped the hood to check it. Anthony, my boy, was around, playing with the man's son. Both boys came over to admire the car. The man turned to me, and asked if I wanted to take the car for a run. At first, I thought he was saying that he was going to try out the car and was inviting me to come along—which would have been fine. But no. He handed me the keys and told me the car could use a good run.

"It was so unexpected, so…generous. I felt the way you do when something good just happens to you, out of the blue. I asked Anthony if he wanted to go for a ride. He did. We belted in, and off we went. The top was down, which made it hard for us to have much of a conversation. But I could see the expression on his face. He wasn't that old, maybe eight or nine. He was putting on his best serious face. I'd never included him in anything like this, before, and he was trying to show he understood it—its importance. The sheer pleasure lit up my face. I loved to drive. I didn't get my license until I was in my twenties, but the minute I did, it was as if the driver's seat was where I was born to be. My son had a toy: I can't remember what it was called, but it was a kind of a space-age centaur, except, instead of horse's legs, it had four tires. My wife said that was me.

"Anyway, I took the car to a highway and went all the way up to fifth. Probably too fast. Definitely too fast. If there had been a cop there, he wouldn't have had to use his radar gun. There weren't any cops. I don't think there was anyone on our side of the road. To the left, there was a mountain, leaning back to a round peak. On either side of us, the scenery whipped by, but in the distance, that mountain turned very slowly.

"I could have kept going, would have driven all the way to Canada and back. I wonder if Anthony remembers it." Lynch shook his head. "What is this car doing here?"

"Waiting for you to drive it," Melinda said.

"You know what I mean."

"I can't tell you."

"More information that's above my pay grade?"

"Probably, but that isn't why. I don't know why this particular car was waiting for us. I do know that we don't usually use cars because of the risk of drawing undue attention to ourselves. We exist beyond the limit of most people's perceptions. Give us a car to roar around in, and we move that much closer to visibility, which causes all kinds of complications. That we're sitting in this vehicle tells me how serious the situation with this creature has become."

"All right," Lynch said.

"I heard a theory, once," Melinda said, "that your impression on the subjectile can form a kind of bond with other impressions. Doesn't work for people, otherwise, you'd be surrounded by your loved ones, right? But maybe it applies to objects."

"Huh," Lynch said. "It's a pity I never owned a bazooka. You?"

"Closest I came was a shotgun, which, I think you'd agree, is not up to the task."

"No," Lynch said. "Where are we going?"

"The battleground. Think you can find it?"

"We'll see." He let out the clutch, and steered onto the street.

IV

What Melinda called the battleground was a shallow bowl in the landscape maybe five hundred yards across. It was five miles north-northeast from town, along a narrow road that followed the twists of a wide creek. Melinda had taken Lynch to the place the third day after his arrival, as a lesson in blending in with the living. A small tour bus ferried interested tourists out to the site, waited a couple of hours for them to wander its grounds, read the plaques positioned around it, and visit the gift shop, then carried them back to town. The bus was never full, Melinda said, which allowed the two of them to steal aboard and take one of the seats at the rear, where they found it relatively easy to escape detection, except for a toddler, a girl in blue overalls, who would not stop staring at them.

Not to worry, Melinda said, kids—little kids—saw all kinds of things adults didn't.

When he and Melinda had exited the bus, Lynch had been struck by the noise, a cacophony of screams, shouts, cracks, and booms, which none of the other passengers appeared to notice.

It filled the air this bright morning, as he and Melinda stepped out of the MG. Per her instructions, he had driven the car to the far end of the parking lot—empty at this early hour—then up the access road that led the short distance to the bluff that overlooked the large dip in the earth. Lynch parked there; though he observed that a dirt version of the road continued down into and across the snowy expanse.

"Well," Melinda said, "what do you think?"

Lynch couldn't remember what the name of the battle was. It was part of the larger struggle between the United States Army and the natives of the northern plains that had flared in the decade following the Civil War. Some thirty or forty cavalry had ridden straight into a significantly larger contingent of Lakota and Cheyenne. The physical engagement between the forces was over in less than an hour, and resulted in the devastation of the Army forces. Its place in the history books had been overshadowed by the events at the Little Big Horn, a short while after. Here, however, in this intermediate existence, the battle had not ended. Lakota warriors, their bodies dyed yellow and red, their feathered headdresses streaming behind them, rode their horses between cavalry officers who struggled to draw a bead on them with their long pistols. A handful of soldiers fired their rifles from behind the barricade they had improvised of their dead horses. A trio of Cheyenne warriors shot the soldiers who were attempting to position a pair of small cannons near the top of the slope opposite. Men shouted commands and obscenities. Clouds of gray smoke floated across the ground, over puddles and pools of blood. Holes burst open in men's heads, their chests, where bullets struck them. Arms, feet, hung dangling from where they'd been shot. Unhorsed Native warriors swung heavy clubs at the soldiers who swung the butts of their rifles at them. Men screamed in exultation and agony. Rifles snapped. The cannons thudded. In ones, twos, more, men died—then continued the battle, rising unwounded to attack one another anew. Above the scene, the smoke gathered in a great knot whose contours suggested a fist.

The first time Lynch had seen this place, had watched the tourists wandering its grounds, blissfully ignorant of the horror continuously unfolding around them, he had demanded an explanation from Melinda. For once, she had answered him directly. Some events, she had said, were sufficiently traumatic that their participants remained caught in them, long after they occurred. War, violence, tended to produce that result. Did that mean these men were trapped here, like this, forever? he'd asked. Melinda had shrugged. They'd been here this long.

The cannons boomed, dirt geysered, and Lynch understood what Melinda was proposing. Here was an army for them to employ. "Would that work?" he said.

"If we could lure it here, maybe."

"But," he gestured at the combatants. "It hasn't stopped any of them."

"That's because they're caught in this event. Bring someone, or something else into it, and the situation becomes a lot more dangerous."

"What about all of them?" He nodded to the men.

"I suppose it'll rip most of them to shreds; though the horses might help. I'm not sure how fast the thing can run."

"What'll happen to them?"

"They'll cease to exist," Melinda said. Before Lynch could voice the objection forming on his lips, she added, "Which is harsh, yes. But is it any moreso than what they're trapped in, now? Who was it said that hell is repetition? What do you think this is for these guys?"

"And who says you get to make that decision?"

"If you have a better idea, I'm all ears."

A half-dozen proposals flitted through his mind, each relying on a crucial detail whose impossibility rendered the rest of the plan useless: he and Melinda revealing themselves to the town's authorities; those men and women understanding and accepting what actually was happening; detonating the fuel tanks of one of the gas stations in the center of town; procuring an M1A1 Abrams tank. He shook his head. He'd already figured out who was going to be leading the beast here, too.

V

As he turned out of the parking lot, Lynch said, "I'm pretty sure I know what this creature is."

"A Tyrannosaurus, right?"

He nodded. "T. Rex."

"It looked different in the movies. Less of those little feathers. What makes you so sure?"

"Science projects. For school: my kids."

"Huh," Melinda said. "Okay."

Science projects: the words were keys, unlocking the padlocks on a cache of memory. He had helped all of his children with their annual entries for the school science fair, which he recalled describing (to whom?) as the bane of his existence, elaborate posters and models whose design and construction were inevitably delayed until the night before the event. (One of the girls—Katie?—had been somewhat more responsible, beginning her projects a weekend or two early.) Anthony, in particular, had little interest in science proper. Hadn't Lynch encouraged him to build a basic pulley, and hadn't he rejected the idea through his apathy towards it? The topics in which his oldest was interested: The Loch Ness Monster, UFO's, Bigfoot, had skirted the edge of legitimate science, to put it mildly, and while Lynch had built models for him in his basement workshop out of Plaster-of-Paris, he'd done so with a dull annoyance souring the process.

A patch of ice on the road ahead burned phosphorous-bright with sunlight. Lynch squinted and eased off the gas.

163

The exception had been Anthony's third grade project, when he had selected dinosaurs as his topic. Lynch had known his son was interested in the great beasts; the enthusiasm appeared general amongst the boys his age. Certainly, Lynch had purchased enough plastic and rubber replicas of the creatures for Anthony to have a plentiful supply with which to populate the diorama they fashioned on Lynch's workbench. What he hadn't counted on was Anthony's passion for actual dinosaurs, which had resulted in his son attaining what seemed to Lynch an encyclopedic level of knowledge of the vanished animals, from their Latin designations to their habits to the precise eras during which the various species had roamed the planet. A pair of figurines he'd assumed showed the same bipedal carnivore did not: the one with the slightly more-developed forelegs was Allosaurus, who had lived tens of millions of years before the larger-headed Tyrannosaurus Rex. Lynch had held Tyrannosaurus up for inspection as Anthony described its six-foot skull, its long jaw lined with six-inch fangs. Believe it or not, Anthony had said, paleontologists weren't sure if T. Rex hunted its prey, or if it was a gigantic scavenger, like a vulture or hyena.

The monster whose teeth had bit a man in two was Anthony's Tyrannosaurus, and from the way it had snapped at the men and women fleeing from it, it had no trouble chasing its meals down. "How is this even possible?" Lynch said.

"You do realize the irony of your question," Melinda said.

"By that logic, this place should be overrun by thousands more creatures like that one. Not to mention, all the animals that have lived here since then."

The road veered towards the creek, whose surface consisted of thousands of shards of light. Lynch accelerated through the curve.

"Touché," Melinda said. "From what I understand, the subjectile consists of layers. It's like the bottom of the sea: things drift down and settle there and, over time, you wind up with this stratified structure. What belongs to a particular era tends to remain at that approximate level, so to speak. There's some movement possible between levels if they're relatively close, but beyond a certain, limited range, you're pretty much stuck where you are."

"So eventually we'll become what? fossilized ghosts?"

Melinda looked away. "Not exactly. It's more a case of, we'll be sealed off within our layer."

"That doesn't sound much better."

"Don't worry about that. What matters is, this is why you haven't been chased by hordes of hungry velociraptors, or stalked by a saber-toothed tiger."

"However," Lynch said, "I have seen more than I would have liked of a Tyrannosaurus." The things you'd never think you'd say.

"True," Melinda said. "There are fissures in the subjectile, cracks that extend deep—very deep, in a couple of cases—into it. They're dangerous—unstable—but if you could navigate one, you might be able to cross a tremendous part of the structure."

"That would have to be a pretty significant break, for a dinosaur to come up it."

"There are a couple that go back a ways, and a new one could have formed. It's also possible the T. Rex found its way along a series of smaller cracks, like a rat solving a maze."

"What happens if we don't stop it?"

"It continues to chow down on the living, gaining strength as it does."

"But eventually, the Army—the modern Army—will come in and blast it."

"Eventually," Melinda said. "In the meantime, people continue to die horribly, deprived of any chance of a continuing existence. Even after the Army shows up, depending on when exactly this is, they may find it harder to deal with the thing than they'd expect. By then, the T. Rex will have ingested a lot of energy from its victims, which will tend to make it more resilient."

"You make it sound like some kind of vampire."

"That isn't too far off."

"That..." In front of him, the road wavered, as if a sheet of water had slid over the windshield. Instinctively, he downshifted, tapping the brake as he did. The engine whined at being forced into lower gear. "A..."

As clearly as if he was standing beside them, he saw Anthony and his son, Jordan. They were in a narrow room, its walls peach, its floor carpeted (cream), one end occupied by a small bed whose blue frame was the shape of a sports car—Jordan's bed—they were in Jordan's bedroom, in the house Anthony and his wife were renting in that village with the French name (Arles? St. Marie? Lyon?). Anthony was lying on the floor, on his left side, his head supported with his left hand. Jordan was sitting across from him, all of his five-year-old's attention focused on the assortment of toys spread out between them. Lynch saw rows of plastic cowboys and Indians, all cast in the same bright red and yellow. Opposite the figures, a handful of Matchbox cars and trucks lay overturned. Jordan's small hands gripped a plastic Tyrannosaur that was almost too big for him. It was painted red, with almost fluorescent purple stripes wrapping its back. Between its shoulders, a rectangular button protruded which, when Jordan pressed it in, opened the toy's mouth and caused it to emit an electronic roar. Anthony held a Matchbox car between the thumb and index finger of his right hand that he drove in circles over the carpet, making revving-engine and squealing-tire sounds as he did. "I'm gonna get you!" Jordan shouted, shaking his dinosaur.

"No way, man," Anthony said, grinning. "This is an MG, the fastest car ever made."

"I have T. Rex!" Jordan said. "Rawr! Rawr!"

"MG's faster than T. Rex," Anthony said.

"Oh no he isn't," Jordan said.

"Oh yes he is," Anthony said.

"Well—he's a vampire!" Jordan shouted.

"A vampire?" Anthony said. "Uh oh..."

"LYNCH!" Something slapped his right cheek, hard. "We're in the middle of the freaking road!"

"What?" He turned, and, for a moment, did not know the woman sitting next to him. Face stinging, he closed his eyes, certain that, when he opened them, he would be someplace else: a hospital bed, most likely, wired to a dozen different devices charting his steady decline, surrounded by his wife and children, their faces forecasting the grief due to arrive. But the sight that greeted him was the same as the one he'd left, the woman he knew was Melinda facing him across the interior of the MG whose engine was rumbling away, while the air outside filled with snow. The expression on Melinda's features blended concern with irritation. "Whatever's happening to you," she said, "can it wait long enough for you to move us out of the path of any oncoming traffic?"

Already, this existence had settled upon him like a cat that rises from your lap, only to position itself there more comfortably. "It's—I'm fine," he said, and put in the clutch.

VI

Here the road ran straight through the plains. Had the remainder of the drive to the town been longer, Lynch supposed Melinda might have spent more of it quizzing him about what had happened. As it was, he answered the single question she put to him by saying he'd just remembered something—a memory he didn't care to discuss, he added—and that seemed to be enough for her. It was far from sufficient for him, in no small part because it wasn't true. Enough of his life, his previous life, his living life, remained opaque for him to not be sure, but he didn't think he'd witnessed the scene of Anthony playing with Jordan. It didn't have the familiar, the comfortable feel of his actual memories. At the same time, some quality of the exchange he'd observed struck him as authentic. Which meant what, exactly? That his son and grandson were aware of the posthumous drama in which he found himself an actor? Or that Lynch was in some way playing out the situation they were enacting? It could be a coincidence, but if so, it was such a one as to push the idea past the point of breaking.

Ahead, on the right hand side of the road, sat the single trailer that marked the furthermost limit of the town in this direction. Although the snow had picked up, the great rent in its middle was clearly visible. A ribbon of black smoke wound up from the trailer's interior to the clouds assembling overhead. Lynch slowed, glancing at Melinda.

"There's no point," she said. "We know what we'll find."

"All right," he said, "where to, then?"

"The Highway. Maybe someone will have seen something."

What Melinda called the Highway ran due north out of town. The name was as much metaphor as description. A path wide enough for a half-dozen people to walk abreast, the Highway rode the contours of the land out to a junction that was lost in the distance. An irregular but unceasing flow of people left the town walking the route, most of them finding their way to it from the rest home on the west side. Their ultimate destinations were unknown to Lynch and, so she claimed, to Melinda. It was the Highway that had brought him to this place that, yes, he had mistaken for Heaven, because where else could the journey he'd taken have led? In the days since, he had avoided the path, half-afraid that, were he to stray too close to it, he would be caught by it and find himself embarked on a fresh odyssey.

Given what Lynch recalled of his early moments on the road that had led him away from the place of his decease, he was skeptical of Melinda's plan. On the other hand, he hadn't encountered any dinosaurs on that route, so maybe it was worth a try, after all. He turned right at the first intersection. To his left, a dozen streets deeper into the town, the firehouse's siren sent up its mournful call. The falling snow seemed to dampen it.

"The trailer," he said.

"You hope," Melinda said.

A left onto a side street, a right onto a road that ran between rows of weatherbeaten houses, another left onto a long driveway that dead-ended in a small parking lot, brought them there. The Highway commenced at the other side of the parking lot, a flat path whose dull white surface appeared to consist of some kind of rock. Lynch did not see anyone in the parking lot, nor on the road. He pulled the parking brake, went to turn the key. Melinda said, "Wait."

He did. "What?"

"Take us out there," she said.

"Is that allowed?"

"Is there anyone stopping us?"

"That's not the same thing," he said, but he released the brake and rolled the car onto the Highway. The snow was streaming down, large white flakes whose individual designs he could almost pick out. Although they eddied around the car, none of them landed on the windshield, the hood, or stuck to the windows. On either side, the plains were veiled by white.

Lynch felt the dash for the controls to the radio. "What are you doing?" Melinda said.

"Trying to find the radio."

"You want to listen to music, now?"

"It calms—"

"Hang on," Melinda said, "what's that?"

"What?"

"That." She pointed at a spot on the road maybe ten feet ahead on the right. Lynch slowed the car to a crawl as he followed the direction Melinda indicated. For a moment, he could pick out nothing except snow falling behind snow, then the shape Melinda had noticed came into focus. The size of a small bird, it appeared to be floating a couple of feet off the ground with a lazy motion that reminded Lynch of a balloon. Which was ridiculous. He brought the car to a stop and flipped on the headlights. The snow caught most of the light and flung it back, but the shape did not. By the glow of the headlights, Lynch saw that it was a human hand, an adult's, most likely, severed at the wrist. Palm up, fingers outstretched, it rotated in a slow circle.

Nor was it alone. Suspended at different heights along the road in front of them, a variety of body parts formed a grisly constellation: a pair of hands, one clenched, one open; a foot, toes pointed down as if for ballet; an arm and part of a shoulder, ribbons of blood trailing from its ragged edge; and a head in the approximate center of everything, the open eyes reflecting the headlights, the mouth slack, the heavy white hair swaying around it.

"God…" Stunned, Lynch did not register the massive shape looming behind the carnage. When the Tyrannosaur lunged forward, sending body parts spinning off like marbles, its vast jaws open, he hesitated, shocked, before dropping the car into reverse. The MG jolted to the right as the beast's jaws smashed the windshield and tore the roof. Lynch cried out and threw his arms in front of his face. With a shriek of torn metal, the T. Rex pulled its head up, taking the roof and half of the windshield with it. Snow rushed into the car. Lynch simultaneously let out the clutch and floored the gas. The car lurched backwards, heading for the edge of the road. He caught the steering wheel, cut it to the right, and once the car was in the center of the Highway, straightened out. He half-turned in his seat, to see the direction he was reversing. As he did, he saw Melinda's seat empty, the top half of it bitten away.

VII

Lynch crested the bluff overlooking the battlefield, downshifted into second, and plunged down the dirt road that led into the thick of the continuing battle. The road was smoother than he had anticipated; though not enough for him to shift to third. At least the snow seemed to be abating. Hooves thudding on the ground, a brown horse carrying a painted Sioux warrior galloped in front of him. A trio of soldiers fired their rifles after the man, and Lynch heard the bullets zip overhead. The stink of gunpowder clotted the air. A Cheyenne warrior aimed his rifle at the three soldiers, and his shot struck the MG's trunk with a hollow ping. On the left, a pair of cavalry officers, their pistols held out in front of them, raced past.

He had been hoping to cover half the battleground before the Tyrannosaur arrived. He was maybe a third of the way when its roar split the air. A glance over his shoulder showed the creature already rushing down the road after him, its great head swaying from side to side as its powerful hind legs propelled it forward, its tapered tail out behind it as ballast. Big. It was so big. He had never appreciated how stupendously big these animals had been. He heard young Anthony's voice saying that a full-grown T. Rex would have been longer than a city bus, but that had been an abstraction, an illustration on a page, two-dimensional. In no way had it prepared him for the beast in 3-D, its bulk, black and yellow, the back ornamented with what appeared to be feathers, its mouth jammed full of razored fangs, its sheer, relentless vitality. He had assumed he would have to drive slowly enough for the Tyrannosaurus to keep up with and keep its interest in him. He had been wrong. From the start, the creature had moved with a speed and stamina that had required what skill he possessed as a driver to outrun, even as he steered the road winding out here. Now, hampered by this dirt road he was struggling not to skid along, he was losing the slender lead he'd maintained on the animal.

A bullet chipped a piece off what was left of the windshield. Lynch flinched. A Cheyenne warrior leapt his horse across the car. The Tyrannosaur's roar drowned out the rifles cracking around him. He looked back, saw its jaws almost at the trunk. He stomped the gas, heard the bite crash where he'd been. He shifted to third, fighting to hold the car to the road as it bumped and bounced over it. Bullets rang on the passenger door. With a thunder of hooves, half a dozen cavalry flanked the car, keeping pace with it. Lynch saw the men looking at him, seeing him, attempting to fit him to the scene in which they'd acted for so long. In a few of their expressions, a terrible knowledge hovered. One man waved his pistol at Lynch, who couldn't tell if the gesture was intended as threat, or request for him to pull over. The T. Rex bit the man off his horse, taking a chunk of the horse's back with him. The horse screamed and thrashed, mortally hurt. The other riders peeled away, only to circle around and begin firing their guns at the creature. In an instant, it was off the road and among them, knocking one soldier and his horse to the ground with a blow from its head, then falling on them. A swipe of its tail took the legs out from under another horse, rolling it over on top of its rider. A quartet of soldiers bunkered behind the carcasses of their horses shifted their aim from the Sioux warriors racing past them to the beast and delivered a volley into its flank. It wheeled and leapt at them. For their part, the Sioux swung their rifles away from the soldiers and sighted on the thing's head.

Halfway across, the access road leveled off and ran straight to the foot of the slope where the twin cannons were positioned. Lynch saw the soldiers stationed at them pause in their duties to consider the situation unfolding below them. To either side of him, Native warriors and U.S. soldiers had stopped their bloody routine to observe the monster fighting their colleagues. A few were riding or running in the direction of the new threat. The MG's engine whined as Lynch raced the remaining distance to the bluff. Behind him, the Tyrannosaurus roared in answer to waves of gunfire. Funny, he thought, how in movies, you were supposed to find these creatures sympathetic, even root for them against the humans—whereas his sole desire at present was to return this example of the species to the extinct category.

When the road climbed the far slope, Lynch put in the clutch and let the car's momentum carry it part of the way up; then, before it slowed too much, he dropped into second and closed the rest of the distance to the cannons. Once he was beside the artillery, he braked hard, letting out the clutch too fast and stalling the car. It didn't matter. He flung open his door and ran to the handful of men in sweat-stained blue shirts and grimy grey pants. They watched him approach, their eyes enormous. Young—most of them were Anthony's age, younger; the oldest couldn't be more than thirty. *Orders*, he thought. *These boys are soldiers. They need orders.* "Who's in charge, here?" he said.

A fellow with yellow sergeant's chevrons on his sleeve stepped forward. He had a long nose, a droopy mustache, a checkered bandana knotted around his neck. Voice raspy, he said, "I am."

"How good is your aim?" Lynch said.

"Good enough."

Lynch pointed toward the T. Rex. "If you can hit the head, do it. If not, the chest. I don't know how fast you are; I do know how fast that thing is. If you miss the first time, you might have a second. The beast won't give you a third."

The sergeant nodded. Turning, he said, "All right: you heard the man."

While the soldiers prepped and aimed the guns, Lynch surveyed the battlefield. As far as he could see, every last man on it had forsaken the round of actions that had occupied him the last century and a half to join the attack on the Tyrannosaur. Sioux, cavalry, Cheyenne rode this way and that around the animal, weaving in and out of one another's paths as they emptied their rifles and pistols into its hide, searching for weak spots. From positions farther out, men on foot maintained a steady stream of fire at the animal. For its part, the Tyrannosaurus ranged amongst its attackers, darting its head to bite the head from a horse, catching a man under one of its rear legs and crushing him to the ground, spinning and knocking a pair of men from their mounts with a blow from its tail. In the short time it had been on the field, the creature had cut the number of men on it in half. Bodies and pieces of bodies lay strewn across the earth. Overhead, the low, dark cloud that Lynch had observed during his previous visits to the site seemed to draw down closer to the earth.

Someone tapped his shoulder: a private, his features waging their own struggle to keep up with what was happening. "Sir?" he said. "Sarge says you may want to cover your ears."

Lynch clapped his hands to his head a second before the cannons erupted, venting fire and smoke in a pair of blasts that buffeted him. One shot went wide, but the other struck the T. Rex on the right hip, staggering it almost off its feet. Enraged, the creature swung in the direction of this new assault. Sighting the soldiers hurrying around the cannons—as well, Lynch thought, as the car it had chased here, in the first place—the thing bellowed and began a halting run towards them. What men remained on the battlefield, realizing the hurt that had been done the Tyrannosaur, renewed their efforts. A group of Sioux and Cheyenne ran at the animal's wounded leg, long clubs and knives out in their hands. A cavalry officer shot close enough to the dinosaur's left eye for it to whip its head around and bite him in half. Next to Lynch, the soldiers loaded the cannons. A Sioux warrior drove his knife into the creature's right foot; it jerked the foot up and out, impaling him on its claws. Despite its injuries, the beast was almost at the start of the bluff. It was met there by the dark cloud, which had been descending from its place above, drawing in on itself as it went, gaining in definition, until what crashed into the T. Rex was almost the same size, a smoky assemblage of limbs that reminded Lynch of nothing so much as a great hand, seizing the Tyrannosaur in its outsized grip.

A vision of Anthony and Jordan at play flickered before his eyes. Anthony was on his back, laughing, the Matchbox MG held aloft in his left hand, his right hand grabbing Jordan's toy Tyrannosaurus, which Jordan, who was sitting on Anthony's stomach, was pushing forward with both hands.

The cannons boomed, the slap of sound deafening. The first shot punched through the cloud-thing and the Tyrannosaur's chest behind it. The second shot struck the dinosaur high in the throat, blowing out the back of its skull. The combined force of the impacts toppled it onto its side. The cloud-creature fell with it.

VIII

Afterward, there was no cheering, no celebration. Looking as if they had awakened from a particularly savage nightmare, the few men who remained began to walk in the direction of the town and, Lynch supposed, the Highway. His hearing had not returned to normal, so he was startled by the soldier who appeared beside him. His mouth moved, and Lynch heard his words as if through ears stuffed with cotton. "Sir," the young man said, his eyes darting between Lynch and the MG, "are you an angel?"

What would Melinda have said to that? The memory of her stilled his urge to laugh. Instead, he shook his head. "Just a man. My name is Tom," he said, "Tom Lynch."

"This," the soldier said, the word straining to carry the weight of the men lying in whole and in part across the landscape, the enormous ruin of the Tyrannosaurus, the cloud-thing draining into the earth, even Lynch and the car. "What is all this?"

How should he answer? A game played by his son and grandson? A dying hallucination? The posthumous firing of a few, random brain cells? He considered the soldier standing there, swaying as if drunk. Whatever fantasy this might be, Lynch decided, he could remain loyal to it.

"I suppose," he said, "you could call it an exorcism."

TRAGŌIDIA

Dying—he was in sufficient pain to suppose—James Bourne lay in the back of Pascal's ridiculous half-van, his Kangaroo, being driven along the road east from Aigues-Mortes. He had not been to the local hospital often enough to be certain, but he had a strong suspicion Pascal was not headed in its direction. At a guess, they were racing for Provence, for the Camargue proper. That was all right: he could die there as well as anywhere.

The worst part was his teeth. As much as anyone could, Bourne had become accustomed to the pain in his shoulders, his hips, his knees. He had taught himself how to move in ways that did not add to his discomfort, and when such discomfort was inevitable, how to move quickly and calmly. He had accepted the shriveling of his desire, and of his cock. To be frank, now that the chemo was done, and his gut no longer felt as if it had been scraped raw, he could tolerate the disintegration of his bones in much better spirits.

His teeth, though: none of the doctors had been able to account for the ache that spread from them through his gums into his face. It prevented him from reading for any length of time. Such pain was not part of the general list of symptoms for Metastatic Osteosarcoma, so they had blamed it on the chemo—until he finished the treatment and his teeth showed no

175

improvement. For the doctors, it was one more reason for the "Atypical" with which they prefixed his diagnosis. Already, he had had the sense that he was moving from a patient to a paper, an interesting case to be presented at their next professional conference. They increased the dosage of his pain medication, and the most honest among them estimated that, at the rate the disease was progressing, his teeth wouldn't be a concern for much longer.

For a short time, the stronger pills had helped to quiet his teeth, had allowed him to concentrate sufficiently to complete his arrangements for traveling to Provence, to finish his final re-reading of Keats's poems. By the time the flight attendant rolled him off the plane in Marseilles, however, two of the pills were barely adequate to the task. (He had tried three, but they had plunged him into a thick blackness through which the pain had stalked him like a hungry beast.) After he had arrived at the Auberge, Pascal had brought him pitchers of sangria, and these, combined with the medication, had allowed him to savor a plate of Pascal's *daube*, served the creamy rice particular to the region. "It's a miracle," he'd proclaimed to Pascal through a mouthful of beef. Pascal had grinned broadly.

It wasn't, of course. The time for miracles, if ever it had been at hand, was long past. A few days after his arrival, the mix of wine and medicine began to lose its efficacy. He experimented with increasing the amount of sangria he drank, but it had little effect, and anyway, it was a shame to treat the wine as a means to an end, and not an end in and of itself. A brief period of grace had been his: he would try to be satisfied with that.

There were five of them. One grabbed his chair from behind and dumped him onto the alley's cobblestones. The rest set to work with their feet. They were holding long sticks, which they also used. Bourne struggled to shield his head with his arms. The sticks struck his body with dull thuds. He could feel his bones not breaking, but pulping. His attackers were men, far older than the late-adolescents he would have assumed would mug an old, crippled professor. One of them was wearing an expensive-looking leather jacket. He wanted to tell them to take his wallet, it was in the knapsack draped across the back of his chair, they were welcome to its meager contents. But one of the sticks had connected with his jaw, and his mouth was numb.

He imagined Pascal had run for the police. He would not have blamed him if he had run away at the sight of five men armed with sticks.

The world withdrew. He wondered if it would return. Perhaps it would be better for everything to end like this, unexpectedly, quickly.

When the world came back, it brought Pascal's worried face hovering over his. A group of men surrounded him. He did not think they were the same men who had beaten him. At Pascal's command, they knelt beside him, took hold of his arms and legs, and hoisted him off the ground. An avalanche of pain swept over him. By the time it had passed, he was sprawled in the back of Pascal's Kangaroo, and they were driving east.

Most of the time, Pascal was too busy running the Auberge to spend much time with him. A week after his arrival, though, while Bourne was sitting outside his room by the pool, soaking in the heat of the midday sun, Pascal appeared with a narrow glass bottle half as long again as his forearm and a pair of plain glasses. Hissing when his fingers touched the hot metal, he grabbed one of the chairs scattered on the concrete apron surrounding the pool and dragged it next to Bourne's wheelchair. He unstoppered the tall bottle, and poured not insignificant portions of its clear contents into the glasses. Bourne accepted the glass he was offered, and returned Pascal's silent toast.

The *eau de vie* hit him like a blow from a big man. He was sure his expression betrayed him, but Pascal pretended not to notice. Instead, he leaned in close and said, "It's bad, this sickness."

"The worst."

"That's why you come back here?" The sweep of his hand took in the Auberge, the Camargue, Provence.

"Yes."

"For the Marys?"

"The town?" Bourne said. "Or the church?"

"The church."

"Why? Have there been reports of miracles performed there?"

Pascal shrugged.

"No," Bourne said, "I was never that good a Christian. I used to tell my students I found the Greek gods more to my liking. I fancied I could feel them here, next to the Mediterranean where they had flourished for so long. But now… 'Great Pan is dead,' eh?"

"What does that mean?" Pascal said.

"Nothing. It's a line from Plutarch, his piece on the failure of oracles. A sailor whose name escapes me heard a voice from shore instructing him to announce the death of Pan to his destination. I think it was his destination. He did so, and there was great lamentation. Report of the incident reached the Roman emperor's ears, and he took it seriously enough to establish a commission to investigate it."

"Bullshit," Pascal said. His cheeks were flushed.

"I—"

"You know who Pan was? Everything." Another sweep of the hand. "He was one of the old gods—as old as Zeus, maybe older. You think something like that dies?"

"I never knew you were a pagan."

"Eh." Pascal looked down. "My father had many books about these things. He told me about them."

"He was a scholar?"

"Something like that. He is dead many years."

Another sip of the liquor brought more words to his tongue. "I was going to write a paper about Pan—about his presence in the literature of the last couple of centuries. English literature, I mean. That's why I read the Plutarch, for background. I was going to start with Keats, 'Endymion.' There's a hymn to Pan near the beginning of it. Keats calls him, 'Dread opener of the mysterious doors / Leading to universal knowledge.' It's the culmination of a series of descriptions of his role in the natural world. I thought I might talk about Forster, too: he has a piece called 'The Story of a Panic,' about a group of English tourists who go out for a walk in the Italian countryside and are overcome by a feeling of inexplicable terror. It's clear they've had a brush with the god. Oh, and Lawrence—he refers to Pan in a short novel called *St. Mawr*. A failed artist described him as 'the God that is hidden in everything;' he's 'what you see when you see in full.'"

"Yes," Pascal said. "Exactly."

"Something else I'll never get around to. I remember thinking I needed to look into Swinburne, to see if I could use him as a bridge between Keats and the Moderns. Ah, well." He finished the last of his drink. "We have discussed it, so it will not vanish from the world, entirely."

"Nothing does," Pascal said. He refilled their glasses.

When Pascal turned right off the main road, Bourne thought it was into a driveway, that he had eschewed the hospital in favor of a familiar clinic or doctor. But they continued driving, deeper into the marshland bordering the road. He had the impression that they were traveling a considerable distance; though it was hard to be sure, because they were moving more slowly, and the road they were following bent from left to right and back again, and every time the wheels jolted in and out of a pothole, a white rush of pain filled him.

The road they were on ended in a small clearing. Pascal parked the Kangaroo at the entrance to it. Before he had finished stepping out of the car, its rear doors swung out. The men who had attacked Bourne were standing there. He was too surprised to speak. They grabbed his useless legs and hauled him forward, catching his arms and lifting him out of the car. Led by Pascal, they carried him to the other side of the clearing, where a gap in the wall of marsh reeds admitted them to a footpath. His ruined bones ground together. Pain as immense as the sunlight washing the sky surrounded him.

Mosquitoes whined about his head. Reeds clattered to either side. The men bore him to the foot of a spring the dimensions of a bathtub. Grunting, they turned around, so that he was facing the direction they had brought him, and lowered Bourne to the ground. His head tilted back, and he could look over the water at the stone from which its source poured. Gray, grainy, the rock had been carved into a face whose features had been weathered to the limit of recognition. What might have been horns, or might have been hair, curled above a wide face whose blank eyes seemed to stare into his above the water that poured from its open mouth.

A hand slid under his head, raised it to Pascal crouched beside him. He was holding a dented tin cup which he raised to Bourne's lips. The spring water was cold, a benediction. He felt as if he could almost speak.

The hand was yanked away, and his head flopped backwards. Pascal pressed a knife to his throat, and cut it.

A couple of days after his arrival at the Auberge, once the worst of the jet lag had passed, Bourne rolled himself down the handicapped ramp at the front door to the dirt lot where the guests parked their cars. The lot was empty. He pushed across it to the thick lawn that reached to the marsh. The chair jounced as he wheeled it over the grass to one of the short trees stationed around the space. Once he was under its branches, he halted. His chest was heaving. His arms and shoulders were searing. Sweat weighted his shirt. He sat gazing at the island of green, where Pascal would hold cookouts if the mosquitoes weren't too bad. Sometimes, he hung lanterns from the trees. Bourne looked at the tall reeds that marked the lawn's perimeter. How long ago was it he had ventured into them, felt the ground slant steeply down to the water?

A chorus of insects was buzzing its metallic song. In the distance, a white bird lifted into the air. He did not know the name of the insects, or of the bird.

Dying was not as hard as he had feared. There was a burning across his throat, and something leaping out of it that must be his blood venting into the air. His body shuddered, too injured already to do any more. Far overhead, the sky was pale blue, depthless as pottery. Closer, water chuckled as the pool was replenished. Then everything went away.

Bourne heard water, and realized that he had never stopped hearing it. He was in water, floating, but when he attempted to stand, his feet found the bottom easily. He rose into darkness—into the night. A crescent moon hung low in the sky. *Artemis's bow*, he thought. He stepped out of the pool and found his legs strong, the thick hair on them saturated. The joints seemed different, as did his feet, which felt hard, almost numb, but he adjusted to the change without difficulty. His arms, his chest—his cock—were large, bursting with life. Something weighted the sides of his head, but his neck was thick enough to bear it.

In front of him, Pascal and his five accomplices were prostrate on the ground, uttering words in a language he shouldn't have been able to understand but did. They were welcoming him, imploring his blessing. They were the reason for the shape he had assumed; their belief held him to it. It would be simple enough to shuck it, to assume the form of a horse, or bird, or tree, or reed—of anything, of all. *Pan.*

For the moment, this form would do. He caught Pascal by the neck and lifted him one-handed, bringing him face to face with what he'd summoned. Pascal's eyes bulged. The acid stink of urine filled the air. He supposed he owed him a debt of gratitude. He lowered but did not release Pascal. He opened his mouth. It was full of enormous teeth. They bit through Pascal's skull with ease. It crunched like a crisp, fresh apple.

The rest of the men were shaking. Their fear clouded the air. He inhaled it, then brought their god to them.

YMIR

I saw how the night came,
Came striding like the color of the heavy hemlocks.
                                                    —*Wallace Stevens*

I

There was a child standing in the road.

Even as Marissa was jerking her foot from the gas, feathering the brake so as not to throw the Hummer into a skid, she was registering the child's threadbare clothes—rags, really—its bare arms and legs, its uncovered head, all impossible here, a hundred some miles south of the Arctic circle. The Hummer shimmied on the ice. From its back seat, Barret—Barry, he insisted she call him—said, "What is it?"

The child's hair was thick, black, long enough for a girl but not too long for a boy. Its wide eyes were brown; its exposed skin was an olive that had been sun-darkened. Although the Hummer was slowing, it was not doing so quickly enough to prevent it running over the child, the child who could not be here, in the middle of a road across a wide, frozen lake in northwestern Canada, twenty miles from the nearest human settlement.

183

"Marissa?" Barry said.

What else could it be but a hallucination, a manifestation of the PTSD she'd prided herself on managing so well since her return from the sand, from Iraq? "It's nothing," she said; though she did not return her foot to the gas, yet. "I thought I saw something in the road."

"Up here?" Barry said. "Not likely. At least, I don't think it is. Do they have caribou in these parts?"

"I don't know."

The child was ten yards in front of her. History prepared for its first, tragic repetition.

"It wasn't a polar bear?" Barry's voice betrayed his eagerness that it was.

"It wasn't."

She lost sight of the child beneath the hood. There was no thud of metal striking flesh, no barely-perceptible tremor in the steering wheel. When she checked the rearview mirror, no small form lay crumpled and bloody on the ice. Her vision wobbled as her heart surged with relief. She let the Hummer coast until her pulse did not feel as if it were going to burst her throat, then put her foot back on the gas.

II

"You saw some crazy shit over there," Delaney said. They were on the beach, sitting on the lounge chairs the resort stationed there, passing a bottle of Kahlua back and forth. Delaney had wrinkled his nose at the sight of the liquor, said he preferred his alcohol to taste like alcohol, not candy, but Marissa said it was what she had at hand, and if he didn't like it, he didn't have to drink it. After a night of screwing in her air-conditioned hotel room, they had ventured into the steaming air to watch the sun rise over the Gulf. A pleasant lassitude, yield of the last week's drunk and the last three night's furious sex with Delaney, suffused her.

His words, however, curdled her satisfaction. She said, "Says who?"

"Says you." He drank from the Kahlua, grimaced. "Jesus." He held the bottle out to her. "You talk in your sleep."

Marissa took the liquor. Across the Gulf, the line of the horizon was becoming more distinct, the sky fading from navy blue to pearl. "What did

I say?"

Delaney shrugged. "Nothing too specific. You sounded pretty upset."

The drink was suddenly too sweet. She swallowed hard and returned the bottle to Delaney.

"I'm guessing you were Army," he said once it was clear she wasn't speaking. "I know women aren't supposed to be in combat roles; I also know things don't always work out that way. What was that girl's name? Jessica something."

"Lynch—Jessica Lynch."

"Right."

In the thickets to either side of the beach, songbirds were anticipating the dawn, their whistles long and liquid. She said, "I wasn't in the Army. I was a driver—private contractor for a group called Stillwater."

"Weren't they—"

"They did a lot of security work around Baghdad. But they had their fingers stuck in all flavors of pie. I was in West Virginia, Charleston, driving tankers full of you-don't-want-to-know-what from one coal plant to another. The money wasn't nearly as good as you would have expected. Stillwater put out the word they were looking to hire drivers to transport supplies from Baghdad to points all over. Starting pay was three times what I was making stateside, with gold-plated benefits, as well. It was no secret the situation over there wasn't nearly as rosy as the President and his cronies were claiming, but the Stillwater rep assured me we'd be using only secure roads. I knew it was a risk, but I figured I'd do it for a year, two at the outside—long enough to accumulate a nice little nest egg for myself. I thought I might be able to parley this position with Stillwater into a better one, maybe driving a limo for some corporate bigwig. I had my livery license; just wasn't anyone interested in hiring me to use it in Charleston.

"Anyway, Iraq was a fucking disaster. Since the roads we were driving were supposed to be safe, they were lightly-guarded, if at all. How long do you suppose it took the insurgents to figure that out? The second day I was in Baghdad, the guy who was in charge of my convoy, a big Texan named Shea, took me aside and handed me a duffel bag. Inside it was an AK-47, with half a dozen magazines. 'This'll come out of your first paycheck,' he told me. Called it a mandatory expense. He offered to show me how to use it, but I said I was fine. My Daddy'd taught me how to rifle-hunt; I guessed

I could work out this thing if I had to. Shea had no trouble with that. He insisted, on penalty of automatic dismissal, that I have the AK on the seat beside me for the duration of any and all runs I made as part of his team. If we stopped at any location that was not secure, which was everyplace between Baghdad and our destination, I was not to leave my cab without that weapon. Doing so was a fire-able offense.

"Intense, right? Most of the guys I drove with were like that. The Army said they'd do what they could for us, but they'd invaded with too few troops in the first place, far from enough to occupy the country, and with the insurgents popping up all over the place, there generally weren't enough of them available to accompany us. Once in a while, we'd luck into a couple of Humvees with .50 cals. They didn't do much to reassure me, themselves, but I assumed if we came under fire, we had a better chance of getting rescued with them than we did without them."

Above, clouds caught the light of the imminent sun and kindled white and gold. Below, the ocean went from slate to deep blue. Marissa held out her hand, and Delaney pressed the bottle into it. She raised it to inspect its contents, said, "When I started drinking alcohol, this was my drink of choice, this and Bailey's. This was in high school, senior year. Girly drinks, the guys called them, but what the fuck did they know. Girly," she pfffed her disdain. "They'd stand around someone's car or pickup, drinking their cheap, crappy beer, showing off their varsity jackets like a bunch of god-damn peacocks flaunting their tails. One kick, and the biggest of them would've been down with a broken leg, a set of busted ribs."

"Tae kwon do?" Delaney said.

"Tang soo do," Marissa said. "Third degree black belt. Sam Dan."

"Huh. You keep up with it?"

"Not formally. I train on my own, for what it's worth. What about you?"

"A little of this, a little of that. I'm more a learn-as-you-go kind of guy."

"Is that so?"

"It is."

The Kahlua was still too sweet, but drinking it no longer made her feel as if she was going to vomit.

"I'm wondering," Delaney said, "if you'd be interested in a job."

III

The Eckhard Diamond Mine was a collection of Quonset huts set back from the rim of a titanic hole in the endless white. Barry leaned forward for a better view of it, whistling appreciatively. "Isn't that something? How far across would you say that is?"

"A quarter-mile," Marissa said.

"I expect you're right."

She stopped the Hummer at the front door of the metal shed closest to the pit. The light green paint that had coated the structure was visible only in scattered flakes and scabs. She left the motor running: the digital thermometer on the dash measured the outside temperature at forty below, and she didn't want to risk the engine not starting. For the same reason, she was carrying the heavily-oiled .38 revolver in a shoulder holster under her coat. She zipped and buttoned the coat, pulled on the ski-mask and shooting mittens lying on the passenger's seat, and tugged her hood up. She half-turned to the back seat. "You ready, Barry?"

He had encased his bulk in a coat made of a glossy black material that made her think of seal skin. The gloves on his large hands were of the same substance. He drew a ski-mask in the gray and electric green of the Seattle Seahawks down over his broad, bland face. "Ready," he said. "Let's go look at my new investment."

Marissa had expected their arrival to draw some kind of reception from whoever was inside the hut. The moment she stepped outside, however, into cold that shocked the air from her lungs, that she felt crystallizing the surfaces of her eyes, she understood why those inside and warm might prefer to reserve their greetings for her and Barry joining them. The cold seemed to take her out of herself; it was all she could do to keep track of Barry as he lumbered the fifteen feet to the hut's entrance. Without bothering to knock, he wrenched the door open and squeezed through the frame. Marissa followed, giving the area surrounding this end of the building a quick once-over. She wasn't expecting to see anything besides the Hummer with its schoolbus yellow paint, a steady cloud of exhaust tumbling from its tailpipe, the great hole in the earth in the background. Nor did she.

IV

"His name is Barret Langan," Delaney said. "He was friends with a guy I used to work for."

"Why don't you take the job, then?"

"I'm happy where I am."

"What makes you think I'm not?"

"Maybe you are." Delaney accepted the bottle from her. The rising sun had ignited the sea to platinum brilliance.

She said, "What's the job?"

"He's looking for a driver, mainly. But it wouldn't hurt if you knew how to take care of yourself, which it sounds like you do."

"Why? What is this guy, some kind of gangster?"

"He's a man with a lot of money," Delaney said, "a little of which he inherited, more of which he married into, and most of which he made by taking the money that had come his way and investing it."

"So he needs, like, executive protection?"

"Not exactly. From what I understand, the guy spends maybe fifteen minutes a day working—talking to his investment manager, that kind of stuff. The rest of the day, he…wanders around."

"What do you mean?"

"I mean he wanders around. He's in Olympia, right? in Washington. Say he watches something on TV about a donut shop in Portland: he goes to Portland."

"In Oregon?"

"Yeah."

"Is that far?"

"For a fucking donut, it is."

"Is he married?"

"Macy, yeah."

"And she's okay with him taking off for Boise?"

"She's got her own things going, charities, mostly. She's out of the house as much as he is."

"Is this her idea? Get him a babysitter?"

"Don't know. From things I overheard him saying to Wallace—my old boss—he's walked into some pretty dodgy places. Bars so far off the beaten track, they aren't even a rumor. Ghost towns that were never on the map to begin with. Old industrial sites. I gather he's run into some less-than-wholesome characters. Could be he's just being prudent. Funny thing is, the guy's enormous, six eight, three-twenty, easy. Hands like canned hams. You'd think the sight of him would be enough to steer most trouble in the other direction."

"Size isn't everything."

"That's not what you said last night."

"Really?"

"Anyway," Delaney said, "the job's there if you want to look into it."

The sun had lifted over the horizon, lighting the landscape to gold-tinted colors. Marissa said, "If I were interested in this position, how much are we talking? Fifty? Sixty? I heard some of the guys who ferried around the Stillwater execs drew down as much as eighty."

"You'd have to do your own negotiating," Delaney said, "but I can guarantee you'd be making three times that, at least."

"Jesus," Marissa said. "Are you serious?"

He nodded. "Understand, you'd have to be available twenty-four/seven."

"For that kind of money, I'll sleep at the foot of his fucking bed."

"You want me to put you in touch with him?"

"Might as well. What's the worst that could happen?"

"Don't say that," Delaney said.

V

Inside, the Quonset hut was a poured concrete floor and metal ribs arching overhead. It had to be warmer than outside, but not by enough to matter. By what light the cloudy windows admitted, Marissa saw that, with the exception of a large, metal cage at its center, the structure was empty. Without hesitation, Barry strode to the cage, which appeared to contain another cage—an elevator, Marissa realized, it was an elevator. Barry swung open the cage door, and stepped into the car, which creaked with his bulk. A black box with a row of rectangular switches had been mounted to his right; he snapped all up at once. Within the elevator, a pair of halogen lights hung in opposite corners flared to life, while the air filled with the nasal hum of electricity. After making certain the door to the place was shut, Marissa crossed to the elevator. It shifted slightly with her weight. A narrow black box with two buttons set one below the other attached to the wire to her left. Barry nodded his ski-masked head at it. "If you would…"

She stabbed the lower button with a mittened finger. The car clattered, shook, and commenced a shuddering descent. Although her face was covered, she supposed her skepticism was evident. She said, "I was under the impression this place was more of a going concern. How long has it been since it was active?"

"As a diamond mine, thirty years, give or take. From the start, it was never as productive as its backers predicted. What diamonds were here were dug out almost immediately. The operation chugged on for a few more years, after which, it was leased to a pair of scientists."

"Scientists?"

"I met one of them; though I didn't know it at the time. At one of Manny and Liz Steiner's parties, a Dr. Ryoko. He and his colleague used the lower reaches of the mine for some type of subatomic research. Had to do with exploiting the layers of rock to slow down the speed of some exotic particles enough for them to be measured. After they left, the mine lay dormant for a decade and half, until a man named Tyler Choate paid a ridiculous sum of money to have the use of the location for three months."

The elevator lowered past an unlit tunnel. Marissa said, "What for?"

"That is a very interesting question. No one I talked to—and I spoke with a number of people—could answer it. I had to turn to a woman who's good with computers to find out exactly how much his rental cost Mr. Choate. I'm used to large amounts of money. This was enough to impress me.

"To make matters more perplexing," Barry said, "Tyler Choate undertook this course of action while an inmate at a maximum-security prison, where he was serving twenty-years-to-life for some especially nasty sex-crimes. Where, as far as I've been able to ascertain, he continues to pay his debt to society."

Marissa was about to ask him if he was sure, stopped herself. Of course he was. When Barry became interested in something—truly interested—he researched the subject as thoroughly as any scholar. Instead, she said, "I'm guessing that Tyler Choate led you to this place, and not the other way around."

"That's right, Barry said. "You're wondering why."

"Yeah."

"When Delaney informed you I was looking to hire someone, he told you that he knew me through his employer, Wallace Smith. Did he tell you what happened to Wally?"

Another dark tunnel rose in front of the elevator door. "Just that he was dead. And," she added, "that he had nothing to do with it. To be honest, he seemed kind of spooked by the whole thing."

"As well he should have been. No one has been able to say with any certainty what became of the man—of him and Helen, his wife. She had suffered a grievous injury and was being cared for at their house. One morning, she, Wally, and her nurse disappeared. Most of them did, anyway. There were…pieces of them left behind. Strictly speaking, there's no definite proof that Wally is dead—that any of them is. But it doesn't look good. The police were treating it as a probable multiple homicide."

"So Tyler Choate's some kind of crime boss, and your friend crossed him."

"That sounds as if it should be what occurred," Barry said. "I'm pretty sure it's the theory the cops are working from. From a distance—from what I've told you—it's the reasonable explanation. Wally's wife was injured in a barn that was connected to the Choates. This set him off in search of information about them. He hired a private detective, a man named Lance Pride; he was the one who located Tyler Choate."

"Wait," Marissa said, "the guy's wife was hurt in a barn? What happened?"

Barry considered the latest tunnel that had opened before them. "A horse kicked her in the head. Split her skull open. A freak accident, but it left her with massive brain damage."

"Ouch. I guess that explains why he was so keen to get hold of whoever owned the barn."

"The horse kicked Wally, too—ruined his hip, left him unable to walk without a cane. That didn't matter as much as the wound to Helen, though."

"What became of the horse?"

"Delaney shot it."

"Oh."

"Anyway—what I started to say was, when I began to poke around into Wally and Helen's disappearance, into the weeks leading up to it, what appeared to be the reasonable explanation fell apart right away. For one thing, the Choates weren't your typical crime family. Almost the opposite, in fact. Pig farmers and super-scientists. I know, it sounds bizarre, but several of the men in the family had careers of some note. In physics, mostly. They also raised pigs on their property, to no great profit, from what I could determine. Members of the family came and went from view. Sometimes this was because they were visiting universities, research labs, think tanks, consulting on theoretical problems and their practical applications. I'll be honest: I couldn't tell you what the hell they were studying, and I flatter myself I'm intelligent. Some of the projects had to do with fairly exotic subatomic particles, which may explain Tyler's interest in this mine."

"You said he was in prison," Marissa said, "Tyler."

The air had warmed sufficiently for them to remove their ski-masks, which Barry did, leaving tufts of his fine hair half-raised. "He is. I gather he was as gifted as the rest of the family, but chose a career in law enforcement, instead. Presumably, to allow him a safe vantage point from which to pursue his less-wholesome activities."

"He was the bad apple," Marissa said. "The rest of the family was okay—weird, but okay—and he was into bad shit. Your friend messed with him, and Tyler had him taken care of. If he's important enough, then him being in prison doesn't matter. He wants to reach out and touch someone, he can do it."

"All very rational," Barry said, "except, there's no evidence linking him to any larger criminal network, not even in rumor. He appears to be a model inmate; at least, his warden thinks so."

Marissa pulled off her ski-mask, stuffed it in her coat pocket. "Okay," she said. "I want to say maybe the Choates are a dead-end, but we're here, so I assume they're not."

They passed the entrance to a larger tunnel. "He called me," Barry said. "Tyler Choate. Last week. I've spent a lot of time and treasure on this matter. I've investigated the Choates as extensively as did Wally. Hell, I succeeded in laying hands on the transcript of a cassette tape Lance Pride sent to Wally about a supposed visit he paid to Tyler Choate in his prison cell. It's nonsense, but I read it half a dozen times. I've had Wally and Helen's histories put under the microscope, too. I've stood in the room where the pieces of them were found. It's been scrubbed clean, of course, but I swear, there is a feel to that space…It's as if, when you notice the walls and ceiling out of the corners of your eyes, they aren't meeting the way they should. But what other effect would you expect the site of such violence to have?

"The problem is, none of what I've found fits together. Despite my best efforts, I been unable to arrange the information I've gathered into a coherent whole that will explain my friend's fate. From what I understand, the police have encountered the same difficulty. I've kept on searching—it was what led me here, to Eckhard. I did my homework; I knew that the mine was tapped out decades ago. I suspect the consortium who've purchased it intend to set it up as some type of tax dodge. I don't judge them; I've done the same thing, myself. What caused me to reach out to them was the fact that Tyler Choate had made use of the mine. In turn, this drew his attention to me."

"What did he say?"

"He asked me if I was a student of mythology."

The entrance to the next tunnel was smaller. "Mythology?"

"I said I'd read Bullfinch when I was younger, Edith Hamilton. Good, he said, I was familiar with the story of Ymir."

"Ymir."

"It's part of the Norse creation myth. Ymir is a giant, inconceivably huge. The god, Odin, together with his brothers, Vili and Vé, kills Ymir, then uses the pieces of his corpse to build the world. His skull becomes the sky, his blood the sea—you get the idea."

"Lovely."

"These are the Vikings we're talking about. They weren't famed for their refined sensibilities."

"Okay—what does this have to do with anything?"

"Picture, Choate said, a being that size, vast enough that the inside of its skull could form the entire sky. How long did I suppose it would take for a creature that enormous to die? Eons as we measure time, even as our gods do. All the time Odin and his kin were carving up Ymir, tossing his brains up into the air to make the clouds, they were surrounded by his dying thoughts. When Ragnarok—their apocalypse—came, and everything went down in fire and ruin, it was only the last of those thoughts, coming to its end."

"That's pretty trippy," Marissa said, "but I don't—"

"Suppose," Barry went on, "you could drill into that giant skull, through to whatever remained of its brain. A sublime trepanation, he called it. Wouldn't you need a plane for that, I said, if we were inside the giant's head? That was taking the myth too literally, Choate said. What it described was the fall of a being—the catastrophic fall, the Big Bang as the original murder—in whose remains all of us were resident. We—everything was living inside this dying titan. Our solar system was a bacterium subsisting on its cooling flesh. Quite a hopeless situation, he said, no less for him and his family. The Choates had scaled the evolutionary ladder, climbed so high above their fellow apes they could no longer see them below, but for all that, they were little better than tapeworms gorging themselves in the loops of the giant's rotting intestines."

How many tunnels had they passed? All full of darkness that had a curiously flat quality, as if it had been painted on the rock face. Barry said, "There are points, however, where the tractability of the quantum foam might permit you to pierce the giant's forehead, to expose the surface of that great brain. You might stand at one end of an unbelievably long tunnel and watch thoughts light Ymir's cerebrum like chains of bursting suns. If you could decode those lights, who could say what you might learn?"

"All right," Marissa said, with sufficient force to interrupt Barry's reverie. "We've moved from trippy to batshit insane."

"I know, I know." Barry shook his head. "The man's voice…it was as refined, as precise, as an Oxford don's. It seemed to surround me. I wanted to ask him about Wally, say, How are you connected to my friend's death? But as long as he was speaking, I couldn't force the words out. They were trapped by Choate's voice. I had the sense that he knew exactly what my question was, but he never answered it. Instead, he invited me to meet him here, today. I agreed. I knew he was still in prison—and I double-checked, after the call ended—but I also knew I would keep our appointment. And," Barry opened his hands to take in the elevator, the surrounding rock, "here we are."

Half a dozen comments competed for Marissa to voice them, ranging from piteous ("Oh, Barry.") to scornful ("Seriously? This is why we drove to the ass-end of nowhere?"). All were choked off when movement to her left drew her eyes to that corner of the elevator, where she saw the same child who had stood in front of her on the ice road. Its eyes were wide, its mouth open.

194

VI

After her breathing had returned to normal, Marissa rose from the bed, pulled off the baseball cap and sunglasses Delaney had asked her to wear, and tugged on a t-shirt. Rather than returning to the king-sized bed, she settled in one of the chairs beside the small table that served as her personal bar. Most of the bottles ranged on it were down to a film tinting their glass bottoms, but the Bailey's sloshed when she hefted it by the neck, and that was fine. She wasn't certain Delaney was awake; she didn't bother checking before she started to speak.

"On the beach," she said, "earlier, I never finished what I was saying to you."

He mumbled what could have been, "Doesn't matter," his words already half a snore.

She swallowed a mouthful of Bailey's. It had been a week since she had not been drunk. Each day's biggest challenge lay in consuming enough alcohol to maintain the pleasant version of the state, without tipping over into anger and self-pity. She said, "This one day, my convoy was caught in an ambush. Textbook example of how to spring one. There were eight of us, traveling west to one of the bases, there. I was third in line. The country was flat, which somehow registered in how big the sky felt. We stuck to the middle of the road, which ran through neighborhoods of squat, sand-colored houses, past palm trees and these big bushes whose name I couldn't remember. The ground was dry; the rigs pulled up rooster-tails of dust as they went. There wasn't any speed limit—well, none that we kept to. In front of some of the houses, groups of men in white robes and red headscarves watched us pass. A few of them threw rocks; although it was more the kids, teenagers and younger, who did that. They had a pretty good aim, too. I'd adjusted to the crack of a rock striking the windshield, the bang when it struck the door. We hadn't been driving that long when the guys ahead of me slowed, fast. Over the radio, I heard Grant, in the lead truck, say, '—in front of me,' and then the IED detonated.

"I saw the explosion, the jet of smoke; I heard the boom, like one of those big fireworks they set off towards the end of Fourth of July displays, the kind of sound you feel deep in your chest. It blew out Grant's windows, shredded his tires, tore the shit out of his engine. Probably concussed Grant, too; although, the insurgents shot him, so who knows? Everything came to a halt. I knew we'd been hit, and when the shooting started, I knew it wasn't over. After the bomb, the gun sounded almost tiny, like strings of firecrackers. I wasn't sure, but I thought we were being targeted from the windows of a couple of houses on either side of the street. Crossfire, right? Most of the fire concentrated on the first truck, but I heard McVey, who was in the second truck, screaming that his windshield was full of holes, and he was pretty sure they'd hit his engine, too, because it was dead.

"Everyone was on the radio at the same time. Shea, the head driver, who was fifth in line, kept trying to raise Grant. 'Grant,' he said, 'move ahead.' Finally, McVey told him Grant was dead, and things weren't looking too good for him, either. 'All right,' Shea said, 'you're going to have to pull around him.' 'No can do,' McVey said, his rig was not moving. Shea couldn't—this was the guy who'd come off as such a badass the first time I met him. Now that the shit was burying the fan, he couldn't process what was happening. He must've told McVey to drive around Grant half a dozen times. McVey said he would love to, but his truck wouldn't move.

"The whole time, the insurgents kept firing, pop pop pop. A bullet punched through the top of my windshield. My AK was on the passenger's seat; I was waiting for Shea to tell us we were going to have to leave our trucks and take the fight to our attackers. At the very least, I was expecting him to direct us to rescue McVey. Because it would have to be us. Someone had radioed the Army for assistance—it must have been Shea—and the woman on the other end told him to wait for an answer that still hadn't come. My heart had shrunk somewhere deep down in my gut. The base of my throat hurt. I was wearing the flak jacket and helmet the company had issued us, but I didn't rate its chances of stopping a bullet from an AK too high. Any minute, I expected the insurgents to leave their windows, or start targeting the rest of us. But all they did was empty magazine after magazine into Grant and McVey's rigs. McVey had gone from demanding help to repeating this kind of prayer, 'Jesus, Jesus Christ, oh Jesus, save me, Jesus Christ.' There was room to the right of his truck, maybe enough for me to squeeze through. I thought I might be able to roll up beside him, use my truck as a shield to let him escape from his and climb in beside me. I could picture myself doing this, but I couldn't do anything to make it happen. My left hand was on the wheel, my right was on the gearshift; my left foot had the clutch pressed in, my right was over the gas—and I sat where I was. Shea was speaking to me, had caught up with the situation and was saying I had to pull around McVey and lead the group out of there. I didn't."

Her throat was dry. She took a generous pull on the bottle. "They had started kidnapping contractors, the insurgents. They were posting videos to YouTube of these guys sitting cross-legged on the floor, their hands tied behind their backs, surrounded by men in black ski-masks. All of them denounced the occupation, a few made requests for ransoms. One guy was murdered, there, on camera, his throat slashed and his head cut off while he was dying. Afterwards, the murdering fuck who'd done it held up the poor guy's head like it was some kind of trophy. There was this expression on the dead man's face...I don't know how to describe it. He looked sick, as if he'd been choking on his own death. I want to say that this was what was keeping me from moving. Maybe it was. Shea was telling me to put the truck in gear and step on the gas. McVey was crying, 'Jesus,' over and over again. My nostrils were full of the burnt stink of gunpowder. The insurgents' guns rattled on, blowing out another of McVey's tires. 'Move,' Shea was saying. I couldn't believe how level his voice was. 'You have to move.'

"Then I was. I can't say what happened. One moment, I was paralyzed; the next, I had the truck in first and was spinning the wheel to the right. It was a tight fit between McVey's truck and a couple of those heavy bushes, but I cleared it. Bullets smacked the passenger door. One punched through and drilled the seat beside me. I didn't slow beside McVey's cab. I didn't look over at it, or at Grant's rig, still burning. I focused on the road before me, and that allowed me to see the child standing in the middle of it in plenty of time. I couldn't say if it was a boy or a girl. It was young—six, seven—dressed in rags. Barefoot. I thought about Grant's sudden stop. There had been reports of insurgents putting children in the way of approaching convoys and, when the trucks slowed, hitting them. I hadn't believed the stories—hadn't wanted to—but it appeared that was precisely what had occurred, here.

"Passing Grant's truck, I steered left, in an effort to avoid the remains of the IED scattered across the road. This set me straight towards the child. I wanted to turn right, but I had to wait for the truck's back wheels to clear the bomb wreckage, and by the time they did, I was already too close. I pulled the wheel around, anyway, shouting at the kid to get out of the way, but even if it had heard me over the roar of the engine and the popping of the guns, I doubt it understood English. It stood there, its eyes wide, its mouth open, its arms hanging at its sides. I could have stomped the brake and done what I could to miss the child, but I didn't. It was like, now that I had put myself in motion, I wasn't about to stop.

"There should have been no way for me to feel the truck striking something that small. Yet I'm positive a slight tremor ran though the steering wheel as I sped past the place where the child was standing. I didn't check my mirrors for anything lying in the road.

"Later, after we'd pulled into our destination and were sitting around the mess hall, I asked Shea if he'd noticed a child's body a little way past Grant's truck. Yeah, he said, he'd seen a body there that must have been a kid's. Motherfuckers must have stationed it there to stop Grant, then, when they set off the IED, it was killed in the blast. 'Savages,' he said. 'Motherfucking savages.' I said nothing to contradict his version of events."

The bottle of Bailey's was empty. Marissa turned it in her hands. She thought Delaney was asleep, but she wasn't certain. She sat where she was, and did not say anything else.

VII

With a shuddering clash, the elevator came to a halt.

"End of the line," Barry said, and slid back the door.

The child was still in the car, its expression of horror unchanged.

Barry stepped out into darkness. For a moment, Marissa was alone in the car with the child. *Not real*, she thought. *It's not real. There is nothing standing there.* Then the tunnel at whose end they had arrived filled with pale, flickering light as Barry flipped the switch that turned on the fluorescent lights set in its ceiling. "It's this way," he said and, without waiting for her, set off.

Pulse thudding, she fled the elevator, rushing ahead of Barry. She swallowed, said, "You should let me go first."

He grunted.

To give her hands something to do, she unsnapped the row of buttons

198

fastening her jacket over top of its zipper, pinched the zipper's tongue, and eased it down far enough to allow her access to her pistol in its shoulder-holster. She considered tugging off her mittens, but decided that the air, while warmer than it was at the surface, was not that warm. Although she could sense the child at her back, she did not turn her head. Instead, she said, "This Wallace—you guys must have been pretty close."

"Oh?" Barry said. "What makes you say that?"

The tunnel was surprisingly finished, its floor and rounded walls concrete. The lights buzzed. "Well," she said, "I mean, here we are, right? I'd have to check the odometer for the exact mileage, but we've come pretty far. Not to mention, all the other stuff you've been up to. You don't do that for just anyone."

"I suppose not," Barry said, though the tone of his voice was threaded with doubt. "Wally was a friend, of course. We certainly drank enough of one another's Scotch. There wasn't a function amongst our set that the two of us didn't attend, and exchange a few words at. He'd traveled quite a bit, and if we were stuck for conversation, we would compare notes on Finland, or Egypt, or Mongolia. We were forever going to do something together, plan a return trip to one of those countries, take our wives someplace new. We got along all right. I had the sense that, wherever we went, we'd have a fine time, together."

The tunnel curved to the left. Marissa wondered how far down the pit—or beneath it—their ride had taken them. She did not look behind her.

"I'm sorry," Barry said. "'A fine time together:' sounds like something out of bloody F. Scott Fitzgerald, doesn't it? Chin chin, old boy, jolly good. Or maybe Wodehouse. The fact is, we weren't especially close. After he died—disappeared, but who is anyone kidding?—afterwards, I was waiting for one of Wally's other friends, the fellows I considered his close friends, Skip Arden or Randy Freeman, to step forward, keep up with the police investigation, ensure that everything that could be done was being done to locate whoever was responsible and bring them to account. No one took that step—Skip and Randy seemed to have fallen off the face of the earth—so eventually, I did. I picked up the phone and dialed the police because I could, because it was necessary that someone should do so and I was available. You could call it loyalty, I suppose. It's difficult to speak about without sounding ridiculous to yourself."

"It's okay," Marissa said, "I understand loyalty."

In front of her, the tunnel dead-ended in a concrete wall in which a flat, grey metal door was centered. Marissa said, "Through here?"

"I assume so."

She pulled off her right mitten and reached inside her coat for the pistol. She withdrew it from its holster, and let it hang muzzle-down in her hand as she approached the door.

"What is it?" Barry said.

"Just being cautious."

A simple doorknob swung the door in. A wave of warm, humid air spilled over her. A rough, unlit corridor stretched maybe fifty feet to a doorway full of soft, yellow light.

"Well?" Barry said.

Before she could answer, the silhouette of an enormous man occulted the doorway. Marissa raised the .38. Mouth dry, she called, "Hello?"

The voice that answered made her want to scream. "Is that Barret Langan?" it called.

"It is," Barry said. "Is that Tyler Choate?"

"The very same," the voice said. "And you brought a little friend."

"Ms. Osterhoudt sees to my well-being," Barry said. "I'm sure you have employees who do the same for you."

"Not employees, no," Tyler Choate said. "I prefer to think of them as associates, fellow-travelers who have not progressed as far along the particular road we walk. Nonetheless, your point is taken. I would consider it a favor, though, if she would lower her pistol. Good manners, you know."

"Go ahead," Barry said, "but keep it handy."

Whatever rock the corridor had been carved from was full of tiny crystals that caught the lights shining at either of the passageway and glowed like stars. Some peculiarity of the walls' contours leant the crystals the impression of depth, so that, in walking the passageway, Marissa had the impression of crossing a bridge spanning the stars. The sensation received a boost when she noticed that certain groupings of the lights seemed to align into patterns, constellations; albeit, none of them familiar. She could not hear her boots scraping the floor. She glanced down, and saw a ball of light streak from left to right, apparently far below her. *Shooting star*, she thought, then, *That's ridiculous.* All the same, the relief that suffused her on reaching the other end of the corridor—from which Tyler Choate had withdrawn—was palpable.

She stepped out onto a white marble floor. Directly in front of her, plush leather seats ringed the base of a sizable marble column. A newspaper lay folded on one of them. A mural whose brightly-costumed figures suggested Renaissance Italy decorated the walls before and to either side of her. On her right, a rectangle of black marble, set lengthwise, formed a counter atop which sat a gold pen in a polished wood holder and a small crystal bowl full of candies in gold wrappers. The entire space was suffused with the buttery glow of the sun descending the sky, which appeared to originate from the wall in which the doorway was set. Marissa leaned forward, and saw rows of tall windows bracketing the entrance, each one brimming with daylight. "What the fuck?"

Barry had followed her into the room. "Why," he said, "this is the Broadsword. What are we doing here?"

"This is the Broadsword," Tyler Choate said. He was standing to the right of the marble column. How, Marissa thought, could she possibly have missed him? The man was a giant, easily eight feet tall, five hundred pounds at minimum. A sleeveless white robe draped him to the tops of his thighs; the garment looked to be a sheet in whose center a hole had been cut for Choate's outsized head. An assortment of astronomical symbols—stylized suns, moons, stars, planets, comets—had been written on the material in what appeared to be black magic marker. The body under the robe was exaggerated, swollen with muscles traversed by rigid veins. Nor was the face any better, the almost-delicate features situated in an expanse of flesh bordered by glossy black hair that draped Choate's shoulders. What Marissa took to be a white dunce cap rose from his head—a wizard's hat, she realized, to match the robe. A single symbol was inscribed on its front, a circle, its circumference broken at about the three o'clock mark.

There was no way for Marissa to have missed him, and yet, she had. It was as if he'd stepped out from behind the creamy light. His voice something with too many legs skittering over her, he said, "To be precise, this is Olympia's famous hotel as it was mid-afternoon on March 5, 1927."

"It's an excellent reproduction," Barry said. "I could almost believe I'm standing in the Broadsword at that exact moment."

"You are," Choate said, "although, the moment has been sliced from its context and slotted here."

Wonderful, Marissa thought, *guy thinks he's a supervillain. Must be all the steroids he took to get this big.*

"Why?" Barry said.

"My father was very fond of the Broadsword," Choate said. "His father took him to dine at it when he was a boy, and he retained a lifelong affection for the establishment. Call this an act of filial piety."

"All right," Barry said. "Why are we meeting you here? What does this location have to do with what happened to Wallace and Helen Smith?"

"Truthfully, not much," Choate said, "although, given its association with my father, it is not completely inappropriate."

"Wallace ran afoul of your father?" Barry said.

"Father developed an unusually...*intimate* relationship with Helen Smith," Choate said. "In the end it tore her—and her husband—apart." He grinned at the obvious pun.

"I was hoping for a more detailed explanation," Barry said.

"He split her head open," Choate said. "He crushed her husband between his teeth. Is that detailed enough for you?"

"Where is he, now?"

Choate waved his enormous hands to take in the surrounding luxury. "Father was much further along in his development than either me or my brother, Joshua. While he could still appreciate the immediate pleasures of your friend and his wife, his form had become more subtle in nature. It was an ideal substance for the process I described to you in our chat. You remember: the sublime trepanation."

"Drilling a hole in the skull of a dead god," Barry said.

"It's a metaphor, of course; except, it's also true. You can imagine, an enterprise of this magnitude requires unprecedented tools. Together, my brother and I were able to fashion such a device from our sire's form."

Great, Marissa thought. *We're in the underground lair of a crazy, giant sex-offender who, from the sound of it, is also a patricide. And who knows? He's probably a cannibal, too.*

As if reading her mind, Barry said, "You killed him? your father?"

A look of almost comic frustration twisted Choate's features. "Come in," he said, beckoning them toward him. "Come in, and have a look out the windows."

Marissa glanced back at Barry. He nodded. She advanced three steps across the floor, and half-turned to view the wall in which the door opened. There were seven to eight windows to either side of the entrance. Tall, wide, arched at the top, they shone as if their very glass had been ground from light. It was a good trick, but not nearly as good as what she saw through the shining panes. A cratered plane of black sand stretched away to blackness. The sky was black, too, with the exception of a scattering of stars, several of them much larger and brighter than any she knew from the night sky. While she watched, one of the stars swelled, two, three times its diameter, more, before contracting to half its original size, then bursting in a phosphorous-flare that jerked her hand in front of her eyes. "Jesus!" she shouted. Behind and to her left, she heard Barry murmur, "Fuck!" Vision bleached, lids fluttering, she pivoted towards Choate. If he wanted to make a move, now was the time. She raised the .38 in his general direction.

Someone was standing next to him, equally tall, wearing a plain robe whose hood had been raised. *This must be the brother*, she thought, *Joshua*. When he lifted his hands and drew back the hood, she saw that she was right; although this sibling seemed much thinner, the skin shrunken around the contours of his enlarged skull. "Can you see anything?" Barry said. She could. She could see Joshua Choate reach his right hand into the left sleeve of his robe and withdraw a knife that was more a machete, a sinister bit of sleight-of-hand. He exchanged a nod with his brother, and started towards her and Barry.

Marissa shot him five times, centering on his chest and tracking up to his head. The first two shots cracked the air and puckered the tops of Joshua's robe. The third shot rung in Marissa's ears like a hammer striking an actual bell; she didn't hear the fourth and fifth shots, only felt the revolver buck in her hand. Holes opened in Joshua's throat, his right cheek, his forehead. His knife bounced on the marble floor where he dropped it; he collapsed next to it and did not move. Marissa swung the gun at Tyler Choate, who had not strayed from his position. His lips were moving, but whatever words were leaving them were kept from her by the ringing in her ears. She shook her head. "I can't hear you."

Tyler nodded, held up one paw with all five fingers extended.

"That leaves me one," she said, "and I'm betting I can put it someplace that will hurt."

A hand pressed her shoulder: Barry, his cell-phone out in his other hand. She did not need to hear what he was saying to know the threat in it.

Choate, however, grinned and gestured at the windows with their special-effects scene. Marissa looked at Barry, who was frowning at his phone. Were they too deep underground? Speaking in the too-loud voice of someone whose hearing was still stunned, Barry uttered a retort that was on the verge of being audible. Marissa thought he was accusing Choate and his brother of luring him here to murder him, to put an end to his investigation into Wallace and Helen Smith's deaths.

That she could see, Choate did nothing. But the roof, the walls, the furniture of the room in which they were standing flew off in different directions, as if yanked away on enormous strings. Now nothing separated them from the desolate plane she had viewed through the windows. In the blackness overhead, a trio of stars flashed one-two-three, strobing the black sand with silent light. Joshua Choate lay where he had fallen; though his knife had been swept away in the disassembling of the room. Tyler Choate also remained in place. Marissa had the impression of something vast looming in the dark landscape behind him, a great, tumorous mass to which he was tethered by a fine thread that floated up from the back of his head and corkscrewed over what she judged a considerable distance.

This time, when Choate spoke, it was as if he was whispering in her ear. "You?" he said. "Barry, my friend, you're incidental. Your companion is the reason you're here."

It was perhaps more shocking than anything Marissa had witnessed. "Me?"

"I required someone to kill my brother." He tilted his head at Joshua's remains.

His words still half-shouted, Barry said, "What?"

"This was a hit?" Marissa said. The notion was laughable, completely out-of-keeping with the madness surrounding them.

"A sacrifice," Choate said, "of himself to himself. Like Odin on Yggdrasil's branch. The only way out of this festering cosmos, this heaving meatwheel. My brother underwent a *kenosis*, an emptying; he divested himself of all he had become. He learned, you understand. From the vantage point we established, here, my brother taught himself to decipher Ymir's dying thoughts. Spelled out in a language of dying suns, he found the key that unlocked the exit to this cadaver universe. That key was nothing, the place that is not a place, the state that is not a state. There, where all things are equally non-existent, he would have parity with Ymir, and might discover what the ancients called the *Ginnungagap*, the breach that birthed the giant.

"Funny," Choate said, "it all sounds rather Eastern, doesn't it? The renunciation of everything and all that. I had always dismissed such notions as so much hippie nonsense. According to my brother, though, those fellows were onto something.

"I helped him to expunge the more…developed aspects of his self. But when it came to helping him out of that most fundamental encumbrance, his life, I could not bring myself to offer him that assistance." Choate smiled tightly. "I will admit, of the multitude of vices I might have numbered amongst my practice, sentimentality, family-feeling, would not have been one of them. Well. I could not take my brother's life; any more, I suspect, than Joshua could have taken mine. I searched for a suitable vehicle to deliver my brother's death to him. You may imagine, I have a substantial list of potential names. By this time, however, Barret's interest in me and mine had drawn my attention, and after I conducted an inquiry into him, I discovered Ms. Osterhoudt in his employ. Further research into the particulars of her history convinced me that she was the person for the job. It seems I was correct."

"All right," Barry said, "all right." The words quivered with strain. "We've done what you brought us here for. It's time for us to go."

The great, dark shape behind Tyler Choate rushed forward, as if the distance between it and him had collapsed. His body rippled, the skin tearing up and down his arms and legs. His mouth split at the corners, widening across his considerable face. Curved teeth that would have been at home in a tiger's jaws burst from his gums. A hellish light ignited within his eyes. "Go?" he said, and the single syllable contained a brief monologue's worth of sinister statements. *My brother may have believed in renunciation, but as far as I'm concerned, the jury's still out. He may have wanted it, but you killed my brother. We haven't had anything to eat, and I'm* starving. Blood streamed from his body, steaming with whatever energy was burning through it. He stepped towards them.

Would the single bullet remaining in her pistol be any use against whatever vision of raw appetite Tyler Choate was becoming? Even allowing for a miraculous shot to the eye or forehead, she doubted it. She raised the pistol, turned, and shot Barry in the head. His expression blank, he fell dead. She tossed the gun down beside him.

Choate's face was mostly a gaping maw; the look on what was visible of the rest of it was unreadable. Marissa said, "Loyalty."

He gave a wet, barking cough she realized was a laugh.

"Fuck you," she said.

And he was gone. In his place was the child, the one who had traveled with her in the elevator, the one who had been standing on the ice in front of the Hummer, the one whose death she had felt tremble the steering wheel of her truck. Its mouth was open, alight with unearthly fire.

"You," she said. "Okay. I'm ready for this. Okay. Let's go. I'm ready."

As it turned out, she was not.

IREZUMI

I

When the situation reached the point we were going to have to call in an outside consultant, and not just any consultant, but her, Noomi Baul, Lindstrom summoned me to the office. I wasn't nervous: I'd already decided that, if they were going to fire me, he and Molloy would have done so within fifteen minutes of my opening the attachment that pollinated the office network with the latest pictoglyph virus. If I had been another programmer, my cubicle might have been empty shortly thereafter. But as Lindstrom was fond of saying, a good—a truly *good*—office manager was worth at minimum a dozen programmers, so once the initial volley of expletives had flown from their office without a follow-up charge from either partner, I relaxed. Truth be told, while I appreciated the inconvenience my faux-pas had caused, I assumed Sunya or Kal would be able to contain the virus and repair its damage by late morning, early afternoon at the longest, after which, my double-click would have moved from the category of "disastrous error" to "amusing anecdote." I mean, these were the people who worked on the Continuing Life projects, and not the simple stuff, either: they handled the refinements of the sensory analogues. If your grandma was enjoying the best sex of her after-existence, she could thank my fellow-employees and the array of ports and windows that decorated their heads.

By the end of the day, though, the screens of the office computers were still showing the mix of constantly-changing symbols. Everything else had been put on hold—had had to be—and everyone had been reassigned to the task of getting ahead of this bug. There was no question about staying late. Throughout the afternoon, discreet calls had been made to various competitors, some enemies, some mortal enemies, none of any help. After dinner, Molloy had contacted Homeland Security, which either he or Lindstrom should have done hours before. But Homeland was busy with something else, and once they'd ascertained that we'd implemented proper quarantine, they were the ones who recommended we talk to Noomi. I figured that was why Lindstrom had called me to the office, so that I could contact her, find out what it would cost for her to come over immediately, negotiate if I could, and set the wheels in motion.

As it turned out, I was wrong. Lindstrom had made the call himself, with Molloy beside him. There had been no negotiation, only a flat fee that would have allowed me to retire on the spot, relocate to the mountains for the rest of my natural life, and very nearly afford one of the better Continuing Life packages. In return, Noomi Baul had guaranteed that, by the time the first employee was supposed to walk in the following morning, the office system would be free of the virus and up and running. "So what do you need me for?" I asked.

"Someone has to stay here with her," Lindstrom said. He was looking south out of his office window, where the bay, still frothing from Hurricane Clarence, was lipping the top of the Manhattan seawall. "Supervise," Molloy added. The fingers of his left hand were spidering over the dermal interface on the back of his right.

"What? I don't know anything about this."

"This level of programming, neither does anyone, here," Lindstrom said.

"Well," Molloy said.

"Do you know who this woman is?" Lindstrom said. He turned from the window, and I saw his left eye shining with the blue light of a Monarch lens. *Damn*, I thought, *he's actually gotten off his ass and gone in for this one.*

"I've heard of her," I said.

"Then you're aware she's likely behind this attack in the first place. I'm not sure this is anything more than an elaborate shakedown, and believe you me, if there were any way I could avoid letting her set foot in this building, I would leap at it."

"But there isn't," Molloy said. "For better or worse, we need her. And we need you to keep tabs on her."

"If you're that worried about her being here," I began, but Lindstrom cut me off. "I can't stand her," he said. "I couldn't stand talking to her on the phone, and there's no way I could take actually being in the same room as her. I'd murder the bitch."

"Nice," I said, "nice talk."

"You are the one with the military experience," Molloy said.

"Seriously? I was an MP. You want to manage a crowd of angry North Koreans, I'm your girl."

"Are you saying you never dealt with drunk soldiers?" Lindstrom said.

"Plenty," I said, "and I had lots of help, plus things like pepper-spray and tasers."

"Look," Molloy said, "Angela: we're exhausted. We're strung out. Not to mention, neither of us likes this chick much, to begin with. It's the perfect recipe for disaster, and we cannot afford any more disasters right now."

"What makes you think I'm not exhausted and strung out, too?"

"I'm sure you are," Molloy said. "But you obviously don't have the baggage with this girl that we do. Plus, you are kind of the one who caused all of this to happen."

"Ah," I said. "You realize that was an accident."

"An accident that's practically wiped us out," Lindstrom said.

"That's a little melodramatic," I said.

"Angela," Molloy said, "we need you to do this. Okay?"

What else was I going to say? "Okay."

II

Noomi Baul didn't step out of the elevator until quarter to one. With no web access, there was nothing for me to do except page through the tablets in the waiting area. There was an article I'd wanted to read about the Mob's involvement in the construction of the Brooklyn seawall, so I caught up on that over a takeout from the better Indonesian place. By the time the elevator door retracted, I'd also finished a piece about how the continuing fallout from the Indo-Pakistani nuclear exchange was complicating efforts to reclaim Bangladesh, and a review of the second *Star Wars* opera. The cleaning bots had completed their circuit of the office, and I was brewing a pot of the good coffee. Behind me, an accentless voice said, "You're Angela?"

I hadn't been completely forthcoming with Lindstrom. I hadn't just heard of Noomi Baul: since her name had first appeared on my personal radar, in a report on the Big Hack of Chinese State Security, I'd read, watched, and plugged into everything I could find about her. Not out of concern for our security: for one thing, there were a couple of guys, Zilur and Rab, who were paid a good deal (maybe too good a deal, considering the day's events) to attend to the office network's protection. It was not, as Lindstrom liked to remind me whenever I expressed my concerns, my purview. For another thing, I didn't think that Lindstrom and Molloy, Inc., qualified for Noomi's attention. While the projects for which we were contracted had applications beyond—sometimes far beyond—their avowed purposes, there were plenty of other companies whose activities placed them several steps closer to the realm of the out-and-out unethical. Of the various movements to which she'd been linked, none had expressed anything more than vague disdain for the Continuing Life set-ups (and how much do you want to bet half their own grandparents and parents were either signed up for or already in one?). For a third thing, the more I learned about her, the more convinced I was that, were Noomi Baul to crosshair us, we'd be so many blue screens.

She looked like her pictures. Dressed in black, from her Doc Martens to her jeans to her short raincoat, she almost could have passed for a Manhattan hipster, except that on her, the color wore differently. Most people choose black to make them appear taller, paler, and of course, thinner. Noomi Baul's clothes added substance to her, made it seem as if she occupied more space than she actually did. Even with the hood of her raincoat up, shadowing her face, the row of silver rings threading her left eyebrow, the silver stud raising from her right nostril, shone. In an environment where the personal ornamentation of choice was the data port, the broad-spectrum window, her jewelry seemed retro to the point of antique. She stood with her right hand extended, and as I took it, I felt the collection of rings crowding her fingers. "Hi," I said, talking too fast, "you must be Ms. Baul. Thank you so much for coming on such short notice." I released her hand. "Can I offer you anything? Coffee? I just put on a fresh pot."

"That would be lovely."

While I retrieved a mug from the cabinet, I said, "So I'm sure Ethan and Seth told you, but our network's infected with some version of the pictoglyph virus. I assume it's the latest one, because no one here had any idea how to deal with it. And before you ask, I'm the idiot who clicked on the message that infected our system. How do you take your coffee?"

"Black, two sugars."

"Right. But now you're here, and everything's going to be fine." I handed the mug to her. "I assume you'll want to get started right away, so if you'll follow me…"

Sunya's station had been selected for Noomi's use, in part because she preferred her screen on its largest setting, thus making my surveillance of Noomi's work on it at least slightly less obvious. Placing her coffee to the right of the touchpad, Noomi lowered herself into Sunya's chair. Hands in her lap, she stared at the columns of symbols effervescing on the screen. At various points throughout the day, I'd done the same thing, watched characters come and go almost too fast to register. A capital A gave way to a cartoon eye, which left to make room for a piece of Kanji, which surrendered to an equals sign, and so on. The longer I'd gazed at the shifting symbols, the more convinced I'd become that there was some kind of pattern, some kind of logic, at work in what I was witnessing, and if only I could see through to it, the apparently random information in front of me would yield to sense. It was an additional danger of the virus, what the news was calling logarithmic hypnosis; fortunately for me, no one in the office had let me stay in one place long enough for it to take hold.

Noomi's fingers fluttered on the touchpad. At half a dozen points on the screen, blue highlighting boxed symbols. Although they quivered, the characters remained in place, as did the ranks around them. Noomi leaned forward. A wave of her hand over the touchpad, and everything except the highlighted figures blanked. I stepped closer. Noomi arranged the symbols in a horizontal line. I couldn't identify them, couldn't guess at what part of the globe had produced them—if they were even language in the first place. They as much resembled the kinds of esoteric marks you run across in exotic physics equations. Noomi slid her fingers on the pad, and the characters moved one in front of the other, until only the second symbol from the left remained untouched; to its right, its fellows had been layered into a new figure, a kind of lattice whose margins were a mess of loops and squiggles. Noomi reached for her coffee.

I had no clue what she was doing. To be honest, I was trying to remember how to subdue an unruly individual. I'd only had to do so once, in Pyongyang, to a former North Korean army officer who'd become violent when the relief supplies ran out before he and his family reached the head of the line. He'd been too malnourished to be much of a threat. I was less certain about Noomi Baul. Assuming she was intent on causing trouble, she wouldn't have walked in here without thinking she could defend herself. She wouldn't have been able to carry traditional weapons past the building's security system, but there were a host of low-detection options available to whoever cared to seek them out, from a paper-knife to a zipsword. Should a network alarm sound, I judged my best move to step in behind Noomi and clap her ear; if that wasn't enough, and especially if I saw her reaching for a weapon, a hammer fist to her collar bone would render that arm useless.

All of which was predicated on her tripping one of the alarms. From what I understood, Zilur and Rab had mined the most important areas of the network with safeguards obvious and imposing and safeguards hidden and fiendish. Considering the course of the day thus far, however, I was less optimistic than I might have been; at this point, it would be just my luck to have Noomi Baul wreak havoc on our system while I sat and watched her.

Her coffee finished, Noomi returned the mug to the desk and began to work the rings off her left hand, placing each one beside the mug. When the fingers of that hand were bare, she did the same for her right hand. The mug surrounded by silver circles, she reached up and drew back her hood.

Despite myself, I gasped. Of course I'd read about the tattoos—without fail, every article about her, no matter how brief, mentioned them. Still photos of them, let alone any kind of video, were impossible to find. Noomi refused all requests to photograph them, and thus far had frustrated efforts to sneak an image by keeping her head covered, with either the hood of whatever jacket she was wearing, or a knit black cap. An artist for the *Times'* Sunday magazine had drawn her head in pen and ink, but she'd done so in three-quarter profile, spending more attention on Noomi's brow- and earrings, her nose stud, than on the tattoos that wrapped her shaven head. They were—positioned where I was, I could see how the slender black lines arced across the bare expanse of her skin, curling back on themselves, leaping ahead to intersect one another. The overall design was impossible to grasp. I had read the tattoos compared to vines, to script, to the coils of a snake or dragon, once to the tentacles of a jellyfish. Seeing them in person, I could understand each of those figures. It was as if her skin had been imprinted with a language that was itself a living thing. She had appeared on the New York scene with the tattoos, and yet they shone as if they'd been inked last week.

"Come here," Noomi said, waving me towards her. "This is unusual."

"What is it?" Even as I moved beside her, I was thinking, *Terrific: so we have the version of the virus she can't deal with. And her fee's non-refundable.*

"There." With her left hand, she pointed at the pair of symbols on the screen; with her right, she caught my wrist. Her skin was fever-hot. I looked down, and saw the black lines rushing over the back of her hand, spilling along her fingers. The sight was enough to freeze me for a second; by the time I was pulling out of her grip, it was too late: the streams of ink had run onto my wrist. There wasn't much pain, but all control of my muscles left me. I watched the tattoo writhe up my forearm, and then my vision dimmed, like a screen being dialed off.

III

Although I wasn't exactly conscious, I retained sufficient awareness to sense time passing. Somewhere deeper in my brain, my sergeant berated me for having fallen for so obvious a ploy. "You could at least have made her work a little bit," she shouted.

When my surroundings brightened, I expected to find myself in the office, Sunya's station empty, some kind of neo-anarchist slogan scrolling across her screen. Instead, I was in a low-lit space whose dimensions I could not estimate but which gave the impression of considerable size. Directly in front of me, Noomi Baul, her hood up once more, sat behind a bulky wooden desk whose thick coat of varnish looked sticky as molasses. To her right, a man and a woman stood side-by-side, unmoving. He was tall and lanky, Scandinavian-pale; she was short and slender, Southwest-Asian dark. Both were dressed in clothes that had been less out of fashion ten years ago. To Noomi's left, a metal chair shone dully.

My heart was pounding, my mouth dry. I tried speaking. "Where is this? Where have you taken me?"

"Nowhere."

"Look," I said, "this is not the time to be cryptic. I don't know what you think you're doing, but the moment you and whoever else dragged me out of the office, you set off a metric shit-ton of alarms. Wherever this is, I'm guessing you have about two minutes left before our security come crashing through your front door. These guys do not fuck around. Do yourself a favor, and let me go, immediately."

"We haven't left your office," Noomi said. "No alarms have been tripped."

It's kind of embarrassing to admit that it took me this long to understand. "This is virtual?"

Noomi touched her finger to her nose.

"The tattoo."

She nodded.

"Goddamn," I said. For someone working for a company whose major stock-in-trade was refining the virtual experience, I hadn't been inside much for years, since the training scenarios they'd run us through in the Army. Ironic, I know. At Knox, the simulations had seemed fairly realistic, although I'd never mistaken any of it for the real thing. This was different. Had Noomi wanted to feed my initial impression, encourage me to believe I was in some warehouse down by the seawall, I'm reasonably sure I wouldn't have detected the lie. I said, "Pretty good. You keep me here while you do whatever it is you're doing. I'm out of the way, but you haven't triggered the alarms. Then—what? You wipe my short-term memory when you leave? Or replace it with something innocuous?"

She did not answer.

"So this was all a set-up?" I asked. "That's what my bosses think. I wasn't sure."

Noomi said nothing.

"I mean, it didn't make sense. Why target us? Is it some kind of financial thing? Everyone's sure Lindstrom and Molloy have offshore accounts; are you going to empty them?"

"You don't seem particularly nervous," Noomi said, less menace in her voice than cool bemusement.

"Why should I be? If you're planning on scrubbing my memory, then I'm not a threat. Dead, I'd be much more trouble to you. If there's some kind of information you want from me, I'll tell you what I know. These guys pay okay, but not that okay. Besides, I won't have any recollection of having disclosed anything. Although," I added, "if you want something from me, I'm not sure why you need this." I found I could move my hands, gestured at our surroundings. "Couldn't you just, you know, take it?"

"Some things, yes."

"And you haven't answered my question. Did you set us up?"

Noomi shook her head. "My being here is entirely legitimate."

"Then why am I in this place?"

"I don't like being watched."

"What did you expect? This isn't the first time you've consulted on this kind of thing."

"It isn't."

"And you've pulled this before?"

Rather than respond to my statement, Noomi inclined her head to the desk, on which a manila folder had appeared. She opened the folder, and spread its contents over the desktop. Hard copies of newspaper articles, magazine essays, a few photographs, fanned across the wood. Their subject was the same, her. I recognized them as pieces I had read. Her eyes on them, Noomi said, "Once you'd been quieted, I surveyed your short term memory. Call it a security protocol. Not much there of any interest, except for these. I assumed you must be company security, or law enforcement, or…something else. It's not unheard of for them to have training in camouflaging their memories, so I searched more closely. Ex-military, but your connection to the Army ended when your service was completed. Interesting that you deployed to Korea, but not much traveling while you were there. The jobs you've held since returning have been more or less of the same, office-management variety. None have dealt with safeguarding your company's network. That isn't your purview, is it? No serious effort to collate what you've read, profile me, formulate a response should you find me your adversary. From what I can tell, you don't believe your associates could defend themselves against me. You're right. They couldn't. I'll say it:

215

you made me curious. I could have spent more time sifting through your brain. But it seemed more expedient to bring you here and speak with you, directly. So—"

"You want to know why I've read so much about you."

"Yes."

"I don't know. Because you interest me."

"Obviously."

"Yeah." After a moment, I said, "When the news started coming out about the Big Hack, everyone was sure the U.S. was behind it. I had just completed basic and all of us were talking about it as a major win for the cyber guys. Of course we weren't about to acknowledge what we'd done, but that was all right. After years of attacks by China, we'd struck back in one blow that had crippled their offensive capabilities—that had driven them to EMP their own hardware. People were saying this was it for the communists, which, in retrospect, was a little pie-in-the-sky. Even when you and that guy—Yoshio? Yoshiro?"

"Yoshida."

"Yoshida, right—even after the two of you were implicated in the Hack, everyone was sure you'd been acting in some kind of official capacity. My guess was NSA, deep cover. That no one ever got to the two of you seemed to confirm that you were under protection, because I could not believe that Chinese State Security would not have put taking you out at the top of their 'To-Do' list."

"You weren't wrong."

Despite the situation, I felt a twinge of pleasure. "Honestly, I wouldn't have been surprised if some of the folks on our side had been willing to look the other way while the Chinese went after you. Too dangerous should you decide to turn against us, that kind of thinking."

Noomi nodded; I couldn't tell whether to confirm my further speculations or to encourage me to proceed. "After that," I said, "I kept an eye out for stories about you. I assumed there had to be a horde of reporters at work filling in your history. I was right, only, no one could find anything. Prior to your appearance in Manhattan, you did not exist. Well, there was no record of you, not even a random street-camera pic, which is pretty much the same thing. I took this as further proof that you were covert ops. What with everything that had been happening in India, Pakistan, Bangladesh, there must have been a host of opportunities for a programming prodigy to be recruited by the U.S. Or, I don't know, maybe you were from Des Moines and you crashed one of the Pentagon's locked sites, earned a job offer and a new identity from the men in black. Either way, I was more interested in where you were going than where you'd been."

"And how did my itinerary impress you?"

"At first, not much." Her brow lowered. I hurried on: "I mean, sure, for the next couple of years, it seemed like you were connected to every major computer-related event. The Mac Wars, the Google/BM thing, the Halliburton Raid—it got to the point that, after the first couple of lines of an article, I could predict whether you'd been involved or not, especially if someone had had to EMP their servers. It was—I wasn't sure why you were spending so much time in the corporate world. I expected the woman who'd brought down the Chinese to have bigger fish prepped for the frying pan, the Russians, say, or the Saudis. To be fair, though, it's been a long time since there's been any daylight between the multinationals and the government. When I was in Korea, there were moments, I swear I wouldn't have been surprised to see the Hyundai logo stenciled on the tank turrets. Cutting the legs out from under Mac East, shutting down the BM part of Google/BM, imploding Halliburton, were all political acts. It was just, it was hard to figure out the ideology that knit together your choice of targets.

"It must have been after Halliburton that the *Wall Street Journal* ran that editorial, 'The Most Dangerous Woman in America?' Except that the title wasn't a question, it was an assertion, and a pretty panicky one at that. What the *WSJ* was forgetting was that there were plenty of rival corporations who were only too happy to watch Mac East disintegrate; beyond Mac Pacific, I mean. Those guys could bankroll their own pundits to argue that what had happened to Google was a normal part of the capitalist ecosystem. Maybe it was; I'm no economist.

"But to have the ability to affect those multinationals, those governments, to the degree that you're a threat to them, so that they have to pay attention to you—not you as part of this or that consumer demographic, but you as *you*, as a private citizen—that's more than power, it's mass, solidity. Like the song says, we're living in an immaterial world. We're all ghosts, except for you. You're real."

Noomi Baul's brow had relaxed, her cheeks reddened. "You're very flattering," she said. "And stupid."

"Why?" I said. "Because someone gave you your tech? I assume that's what happened. I admit, I had no idea anyone was that far along on—I'm not even sure how to describe it. Your tattoos. Who cares if you weren't the one to develop them? You're in the driver's seat, now."

There was no change in Noomi's expression, but the already-dim lighting in her private space dipped to complete dark. A pillar of white light leapt up around the metal chair to her left. I raised my hand against its brilliance. Squinting, I could distinguish a child-sized figure seated in the chair, a trio of taller forms encircling it. Except for the fluttering thump of a heartbeat, there was no sound. The light jumped and danced, a stream of phosphorous submerging the tableau, simplifying its subjects to charcoal sketches. The tall forms moved their hands over the seated figure's head and neck. Each might have been holding something, a syringe or a scalpel, or their fingers might simply have been too long. The heartbeat raced faster, the thump verging on a hum. It was hard to be certain with all the hands scuttling over it, but the seated figure's head appeared to be shifting, as if its skin had become sticky and were adhering to the tall forms' fingertips.

The stream of light vanished, the heartbeat ceased, and the metal chair was once more empty. The area behind Noomi, to either side of me, filled with the glow of dozens of screens. From movie-theater large to personal-entertainment small, they overlapped, forming a virtual mosaic around us. While each screen played different footage from those adjacent to it, the general subject was the same: the inundation of Bangladesh during what came to be called the "*Ek, Dui, Tin*," the One, Two, Three, the trio of super-cyclones that had followed so close on one another's heels as to constitute practically a single storm of almost two and a half weeks' duration. To my right, one of the runway cameras at Sheikh Majib International caught a British Air Dreamliner riding an ocean swell, for all the world like an enormous surfboard, straight into the slender control tower. To my left, a Bangladeshi sailor recorded the pileup of cargo ships and supertankers as the Sanadia Island port was overwhelmed. Directly in front of me, a tourist standing on the fifth or sixth storey of their hotel filmed the first wave to reach Dhaka, a mass of water whose churning edge rose over the white wall surrounding the hotel and raced across the green lawn between the wall and the hotel. Here was the Dhaka Metro being shoved off its elevated tracks.

Here was the interior of a grocery store, its windows bursting inwards in a torrent of water and glass. Here was a family crowding the roof of their house as the steep prow of a fishing boat, freed from its moorings, swung lazily towards them. Here was a satellite photo showing the new northern shore of the Bay of Bengal, a margin that encompassed eighty-nine percent of what had been Bangladesh.

I had seen the videos, the photos—first when they dominated the major news outlets, and then, after the majors had moved on to the next shiny object, when I sought them out on an assortment of local and micro news sources. I'd listened to experts insist that this was no surprise: given the rise in sea levels the past couple of decades, plus the increase in intensity and duration of severe weather events, it didn't take a genius to predict that a low-lying country with a history of cyclonic activity had been painted by the targeting laser. Yes, precautions had been taken—seawalls put up, building codes improved, evacuation routes planned—but against a disaster of this magnitude and length, none of them had been enough. Weeks, months after the end of the storms, the typhus-3 outbreak, the convoys to India and Myanmar, I continued to search for news of the area. I'm not sure why. I was a high school junior; there wasn't much I could do aside from contribute money to the Red Cross/Red Crescent. Keeping up with what was happening seemed a way to maintain some semblance of responsibility; not looking away, I thought, had to count for something.

Behind me, the space lightened. A glance over my shoulder showed what I took to be another screen, the size of a large window. The image displayed on it was unfamiliar. In fact, it was so different from everything else connected to the Bangladesh catastrophe that I could not process it. I turned, and my head swam with vertigo, making me step back from an actual window, one so high clouds formed a carpet far below it. A late afternoon sun the color of molten bronze had sunk almost completely beneath the clouds, swelling them with orange light. Overhead, the sky was a blue-black cloth, a handful of early stars studding it in place. This had to be one of the top floors of the Al Burj, or that other building, the one in Rio whose name was not coming to me. *This isn't real*, I told myself. *You're inside.* The problem was, inside felt exactly like outside, and if the only thing delineating the fantasy of one experience from the reality of another was my say-so, that standard seemed distressingly weak. Dropping my gaze, I did a careful about-face.

The screens, desk, Noomi: everything was gone. In its place was an office whose downscale furnishings were distinctly out of keeping with what the rent on a location like this had to be. Shelving units, some tall and thin, some short and squat, filled the distance between me and a trestle table behind which sat an old man. Toys crowded the shelves, the table, the vast majority of them the bright, cheap productions of whatever emerging economy they had been outsourced to. Similarly shabby, the old man was wearing a battered porkpie hat and a threadbare tweed jacket over a red and white checked shirt buttoned to the top. His face was long, his ethnicity indistinct. His large hands fumbled with the cap of a small, purple bottle. I thought of a vendor at a flea market. The old man succeeded in twisting the cap off the bottle, whose contents he tipped into a shallow dish in which rested an elaborate yellow bubble-wand. He swirled the wand in the soapy mixture, lifted it, and blew into its filmy spaces. Quivering, the liquid belled into a sphere which clung to the wand as the old man continued to fill it with his breath. From its shining surface, another bubble raised, and another, until the first sphere had become the center of a cluster of spheres. The old man gave a final puff, and the bunch floated free of the wand, across the table, and towards me.

To my left, a voice said, "You are Ms. Rasmussen." From what my peripheral vision had registered as a block of shadow but which I realized was an unlit passageway, a second man stood observing me. His suit, shirt, tie were of such a piece with the shadow that, had he not announced himself, he could have remained there without me noticing him indefinitely. His face was dark. I don't mean African; I mean it was difficult to see, as if there were a veil floating in front of it. The man didn't wait for me to answer him. He said, "I understand that you have adapted to the graft."

I'd already figured out that I was viewing one of Noomi's memories up close and personal, which meant there was no point to my talking or otherwise attempting to interact with the characters before me. I did not anticipate the images that would surge through me at this man's words: an elderly Asian woman's face, its benign expression set askew by the mono-goggle slowly rotating over its left eye; a thick, transparent wall whose outer surface was covered in what appeared to be red graffiti; a pair of slender bare arms under whose skin black lines spread like vines. Accompanying the scenes was a spasm of plasma-hot rage that trembled for me to express it.

If the man in the shadows noticed the emotion, he chose not to acknowledge it. He said, "You are ready to enter the employ of my associate and myself." He nodded to the man at the table, whose hands roamed its top, pushing toys this way and that. "You may consider this your introduction to your new position. You join us at a time of some crisis. For several years, now, my associate and I have been at loggerheads with a former partner of ours. Perhaps you are aware that there are no feuds fiercer than those between old friends; certainly, that is the case, here. Our conflict stems from a plan the three of us developed for putting the interests of ourselves and a select few in a position of permanent advantage. As we saw it, our prosperity could best be secured through extensive and fundamental modification of our surroundings. The project's details are unimportant. Suffice to say, it was ambitious and, like all such undertakings, utterly ruthless. My associate and I trusted our colleague with the implementation of the plan's finer details; although I was not averse to dirtying my hands when necessary. Indeed, there were moments I rather enjoyed it."

Without looking at it, the old man picked up an oversized, neon-green, plastic egg that snapped open at the middle, releasing a mass of bright blue goo all over his fingers. Thick, mucousy, the goo dripped and dangled from his hands. He smeared it over the tabletop, wiped what was left off on his jacket.

"That was the problem," the other man said, "in a word, *pleasure.* As we conceived it, our interests would best be served by a more…austere setting, one scoured clean of all manner of…" the man waved his hand, "everything. How could we know—posed of us, the question sounds absurd, but how could we know that the same circumstances we sought to develop to our preferences would be transformed in ways vastly more conducive to our ongoing success by the agencies of—well, of essentially the lab rats? Left to their own devices, driven by nothing more grandiose than ignorance and venality, those in authority had shaped this environment into one in which we could thrive. The swollen seas, the heated air, supersaturated with two centuries' worth of industrial by-products; the blackened earth, charred and cracked by the weapons of your wars large and small; the crumbling cities, overcrowded with the hapless and destitute: for variety, your accomplishments could not be surpassed. Nor had we anticipated the brute satisfaction we would take wandering through your achievements. Neither my associate nor I like to be precipitous in our actions, but neither do we like to remain on a course that has so clearly been superseded. Accordingly, we abandoned our original designs in favor of what had been dropped in our laps."

Wait, I thought, *what is he saying?* I tried to concentrate on the man's words, but the rage that had shot through me had pooled high in my chest, where it glowed like so much magma ready for eruption. I was aware of myself—of Noomi—struggling not to contain, but to delay, its venting.

The man in the shadows said, "The majority of our fellow travelers accepted our decision. When all was said and done, a single holdout remained, and that was our old colleague. Always the project's most enthusiastic supporter, he had become zealous in his adherence to it. Our relations with him deteriorated, until our one-time friend departed the company to continue his implementation of our discarded plan. I suppose we might have gone our separate ways and let that be that, but there are no truly separate ways, are there? From the moment he attempted to realize what had become his project, our former colleague had come into conflict with us. It does not do to be sentimental: we initiated a range of countermeasures. Embarrassing as it is to admit, the Zealot, as we had come to call him, anticipated our moves and thwarted them."

With a grunt of what might have been satisfaction, the old man held up a pocket-sized transistor radio. He ran out the antenna and rolled the volume dial. High-pitched, atonal trilling spilled out of the speaker—flutes, I thought, although you couldn't call the sounds they were producing music in any but the broadest possible sense of the word. Nodding, the old man pressed the radio to his right ear.

Up and down my arms, skin raised and lowered as if I had the worst case of goosebumps, ever: the tattoo, I realized, shifting.

The man in the shadows said, "During his time with us, the Zealot recruited a considerable number of assistants. When he split from us, his acolytes left with him. This was no surprise: from the start, our former colleague had offered a…generous benefits package to his assistants. They gave him a tremendous tactical edge, which he employed in a wide range of situations. My associate and I were running from one place to another continuously, putting out the fires they were starting. This would not do. We began a recruitment drive of our own.

"It was as part of this ongoing process that we encountered the work of

Dr. Akihiro. These last few decades, the Zealot's people have focused their energies on the internet, whose possibilities they have exploited to their considerable benefit. The doctor's work on more sophisticated user interface systems promised to shift the balance of what had become a costly and difficult campaign in our favor. All that she required was a suitably responsive technology. She had experimented with organic machinery, only to reject it as too intractable. It so happened that my associate and I numbered among our holdings an organism uniquely adapted to the doctor's needs. Overtures were made, offers accepted, and she was brought into our service. With our resources at her disposal, Dr. Akihiro was able to succeed with what she called her *irezumi*. All that was left was to locate and secure an appropriate recipient for the doctor's special tattoo.

"This proved a challenge. We—I don't imagine the history of our clinical trials will be of much interest to you, except insofar as it encouraged us to direct our attention to younger subjects. Our requirements received an unexpected boost when your native land was submerged, not to mention, when its larger neighbors finally allowed their cold war to heat to thermonuclear temperatures. Suddenly, it was, you might say, a buyer's market. With an abundance of prospective recipients lined up outside her door, Dr. Akihiro was able to move forward with widespread testing."

Another string of images flickered behind my eyes: looking down at the heavy bodysuit restricting my motion, its yellow surface studded with blinking white lights; a forest of pins rising from my arms, the top of each sprouting a thread of wire that tethered it to a bulky console to my right; an ocular jack lowering towards my left eye, the half-dozen needles ringing its circumference locking into position. The pool of magma in my chest swelled.

The man in the shadows said, "For a time, it did seem as if, the nearer we drew to success, the slower grew our approach. One moment, all would be proceeding apace, and then the interface systems, the doctor's *irezumi*, would…rebel. Sometimes the test subject was complicit, sometimes not. Either way, their final moments were not pleasant.

"That, however, was before *you*. I will admit, when the doctor showed me your results on the upper-level training exercises, I was dubious that such consistent ferocity could lead to anything other than another failure; indeed, I almost suggested we excise you then and there. Had it not been for Dr. Akihiro's pleading... What a pleasant surprise to find that someone so young—and, let us be frank, so traumatized in so many ways—could muster such self-discipline. You have resisted the temptation to foolish action that has undone so many of your predecessors, and while I am vaguely curious to know why, your motivation is of less consequence than your ability. That ability has brought you here." The man nodded at the office, its shelves of cheap toys, his associate hooting softly as he continued to press the transistor radio to his ear. The muscles in my face trembled with my effort to withhold emotion from it. The tattoo—the *irezumi*—prickled with what I recognized as anticipation.

"You," the man in the shadows went on, "are to be our left hand. You will defend our interests. You will frustrate and stall our rival's designs. When the opportunity presents itself, you will strike at his interests. You will be permitted considerable latitude in your approach to individual situations, as long as the final result favors us. There is no need for me to threaten you against failure: should you fall short in any of your contests with the Zealot's forces, they will see to your disposal. Undoubtedly, at some, future point, they will get the better of you. Even so, it's not as if your prospects as a refugee were significantly brighter, and in the meantime, you can enjoy a comfortable existence. If you are the kind of person who takes comfort in such things, then you can console yourself with the knowledge that you will be spending your time serving a worthy cause.

"Of course, I suppose our former colleague would offer much the same solace."

My muscles tensed, and in a burst of images that she had kept under lock and key until this moment, Noomi's plan was disclosed to me. A lunging backfist to the man in the shadows' face, followed by a stepping chop to his throat. Press her hand to whatever portion of his flesh was available; inject the *irezumi* and use it to trip his nervous system into seizure. Go for the old man and repeat the process. Raid the partners' thoughts for whatever information might come in handy, fibrillate their hearts, and get out of here. A moment more, and the rage in my chest would come streaming out.

The man in the shadows said, "The details of your new life will be explained to you in mind-numbing detail by Ms. Lindsay when she returns to fetch you. You are here—to be candid, you are here because my associate and I wished to indulge a desire to see you in the—enhanced—flesh. Having forged our blade, we wished to admire it, to observe our reflections in its surface. That, and we wanted you to see—"

For a moment, my surroundings lost focus. Then, it was as if I were at the eye doctor and she rotated the correct prescription into place. The office was gone, replaced by a vast, dark plane. Both the man in the shadows and the old man had remained, but behind each, an enormous black shape loomed. The man in the shadows stood at the foot of a monument that would have put the Statue of Liberty to shame. Struck from obsidian polished to trap what light there was within its acres of skin, the statue was of a man wearing a giant, gold mask whose design suggested the burial mask of an ancient pharaoh. Huge as the thing was, it was dwarfed by what raised in back of the old man, a jagged heap of rock that looked as if it had been torn fresh from the Himalayas. The air was full of music, the same atonal cacophony the old man had been listening to, but exponentially louder, as if played on flutes carved from redwoods. I did not understand what was happening. Obviously, Noomi had been flipped into some kind of virtual setting, but through what means, I couldn't tell.

Under my feet, the ground trembled. The great, golden head of the statue was moving, tilting its blank face downwards. At first, I thought the structure was breaking apart, but the head remained attached as its titan eyes rolled in their sockets. I could feel its gaze churning across the plane in my direction. It crashed over me like a wall of water.

Submerged in its notice, I was submerged in it. The statue vanished, as did the man in the shadows, each of them no more than a mask, a mediation for something that enveloped me like a great, dark ocean. I saw—I didn't see so much as my brain translated what I was experiencing into sight. I was shin-deep in what might have been the foam of a wave's furthest reach up the beach, except that this foam spread in all directions, indefinitely. Nor was it composed of water; instead, rings of light, each barely wide enough to fit my pinky, shook and shimmered one beside the other. There were thousands of the rings in my immediate vicinity, hundreds of thousands a little farther out, millions and hundreds of millions beyond that, a billion, a hundred billion, more numbers too large to be any more than abstractions, in the distance. Where the individual rings blended into a glow, something hung above them. It was too distant and too dim for me to see too much of; what caught the light reminded me of one of those fractal screensavers you still run across, lopsided globes that flatten and drain down their own centers. Even this far removed, most of it invisible, it nauseated me, the little of it I glimpsed making me feel as if I were folding in on myself. I looked away, and saw movement nearer. From the gaps between the rings of light, slender tubes rose into view, swaying with the lazy motion of undersea plants swept by the tide. At first, that was what I took them for, some kind of flora native to wherever this was; then one of them corkscrewed forward and down, sinking its top into the space between two rings and lifting what had been its base into view. Other tubes repeated the motion—all of them were repeating it—the mass of them was crawling towards me. I thought of a clump of earthworms squirming across a muddy field. I'm not sure what it was, what hitch in their collective movement, that made me realize what I was looking at was not an abundance of individual organisms, but a single creature broken into an indefinite number of segments. Organism wasn't even the right word, but I didn't know what was. A sensation too primitive to be emotion poured off the thing in waves, a lack so fundamental as never to be met, no matter what the remedy. It struck the rage molten in my chest like a blast of liquid nitrogen, cooling, hardening, and crumbling it to powder in an instant. The thing hungered, and its hunger was a great whirlpool spinning down to the ocean floor, threatening to sweep me into it like so much flotsam. A want that profound wouldn't even notice when it consumed me. It could strip the flesh from my bones, drain the air from my lungs, taste my final thoughts as they sparked between neurons—more, it could peel my experiences from their settings, scrape the meat out of them, suck the last sensation off their husks, and it wouldn't matter. It would be like trying to satisfy a starving man with a grain of rice. The absence the thing encompassed pulled at me. On my arms, my scalp, the *irezumi* writhed, a nest of snakes trying to tear through my skin. The pain was awful, and then it tore me apart.

IV

The office coalesced around me to the sound of someone speaking, a stream of words that went, "Oh God oh Jesus oh Christ oh fucking Christ what the fuck what the motherfucking fuck oh motherfucker oh you oh God oh

Jesus," and so on. I was seated in Sunya's chair, at her work station. Noomi Baul was standing to my right. Sunya's screen was up, the Lindstrom and Molloy logo centered on it. "What the fuck what the motherfucking fuck." I looked at Noomi, but her lips were not moving. Mine were. Once I realized this, my litany of invectives gave way to, "They're not—"

"They aren't," Noomi said. "They more aren't than are. You could call them aliens; although even that makes them sound more familiar than they are. As far as I've been able to work out, they're…dispositions in the structure of things, distortions proximate to the quantum foam that analogize intelligence. If you were to call them gods, you wouldn't be completely wrong; nor would you be if you called them devils."

"How did they—"

"I don't know."

"You—you're—"

"A weapon," she said. "I've come to take a certain pride in being a highly effective one, but that's all."

"I…"

"The pictoglyph virus builds and opens a gate," Noomi said, "which allows a stream of self-organizing, self-directing information to manifest within a network. Left unchecked—you don't want to leave it unchecked. The only solution to a full-blown manifestation is to EMP the hardware. The problem is, once the virus has been accessed, there's no way to stop it constructing its gate; at least, none I've found. What you have to do is reroute the gate's destination to a closed network, so that when the information passes out of it, it's confined to a single location long enough for it to be diagnosed and wiped. The internal system of a repressive state security apparatus will do nicely, as will the private preserves of a multinational corporation—or a virtual afterlife."

"What—wait—you sent the virus to Continuing Life?"

"Don't worry: no one will be able to trace it back to here. It should take another day for the information to achieve its optimum form, and maybe six hours after that for the decision to be made to EMP it."

"But there are people in there," I said. "There are people's grandparents, their great-grandparents, and children—there are children, and people who were in comas, who've gotten a whole new life, inside." I hated that I sounded like a sales rep for De Leon, Ltd., but what I was saying was true.

"Simulacra," Noomi said. "Sophisticated replicas with which you can delude yourselves that your loved ones are not really lost to you."

"From what I understand, the jury's still out on that. Even the Vatican's stepping more lightly, these days."

"What does it matter? Even if those…things are some form of continuation of the human, what gives them the right to extend their existences when so many others have had theirs ripped away from them?"

I wasn't in any state to argue the final ethical points of a virtual afterlife. "I'll tell," I said. "If the office network's up and running, then I can have Lindstrom and Molloy on the phone, instantly. I'm guessing I can't stop you from walking out of here, but I can make sure everyone knows what you've done."

"You might want to take a look at your right hand, first."

"What?"

"It's not a trick—go on."

The tattoo was discreet, a black mandala on the meat between my thumb and index finger. As I watched, it wriggled ever-so-slightly, as if settling in to its new location. My stomach squeezed, my takeout burning at the base of my throat. I groaned.

"That is my insurance policy," Noomi said. "If you should make any unwise decisions regarding what you've learned of me, that mark will allow me to open a gate very much like the one the pictoglyph virus builds in the middle of your brain. What will come through—to everyone around you, it will appear as if you died a very difficult and painful death from an aggressive species of brain cancer. Which will be close enough to the truth for it not to matter too much."

Only when she went to walk away from the work station did I say, "Why? Why show me all that—tell me—let me remember it? Wouldn't it have been simpler to wipe my memory?"

"You're not without skills of your own," Noomi said. "I may have need of them, sometime. Chinese Security has a long memory. This way, it will be easier for me to call on you. Anyway, you were curious, weren't you? And why shouldn't you have to live with what you know? The rest of us do."

V

One of the selling points for Continuing Life is what its developers call the At Last factor. Because of processor speeds, everything in a virtual environment happens in slices of time so small their names sound like something out of Dr. Seuss: attosecond, zeptosecond, yoctosecond. It's not quite instantaneous, but it means you can pack an awful lot of subjective experience into a little quantity of time. Combine that with a setting that maps onto the real world so closely as to leave no gap apparent between them, and in your virtual afterlife, you finally will have world enough and time. Provided you and/or your family have purchased at least a mid-level package, you can spend a week walking the corridors of the Louvre, or diving the remnants of the Great Barrier Reef, or taking a submarine tour of Venice. If you did well enough in this life to buy the next life you want, then you can try to scale Everest, or visit the Marianas outpost, or board a shuttle to one of Virgin's orbital hotels.

What most people—including, you can be sure, a good portion of the system's current and future residents—don't realize is that you spend almost all of each day in Continuing Life inactive—in power down mode, if you like. This allows your time inside to maintain parity with time outside, which is especially important if you have family or friends with whom you want to continue relations. From what I understand, the test versions of the system experimented with permitting occupants more latitude in the amount of their subjective experience, and it did not end well. Whatever human consciousness might be capable of in theory, there's nothing in our daily lives that prepares us for a thousand, for ten thousand, years' worth of life. It doesn't say much for your virtual afterlife if it causes its inhabitants to invoke their annihilation clauses, so the time ratios were scaled back and regularized.

Continuity with the life they left was more important to the system's residents than anyone anticipated. It turns out that, whatever afterlife they may have been promised by their assorted faiths, given the choice, the typical person will opt for a situation that's more or less a continuation of what they've known—maybe with a few improvements here or there, but otherwise the same. Thus the meticulous construction of a virtual world indistinguishable from the actual one. The idea is to make it as easy as possible for the inhabitants of Continuing Life to convince themselves that their lives haven't changed that drastically.

What all of this means is that, when the gate Noomi Baul re-routed opens, the consequences for Continuing Life's residents will look and feel about what they would for you or me, were such a gate to admit something to this world. It was Noomi's parting gift to me, a look at what's already unfolding in the system. Most likely, it began with one of the inhabitants clicking an e-mail they shouldn't have. If it worked once, right? Maybe it blanked the screen, crashed the resident's interface, or maybe it did no more than cause the lights to flicker. Either way, information will pour into the network like water out of a firehose. At first, the system will treat the influx as it would a large-scale upgrade, by shunting it to those zones of zero population—the South Pacific, say—so that, should there be any problems with the information, they can be identified and addressed before they affect any of the inhabitants.

So while she drinks her morning coffee, the news channel your grandma keeps on for background noise will report seismic activity in the deep ocean. It's unlikely she'll find this cause for much alarm. Continuing Life is marketed as a dynamic environment, one whose occasional storms and even mild earthquakes provide a stimulating variety to the setting. Besides, the chances are good that she'll have selected a primary residence far inland and well-above sea level, the habits of an actual lifetime having persisted into her virtual one. The next she hears of it may be during lunch at Applebee's, when the screen over the bar will be showing satellite photos of the new land mass that's pushed up through the ocean. She won't be especially concerned. If this is supposed to be happening, then there's no reason for her to worry; if it isn't, there's a university of talented young women and men to deal with it. By the time she's discussing the island with her neighbors over dinner, and whether what appear to be buildings on its sides could be the work of human hands and not natural formations, your grandma may be as much annoyed as anything. This was not what she paid for, some kind of science-fiction scenario, Atlantis rising from the depths. She's here because her life ran out before she was done with it. Her intent is to watch her grandchildren grow up, and to take a refresher class in French at the local college, so that when she visits Paris, she'll be able to ask for directions to the Eiffel Tower, herself. If this current situation continues, she may have to speak to someone.

IREZUMI

Were she told, your grandma would take little comfort in the knowledge that, as she's turning in for the night, a room full of those talented young women and men is scrambling to deal with the threat to her home. In a matter of seconds, the information whose admission to their network none of them can explain has thwarted the system's extensive safeguards and begun reconfiguring significant portions of it. When your grandma next wakes, ahead of schedule—the result of a programmer's hypothesis that they might slow the invading information by returning the system to active mode early—it will be to disaster. The morning's news, which she will watch attentively, will struggle to keep up with events. More, and more significant, earthquake activity throughout the Pacific, pushing tsunamis towards the Hawaiian Islands, the western coast of North America. Seawalls topped, breached. Houses collapsed, swept away. Lava running out of Hualalai, Mauna Loa, and Kilauea. Mountains from the Volcan Fuego in Colima to Volcano Mountain in the Yukon spewing smoke and fire like gigantic fireworks. Mount St. Helens bursting. The Yellowstone caldera rising. She'll remain in front of the TV for the rest of the morning.

Around lunch, your grandma will attempt to contact her middle daughter, your aunt, who's typically the child she calls on when she needs reassuring. Leading with an apology, a pleasant woman's voice will tell her that the outside interface is currently unavailable and she should try it again, later. Only after she has no better luck reaching her other children, her older grandchildren, will she accept that, for the moment, she is cut off from everyone she knows in the actual world. The unease this occasions will be nudged into anxiety by her lunchtime conversation with the members of her book club, none of whom makes the slightest pretense of discussing *Persuasion;* instead, the three women and two men trade rumors like children showing off their latest toys. Underneath their sometimes fanciful particulars—the Chinese are doing this, as revenge for the Big Hack; it's Mac Pacific, sabotaging the competition for their Next Phase; it's that solar storm, messing with the hardware—the explanations share a recognition that something in their environment has gone profoundly wrong. The six of them will still be debating whether you can die in this place when the Yellowstone supervolcano explodes. It will sound as if a sizable bomb has detonated a mile or so away. The noise will send them to the TV, on which the news anchors will be trying to re-establish contact with the crew whose helicopter was circling the caldera moments before. One of the book club members will run out the front door onto the lawn, where he will look up in all directions, until he finds what he was seeking and calls for the others to join him. When they do, and turn their collective gaze in the direction he's pointing, north-northwest, they'll witness what appears to be the top of a great, round cloud in the distance, beyond the nearer peaks. Those same peaks and their more distant brethren will take the brunt of the pyroclastic flow that radiates from the blast, but within the hour, heavy flakes of what your grandma at first mistakes for snow will be tumbling through the air, and an hour after that, thick clouds will roll across the sky, plunging the day into gloom.

What your grandma won't know—what none of her friends, none of the system's other inhabitants will know—is that Continuing Life has been locked into active mode. How, the programmers won't be able to say with any degree of certainty; though there will be plenty of theories—and blame—darting around the room. Your grandma will stay up well into the night, as the TV ricochets from disaster to disaster. The fault lines that have zigzagged up the centers of major cities, collapsing buildings as if they were made of cards. The volcanoes around the globe that have started spraying lava like fountains. The flooding that's followed the failure of seawall after seawall. There will be reports of other things happening, too. None will be especially coherent. A picture of Kilauea, a net of lightning joining its flaming crown to the black clouds roiling above, will be scrutinized for the figure that (allegedly) can be seen through the gaps in the electricity, a conglomeration of shadow that would stand skyscraper-high were it real. A short video clip of the latest tsunami swelling towards Los Angeles will be slowed to examine the dark object that appears to be moving beneath its crest. A fragment of a phone call from Vancouver will be subject to inconclusive analysis to determine the nature of the roaring in the background. Even as one of the programmers will voice the fear that no one wants to be the first to utter, that they aren't going to be able to beat this, your grandma, responding to what sounds like an avalanche, will switch on the outside light and open her front door. She'll see the foot of mud that's buried her lawn, the flakes of it that have not stopped drifting down, tinted orange by the sodium light. Despite everything, she will find the scene momentarily beautiful, and her ability to do so will lift her spirits. Not until she's about to shut the door will she register the mountain looming in the woods beyond the lawn. There's never been a mountain there, before. Sick with dread, she'll go to close the door, already having noticed the mountain's silhouette. Before the door shuts, she'll see the giant shape taking a step in her direction.

Once the decision has been made to EMP Continuing Life's servers—the internal debates conducted; the necessary requests filed with, reviewed by, and greenlit by Homeland; the delivery of the pulse generator arranged— the actual process will take no more than thirty minutes, from the moment the agent to whose wrist the device has been shackled steps out of his car in De Leon, Inc.'s underground parking lot to the one he turns to the CEO and announces, "It's done." For your grandma, as for the system's other inhabitants, twenty thousand years of subjective time will have passed. She will have witnessed her world transformed beyond recognition, its every last familiar detail washed or burned away, buried under layer after layer of igneous rock. She will have fled across the ruin of her afterlife pursued by creatures beyond her ability to apprehend, enormous things whose outlines keep shifting but whose eyes are alight with malice and delight. She will not have escaped them, and the torments they will have inflicted on her will have driven her from sanity, through insanity, and out its other side. Her body will have been molded like so much clay in the hands of a mental patient, stretched and compressed and bent and twisted into forms grotesque and awful. At last, the material that used to be your grandma, what remained of her, will have been incorporated into the walls of the structure the rulers of her world have raised on the top of the planet, a travesty of angles whose reflection crowns the globe's southern pole. She will have suffered so much for so long as to have forgotten the difference between pain and herself. Were she capable of understanding what is on its way, the burst of electromagnetism that will wipe all of this away, rendering her and her world down to their constituent atoms, she would weep with gratitude.

THE HORN OF THE
WORLD'S ENDING

I

The young officer knew his Homer; he knew Virgil, too. More importantly, he had read Herodotus, and so from epic and history together learned that the gods sometimes walked amongst men. When he imagined himself encountering a god, it was usually in the thick of battle. He would be on horseback, slashing right and left with his sword, and a flash of metal would draw his eye to a tall man in shining armor whose sword was cutting a bloody arc through the foes around him. Mars would pause in his gory work long enough to nod his approval at the officer, and then the battle would separate them. Brief as he pictured it, that gesture would cling to him, lighting his way along a magnificent career. The opportunity to position himself closer to that (possible) encounter had led the young officer to request duty here, Judaea, where a surprisingly successful revolt had led to the defeat of a legion and the proclamation of an independent Jewish kingdom. In response, the emperor had summoned the governor of Britannia, Sextus Julius Severus, to command the army that would re-establish imperial control of the province. To that end, Severus had called on a full half-dozen legions, and supplemented them with elements drawn from another half-dozen, including the young officer. Finding himself part of an enterprise so vast, the young man's pride had swelled, and he had felt sure that the weeks and months ahead would bring him the meeting for which he yearned.

What he had met thus far, however, had more in common with the life of the farmer than it did that of the soldier. At least, that was the comparison his commanding officer made. Old Lucian had left a considerable farm in southern Gaul to be part of this force, and he tended to treat that occupation as the measure by which all other things might be described. Judaea, Lucian had said to his junior officers, was like a field that had been neglected, so that weeds had taken root in the soil, and wild animals had claimed it for their territory. If you did not want to cede your land to such things, the only remedy was fire and the blade. You must burn the weeds, and you must kill the animals. The young officer was not certain how sound his superior's views were when it came to agriculture—his own family had been scholars and wine merchants. Applied metaphorically, it meant razing smaller settlements, setting the torch to whatever would take its flame, and cutting down any who did not flee quickly enough. He had no moral objection to his prescribed course of action: these people had not been Roman to begin with; worse, they were actively hostile to the Empire. Whatever fate was theirs, their actions had purchased them. Rather, his objection was an aesthetic one. Burning fields, slaughtering livestock, pillaging then knocking down dwellings, killing those who put themselves close enough for it: none of it was especially heroic, especially glorious. Elsewhere, to the north and east, there was fighting. He had heard accounts of battles between elements of other legions and Judaean forces, fierce contests whose victors could feel well-satisfied. It was in such clashes as these, and not the slaughter of sheep, that one might hope to see, and be seen by, a god. His lack of satisfaction with the action he directed was matched by his unhappiness with the place to which he'd come, the people who inhabited it. Granted, no place could match Rome, but this country seemed almost exactly its opposite: what greenery there was hemmed in by arid land; the trees little better than bushes; the buildings only a few steps up from hovels. The men wore thick beards; the women dull robes; and few if any would or could speak Greek. It hardly seemed a place worth contesting.

Old Lucian had warned his junior officers to be careful of traveling anywhere alone, especially in the larger towns and cities. The Judaean troops had carried off raids astounding in their brazenness, helped in no small part by a civilian populace ready to aid and abet them in ways large and small. Stroll through a market by yourself, and you were likely to find yourself distracted by the merchant who spilled his wares in front of you, so that a Judaean soldier could slip up behind you and treat your armpit to his dagger. The young officer did not doubt the caution; indeed, it was his very belief in it that had brought him to this inn outside Bethlehem. Apparently, walking in the front door, his cloak swept back so that his armor and sword were plain to see, and demanding seating and wine was his best chance to put himself in harm's way. He did not object when the innkeeper placed him in the center of the large dining room; instead, he took in the drinkers and diners around him with a level gaze that he meant to serve as a challenge and a caution. Nobody looked immediately threatening, which was to say, everybody did. He loosened his helmet, set it on the rough table in front of him, and waited for his wine.

He had his first cup to his lips when the two men seated to his right stood. Heart surging, he threw down the cup and sprang to his feet, kicking back his chair and drawing his sword. The men put up their hands—reaching for weapons, he guessed. Already, he was moving to stab the one to the right, who was closer and whom he could turn to use as a shield against his friend. But the men were not producing daggers; they were holding their hands over their heads and scrambling back from his lunge. Afraid that this might be a feint, he spun, his sword out before him, the light quivering up its blade. The rest of the patrons were frozen at their places, their eyes wide. He covered the room again, more slowly this time, pretending that the flush he could feel climbing his cheeks was a result of his sudden movement.

Later, after he had returned his sword to its sheath, the mess had been cleared up, and he had resumed his seat, the young officer would wonder how it was that he had surveyed the room thrice and not taken notice of the man seated in front of him, in the corner to his left. He might have been the oldest in the room; though it was difficult to be certain, since he was clean-shaven and wore his hair stubble-short. The eyepatch covering his right eye drew attention, but was hardly unique; while his robes were remarkable only for their wear. Where the man's table was, the room was noticeably darker—almost more so than it should have been—and the man seemed *dim*, of a piece with the shadows gathered there. It was as if, the young officer thought, the darkness behind the man was casting him forward, and not the other way around. Even after he had noticed the man, he remained difficult to see, on the verge of merging with the shadows. None of the other patrons was looking at that part of the room, which the young officer at first assumed was because none of them could see the man; with further scrutiny, however, he saw from their positions relative to the corner that every last one of them was aware of the presence sitting with them. Surely, the young officer thought, this could not be a god. Whatever the man was, staring at him so directly couldn't be the wisest action, and yet the young officer seemed unable to direct his gaze elsewhere.

When he spoke, the man's voice was high, nasal; his accent not local. He said, "Come over here, boy."

It was hardly the way to address a Roman officer, and would have earned another speaker a blow to the face. The young officer opened his mouth to correct the man, but could not find the words to do so. Instead, his legs raised him from his chair and walked him to the corner. There was an empty chair across the table from the man; he nodded at it, and the young officer lowered himself onto it. Though his back was now to the rest of the room, the young officer was not concerned; what worried him was this figure whose merest words could compel his obedience. He debated attacking the man—shoving the table into him, following with a thrust of his sword—but all the man would need to do was shout, "Stop!" and he would be left at his mercy. For the moment, it was better to remain still and allow the situation to unfold. No doubt, old Lucian would have an applicable farm reference for him, something to do with letting the crops come up or watching to see what the fox does.

The man nodded at him, again. "Your emblem."

"This?" The young officer touched the small image of the bull that fastened the ends of his cloak.

"What legion?" the man asked.

"The Ninth," the young officer said. "The Hispana."

To his surprise, the man's face split in a grin. "I wondered," he said, almost to himself. "It seems every last soldier in the empire's been sent to this place." There was a jug of wine and a pair of cups on the table. The man filled one of the cups and placed it in front of the young officer. As he did, his sleeve slid up, uncovering the SPQR tattooed on his forearm. His eye met the young officer's. Its center was black—not dark brown surrounding black, but entirely black. The young officer had the impression he was peering through an opening to an immense darkness. He swallowed and said, "What are you?"

The man tugged his sleeve down. "One who has been counted amongst the ranks of the Ninth," he said. He lifted his cup. "Join me in drinking to it."

The wine was thick, almost cloyingly sweet. The young officer took a mouthful, and returned his cup to the table. "You served in the Ninth," he said.

"I did." The man refilled his own drink.

"It cannot have been that many years ago."

"Nor was it."

"You do not appear to have been too grievously-wounded."

"You mean, aside from this?" The man pointed to the eyepatch. Before the young officer could stammer a reply, he said, "You're correct: even missing an eye, I could best any man in this room."

Ignoring the taunt, the young officer licked his lips and said, "But you have refused the emperor's summons to aid in the defeat of his enemy."

"I have," the man said. "I have done Rome a mighty service, already. Indeed, it has not ended. Hadrian can spare me for this adventure."

The young officer's hand had found the hilt of his sword. "What service," he said, "is it that allows a legionnaire to speak so casually of his emperor?"

"The same," the man said, "that allows him to keep that handsome blade safely in its scabbard. And that allows him to ask you to place your hands flat on the table."

There was no change in the man's voice, yet for a second time, the young officer found himself following its instruction, as if it had only described an action he was about to perform, anyway. "That's better," the man said.

"There are half a dozen men stationed outside this place," the young officer said. "If I raise the alarm, they will answer."

"By all means," the man said. "Invite them to join us." When the young officer did not, he continued, "Never travel alone: has no one told you that?"

"In the name of your oath as a soldier," the young officer said, "I command you to release me."

He might as well not have spoken. The man said, "You came here in search of trouble, didn't you?"

Face flushed, the young officer did not reply.

"And instead," the man said, "you found me." Leaning back in his chair, he slid his right hand in amongst the folds of his robe. The young officer tensed, anticipating the appearance of a knife. He weighed calling for assistance from the other patrons, but could he reasonably expect them to help him? His hands stubbornly refused to leave their places on the table. Perhaps he could kick the man, break whatever hold he'd established over him.

Instead of a blade, however, the man withdrew a short, black horn, such as might have ornamented the skull of a not-especially-large goat. He set it on the table, and the young officer saw that it had been hollowed, carved into a horn of another sort. Its surface had been polished to a fine sheen, so that the figures incised up and down it appeared to float beneath its surface. The young officer did not recognize any of the symbols. A few suggested Greek characters, a few more Latin, but they were mixed in with other arrangements of lines and circles to form a code alien to his experience. The writing seemed to shift as he studied it: whatever his gaze fixed on held steady, but he had the overwhelming impression that the symbols at the edges of his vision were moving, turning like carvings to show themselves from a slightly different angle.

"This—" the young officer said.

"This came into my possession in Britannia," the man said. "The man who had it before me swore it was a relic of lost Atlantis, which I judged so much horseshit the first time I heard it. Later…my views on the subject became more flexible, you might say.

"Could be, there's lesson in it, for you. Listen: this is what happened:"

II

He called himself Bulinas. Said he was from some Greek island or another. Old enough for his hair and beard to be white, but young enough for his back to be straight. A philosopher, was how he was presented to me, a man of learning. The story was, he'd had trouble with Domitian, which had led to him putting a good distance between himself and Rome. That ended with the emperor's assassination. Rumor had it Bulinas had foreseen the death; though you didn't need to be much of a seer to know that it was only a matter of time before the emperor's rivals struck at him. Anyway, the man himself never made such claims. He'd found his way into Trajan's favor, which was how he'd come to us in Britannia.

That's where we were, at Eboracum, rebuilding its wooden fort in stone. Hard work, but it was a dangerous land. The Brigantes were forever on the verge of attack, and the Votadini were happy to sweep in for a quick raid if the mood took them. A couple of the older men had been with Agricola when he'd taken his trip up into Caledonia, and they told stories of the northern tribes would freeze your blood and have you shitting your pants. As they were no doubt intended to. It was no secret that Agricola's invasion hadn't defeated the Caledonians in any kind of lasting way; already, some of the forts that had been put up in the southern part of the place were being abandoned. It was our luck that the Caledonians and the Votadini, not to mention, the Brigantes, were as happy to slaughter one another as they were us. Had they been able to unite under a strong leader—well, you see how well the Judaeans have done, and they don't have a tenth the men those tribes did.

What it all means is, the prospect of a stone fort appealed to us, so we labored as fast as we could and prayed the locals would hold off attacking us for one more day. At first, when Bulinas rode in at the center of a sizable guard, we assumed he was some official or another, up from the south or maybe from further away to inspect our work. A great one for building, was Trajan, and there appeared to be no shortage of functionaries available to assess our construction's progress. Most were trying for a bribe. If they were of consequence, they received a decent meal at the general's table and a modest token of our esteem for their service to the emperor. If they were not of consequence, their hints earned them a bowl of whatever the men were eating and a blank stare.

Within a day of this man's arrival, though, my centurion had summoned me to his tent and told me to name the eight best men in the century. I did. Could each of them handle a horse? At least as well as could I, I said. That was good, the centurion said, because I was going to be riding out with them in another hour. We'd be accompanying our new visitor north, into Caledonia, with all due speed, until we'd delivered him to the fort at Loucovium. There, we were to wait with the man until he was ready to return.

It was not the first time a group of us had been assigned to guard a dignitary on his travels. But such a small group for so hazardous a destination seemed ill-advised. Loucovium was stationed by a token force; its name was at or near the top of the list of those to be left to the Caledonians. The locals had to be aware of this. There was every chance we'd find ourselves riding into an attack on the place. If not that, the area around the fort was bound to be thick with Caledonian warriors, unafraid to show themselves. I said as much—I said all of this to the centurion, who agreed that the mission was likely to be very dangerous. "Best make sure you choose a fast horse," he said.

I did—so did we all, including the man who introduced himself to me as Bulinas. His speech was plain, but not in the way of some of the visitors I'd had words with. Those men had talked to me as if I were their servant, or an idiot child. This man said what he had to say to me as if he were one man and I another. He asked me how long our journey would take. I told him the rest of today and maybe half of tomorrow. Where would we shelter for the night? That depended on where we were, I said, but I hoped he was prepared to bed down outside. He was no stranger to sleeping under the stars, Bulinas said. Was I sure that I could bear to leave the comfort of my quarters here? His question was more jest than challenge—though there was a challenge in it. It made me smile. "I expect we'll see," I said.

We rode out in the early afternoon. The best of the summer was past, but the days were still long enough for us to cover a good part of the distance to Loucovium before night. We kept a brisk pace, but not so much as to exhaust the horses. We followed the Roman roads, which were in poorer repair the further north we went. Soon, we were through the lands of the

Brigantes and into the territory of the Votadini. They were supposed to be our allies, but it was more a case of, most of the time, they didn't fight us. There were Roman forts along the road, and we might have stopped at any one of them, but our orders were to cross as much ground as we could, so we kept on until the light had left the sky, completely. We could have tried our luck at one of the Votadini towns, but none of us, including our charge, felt inclined to test our luck. We located a decent clearing to one side of the road, next to a small stream, and made camp.

That was where I had my first look at this horn, at the fireside. The nine of us had our weapons out and were tending to them. The swords and lances didn't really need the attention—had we been attacked, I would have counted on my blade to cut a man's arm from his body—but running the sharpening stone along the edge of your sword helped you to feel a little less worried about whoever might be moving in the trees beyond the firelight. We should have outrun any report of our coming—no one had passed us on the road—but who knew who was here, already? There were rumors of Caledonian warriors stationed along the main routes into their land. The Votadini might decide to take offence at our presence and deal with us. Hell, an ambitious gang of bandits might judge our number small enough to overcome. Not to mention, the things that were supposed to prowl the woods: men would could trade their shapes for those of wolves and bears; beasts that looked like dogs but laughed like men; a monster that was said to drop out of the sky and drain the blood from you before you knew it was gone. Yes, most of it was so much horseshit, but at night, surrounded by a strange forest in a dangerous place, the most outrageous tales slide that much closer to truth.

Bulinas had withdrawn a wide, flat box from one of his saddle bags. He sat with it on his lap, as if it were a small table. It was made of dark wood that smelled of spices. The lid bore a mark that I had not seen, a circle broken about two-thirds of the way around. A simple catch held the box shut. Bulinas unfastened it and raised the lid. The campfire seemed to dim. I was seated close enough to him to have a peek inside the box. It was divided into a number of compartments, no two of them, as far as I could tell, the same size. Each held a different object. I saw a thick coin whose copper had greened with age. Below it was a curved fang long as a man's finger; above it was a round stone like an eye. From the lowest slot, Bulinas lifted the horn.

He cradled it in both hands, and nodded over it three times, his lips moving silently. When he finished he turned to me, as if waiting for me to speak. I pointed to the horn, and asked him what it was.

A relic, was what he called it. He said it had come from Atlantis, from the time when its peaks still rose above the waves. In its last days, the kingdom had been besieged by a force of monsters, men with the heads of serpents. What Atlantean troops didn't run screaming at the sight of them were overwhelmed by the creatures. Soon, the serpent-men were within a day's ride of the capital. The Atlantean king wasn't much of a warrior: he was pale, sickly, in need of special medicines to give him strength. But he was a learned man, and something of a sorcerer. He spent his days and nights frantically searching through scrolls and tablets that had been old when Atlantis herself had been young. At last, in a scroll that spoke of the darker gods, the king found what he was after. He called his palace guards to his chambers, and began directing them to move all the furniture to the walls, clearing the center of the room. There, he drew symbols and secret marks on the floor. When he was finished, he ordered the guards out of his room and closed the doors behind them, forbidding them from opening the doors until he summoned them.

The guards kept watch there all night, as the serpent-men drew up to the city walls. At one point, the entire palace shook, as if struck by an earthquake; at another, a smell like charred flesh filled the air. Late the next morning, the king threw open the door to his chambers. The guards were amazed at the sight of him. He seemed to have become an old man overnight, his hair gone, his flesh loose and wrinkled. In the room with him, in the center of the figures he'd chalked on the floor, was a black goat. The king ordered the guards to kill it, which they did, straight away. Its blood was black, too. Only when the goat was lying dead did one of the men notice that its eyes were those of a man, and that its features resembled those of a human more than they did those of a goat. But the king did not give them time to study the thing. He held out his hand for the nearest guard's sword, and with more strength than any of them would have guessed, used it to cut one of the goat's horns from its head. He dropped the sword, and demanded a knife. With this, he scratched symbols onto the horn, then sliced off its tips. He let the knife fall beside the sword, and hurried to the palace's front door.

The Horn of the World's Ending

Already, the serpent-men had pierced the city's defenses and were swarming up its streets, fighting their way to the palace steps. What Atlantean soldiers were left had withdrawn to the palace, where the surviving commanders were trying to organize some form of counter-attack. The king walked down the steps and strode through the ranks of his soldiers until he was standing in front of them, in the path of the oncoming serpent-men. As the officers realized what was happening and shouted for the troops to protect the king, he brought the goat's horn to his lips and blew. "He sounded the horn," Bulinas said, "and the serpent-men were routed."

I waited for him to explain exactly how the monsters had been defeated. He didn't. So I asked him. The children of the gods, he said, had come to the king's aid. Which children? I asked. Of which gods? The offspring of the black goat, he said. Did he mean Pan? He shook his head. There were other gods besides those who called Mount Olympus their home, he said. These were darker powers, ones whose very names it was ill-advised to speak. Among these was the black goat, sire of a thousand young. Those who knew how might call on him, and if it suited the god's purpose, he would dispatch his brood to them.

It would have been outright rude to pronounce the man's story horseshit to his face, but my heart sank in my breast as I realized what the purpose of our journey was. We were going to convey him to Loucovium, where he would produce his horn, blow it a couple of times, and declare that the Caledonians had been defeated by the divine forces he'd sent to them. If we were fortunate, no actual Caledonians would put in an appearance while we were at the fort. I couldn't make up my mind whether the man sharing the warmth of the fire with me was a charlatan who'd found that horn at a market and invented a story to go along with it, or a fanatic whose belief was so thorough as to be compelling. Neither prospect was appealing; although I guessed a fraud might wish to depart the fort as soon as he could, before his deception became apparent. It was disappointing, because I had liked the man; though it was not as unsettling as the thought that the officers and officials above me—up to and including the Emperor, himself, it seemed—had been swayed by Bulinas's words. I knew that the empire under Trajan was as big as it had ever been, and that the Emperor was desirous it should remain so. The Caledonians were and had been an ongoing problem, one that taxed the empire's resources to their limit, if not beyond. To resort to what was so obviously a fairy-story to solve that problem, however, showed a kind of mania at work in my superiors that was not pleasant to contemplate.

My opinion of Bulinas and his horn changed the next morning. The attack came just before dawn, in a shower of arrows that missed the man standing watch, but killed two of the men rising from their bedding and wounded another three. There were twenty-five or thirty of them, and they had surrounded us. I woke to an arrow burying itself in the ground beside my ear. I scrambled to my feet as a second flight of arrows filled the air, and a third. Another man went down, an arrow through his throat. The numbers were too large for bandits, but whether our attackers were Votadini or Caledonians wasn't the most pressing concern. Howling at the tops of their lungs, our foes burst from the trees, our ranks sufficiently thinned for them to deem the odds in their favor, which I guess they were.

From the corner of my eye, I had marked Bulinas awakening, throwing his hands over his head as arrows shot past it. Now, as I drew my sword and prepared to meet the men charging across the clearing at me, I heard him blowing his horn. *He believes*, I thought. I supposed that was better; though it wouldn't make our attackers' blades any less sharp.

Sometimes, in the seconds when you're waiting for an enemy to close, everything seems to speed up. He's on the far side of the field, and then you're raising your shield to block his sword. Other times, the world slows down. He's running towards you, and you note the blue tattoos curled up and around his chest and arms, the bronze necklace like a collar, the notches in the sword he's carrying point up, like a torch. I watched the man nearing me stumble as his foot found a dip in the ground, then regain his stride, his face momentarily swept by embarrassment at his error. All the while, the blast of Bulinas's horn filled my ears, an ongoing scream that rose the hairs on the back of my neck.

Just as I was lowering my sword, preparing to duck the swing I could see coming and draw my sword across the man's belly, the air around me—around us—broke open. It was as if a wall none of us had known was there gave way in several places at once. Black water spilled out of the bottom of each break. It was followed by a herd of demons.

I don't know what other name to give them. Each was the size of one of our horses, covered in thick, black, shaggy hair. Great horns rose from their heads. I could call them goats, but that would be like calling a dragon a lizard. Their faces were more like those of men than those of beasts, and their mouths were full of teeth the size of spades. The sound that came from their throats was the answer to the scream of Bulinas's horn, and the smell that poured off them was of burning pitch. The mere sight of them broke the attackers' charge, and in less time than it takes me to find the words for it, the things cut through them. They trampled men under hooves like axe blades. They smashed into them with their horns. They caught them in their teeth and bit them in two. A couple of the braver ones tried to make a fight of it, and the things tore them to pieces. Even after the last attacker was dead, the things continued to savage them, stamping what remained of them into ground muddied by black water and blood. Their screaming continued, undiminished.

When the eyes of the first one locked onto me, I felt my bowels loosen; I'm not ashamed to say. Legionnaires or not, the rest of the men and I would be no more trouble to these creatures than had been our enemy. Their eyes were not those of goats; though I don't know as I'd go so far as to call them the eyes of men. They were full of something, a hateful intelligence that shone out like a lamp. I tried to shout for the others to stand fast, there was no point in running, but my tongue had gone dead in my mouth.

The note Bulinas blew on his horn didn't sound any different from the one that had summoned the things, but it had the opposite effect. Wheeling on their hind legs, they rushed to the openings that had brought them here and plunged into them. Once the last one was gone, the breaks seemed to flatten, as if becoming images of themselves. Bulinas ceased his note, and the openings fell to the ground in a rain of something like sand.

There was no point in asking him what had happened. I'd heard the story he'd told the night before. I'd been at the sites of enough battles to know that the aftermath of one is never a pretty thing. If I'd never seen men savaged like this, their bodies rent asunder, the remains shredded and flattened, floating in a muddy soup, the air heavy with a scorched reek, that was because the only battles I'd been at had been fought by men, against other men. There was nothing I could do about any of it except vomit, wipe my mouth, and look to the casualties.

Of the three who'd been struck by the enemy's arrows, two were in decent enough shape to continue the rest of the ride. The third man had been struck high in the chest, close enough to the heart to have nicked it. The blood was leaving him fast. All the rest of us could do was attend as he completed his journey out of this life. I hoped those things weren't waiting for him on the other side.

Our party, small to begin with, was down by four. A couple of the men opined that we should give the fallen what funeral rites we could, which I agreed with. As far as I was concerned, that meant laying their corpses in a row, covering their faces with their blankets, and muttering whatever prayers anyone could remember. It was not the ceremony those fellows had been asking for, but in the time it would take us to do any more, we could find ourselves under attack by the next group of warriors with an urge to test themselves against some legionnaires. Worse, Bulinas could put that black horn to his lips again, and admit the demons to our presence a second time. So I pulled what rank was mine to pull and, in short order, we had arranged our comrades' bodies with as much dignity as we could. By the time the sun had cleared the trees, the six of us were mounted and riding north, hard.

After the morning's assault, you may be sure, I saw threats everywhere, figures at the limits of my vision that I was half-convinced ducked behind the nearest tree when I looked at them straight on. At least on horseback, we would make harder targets to hit. You may be sure, too, after the rest of the morning's events, I could not stop thinking about Bulinas and his horn. Here, it seemed, was the solution to Trajan's Caledonian problem. We had been dispatched on a mission of inquiry, to learn how effective the horn and its attending monsters would be against a Caledonian force. Either someone had intelligence that an attack was being planned on Loucovium, or the men stationed there would be tasked with creating an incident that would draw one down on them. From what I had witnessed already, I did not like the Caledonians' chances. No soldier disdains the weapon that saved his life—and I had no doubt that, without the appearance of the demons, none of us would have left the clearing alive—but I was uneasy at enlisting such allies. We had enough trouble with the loyalty of the Brigantes, and they were human. How much less could we trust the creatures that scrambled up from the deepest pits of Tartarus?

The fort at Loucovium had been raised near the eastern shore of a river that flowed out of the southern end of a narrow lake. The surrounding terrain climbed into gradual hills whose crests were too far away to permit the Caledonians positioning their archers on them. Tactically-speaking, it was as sound a location for a fort as I'd seen. As we drew within view of it, I saw the tents pitched on the ground around it. At a guess, five hundred Caledonians were camped there. I pulled my horse up short, my hand on my sword, while I assessed the scene before me. At the near side of the encampment, a group of men were engaged in a game involving long sticks and a ball. Amidst the tents, other men sat talking. Alongside the road to the fort, a few sentries leaned on their spears. It did not have the look of a force ready to attack. A couple of the Caledonians caught sight of us, and pointed us out to their companions, who stared at us, then shrugged and returned to whatever they'd been doing.

Perhaps it was a ruse, an elaborate trap. But it didn't feel like that, nor did we have any option but to finish our ride. We set off at the fastest gallop our horses had left in them. The Caledonian sentries straightened. A couple of them dipped their spears towards us, but didn't follow the move with anything more hostile. The faces of the men who had beset us that morning were in my mind's eye; I wondered if any of them had been kin or comrades of the warriors to either side of us. I saw a man nock an arrow to his bow and lazily aim it in our direction, only to lower it with a laugh when one of his companions spoke to him.

At first, the officer in charge of the fort was overjoyed to greet us. It had been a while since he and the twenty-four men under him had had much in the way of visitors. Once he realized that we were not the advance for the reinforcements he'd never stopped requesting, his enthusiasm waned, but he recovered himself enough to declare his hope that Bulinas's stay would impress on him the need to strengthen the garrison. Since early spring, the Caledonians had set up camp outside the fort in a brazen display he and his handful of men could do naught to dispute. The Caledonians knew this, as they knew that, should they choose, they could take the fort in short order. For the time being, it suited their purposes to remain where they were, their mere presence a daily humiliation, but who could say how much longer that would be the case? Bulinas did nothing to correct the man's impression that he was here to take stock of the situation; nor did I or any of my men. What could we have said that wouldn't have sounded like madness?

For the next couple of days, little happened. Bulinas made a show of inspecting the fort, checking its supplies, mounting its walls to survey the enemy, listening to the commander's plans for an attack on them, but he passed much of his time in the tent that was provided for him, seated cross-legged on the ground, his eyes closed, his hands resting palms-up on his knees. Since my men and I were supposed to be his guards, we kept close to him. Whatever troops weren't on duty drifted by us to catch up on news of the wider world. All of them asked about our charge, but we said that we didn't know anything about him. It was true, or true enough. You can imagine, I was full of questions, as were the rest of my men. We passed them back and forth in low voices as we stood outside the tent. Who was this man? Was he a sorcerer? How had he come by the horn? What about the other items in his box? Could any of those work similar feats? It would have been the simplest thing to duck inside and put our questions to him. He had spoken to me, already; who could predict what else he would disclose? Yet I stayed where I was, my feet anchored by that uncertainty. That Bulinas might answer my queries was not without peril. Thus far, I had been witness to a sight that would plague my memory until my death. Who could say what other, worse things he might show me? That was the riddle that lay underneath all the others: what kind of man has the use of such a thing?

The morning of our third day at the fort was gray, full of fog and a chill rain. Bulinas stuck his head out of his tent, frowned, and returned inside. When he reappeared, he was wearing a black cloak with the hood up. I accompanied him as he climbed the fort's eastern wall, which overlooked the greater part of the Caledonian camp. They were going about their business much as they had been the day of our arrival. They did not appear to like the rain any more than we did. Bulinas studied them for a long time, enough that I thought he might be searching for something in particular, and started to trying to figure out what it could be. The fog rendered large portions of the camp difficult to distinguish. A pair of Caledonians noticed us watching them, but didn't seem to find it of much worry.

When he threw his cloak over his shoulder, I was surprised to see the black horn in Bulinas's hand. I had expected more fanfare leading up to its use against the Caledonians. At the very least, I assumed he'd have the fort's commander with him. No. He lifted the horn to his lips, inhaled deeply, and blew. For all the force he put into it, the note that emerged was no louder than the one I'd heard in the forest clearing. The horn screamed its shrill, strange sound, and everyone who heard it stopped what he was doing. Inside the fort's walls, men scrambled for their weapons, sure that the Caledonians had finally commenced their assault. Outside, on the plain, the reaction was mixed: most of the men stood around gawking at one another, unsure what the signal meant. A few went for their swords and spears, fearing, I suppose, a raid by us. By the time those on either side of the rampart had identified Bulinas as the source of the shriek that scraped their ears, the air was full of cracks from which black water sprayed as if from a breaking dam. The cracks burst, and the demons leapt from them in a hairy mass.

There was an instant, as I was watching the faces of the Caledonians below me, rent by puzzlement and fear, when the grimmest sort of satisfaction suffused me. *Here you go, you murderous bastards*, I thought. *Here's an enemy'll grind you and your irritant kingdom to dirt, to nothing. Let's see what your tattoos and your blue paint do against these things.* As the demons smashed into the nearest Caledonians, I grinned. One of the things tore through a Caledonian shield and the arm behind it. The fog kept me from seeing too far into the Caledonian camp, but I had little trouble picturing what was happening there. These things, the black goat's children, were slaughtering any and all they found.

Because of my closeness to Bulinas's horn, whose shriek went on, I didn't hear the screams coming from within the fort, at first, and once I did, took a moment to place them. I turned, and saw one of the splits in the air hanging in the center of the fort, black water pooling the ground, a trio of the demons killing the men who could not fight them off. Half of the fort's residents lay dead and dismembered, including all but one of the men who'd survived the journey here with me. While I watched, two of the demons caught a man between them and ripped him apart.

My sword was in my hand, and I would have gone to my death had I not remembered the second blast Bulinas had blown three days ago, the one that had sent the monsters away. Stepping closer, I bellowed at him to stop. He had done enough; the enemy was defeated. It was time for him to return these beasts to hell.

Instead of ceasing his blast, however, the man prolonged it. Now the earth began to shake, all at once and violently. On either side of the fortress wall, cracks raced across the ground, black water leaping from them in geysers. The rifts opened, and more of the goat-demons clambered up out of them, joining their brethren in the mayhem. A crack split the wall behind me, releasing further demons before that section of the rampart collapsed. The cries of the things had drowned out the sound of Bulinas's horn; though I could see him continuing to blow it. The shaking of the earth grew stronger, almost knocking me from my feet. Except for us, there was no one alive inside the fort; nor did I see any men living where the Caledonians had been. There were only the demons, galloping through the muddy remains of both forces, their eyes alight with malicious joy, the smell of their smoldering hair floating on the air. And still Bulinas sounded his horn, as the earth gave way in longer and deeper vents, releasing more black water and more demons.

I didn't know what the man intended. A demonstration of sufficient devastation to leave no doubt of his weapon's power? Or something else, something grander, madder? There was no way to ask him: he couldn't have heard me if I'd been yelling in his ear. I steadied myself, raised my sword, and cut his right arm from him. Still grasping the horn, it dropped between us. His eyes wide, Bulinas turned towards me, unbalanced by the loss of his arm. Blood sprayed from the stump. His mouth was open, his lips working to form some word, curse or question, but I did not learn what it was. In two bounds, one of the largest of the demons sprang up the wall, caught Bulinas in its teeth, and leapt off into the fog with him.

It was followed by another, equally big, which landed on the spot where Bulinas had been standing. It stared at me, at my sword dripping blood, and I stared at it, at its mouth smeared with gore. There was more of man than goat in its enormous features, and I saw in them great age, age to compete with that of the mountains, of the sea. Its yellow eyes had watched the waters swallow Atlantis, and even then, had been old. This thing had seen Jupiter overthrow Saturn; it had witnessed Saturn casting down Uranus. My fingers loosened and my sword slipped from my hand. My knees bent, and I fell prostrate before the beast. It snorted.

When I rose, it was with Bulinas's horn in my grasp. The demon's face showed what I am sure was surprise. The note I sounded was a poor copy of Bulinas's, but it served the purpose. The demon resisted it, striving to maintain the freedom it must have thought at hand; it snapped its teeth and pawed the dirt, smoke streaming from its black coat. Whatever spell or compact bound it was too strong, and it hurled itself from the top of the wall through one of the cracks in the air.

III

The man leaned back in his chair. The shadows around him shifted, as if someone had moved a lamp from one side of the room to the other. "Of all the men," he said, "who saw the day break in that place, I was the only one left alive. Already, the remnants of the Caledonians and their camp had slid into the crevasses that had split the earth and were drawing closed, leaving a muddy expanse. The wreckage inside the fort suffered the same fate. I could not stay where I was, so I picked up my sword, tucked the horn in my belt, and made my way down from the wall. I knew I was headed south, but I was not certain of my destination. Why not Eboracum, or one of the closer Roman forts? The thought occurred to me while I was not yet out of sight of Loucovium. It was no great honor to have led a group of men, including an important visitor, to their deaths, but under other circumstances—had that first ambush been more successful—I could have shouldered the responsibility. The horn, though, changed everything. I'm a lousy liar, always have been. Whatever story I attempted about the fates of Bulinas and my men—not to mention, everyone else who'd been at Loucovium—I would not be able to conceal my possession of the horn. In short order, I would be commanded to surrender it, or have it taken from me, and then it would be used again. Perhaps the one to do so would exert more control over it than had Bulinas—or perhaps not.

"Such a wager was too big for me to take. I could try to lose the thing, bury it somewhere, toss it into the sea, but could I be certain it would not be unearthed, washed up on a beach? I couldn't. No matter which way I turned the situation, I could see no solution for it but for me to keep and guard the horn as best I could for as long as I could. I left my armor by the side of the road; though I kept my sword, wrapped in my cloak. My clothes were a mess, and my travel made them worse. I moved south, avoiding the Roman forts along the way, stealing food when I could, buying it with what little coin I had when I couldn't. Though I felt a pain at doing so, I skirted Eboracum. At Londinium, I bluffed my way onto a merchant ship that took me across the Oceanus Britannicus to Gesoriacum. From there, I wandered the empire, keeping to its margins. I hoped I might locate someone to relieve me of my responsibility, but that has not come to pass. I've learned much. I now know that Bulinas kept the horn in his box to shield himself from its effects. Having it next to me for so long has left me…changed from what I was."

The man stood, picking up the horn and returning it to the interior of his robes. "You remind me of men I served with," he said, not unkindly. "If I thought you would take heed of my words, I would caution you against taking part in tomorrow's activities. Since my warning would fall on deaf ears, I'll offer another in its stead: when you see your death approaching, meet it well." The man turned and walked towards the corner behind him. The shadows seemed to surge forward to embrace him. The young officer had the impression of the man entering a long, dark corridor, then it and he were gone.

The young officer glanced around the room, but if any of the other patrons had witnessed the man stepping into the shadows, none offered a sign of it. Nor did any challenge him as he departed the inn. The expression on his face kept his superior officer from asking him where he'd been for so long, and alone, too. It may have been what determined that man to assign the young officer command of a small detachment of soldiers the next day. This group was one of several sent out and tasked with the destruction of local villages. If the young officer recalled the advice he'd received the previous day, he had little trouble discounting it. This was the same duty he'd been performing since his arrival, and if there was one thing it was not, it was dangerous.

When the Judaean ambush erupted from the huts and hovels to either side of him and his men, there was no time for anything except the arrow that had struck his horse's eye and dropped it to the street. He managed to roll free, and to come up with his sword drawn, but there were Judaean warriors everywhere. His men were swiftly and mercilessly overborne. It was all so fast: he swung his blade at a man who parried the blow and returned it, opening himself to a cut to the neck. Like a kick from a horse, an arrow hit the young officer high in the left leg. He staggered forward, and a Judaean fighter lunged at him. His armor deflected the thrust into the meat of his right bicep. He cried out, and released his sword.

THE HORN OF THE WORLD'S ENDING

It was over. His men were dead or lying wounded, waiting for their attackers to finish them. From behind, hands grabbed his shoulder and pushed him towards a man who was drawing a long knife from his belt. The Judaean captain was standing in front of a dim doorway in whose shadows the young officer caught a glimpse of the face of the man with the black horn. As best he was able, he straightened. After the story the man had told, the young officer supposed it was futile to hope that he would intervene, raise the horn to his lips and bring destruction to the Judaeans. At least he was present; if not a god, then not a man, either. Was it sufficient consolation? The Judaean captain pushed the young officer's forehead back and pressed the knife to his throat. He wasn't sure, but he doubted it.

THE UNDERGROUND
ECONOMY

That's not what I want to talk about. If you're interested in hearing about the day to day of a stripper, there are plenty of books you can read. Some of them are pretty good. Or you could watch *Showgirls*. Not, it's not accurate, but it's the kind of movie most of the girls I danced with would have made about themselves. So there's that.

It's a person—Nicole AuCoeur, the girl who told me I should try out at The Cusp, they were hiring and I could make some serious cash. I want to talk about her, about this thing that happened to her.

We weren't friends. We'd been in a couple of classes together at SUNY Huguenot. Both of us wanted to be writers. Nikki said she was going to be a travel writer. I was planning on writing screenplays. We took the same fiction-writing workshops, and were in the same peer-critique group. I read two or three of her stories. They were pretty good. The teacher was into fantasy, *The Lord of the Rings*, *Game of Thrones*, so Nikki turned in that kind of story. She was that type of student. Figure out what the professor likes and play to it.

I didn't know she was working at The Cusp. She was always late for class, and she always showed up stoned. She drenched herself in some kind of

257

ginger-citrus perfume, to hide the smell, but it clung to her hair. She had long, brown hair that she wore in long bangs, like drapes. If anything, I thought she was some kind of dealer. I remember this one time, in the middle of class, she opened her purse and started to root through it—I mean, frantically, taking stuff out of it and piling it on her desk. The professor asked her if everything was okay. She said, "No, I can't find my stash." The guy didn't know how to respond to that. The rest of us tittered.

Anyway. I ran into her the summer after that class. I was sitting in Dunkin Donuts, making lunch out of a small coffee and a Boston cream donut. Nikki sat down across from me. I hadn't realized she was still in town. I assumed she'd gone home for the summer. She said she'd stayed in Huguenot to work. I asked her what she was doing. She said dancing at The Cusp.

I blushed. Everyone knew about the club. It was on 299, on the way into town, a flat-roofed cinderblock building. We used to call it The Cusp juice bar, because they couldn't serve alcohol there, on account of the girls dancing fully nude. I hadn't known anyone who worked there—well, not that I was aware of—but I knew people who'd known people. Although what I'd heard from them had concerned the professors who were regulars at the place. There was a story about this one old guy who'd paid for a girl to come to his place and pee on him, so I guess I had an idea of the place as one step up from a brothel.

Nikki ignored my blush. She said the money was fantastic, and the club was hiring. If I was interested, there were auditions the following Wednesday. We made conversation for a couple of minutes, then she left.

To make a short story shorter, I tried out, was offered the job, and took it. Money—yeah, the money was better than I could make anyplace else in town without a college degree, and in a lot of cases with one. I had been working part-time as a cashier at Shop Rite, but I couldn't get enough hours to cover the rent, my car—which was a piece of shit that spent as much time at the mechanic's as it did on the road—and groceries. Not to mention utilities. And going out. My dad had wanted me to come home for the summer, and when I didn't, he got pissed and said if I wanted to stay in Huguenot so bad, I could find a way to pay for it.

So I did. I had to shave my crotch, which was no fun, and keep it shaved, to give the customers a clear view of what I was waving in their faces. The dancing wasn't, not really. It was wriggling around on stage, teasing I was going to undo my top, wriggling some more, removing my top with one hand but keeping my boobs covered with the other, wriggling some more, etcetera, until I was down to my shoes. Oh, and the garter the guys stuffed their dollar bills into. The air stunk of cigarette smoke, mostly from the dancers. All the same, I smiled at everyone. Not because I was enjoying myself, but because it made me more money if the customers thought I was enjoying myself. It intimidated some of them, too, which did please me. I wasn't especially nervous working at The Cusp. Probably, I should have been. But I was sure I could handle any creeps who tried anything with me. My dad had been a marine, and a martial arts nut, and I had grown up knowing how to punch an attacker in the throat, tear off his ears, and gouge out his eyes. Plus, there were always at least two bouncers in close proximity, in case things in the private rooms got seriously out of hand.

That was where the real money was. Private dances. Lap dances, mostly, which were forty dollars for five minutes plus whatever you could convince the guy to tip you. Some girls could keep a customer in there for two or three dances in a row. I didn't, not usually. There was also a room at the back of the club, the Champagne Parlor. Two-fifty for half an hour with the girl of your choice. And a complimentary bottle of non-alcoholic champagne. That was mainly for the guys whose buddies had brought them to The Cusp for their bachelor parties.

Nikki was the queen of the private dances. She had this routine. The DJ would announce her as, "Isis," which was the stage name she used. (Mine was Eve. I know: subtle, right?) She would walk out onto the stage in a long, transparent gown that trailed along the floor behind her. She danced to Led Zeppelin, "The Battle of Evermore." I think she'd studied ballet at some point. There were a lot of ballet moves in her routine. She stood on one leg and held the other leg out in front of her, or behind her, or to the side. She skipped across the stage on the tips of her toes. She half-crouched, leapt, and came down in another half-crouch. She twirled, sometimes on her toes, her arms stretched above, sometimes with one leg bent behind, her head thrown back, her arms curved in front. The gown floated after, whipped around her. She let it drift away. Underneath, she was wrapped in scarves, each of which she undid and sent fluttering to the floor. Throughout, she went from customer to customer, bending towards them, giving them a closer look at what lay beneath the remaining scarves.

259

By the end of the song, all she had left on was a pair of fairy wings. I guess that's what you'd call them. They were like something from a Halloween costume, one for adults. Sexy Tinkerbell or whatever. A pair of clear straps looped them around her shoulders. They weren't that big, and they were made of thick plastic. When the lights played over them, they filled with a rainbow of colors that slid about inside them like oil. Something to do with the plastic. They weren't butterfly wings, which is what most fairy costumes come with. They were long, narrow, shaped like blades. Hornet wings, or an insect from that branch of the family. If I thought about them that way, they almost freaked me out. Nikki danced stoned—she did everything stoned, from what I could tell—and the glaze the pot gave her eyes made them resemble the hard eyes of an insect. Together with the wings, they lent her the appearance of an extra from a grade-z sci-fi flick, *Attack of the Wasp Women* or something.

None of the customers noticed this. Or, if any of them did, he had a kink I don't want to think about. Nikki never danced more than one song. As Zeppelin faded away, she was off the dance floor, followed by one and sometimes two guys. Most of them went for lap dances, which took place in one of a row of booths set up opposite the club's bar. Yeah, the juice bar. The booths were basically large closets with small couches in them. The customer reclined on the couch, and the dancer did her thing. Each booth had a camera mounted high in one of its corners. For the safety of the dancers, supposedly, and to ensure no one went from lap dance to out-and-out hooking. Part of the bouncers' jobs was to keep an eye on the video feed; although I never saw any of them cast more than a glance in the monitors' direction. I don't think Nikki ever unzipped anyone's jeans, but there's a lot you can do before you reach that point. To be sure, as far as tips went, none of the rest of us could keep up with her.

Not that she was stingy with her money. If it was a night the club closed early, a bunch of us would head into one of the bars in town, and Nikki would cover our drinks. If we were working a late night, once the last customer was out and the front door locked, she'd produce a bottle of Stoli for us to mix with the juice bar's juices. Those times—sitting around the club, shooting the shit—were better than being at an actual bar, more relaxed. Most of us changed into our regular clothes, jeans, t-shirts, wiped the makeup off our faces. Not Nikki. She stayed naked as long as she could.

Except for her wings. She wandered around the club, a drink in her hand, the wings bouncing up and down with each step, clicking together. She would lean against the bar, where I was sitting with a cup of coffee because I had an eight a.m. class I'd decided to stay awake for. We didn't say a lot to one another. Mostly, we traded complaints about the amount of reading we had to do for school. But having her beside me gave me an opportunity to study the tattoo that decorated her back, so I did what I could to keep to keep the conversation going, such as it was.

That tattoo. All of the girls had ink. In most cases, it was in a couple of places, the lower back and the shoulder, say. That's where mine were. I had a pair of coiling snakes on my back, and the Chinese character for "air" on my right arm. There's a story behind each of them, but they're not part of this story. One girl, Sheri, had ink on most of her body, brightly-colored figures that were enacting an enormous drama on her skin. Nikki had a single tattoo, a square panel that covered most of her back. It was difficult to see clearly, warped by the plastic wings lying over it. The artist had executed the image in black and dark blue, with here and there highlights of pale yellow and orange. There was a car in the middle of it, an older model with a narrow grill like the cowcatcher on a train. The headlights perched high on either side of the grill. The car stretched along a foreshortened road, its rear wheels and end dropping behind the horizon. I wasn't sure if the distortion was supposed to represent speed, or just an extra-long car. To the right of the car, a cluster of tall figures filled the scene. There were five or six of them. They were dressed in black suits, and black fedoras. Their faces were the same pale oval, eyes and mouths empty circles. To the left of the car, a steep hill led to a slender house whose wall was set with a half-dozen mismatched windows. Within each frame, there seemed to be a tiny figure, but I couldn't make out what any of them were. A rim of orange moon hung over the scene in a sickly smile. The picture had been done in a style that reminded me of something from *Mad* magazine, exaggerated in a way that was more sinister than comic. It fascinated me. I asked Nikki what it was supposed to be. She said, "Oh, you know, just a picture." Which could have been true, for all I knew. At the same time, that was a lot of investment in a random image.

The customers didn't mind it. Not that I heard, anyway. Most of them were too timid to say anything. They acted as if they were cool, confident, but it was obvious they weren't. It was as if they were tuning forks, and our bare skin was what they'd struck themselves on. They vibrated, made the air surrounding them quiver. There were exceptions, sure. One guy who was a long-haul trucker. Not too big. Kept his hair short, his beard long. Had on a red flannel shirt every time he entered the club, which was about once a month. He was quiet, polite, said, "Yes ma'am," "No ma'am." But there was a stillness to him. It was what you'd expect from a wolf, or one of the big cats, a tiger. The utter focus of a predator. That I know, he hadn't tried anything with any of the girls before I started at The Cusp. He behaved himself while I was there, too. If I'd heard he owned a cabin in the woods, though, whose walls were papered in human skin, I would not have doubted it. I gave him a lap dance, once, and spent the five minutes planning the elbow I'd throw at his temple or throat when he grabbed me. He didn't, and he tipped pretty well. That said, I wouldn't have done it a second time.

The other exception was a group of guys who squeezed into the club one Thursday night. There were five of them, plus a man who said he was their driver. The bouncer who was working the front door said he saw them pull up in a white van. The five guys were huge, the biggest men I'd ever seen in person. I'm going to say seven feet tall, each, three feet and change wide. Three fifty, four hundred pounds. All dressed in the same khaki safari shirts, khaki shorts, and sandals. They had the same style, crewcuts that squared the tops of the heads. Their faces were blank, unresponsive. They stared straight ahead, and didn't so much as glance at any of the girls. In the club's mix of white and blue lighting, their skin looked dull, gray. They could have been in their early twenties. They could have been twice that. They stood beyond the front door in a group and did not move. They reminded me of the stone heads on Easter Island. They weren't still—they were inert.

Not their driver, though. He was smaller—average-sized, really. It was standing in front of his passengers that made him appear diminutive. He was wearing a beige, zip-up jacket over a white dress shirt with a huge collar and brown bell-bottom slacks. His hair was black, freshly-cut and -gelled, but his skin had the yellow tinge of someone with jaundice. He was younger pretending to be older. I figured he was in charge of the five guys. Actually, what I thought was, the five passengers were residents of one of the local group homes, and the driver had decided to treat them to a night out. I know how it sounds, but things like it happened often enough for it not to seem strange, anymore.

The driver didn't waste any time. He spoke to the front door guy, who pointed him to the bartender. She leaned across the bar to hear what he had to say, then motioned to one of the girls who was killing time with a cranberry spritzer to fetch someone from the dressing room. I read her lips: Isis. Nikki. The driver nodded at the bartender, and passed her a folded bill. I'm pretty sure it was a hundred.

Nikki emerged from the dressing room wearing her assortment of scarves, but without the long gown. She looked across the club to where the driver was standing with his hands in his trouser pockets. Her head jerked, as if she recognized him. When she walked up to him, she kept her expression neutral, which only seemed to confirm that she knew the driver. He tilted forward to speak into her ear. Whatever he had to say didn't take long, but she took a while to respond to it. She stared at the driver, as if trying to bring him into focus, then nodded and said, "Sure."

Apparently, what the driver wanted was a lap dance for each of his five passengers, all of them provided by Nikki. He gestured for the nearest of the huge guys to come forward. Nikki took hold of one enormous hand and led the guy to the middle lap dance booth. He had to stoop to enter it; I wondered if he'd fit inside. He did. His four buddies didn't register his departure in the slightest. The driver stationed himself midway between the rest of his passengers and the booth. He gazed into space, and waited.

I didn't see Nikki emerge from the booth with the first giant in tow, because I'd been called to the dance floor. It took me two songs into my three-song routine to sell a customer a private dance. He was a college student. I almost thought I recognized him from one of the big lecture classes. He was free with his money, and it wasn't difficult to keep him in the booth for two dances. We were to the right of Nikki and whichever of the enormous guys she had with her. The walls of the booths weren't thick. All kinds of sounds leaked through from the adjoining spaces. That center booth, though, was silent. I noticed this, but I don't know if it seemed strange to me or not. I'm not sure. I was busy with the college student. I want to say that there was something off about that lack of sound. It was as if it was a gap in sound, a blank spot in the middle of a song, rather than the end of it.

Nikki and I finished our dances at the same time. I didn't notice anything wrong with her, then, standing naked outside the booths. She was flushed, but she'd been working hard for almost thirty straight minutes. She was sweaty, too, which was odd. The club was air-conditioned, in order to keep the dancers' sweat to a minimum. I wondered if the driver was going to ask for his turn, next. He didn't. He passed Nikki the biggest roll of bills I had and have ever seen, collected his giant cargo, and exited The Cusp without another word. Nikki gathered her scarves from inside the booth and retreated to the dressing room.

She didn't stay there long. She dropped the scarves on the floor, stuffed the roll of money into her purse, and returned to the club. The first customer she approached was a middle-aged guy wearing gray slacks and a white button-down shirt. He was sitting back from the stage, so he could watch the show and not have to pay out too much cash. Nikki straddled him in his chair and ground her pelvis against him. Whatever prudence he'd imagined he possessed flew out the window. He trailed behind her to the lap dance booths.

A minute later, he was screaming. The booth's door flew open, and Nikki stumbled out of it. There was blood all over her legs, her ass. She stopped, found her balance, and walked toward the dressing room. As she did, her customer emerged, still screaming. The front of his slacks was dark with blood. Of course I assumed he'd done something to her. His face, though. He was wide-eyed, horrified. One of the bouncers was already next to him. I went to check on Nikki.

She was bent over one of the makeup tables, attempting to roll a joint. The backs of her legs, the cheeks of her ass, were scarlet. Closer to her, I saw that her skin had been scraped raw. It reminded me of when I'd been a kid and wiped out on my bike, dragging my palms or shins across the blacktop. The air smelled coppery. Blood ran down Nikki's legs and pooled on the floor. Blood flecked the bottoms of the plastic wings, the tattoo. She wasn't having any luck with the joint. Her hands wouldn't do what she wanted them to. I pushed in beside her, and rolled the spliff as best I could. I passed it to her with fingers that weren't trembling too much, then held her lighter for her.

I didn't know what to say. Everything that came to mind sounded inane, ridiculous. Are you hurt? Her legs and ass looked like hamburger. Do you need a doctor? Obviously. What happened to you? Something bad. Who were those guys? See the answer to the previous question. I couldn't look away from the ruin of her flesh. When I'd started working at The Cusp, I'd thought that I was entering the world as it really was, a place of lust and money. Now I saw that there was a world underneath that one, a realm of blood and pain. For all I knew, there was somewhere below that, a space whose principles I didn't want to imagine. I mumbled something about taking her to a doctor. Nikki ignored me.

By the time one of the bouncers and the bartender came to check on her, Nikki had located her long gown and tugged it on. She checked her pocketbook to be sure the roll of cash was there, took it in the hand that wasn't holding the joint, and crossed to the fire exit at the opposite end of the dressing room. Without breaking stride, she shoved it open, triggering the fire alarm. She turned left towards the parking lot as the door clunked shut behind her.

The bouncer, the bartender, and I traded looks that asked which of us was going to pursue her. I did. I hurried along the outside of the club and across the parking lot to where Nikki parked her Accord. The car was gone. I ran back towards the building, which everyone was pouring out of. I could hear a distant siren. Most of the customers were scrambling for their cars, hoping to escape the parking lot before the fire engines arrived and boxed them in. I considered making a dash inside for my keys, and was brought up short by the realization that I didn't know where Nikki lived. I had an approximate idea—the apartments down by the Svartkill—but nothing more. I could drive around the parking lots, but what if she'd gone to the emergency room, or one of the walk-in care facilities? I didn't even have her cell number, another fact which suddenly struck me as bizarre. Why couldn't I get in touch with her? Why didn't I know her address? The strangest sensation swept over me there in the parking lot, as if Nikki, and everything connected to her, had been unreal. That couldn't have been the case, though, could it? Or how would I have found out about the job at The Cusp?

I didn't see Nikki for the rest of the time I worked at the club. I stayed through the end of the fall semester, when I graduated early and moved, first back in with my dad, then down to Florida. The five enormous guys, their jaundiced driver, didn't return during those months. The customer whose pants had been soaked with Nikki's blood did. Less than a week later, he appeared at the front door, insisting he had to talk to her. His face was red, sweaty, his eyes glazed. He looked as if he had the flu. The bouncer at the door told him that the girl he was looking for no longer danced here, and no, he didn't know where she'd gone. The guy became agitated, said he had to see her, it was important she know about the cards, the hearts. The bouncer placed his hands gently but firmly on the guy's chest and told him the girl wasn't here and he needed to leave. The guy broke the bouncer's nose, his right cheek, and three of his ribs. It took the other two bouncers on duty to subdue him, and they barely managed to do that. The cop who answered the bartender's 911 call took one look at the guy and requested backup. The cop said they would transport the guy across the Hudson, to Penrose Hospital, where there was a secure psych ward. As far as I know, that's what happened. I don't know what became of Nikki's last customer, only that I didn't see him again.

Years went by. I left Florida for Wyoming, big sky and a job managing a bank. I bought a house, a nice car. The district manager was pleased with my performance, and recommended me for a corporate event in Idaho. I took 80 west to Utah, where I picked up 84 and headed north and west into Idaho. Somewhere on the other side of Rock Springs, a white van roared up behind me and barely avoided crashing into the back of my rental. I swore, steered right. The van swung wide to the left, so sharply it rose up on its right wheels. I thought it was going to tip over, roll onto the median. It didn't. It swerved towards me. I should have braked. Instead, I stomped the gas. The rental surged past the van. As it did, I glanced at the vehicle's passengers. Its rear and middle seats were filled by a group of enormous men whose crewcut heads did not turn from the road ahead. In the front seat, a driver with black hair and yellowed skin laughed uproariously along with a woman with long brown hair. Nikki. Together, she and the driver laughed and laughed, as if caught by an emotion too powerful to resist. He wiped tears from his eyes. She pounded on the dashboard.

I pulled onto the shoulder and threw the car into park. My pulse was hammering in my throat. I watched the van speed west down the highway until it was out of sight. I waited another half hour before I shifted into drive and resumed my journey. The remainder of the drive to Idaho, and all of the way home, I didn't see the van. But I was watching for it.

I still am.

THE COMMUNION OF SAINTS

1. *Cannibale* (Lecter)

To start with, Calasso lets Alter handle the questioning. His partner begins where Calasso supposes he would, too: "So Anthony Hopkins—sorry, *Sir* Anthony Hopkins took your son." He succeeds in making the statement sound more reasonable than Calasso thinks he could.

The woman seated across the table from them is enormous, obesity and diabetes egging one another on. Mrs. Madeleine Connolly wheezed all the way into the room, and after she lowered herself into her chair, needed a full five minutes to catch her breath. Her style of dress is what Calasso thinks of as lower-class-defiant. From a t-shirt that would do most women he knows as a dress, Elvis Presley delivers a heavy-lidded black and white sneer. Pink and yellow floral-print leggings hug thick legs that descend into short black boots with chunky heels. She accessorizes with dangling black and white earrings that remind Calasso of miniature chandeliers, and a tiny hot pink purse that looks barely big enough to contain a cell phone. Yet her short, grey hair has been cut in a contemporary fashion, and her face has been made up in an understated way that accentuates its underlying kindliness. It's difficult to imagine her being responsible for anything happening to her eighteen-year-old son, any kind of violence—but people will surprise you. She furrows her brow at Alter's words and says, "Not him—the one he

267

played. In the movies. The doctor, you know, the cannibal."

"Hannibal Lecter?"

"That's right," she nods. "He's the one who took my boy."

"But he's a character in a film. If you saw him, you would've been seeing the actor who played him."

"Or someone who strongly resembles him," Calasso adds.

"Uh-uh. It was him, the cannibal doctor. He was dressed the same as in that movie with the lambs, one of those orange prison jumpsuits."

"All right," Alter says. He consults his notepad. "You said the, uh, doctor was living in the apartment across from the one you and your son share."

"Had to be," Madeleine Connolly says. "I thought the place was empty. Had been for six months, since Mrs. Lindstrom died in it. She was a sweet lady. Died in her sleep. None of us knew about it for days, until she started to smell. Super hasn't been able to get the stink out of it. Too cheap to pay for a professional cleaning. No one who's come to look at the apartment has come back."

"When did you notice Dr. Lecter living there?"

"I didn't. I didn't think Richard did, either, but could be, I was wrong. He's a deep one, my Richard. Could be, he saw that horrible man opening the door to that place and didn't want to worry me. He's always looking out for me. It makes sense, though. I mean, it's the perfect place for a man like that to live, isn't it? A place that smells like death."

Calasso considers disagreeing. The way the character's portrayed on screen, at least, he seems more of an aesthete. But that's hardly relevant to the matter at hand, so he keeps his peace.

Alter says, "Can you think of any reason why the doctor would have wanted to abduct your son? Did they spend any time together? Did they disagree or argue about anything? Had Richard borrowed any money from him? Had he borrowed any money from Richard?"

The woman shakes her head. "Richard didn't have anything to do with that man. Why would he? He'd seen his movies. He knew what he'd be dealing with."

"Okay," Alter says. "And you're certain Dr. Lecter didn't say anything when he took your son?"

"Not a word. It's like I told the other officers. Richard and I were watching TV. *Wheel of Fortune*. I heard the front door open, which was strange, because I always keep it locked, bolted, with the chain on. I said to Richard, 'Did you forget to lock the door when you came in?' No, he said, he hadn't. Then *he* came racing into the living room. He had on that orange jumpsuit, and his hair was all slicked back against his head, and his mouth was open and awful. He ran right in front of me, over to where Richard was on the couch. He grabbed Richard's hair, and hauled him onto the floor. 'Hey!' I said, 'You leave him alone!' I was so shocked. I fumbled with the remote, tried to turn the TV off. But I hit the wrong button, and put the sound way up. All I could hear was a commercial for Burger King. Richard struggled, grabbed at the man's hand, but I don't think the doctor even noticed. He dragged Richard down the hall, out the front door, and over to that apartment I'd thought was empty. I don't move too fast, on account of my size, but I was up from my chair and at that door in time to hear it being locked. I pounded on it, and shouted for the man to open it, but the only thing happened was, my neighbors stuck their heads out of their doors and yelled at me to be quiet. Can you believe that? I thought neighbors were supposed to look out for one another."

For the remainder of the interview, Calasso half-listens. Madeleine Connolly's story has remained consistent since the first uniformed officers responded to her call. As has her insistence that her son was a good boy, not mixed up in any trouble, working part time at Home Depot and taking classes over at HVCC. It's the stereotypical parent's response to questions about their child's extra-curricular activities. No matter that, in Calasso's experience, the vast majority of serious crimes are committed by criminals upon other criminals, mom and dad maintain their denials. He doesn't hold her belief in her son's innocence against Mrs. Connolly. Were he to be placed in the same position, he knows he would utter similar protestations on behalf of his children. At the same time, it slows the investigation into Richard Connolly's apparent abduction. He and Alter will have to track down and speak to the missing boy's friends and co-workers, which adds time to the investigation that he's afraid young Richard does not have. When the uniforms arrived, located the super, and convinced him to open the door through which the boy had been taken, they were met by empty rooms. Aside from dust and mouse droppings, the apartment's only content was in the center of the kitchen floor, an antique china plate on which sat a slice of liver, bloody and warm. While the lab results have yet to return,

Calasso has a sinking feeling the organ will prove human, and specifically, Richard's. Thus far, he's succeeded in keeping the most sensational details of the boy's abduction from the local media, but it's still early days, and so only a matter of time before reports of the cannibal kidnapper fill the news.

"Anything you'd like to add, Tom?" Alter's question returns his attention to the interview.

He's about to say, "No," and thank Madeleine Connolly for coming in, tell her they'll be in touch, offer a word of reassurance. Instead, he says, "Just one thing. Those movies—the ones with Hannibal Lecter—what do you think they are?" He isn't sure what he's asking.

The woman doesn't hesitate. "Why," she says, "they're documentaries, aren't they?"

2. Calasso: *Per Una Selva Oscura*

Detective Thomas Calasso of the Albany, NY, Police Department is not a happy man. If, aided by a bottle of decent single malt, you were to ask him the reason for his unhappiness, he would tick off the causes on his fingers. His cholesterol continues to be high, which means he is going to have to return to taking the medicine he insists makes him tired, although his doctor swears that this is not one of its side-effects. Despite several years of daily exercise, he has been unable to shrink the belly that pushes down the front of his pants. His sex life has dwindled to practically a seasonal event, as his wife, Theresa, has been harrowed by a menopause that has lasted the better part of two years and has withered her desire. Even when she has been receptive to his advances, as often as not, he has been unable to perform the act to its conclusion.

Nor are his complaints limited to the physical. His career, whose early, upward trajectory was so steep as to be almost vertical, leveled off a decade ago, and has maintained a pretty much constant altitude since. More men and women have clambered around him on their way up the departmental ladder than he cares to remember, many of them pausing to take what instruction they could from him, then continuing without a backward glance. He's contemplated retirement—after twenty-seven years, he's served well past the minimum requirement—but last week's mail brought a letter accepting his youngest to Bard, her top choice, while his oldest is contemplating returning to college to earn her degree as a paralegal, and his wife is insisting that the bathroom needs to be not just painted, but completely gutted and redone—in short, there are plenty of bills headed his way in the short term, the long term, and no doubt the longer term. If he could figure out a path from police work to another, more lucrative career, he would likely take it; a few former colleagues are driving Mercedes and living in Loudonville. But he cannot map a route that will lead him to a five-bedroom, two-and-a-half bath McMansion with a German car in its long driveway and a hot tub on its bluestone patio.

Those who have known him the longest—his younger brother, Mark, a cardiologist who practices in Boston, his cousin, Felicity, an entertainment reporter for *People* magazine—would say that he has inherited the dour fatalism of their Sicilian grandmother, for whom every happy occasion was a promise of imminent calamity, and every calamity a herald of further disaster. Theresa is convinced that he is clinically depressed, and has been urging him to speak with his primary care physician about a prescription for something that would help to lighten his mood. If ever it amused her, his answer that this is what the liquor cabinet is for has ceased to do so for some time. And if he were being honest, with Theresa or with anyone else who cared to ask and had poured him two fingers of Talisker, neat, he would admit that the booze doesn't help whatever is wrong with him, anymore. There is still the loosening in his chest once the whisky warms his stomach, the psychic equivalent of tugging down the knot in his tie, opening the top two buttons of his shirt, but it is as if, underneath his white dress shirt, he is wearing another garment, a vest woven from thick, coarse hair, a relic of his Nonna's austere Catholicism. Here he is, midway through his life's journey (and that's speaking optimistically: his father died at fifty-eight, eleven years beyond his current age, while his father's father lived only ten years after that), and he cannot shake the dread, the outright conviction, that his adult life has been nothing. The feeling is more than the typical policeman's cynicism, the awareness that basically everyone is an incipient criminal, that whatever victories he has won have been local and temporary. No, what plagues him is the sense that his part in everything in which he has been involved, from his marriage, to his children, to his job, might have been played by anyone with as much if not more success. He is a blank, a space around which his life has happened. It's no wonder, he thinks, that he has wound up working missing persons, because that's what he himself is.

Midlife crisis is the diagnosis of the therapist he's consulted on the sly, a pair of words so generic as to be meaningless. (Strangely, it put him in mind of the tumult of his adolescence, which his favorite aunt used to assure him was normal, symptom of a phase he was going through; his mother offered almost identical counsel when he and Theresa hit a rocky patch when the girls were young and seemed to monopolize her time. It's as if life is a series of phases to be endured until the final, phasing-out from it.) The phrase brought with it a set of images equally banal: Calasso with a woman twenty years his junior, her most noteworthy features her vacant smile and the breasts filling her bikini top; him seated behind the wheel of cherry red sports car, a Porsche or Corvette; him, walking hand in hand with his new companion on a tropical beach, the tip of a wave foaming around their bare feet. He is sufficiently honest with himself to admit some measure of truth to the therapist's assessment. In the last few years, a surprising, almost frightening number of the friends of his youth have divorced, started new careers, moved vast distances, embraced religion, quit drinking, battled cancer. (This last he recognizes as no one's choice, yet he cannot help listing the disease amongst the trials to beset what he continues to think of as his class, decades past their high school graduation.) In spite of this recognition, he is convinced that there is more to his feeling than midlife *noia*. It is as if, after a promising start in a couple of moderately-successful films, he is one of those actors who is constantly mistaken for another actor. Like a film, his life possesses the illusion of depth; shift perspective, however, and it flattens out to nonexistence.

3. *Mostro* (Xenomorph)

"I don't know how you expect me to draw this," Maxwell, the sketch artist, says.

"Try a pencil," Alter says.

"Look," Calasso says, "just do the best you can, okay?"

Maxwell shakes his head, but returns to the office where Judge Marcus Ryan is waiting. Once the artist is out of earshot, Alter says, "You know what he's going to come back with, right?" Although Calasso nods, his partner continues, "A picture of the Goddamn monster from the *Alien* movies."

"The xenomorph," Calasso says.

"Whatever. The point is, you'd be as well Googling a photo of the thing and copying that."

"You know who the judge is, am I right? You understand how miserable he can make our lives, and by 'our,' I mean everyone in the Capital District. It's important—it's essential—that he feels like we're pulling out all the stops for him. So allow me to tell you what I told his honor. Obviously, this was someone in a costume. Maybe the costume came from a store, or maybe it was homemade. If the judge can give us a picture of what he saw, then it should help us to figure out what kind of costume the bad guy was wearing. That will aid our investigation."

"You don't think that's taking the long way round this? It's not as if we have the manpower to spare. Shouldn't we concentrate on the judge's driver, find out if he had his fingers in any pies he shouldn't have?"

"Once the Commissioner hears that Marcus Ryan's personal driver has been kidnapped, we are going to have more warm bodies at our disposal than we'll know what to do with. The Captain's going to tell us to leave no stone unturned—you can imagine. We might as well get a head-start on some of those rocks. Based on what Ryan's already told us, I'm guessing the suit was put together by the guy inside it. Could be he has some experience in costume design. I don't know where he'd get the material for it, maybe a junkyard, maybe online. Once Maxwell's done, we'll tell one of the uniforms to start researching what you'd need to construct something like this, and then we'll go from there."

Alter nods. "I'll put Vargas on it."

"She's sharp."

"You think this is connected to that other kid, Connolly?"

"Hard to think it isn't, what with the movie references. On the other hand, it's a pretty big jump from dressing up like Hannibal Lecter to making your own xenomorph suit."

"Like you say, it's a hell of a coincidence."

"Nah, it can't be, can it? What's the alternative, though? A single kidnapper with a closet full of horror movie costumes? A gang whose members dress as their favorite monsters?"

"Sounds like something out of Batman."

"It sounds ridiculous. Maybe this is all some kind of elaborate practical joke."

"Tell that to the Connolly kid's liver."

"I know." Calasso sighs. "And I'm afraid that blood is going to be the driver's."

"Yeah," Alter says. "I'll go find Vargas."

"Do that."

After Alter has navigated the maze of desks and chairs to the exit, Calasso glances at the windows of the office where Judge Marcus Ryan sits on the edge of one of padded chairs, his massive forearms on his knees, his hands clasped, while Maxwell moves his pencil over the page of the sketchbook open on the coffee table between them. The judge's tie hangs unknotted around his neck, his shirt collar is unbuttoned, his sleeves are rolled up to his elbows. A pewter flask stands uncapped on the table to his right. Through the strands of hair combed over his scalp, his skin is flushed, shining with sweat. Calasso's dealings with the man have been mercifully few and far between, but each time, the judge has conducted himself with an almost Olympian reserve, as if his legal authority is indicative of power more profound. The abduction of his driver, however, has deflated him, reduced his long, perfectly-formed sentences to jagged and jumbled fragments. Calasso interviewed Ryan upon his arrival at the station, and struggled to make sense of his story.

The judge had been on his way out of his house on New Scotland to a fundraising dinner for St. Peter's. He instructed Mario (Navarro, his driver) to bring the Cadillac around to the carport. When Judge Ryan stepped out of the side entrance and turned to activate the alarm, Mario was waiting with the back door open. As the judge descended the side stairs, he saw something moving above his driver, descending from inside the carport's roof. "Uncoiling," Marcus Ryan said, "unspooling, unrolling itself from itself." Black, glossy, its skin was more like the surface of the car than the flesh of any warm-blooded creature. He saw arms and legs too, too long, like the limbs of a giant spider, a tail like a string of bone, an oblong head whose face was all mouth, a nest of silver fangs. It was the way it moved, the judge said. He could not tear his eyes from it. Mario saw him staring at a point directly above him and tilted his head back. What was lowering itself towards him made his mouth drop open, the front of his trousers darken. His head lolled on his neck, his body went limp, but before his faint could carry him to the driveway, the thing grabbed Mario by the shoulders and lifted him into its embrace. Once he was secure against it, the creature retracted up, under the carport's roof. Too frightened to move, the judge stood where he was, until a shower of blood slapped the roof of the car, startling him into action. The uniforms who answered his call went so far in their search of the carport as to climb amongst its rafters, but the structure was clear, as were the roof of the main house, the garage, and the branches of the old oaks scattered around the grounds. The only evidence corroborating Judge Ryan's account was the one to two liters of blood drying down the windows of his Cadillac.

Calasso offered to interview the judge at his house, as a courtesy, but the man insisted on coming to the station. "The way it moved," he said. "If you could have…Like nothing…You would understand…Turning…Like nothing you want to see…Twisting… Corkscrewing…Nightmare…Like a nightmare."

4. Calasso: *Città Irreale*

Detective Thomas Calasso of the Albany, NY, Police Department is not a happy man. Sometimes, he blames this on the city where he has lived since moving there to attend the State University when he was eighteen. From the start, he was aware of a certain, odd quality to not only the capital city, but to those around it: Rensselaer across the Hudson, Watervliet to the north, Troy across the river from that. As a college freshman, snug in the self-contained world of the campus, he was not overly concerned with the surrounding community except as a destination for the occasional party, or trip to the movies, or late-night excursion to the diner. Once he had a car, during his junior year, he took to exploring Albany, venturing downtown, to where a cluster of tall buildings gave the impression of a slice of another city, Boston or Manhattan or Chicago, lifted from its setting and deposited on the long hill that led up from the Hudson. Sometimes, he continued towards the river, in amongst the forest of concrete pillars that raised a network of roads into the air. He'd been majoring in American History, with a focus on New York State, and he had read that this place had been the original downtown, a collection of homes and businesses built along the Hudson's west bank. When the spring thaw raised the river, it had flooded the streets, sometimes to a depth of several feet. Now, it was flat, bare earth, in the shadow of the elevated roads whose construction had provided the rationale for the neighborhood's destruction. He would steer to the shoulder of one of the local streets that wove through the support pillars, shift into Park, and try to imagine the place as it had been, to reconstruct the flat brick facades of its buildings, awnings lowered over shop windows, people entering and exiting their front doors. In the rush and boom of cars and trucks passing overhead, he could almost succeed in projecting the images he had seen in old photographs onto the shadowy space.

If there was time, he would return the car to Drive and, depending on traffic, head north or south. North brought him past a short building atop which a giant model of Nipper, the RCA mascot, cocked his head to one side. He was charmed by the enormous dog; it seemed like a detail from the old Batman comics, one of the oversized ads that crowded Gotham's rooftops, made real. Not long after Nipper, the road straightened and broadened, its margins empty of everything but a diner at which he liked to stop for a Coke and the gyro platter. (He'd dated a Greek girl who'd dumped him for a rich French guy but left him with a taste for her country's cuisine.) If conditions were right, heavy fog would roll up from the Hudson over the road, forcing him to drop his speed to almost a crawl until, ahead on the right, the diner appeared luminous in the mist. Something about the stretch of road reminded him of a runway; he wasn't sure what. Its emptiness, perhaps.

Driving the opposite direction, the impression was oddly similar. There, faded brick buildings and two-family homes lined streets that led down to Albany's port, an expanse of warehouses and empty lots surrounded by sagging chain-link fences. It wasn't so much that he expected a plane to drop out of the sky as it was an underlying sensation of imminence, as if all this open space was needed for the arrival of…he didn't know what, something vast, sublime. Struck by the symmetry of his responses to the northern and southern reaches of the city, he was on the lookout for any such parallels between its eastern border with the river and its less well-defined western limit, where he had his first off-campus apartment, in the former attic of a large house. That he could discern, the horizontal compass points were opposites, the east a site of absence, the west a site of presence, of new construction as the shopping centers and malls and office buildings replaced stands of trees and meadows. Although he supposed the stores that populated the malls and plazas were their own kind of blank, national and international chains whose connection to the surrounding community was accidental and contingent.

Not until he had completed his Bachelor's and was working towards his Master's, also at SUNY, did it begin to occur to him that his understanding of the city, of the entire Capital Region, was in error. Rather than take on any more student loans, he had found a job just up the river in Troy, working as the office manager for an eye surgeon. Every morning, he rose early to chip away at the week's reading for his classes, showered, and drove to work. If he was running late, he headed for 787 and raced to the exit for Route 7; if he was on time or ahead of schedule—which he generally was—he took a local route, either along this side of the Hudson to Watervliet and the bridge, or over the river to Rensselaer and north along the Hudson's eastern shore. On his return from his job, he followed another set of local streets home. He viewed the exercise as an extension of his textual research into the area, a way of seeing history on the ground, as it were.

When he decided to leave the Master's program and the Ph.D. for which it was presumably laying the groundwork in favor of the police—a career shift facilitated by his then-girlfriend's revelation that she was, in fact, pregnant—his knowledge of the side streets and out-of-the-way pockets of Albany proved a considerable asset. Indeed, it developed into a running joke, amongst both his fellow officers and his family members, that he was never lost, was incapable of becoming lost. "Mr. Map," they nicknamed him. In the time before widespread GPS, he was frequently consulted by other cops for directions to unfamiliar and hard to reach locations. Even after everyone could look up the best route to an address on their phone, he was asked to evaluate the information, refine it, suggest shortcuts. It was as if he carried a replica of the area in the folds of his brain. It was one of the reasons, he suspects but has never been told outright, that he was assigned to missing persons, because he knew all the places the lost might be found.

He knows something else, too, something he started to learn during those early drives between Albany and Troy. At the time, he interpreted the impression the region made on him as one of openness, of readiness for some great event. Especially once he graduated the Academy and began his time as a patrol cop, he realized that what he had taken for openness was in fact emptiness, that what he had viewed as readiness was actually exhaustion. As he moved from patrol to robbery, then from robbery to homicide, then from homicide to missing persons, what he experienced daily of the city and its surroundings aligned with what he had studied of it before dropping out of graduate school, namely, that its best days had been lit by the sun of years long past, and that since the end of the nineteenth century, the area had been on a steady decline, its only real growth industry the legions of office workers required to keep the state bureaucracy from complete paralysis. Yes, the region had its cycle of booms and busts, but from the long view, these were only the shifts and lurches of a ship that has already slid beneath the water's surface. Years, decades prior, the damage was done, and now, the place was in a kind of living death.

5. *Demone* (Krueger)

Through what Calasso supposes must be some species of luck, he receives the call for the third kidnapping while it's still in progress, at four o'clock on a Thursday afternoon. While he and Alter are speeding to the Catholic charities soup kitchen in Arbor Hill, he's on the radio, calling for roadblocks to be set up at the nearest intersections. Although the initial report is jumbled, with no mention of any vehicle spotted leaving the location, there is no way for the kidnapper not to be behind the wheel of something (Calasso's bet is on a van). If, for some foolish reason, the perp has tried to hoof it, so much the better: the army of police he's about to unleash on the neighborhood surrounding the soup kitchen will find the guy in even less time. It wouldn't be accurate to say that Calasso feels good—there's far too much that can go wrong—but there is satisfaction in thinking that the odds have finally started to favor him.

Three hours later, as the uniforms continue their search of the houses, yards, and lots around the Catholic charities building, and the Captain heads for the press conference for which Calasso and Alter have done their best to prepare her, Calasso struggles to hold onto the feeling that the case has turned in his direction. It was a mistake for the kidnapper to strike during the day, and a bigger mistake to do so at a location as crowded as the soup kitchen. Calasso is familiar with the institution. When his oldest was fulfilling the service hours required for her membership in the National Honors Society, she volunteered here during the Christmas season. He tagged along—to lend a hand, he said, and did; although both of them knew it was to keep an eye on her. Ten years ago, the soup kitchen was busy, and that was before the economy collapsed in the Great Recession, from which this area seems to have taken particularly long to recover. There are regulars at this place, men, women, families, who witnessed the abduction of Sr. Lucy Grace and in one case attempted to intervene (for all the good it did). Calasso has witnesses to spare, and surely one of them has noticed something, some incidental, seemingly-inconsequential detail that is going to unravel this case.

Because what they have from the principal witness, Sr. Christine Aquin, is not terrific. When Calasso pushed past the groups of agitated men and women choking the hallways, to the kitchen, he found a woman younger than his oldest daughter, her face streaked with tears, her wimple gone and her brown hair in disarray, the front of her habit spattered with spaghetti sauce. Her eyes were wide, her face preternaturally still. *Shock*, Calasso thought. Voice trembling, the nun said, "It was the Devil. You must know that. He was the one who took her. We were boiling the water for the pasta. Thursday is spaghetti night. He stepped from behind her. There were four pots on the stove. I said we needed a fifth. The dining room was already crowded. Sr. Lucy said four would be plenty. I couldn't find the sauce. We had a donation of sauce on Tuesday. There was no one there, and then he stepped from behind her. Newman's Own, the sauce, the one that gives the profits to charity. Cabernet marinara. I searched the cupboards and all the cabinets. We had to start the meatballs. I spent the morning making them with Mrs. Allan. Sr. Lucy said one of the volunteers must have put the sauce in the pantry. His skin was burned, all the way through, as if he'd stepped right out of a fire. It smelled like pork, like burnt pork. I heard her in the pantry. The jars clinked together as she shifted them. 'Here it is,' she said. She walked out of the pantry. Her arms were full of jars. Eight of them, at least. He was wearing a hat, one of those hats…a fedora. It was brown. Sr. Lucy didn't see him. He grabbed her by the shoulder, her right shoulder. He used his left hand. He couldn't use his right one, because it wasn't a hand, it was metal. A claw. Sr. Lucy looked over her shoulder. When she saw him—the Devil—she screamed and threw her arms up. The jars of sauce went everywhere. One of them smacked the counter in front of me and exploded. I put my hands up, to shield myself from the glass. The Devil had his arm—his left arm—around Sr. Lucy's throat and was dragging her backwards, out of the kitchen. A number of the volunteers appeared in the hallway. They'd heard Sr. Lucy screaming, the jars bursting. One of them, a young man—I don't know his name, I'm sorry—charged the Devil. Wasn't that brave? Foolish, but brave. One flick of that claw, and the Devil laid him open. No one else tried anything after that. Who could blame them? I'm sure Sr. Lucy didn't."

The nun's story remained consistent through Alter's follow-up; indeed, she repeated it pretty much verbatim. The half-dozen men and women who responded to Sr. Lucy Grace's cry corroborated the latter details, adding that the kidnapper hustled his victim out the front door. None of them followed because they were all busy tending to the young man who had been half-disemboweled. A couple of the uniforms followed the trail of blood the kidnapper's claw left, but it diminished after a hundred yards or so. The perp appears to have been heading east, but that may be where he parked his vehicle.

After they turned Sr. Christine Aquin over to the EMTs, and assigned the last of the search areas to the final uniforms to arrive, Alter said, "You know who she saw, right?"

Without looking up from the screen of his laptop, balanced on the trunk of their car, Calasso said, "Freddy Krueger."

"Mr. *Nightmare-on-Elm-Street*, himself. Doesn't seem to have recognized him, though."

"Kids today: no respect for the classics."

"Is Freddy K. a classic?"

Calasso shrugged. "He's what we have, instead."

"Our boy certainly likes him."

"He likes all the bad guys from that time period, doesn't he?"

"You're thinking…?"

"Nothing. I don't know." Calasso folded the laptop shut. "Actually, you know what I can't figure out?"

"You mean, aside from what an eighteen-year-old, part-time college student, a thirty-nine-year-old Dominican immigrant, and a forty-two-year-old Catholic nun have in common that could make them the targets of a kidnapper who likes to dress himself as horror movie icons?"

"Yeah, aside from that."

"I haven't the foggiest."

"It's the effect his costumes have on the people who see them. Remember Judge Ryan? Even Mrs. Connolly was convinced her son had been grabbed by *the* Hannibal Lecter. And now this young woman. From the way they act, you'd think they witnessed an actual monster in action."

"So you're thinking what? The guy sprays some kind of psycho-active chemical into the air before he makes his move?"

"I don't know what I'm thinking. It's just weird, is all."

"Well, file that under duly noted. And speaking of weird: you know what I found out?"

"What?"

"Something unnervingly similar to this—the kidnapping, the costumes—took place in our beloved Capital District a little over a hundred years ago—hundred and three, I think."

"Seriously?"

"The wonders of Google. Four people with no apparent connection to one another were abducted by a man dressed as different Catholic saints. The papers called it the Communion of Saints kidnappings."

"Did they get whoever did it?"

"They got someone. A Polish guy, worked at a junkyard, which was how they figured he was able to come up with the costumes. Reading between the lines, maybe he did it, and maybe he didn't. No one else was grabbed after his arrest, which did seem to settle the matter."

"What about the victims?"

"Far as I could tell, they were never found."

"Huh," Calasso says. "All right, that is weird. In fact, it's Goddamned spooky. What the hell were you searching for?"

"'Kidnappings in Albany.' It took me a while to find it."

"I never heard of it, and I have a degree in the history of this place."

"You think it means something? Like what? Our boy's a true-crime buff who decided to stage his version of Albany's strangest crimes?"

"Nah. I mean, could be, but how likely is it? It's probably a coincidence. Which doesn't make it any less spooky."

What else can it be but coincidence, one of those moments when the present puts on the garb of the past? Madness to believe anything else; he might as well call in the psychics, break out the Ouija board. He might as well try to answer Sr. Christine's final question to him: "What is the Devil doing loose from Hell?"

281

6. Calasso: *Noi Crediamo Che Presto Le Cose Che Avrebbero Creduto*

Detective Thomas Calasso of the Albany, NY, Police Department is not a happy man. Lately he has been spending time in local Catholic churches, St. James on Delaware and Blessed Sacrament on Central; once in a while, the Cathedral downtown. On his way to work if he's early, or during lunch if he isn't working through it, or on his way home if he isn't too tired, he slips through the front doors into the vestibule, and from there into the church proper, dipping his fingers in the small bowl of holy water affixed to the doorframe and crossing himself as he goes. Inside the church, he genuflects and slides into one of the pews towards the rear. Sometimes, he reaches down, lowers the kneeler, and eases forward onto his knees, resting his elbows on the top of the pew in front of him; other times, he remains seated, but hunches over, as if in prayer or contemplation. He does not attend daily mass at any of the churches, nor does he attend mass on Sundays or holy days of obligation. Though raised Catholic in a devout household, he has not been to mass on a regular basis since shortly after his youngest made her First Holy Communion, a decade ago.

The immediate cause of his first missed mass was, ironically enough, an Act of God, in the form of an early-morning thunderstorm that knocked out the power to the house and left the alarm clocks mute. He and the rest of his family slept right through their usual Sunday wake-up of eight a.m.; in fact, by the time he opened an eye, saw the clock radio's blank face, realized what must have happened, and fumbled for his watch, it was one minute to ten o'clock, much too late for the nine-thirty service. Eleven o'clock mass was not absolutely out of the question, if everybody hustled, and there was a twelve-fifteen service, too, but as he considered the face of his watch with its round of Roman numerals, another possibility occurred to him: brunch at the diner on Central he and Theresa used to frequent when they were first seeing one another. Initially, the girls were wary of his suggestion that, this Sunday morning, they do something a little different, and go out to eat. Of their parents, their father was without doubt the more religious, the more invested in their faith and what it meant. They weren't sure if this was some kind of strange test; for that matter, neither was his wife.

While they had cheerfully described themselves as recovering Catholics early on in their relationship, the moment Theresa told him she was pregnant, he tacked hard towards the faith whose headland, it turned out, was not that far away. It was for the baby, he told Theresa. It was important he or she grew up with the structure religion provided. Although she hadn't shared his sudden change of heart, Theresa hadn't argued with him. That first Sunday he had resumed attending mass, she had accompanied him. She had enrolled in the Pre-Cana classes that were required for them to be married in the Church, and at their wedding, she had promised to raise the baby swelling the front of her dress Catholic, along with any siblings the child might have. She had kept her vow, through Christenings, First Penances, First Communions, and in the case of their oldest daughter, Confirmation. If she had balked at sending the girls to Catholic school, it was as much because of the expense, and because their local public school had a good reputation. Questions of Church doctrine the girls raised, she referred to their father, who never seemed to lack for an answer. Whatever concerns she had about the religion, she kept to herself; although, when whichever priest was delivering that Sunday's homily lashed out at Planned Parenthood, as they did on a semi-regular basis, there was a certain tightness to her mouth that suggested she was holding in an opinion she very much wanted to share. Once, about two years into their marriage, Calasso had asked her what she got out of their weekly visits to the church. She shrugged, said, "It's something we do as a family," which he supposed was as good a reply as he could expect. He was the one who found satisfaction of a less tangible variety in religion.

Until one day he didn't. Cautiously, Theresa and the girls went along with his suggestion that they skip mass in favor of brunch. The following Sunday, they repeated their visit to the diner. He had to work the Sunday after that, so Theresa took the girls to church, but the next weekend, they were back at the diner, and a new pattern replaced the old: Sunday mornings were for sleeping in, then family brunch. At separate moments, surreptitiously, each of the girls questioned the change in their collective behavior; he justified it with as much subtlety of reasoning as he had their questions about Original Sin, the Incarnation. Theresa was less interested in his rationalizations, more concerned that the sudden change in his attitude was symptomatic of other psychological troubles. With her, he was direct. "I don't believe it, anymore," he said. "Any of it. I'm not sure I ever did."

At the time, the admission felt bold, liberating, a step into a new, more honest existence. With the passing years, however, whatever authenticity he seemed to find has proved flat and dull. The faith around which his and his family's life used to revolve has not returned, and while he suffers an ache at its absence whenever his obligations to his nieces and nephews bring him under a church's roof, his nostalgia is usually curdled by the priest's sermon. The child-abuse scandals, the clumsy cover-ups and self-righteous justifications have done nothing to bridge his distance from the religion, but he has retained the ability to differentiate between the actions of the clergy and the tenets of the faith they are supposed to exemplify, and while the corruption is a convenient rejoinder to any sibling or in-law who criticizes his departure from the Church, it is not the root of his problem. What he said to his wife is true: his current lack of belief has brought with it the sense that he never believed, that his return to Catholicism, his setting it at the center of his family's life, was fundamentally panic at the shock of Theresa's pregnancy, an overreaction that continued for years.

Were you to suggest to him that his recent visits to local churches seem to argue against so absolute an interpretation of his history—to hint that his past devotion was not entirely a lie—he would likely shake his head. Churches are quiet places, he would say, they're still, a combination he finds conducive to reflection, which this current string of kidnappings demands from him. Dipping his fingers into the holy water, genuflecting, are camouflage, ways to guarantee he'll be left undisturbed for the fifteen to twenty minutes he devotes to turning over the details of the abductions. Sometimes, he would say, an unfamiliar location can help to loosen your mind, allow you to make connections you wouldn't have, otherwise. He would allow a certain irony to his selection of churches as his preferred location for the examination of a mystery, but he would caution you not to place too much faith in it.

7. *Madre di Lacrime* (Crone)

When they breach the shack, Alter goes first, even though Calasso is holding the shotgun. His sour thoughts about his partner's ambitions are interrupted by a flock of balloons that pour through the doorway, red white yellow, up to the underside of the overpass above. Alter raises his left hand to guard his face, and that allows the hulking figure waiting inside to step forward and chop off his right hand. Calasso sees the machete—practically a short sword—flash, his partner's wrist spout blood. He registers the hockey mask hiding the assailant's features as he pushes Alter down and unloads the shotgun into it. A flash, a thunderclap that stuns his eardrums, the kick of the stock into the meat of his shoulder, but he's already pumped the shotgun and fired a second time at the shape that's staggering backwards. He chambers a third shell, but the perp is on his back, the hockey mask and what lay beneath it a ruin. Calasso circles him to ensure that he isn't breathing, kicks the machete away in case he's wrong, and retreats to where Alter lies writhing. Keeping the shotgun trained on the kidnapper's form with his right hand, he unbuckles and unleashes his belt with his left. He holds out the belt to Alter, who takes it. As his partner is tourniquetting his right forearm, Calasso radios for backup, for aid for a wounded officer. He locates Alter's hand, still clutching his pistol. *At least he held onto his weapon*, he thinks, and has to stifle hysterical laughter. *Keep it together.*

There is no sign of any of the missing individuals in this front part of the shack, but at the rear, the dirt floor slopes steeply down. Calasso should wait for the other officers to arrive before investigating back there. At most, they're two minutes away. If Friday-the-13th here had any friends, they've been alerted to Calasso's presence, to put it mildly. Best to leave them to SWAT. He has nothing to prove. If it hadn't been for him noticing the shack on his and Alter's drive past it, and what's more, the grooves leading through the dirt outside its front door, as if a body had been dragged to it, they wouldn't have discovered the kidnapper's lair. Granted, it was more happenstance than the result of arduous investigation, but he was the one who told Alter to pull over. Whatever else takes place, he is the one who broke this case.

Except, he cannot stop his legs from carrying him deeper into the structure. It's as if he's caught in the grip of something larger than himself, part of a narrative that demands he fulfill the requirements of his role. He is the lead detective working this series of crimes, this mystery: it is incumbent on him to see the thing all the way through to the end. Light enters the rear of the shack from a hundred tiny holes in its siding, making the air glow. In front of him, the floor drops almost vertically. A series of planks jammed into the dirt one under the other forms a treacherous set of stairs. He takes them almost on his side, half-sliding under the ground, the shotgun muzzle up and ready.

The space into which he emerges is a pocket in the damp, dank earth.

Layers of muddy trash carpet the floor. Muddy posters and papers decorate the walls. In the center of the room, a basin dug out of the ground holds a dark liquid whose coppery stench makes his gorge rise. On the other side of the basin, the sculpture of a woman kneels gazing down into it. Executed in gray clay, with the rough technique of either a beginner or amateur, the statue suggests the Virgin Mary, its head draped, its body robed. The face, however, is no maiden's; the opposite, in fact. It suggests profound age, a lifespan of such length that the various features are subsiding into a sea of creases and folds. The kidnapper dabbed blood on the lips, the eyelids. No doubt, it's some private fetish, a replica of the guy's mother or grandmother or great-aunt Rose.

The sculpture sighs. Calasso starts, aims right, aims left, shotgun ready for whomever he's missed camouflaged in the garbage. His eyes dart to the statue's face, where bubbles froth the blood smeared on its lips. His weapon trained on the sculpture, he steps toward it. Its eyelids open amidst the blood across them, and what looks at him through that crimson film causes him to lower first the gun, then himself, until he is prostrate before it.

Later, long after the backup has arrived, and Alter been sped away to Albany Med, and the crime scene been secured, and Calasso debriefed by the Captain, herself, he will attempt to put the sensation that swept over him to words. He will be sitting on the back porch of his house, a sizable glass of Talisker mostly-untouched on the arm of his chair. After asking him again and again if he's sure he's okay, his wife and daughters will have heeded his request for a little time by himself, to decompress.

Staring at a night sky hung with low clouds, he'll think about other nights he's been out taking the dog for the last walk of the day, and an enormous wind has blown up, a change of weather moving in, with such speed and such force that it feels as if all the night is rushing against him. Only, what streamed out the crone in the mud was a torrent of sensations, images. Chief among them was the feeling of time, of decades, of centuries, time laying on him like a robe made of lead, time bending him down to the ground. If only he could let his burden carry him the rest of the way into the soil, from which he has the impression of having emerged, drawn forth from it by means he does not understand. (He had a vision of a hazy, firelit stockade that a distant version of himself recognized as Fort Orange, the settlement the Dutch raised on what would become Albany's location. The hewing of these walls, the laying out of the streets they enclose, the hearths around which those streets were planned: he has the sense of all of this as having summoned him and birthed him.) Exhaustion dulled his limbs, his thoughts. (He saw a succession of bowls scooped out of the earth, some filled with water, some with wine, some with blood. Reflected in the liquids' surfaces, a panoply of faces, the stylings of their hair a gauge of the passing years, their expressions united in desire.) Here is a *noia* to dwarf Calasso's own experience of the emotion, the disgust of a divinity, or of something near enough, a *deus loci*. Buried within the weariness, the boredom, he is aware of a bright thread, a burning seam that might be teased out, channeled to the accomplishment of deeds extravagant and extraordinary, violence of a real and of a figurative sort. All that would be required is an acolyte of sufficient vision, someone more than a high-school drop-out with power fantasies and a fixation on the monsters of his childhood.

That is what he offered her, the crone, the muddy avatar of the place where his life has run aground. The city revealed herself to Calasso, parted her robes, her flesh, to display to him the worn, leathery bag of her heart. In exchange, he promised her himself, mumbled into the dirt and refuse his pledge of something else, something better, he doesn't know what, but it will be more than mere costumery, a re-enacting of tired plots. Was his offer accepted? SWAT found him alone. Tucked into the breast pocket of his dress shirt, Calasso later noticed a tiny wooden figure like the miniature replica of a saint. It was her image, the hem of its robe dark with what he is reasonably certain is dried blood. He turns it over in his hand, his pulse quickening with something like joy.

APHANISIS

When he looks up, the child is standing in front of him, offering a glass of cloudy liquid that he supposes is water. Does it matter? He accepts the drink and, careful not to slice his lip on the jagged edge of the container, samples its contents. Though chalky, it's cold, and he gulps it down so fast his temples ache. Its coolness spreads through his throat and chest, makes him shiver. His breathing is still heavy, but not as labored as it was when he collapsed into a half-sit. Rising on one knee, he pushes himself to his feet, returning the empty glass to the child, who takes it and cradles it against her worn t-shirt.

The null-sword juts from the ground like some sinister Excalibur. He takes hold of its hilt and tugs it loose from the dirt. He has the impression he should feel more self-conscious about this, a grown man well into his middle-age, wielding a sword, and not just any sword, but one whose ornate guard and engraved blade lend in the appearance of a costume weapon, an artist's fancy. Yet he is not embarrassed in the slightest. If anything, grasping the sword gives him an almost primal comfort. And what better for slaying the products of the imagination, than a fantastical weapon?

(If you can say, that is, that the imagination and the unconscious are the same thing, which he's not sure you can. Certainly, they seem to be connected to one another, the imagination the mask the unconscious wears when it wants to make itself known. Certainly, too, the null-sword has proven effective at dealing with the unconscious's productions. He doesn't understand the exact mechanism by which it does this but he doesn't think it matters.)

A few meters away, the ground halts in a ragged cliff that extends to either side as far as he can see. He'd thought the edge of the world a figure of speech, a way for the residents of Spittle to congratulate themselves on their assorted depravities and decadences: *We're as far as you can go; after us, there's only nothing.* Beyond the ragged margin of the dirt, however, is a gulf that reaches the limit of his vision, further. It might be confused with outer space, except that there are no stars visible in its expanse, only vast ribbons of color that undulate into and out of visibility, occasionally intersecting one another and engaging in a twirling dance before rippling out of sight. Less frequently, great spheres of braided light flare into view and, as quickly, wink out. Once, there was a thunderous burst of sound like a chord played on an organ the size of the moon.

It shouldn't surprise him. After escaping the mines and making his way to Moosejaw, where he found the null-sword wrapped in burlap sacking in the back room of an abandoned grocery store, as the woman with the hole in her cheek had said he would, and after witnessing the weapon's effectiveness against the horde of sand-hobos that bushwhacked him outside of Spittle, he should have been prepared to find the literal edge of the world across the barren plain on the other side of Spittle's ash heaps. But it does, which may be why he finds himself monologuing to the child, who appeared at his heels as he was on his way out of the last of the dumps.

"The annihilation of consciousness," he says. "That was what I had decided upon. All the things that brought me to the mines—that made me think I deserved the mines, that they were a punishment I had earned, as if I were subjecting myself to a kind of personal justice, manufacturing justice by acting as if it was real—as far as I was concerned, all of those debts were long paid. I only wanted rest. But they—the overseers—would not permit me to die, which was perverse, bizarre, because plenty of other miners perished on a regular basis. Because I wanted it, because I sought it out, they thwarted me. I believe it amused them to do so. I suppose I should thank them for not allowing me to die before I met her, Merida. When I told her that I was after the annihilation of my consciousness, she said, 'Yes, but what about your unconscious? What are you going to do about that?'

"After first, I thought her question absurd. The moment my consciousness was extinguished, I was certain my unconscious would be snuffed out, as well. No, Merida, said, I was treating the unconscious as if it were an adjunct to the conscious, when it was the other way around. The conscious, she said, sits atop the unconscious like the penthouse suite of a skyscraper. Those top storeys could be removed, and everyone living beneath them would register some disturbance, and then continue with their routines. But, I said, I'll be dead: there won't be any place for those residents to live. They'll continue as information, she said. So will your consciousness, but that breaks down almost instantly. Your unconscious is made of sterner stuff.

"To be honest, it sounded as if she was talking about my ghost, but she said that there were ways for this information to be accessed after my body had been mulched. There were rumors, she said, of a conglomerate in Wire who had worked out a means of collecting your residual information, distilling it, and injecting it, to trip through your unconscious. It was supposed to be a treatment for Black Dog, but she had her doubts.

"Why the prospect of someone ranging through my unconscious should have bothered me, I'm not sure. It's not as if I would be aware of it; although, I guess I might, in some strange way. It was more a case of, I had decided to erase myself from existence, and I meant to do so as thoroughly as I could. Merida took me to the pit-witch, who told me about this," he brandishes the null-sword theatrically, "and where to find it in Moosejaw. She also directed me here, where, she said, the proximity of the gulf would allow me to manifest the contents of my unconscious. Once they had been incarnated, the null-sword would destroy them completely, down to their information. As soon as the last of them had been expunged, I could complete my original plan safely.

"I don't mind telling you, I had a hard time believing the pit-witch. Everything she described sounded like it had been hacked from the plot of a Moorcock. After I escaped the enclave, I did head for Moosejaw, but that was because I figured the trackers wouldn't pursue me that far into it. I didn't expect to find the null-sword there, not really. Even holding it in my hands, I didn't know if it was what the pit-witch had said it was, a blade of irrational metal. It wasn't until I saw the sword in action that I realized the witch had been telling the truth, whereupon, I set out for Spittle, and the edge."

The child has wandered away a few paces, to the milky pool from which she scooped the water she gave him. Embarrassed at having been abandoned by his audience, the man strides to the edge of the dirt and stops there. The drop-off is steep, immeasurable. Gazing at the gulf, he allows his eyes to lose their focus. He doesn't try not to think. That, Merida said, was likely to be his principal danger. In trying not to think you wound up thinking about how you couldn't not think, and in so doing, blocked your unconscious. The trick, she said, must consist in remaining open—to his thoughts, to what was swimming underneath his thoughts—and to fashioning that openness into a space into which the denizens of his unconscious could be coaxed. Once they were contained, the peculiar energies of the gulf would act upon and manifest them. In his time at the edge of the world, he has learned to identify the particular sensation that heralds the beginning of the process, a fullness starting in his belly and reaching up to the top of his throat, as if he has consumed a large, rich meal that is not sitting especially well. As soon as that feeling has established itself, he retreats a safe distance from the dirt ledge and waits.

It never takes long. The fullness becomes a tightness. Sometimes the tightness remains centered on his gut; other times, it shifts to his chest, or his back. Once, it moved to the right side of his neck. The tightness becomes painful, as if the skin is being stretched to breaking from within. His nerves fire white hot. Since the first manifestation, he has continued to promise himself that this time, he will remain standing, he will not permit the pain to get the better of him. He has broken every one of those vows, dropping to his knees and then to his side, his eyes streaming tears, his jaw clenched, his breath hissing through his teeth. The tightness becomes a tearing, as if someone had worked a knife under his skin, taken hold of it, and begun peeling it off him, employing the knife to assist them. His nerves burn so hot, they're freezing, absolute zero. Amazingly, he does not lose his grip on the null-sword. He has the impression of something exiting his body, and the manifestation is accomplished.

Initially, his unconscious released versions of himself, alternate selves he'd long ago dreamed as his future. He found it surprisingly difficult to raise his weapon against them, especially the ones who understood what he was doing and pleaded with him not to. A couple of them had run. A heartening number stood and did their best to fight him. In the end, he cut every last one of them down, the effect of the sword's blows rendering their remains a fine, colorless powder that the next breeze carried away. The unrealized selves were followed by versions of his immediate family members (his mother, young as she was when she sang to his childhood self in the back yard; his father, punctured and pierced by the machines that were keeping him from death), his close friends, favorite film characters, more distant family members, friendly acquaintances, favorite cartoon characters, and on and on through the multitude which inhabited his unconscious. So many, he had not thought his depths contained so many.

Eventually, the recognizable figures gave way, first to generic forms he realized must be early memories, when his child's brain lacked the context to identify a fireman in fire gear, or a clown, or the bishop in his regalia, and then to things at whose origin he could only guess, a figure made of bent and twisted wire netting, its head a tire whose treads opened in a cacophony of mouths, a thing like a short tree, its branches flowered by severed fish heads, their mouths gaping in idiot unison, a form that was little more than a collection of shadows and a sound like nails tapping on glass. Some, he fought for a minute, others, for an hour, a few for the better part of a day. At the end of each contest, he swung the null-sword down in an arc and slew his opponent.

The new adversary his unconscious releases wrenches itself from his gut and side and lower back, as it's been coiled half around him. He cries out, flailing the blade to back it away from him. There's no blood, no visible wound to his flesh, but the pain takes long enough to subside for anything with a notion to attack to do so. As soon as he can stand, before he's ready, he heaves himself up, the blade out at what's in front of him.

Through eyes still awash in tears, he sees what might be a centipede, if centipedes grew longer than a man. Its exoskeleton is dull grey, translucent; beneath its surface, schools of black squiggles like half-written letters stream. The creature's head consists of a cluster of heads taken from baby dolls. All are hairless, their eyes missing. At its other end, the thing dissolves into a puddle of greasy liquid. From somewhere, possibly the doll heads, the creature emits a clicking sound, like the spinning of plastic wheels. At the sight and sound of it, he feels what he's felt with all of the manifestations, no matter how bizarre, how repugnant: a deep sense of the familiar. He shifts his grip on the null-sword, lowering the point, and adjusts his stance.

When the thing lunges at him, he steps to the right, slashing up and to the right, then pivoting to chop down. He retreats as the creature whips around after him. His blows have opened a pair of gaping vents in its armor, through which streams of black liquid swimming with black squiggles pour. The thing darts at him again, and this time he moves left, slicing a long opening in its right side, above the row of its long legs. As it twists after him, he spins and strikes the center of the dolls' heads. A trio of the heads goes spinning; clear fluid sprays from another four. Now he is the one pressing the attack, swiping at the creature's head to force it to rear. He cuts it just above the middle, bisecting it. The thing's halves fall heavily, writhing. What had been a contest has turned to butchery. He severs the dolls' heads from the top section, slices it into three parts, and slices the bottom section into three. Once the creature begins to lose definition, its surface becoming pale, granular, he knows he is done.

There comes a moment, after he dispatches his unconscious's latest sending, when he pauses, sounding himself to determine whether his task is done, whether he has at last emptied the vast region below his conscious of its denizens. How many of them can there be? How many figures are necessary to populate the space? He would know, the pit-witch assured him. The moment his unconscious was clear, he would feel it. Then, it would be a matter of turning the null-sword on himself, and his quest would be completed.

He does not feel empty.

He sighs, wipes the sweat from his brow with the back of his hand. He looks around for the child, expecting her to approach with a fresh glass of milky water. She's nowhere to be found. The jar with the jagged lip rests beside the cloudy pool. He walks over, squats to take the jar and scoop the pool with it. The sediment in the water swirls, makes fantastical shapes.

I must be almost done, he thinks. *I have to be. How much can any person contain?*

GRIPPED

This was maybe '91 or '92. The economy losing its footing, stumbling into recession, the glories of the Gulf War receded in the national rearview. The turn of the century—of the millennium—no longer a description of past events, but a predictor of things on the way, less than a decade's distance. Across central Europe, groups manacled by toppled tyrants massaged raw wrists, regarding one another from the corners of their eyes while reaching for the knives. HIV-AIDS rampaged through the bloodstreams of young and old, rich and poor, celebrity and nobody.

Joe was working as a bouncer at the End Zone, a strip club in Latham. Most of his job consisted of taking money at the door and maintaining a generally hostile expression to everyone who handed him cash, from the college boys up from SUNYA, down from Sienna, or over from RPI, to the truckers and businessmen in town for the night, to the assorted regulars, most of whom knew how to circumvent the club's no-alcohol policy by gulping from their bottles in their cars in the parking lot. He kept the camo patrol cap on because it added to his bellicose appearance, and when he inclined his head forward the bill made it more difficult for the customers to be sure where he was looking. Even in the club's air-conditioned atmosphere, his denim jacket rapidly grew humid, but it lent a good ten pounds to him, and he figured the bigger he seemed, the less chance there was of a random asshole trying anything with him. Plus, the jacket's pockets were capacious enough to hold a flask of rye on the right and a dog-eared paperback of French poetry on the left. The liquor, he treated himself to after locking the club's door behind the last patron to exit. The verse, he read as the alcohol's heat spread from his stomach and the girls changed into their regular clothes and prepared to leave. He murmured the French: "Comme je descendais des Fleuves impassibles," "La lune s'attristait," "A la fin tu es las de ce monde ancien." When it was time for the girls to go, he walked those who did not have rides waiting for them to their cars.

He encountered less trouble than he'd been warned to expect by the man who hired him. In most cases, his arrival was enough to put a stop to whatever bullshit was in progress—usually, a guy who couldn't or wouldn't get the message that the dancer he was crowding wanted him gone. Every so often, he found it necessary to grip the arm of the offender high on the bicep and steer him to another part of the club, up to and including the front door. Although plenty of customers played tough, thrusting out their chests and glaring at him, they were roosters, showing off for the other cocks. The only one who truly made him nervous, to the point he retrieved the aluminum bat he'd propped behind his stool at the front door, was a short guy with curly red hair and a van dyke who entered one afternoon not just drunk but angry drunk, his face flushed, his eyes sparked bright by an altercation with his girlfriend, or the woman he thought was his girlfriend, from what Joe overheard of the tirade the man unloaded on Kelly, the bartender, and then to the mirror behind the bar. Before he was done with his speech, he grabbed the empty glass in front of him and smashed it onto his forehead. When he stumbled off his seat, blood was streaming down his face, shards of glass shining in his hair. He opened his mouth and screamed, a howl of frustration and rage that turned all the heads in the room his direction and sent Joe hurrying for the baseball bat. His fingers had just closed on it when the man burst into tears and sat down on the floor. Kelly was already on the phone to 911, and although Joe hustled to where the man was sitting, the situation was over. During the five minutes the Sheriff's deputies took to arrive, the man screamed twice more, but no one paid attention to him. That night, Joe remained in the club after the last girl had departed, smoking his way through a pack of Marlboros and reading Baudelaire: "Dans des terrains cendreux, calcinés, sans verdure, / Comme je me plaignais un jour à la nature." As dawn was bloodying the horizon, he crept into the backseat of his Dodge and plummeted into dreams of men with glass studding their skin.

A week after that, Joe had his encounter with the shirtless guy. It was closing time, the last girl left from the stage, the music switched off, the house lights raised. Joe had thought all the customers were gone. But when he glanced at the stage, he saw a lone figure seated on one of the chairs that lined it. One sneakered foot propped on the railing that ran the stage's perimeter, the guy had pushed his chair up on two legs. Didn't your mother ever tell you, Joe thought. At some point after entering the club, the guy had doffed whatever shirt he'd worn in, which had escaped Joe's notice—odd, because if there was one thing the patrons of a strip club were absolutely obliged to do, it was to remain clothed, themselves. The guy was skinny, but his flesh was roped with muscle. None of the girls had mentioned a ride waiting for them inside, so it was likely Mr. Shirtless was waiting to surprise one of them with his attentions. Joe approached quickly and quietly. He considered kicking the guy's chair out from under him, but on the off-chance he wasn't there for some nefarious purpose, Joe opted for the usual bicep grab, ready to ease the guy to the floor should he startle and topple the chair.

Instead of closing on the man's arm, however, Joe's fingers grasped the man's right hand. In a move whose serpentine specifics happened too fast for him to follow, the guy corkscrewed to his feet and twisted to catch Joe's grip in his. Joe's brow lowered, his frown becoming a grimace as the shirtless man tightened his hold. The guy couldn't weight more than one-fifty, and that was assuming you threw in the sneakers and black corduroys hanging from his hips, but he possessed circus-strongman strength. As best he could, Joe returned the pressure, but it was no contest. The man squeezed his hand, pain lighting Joe's arm as his bones gave to the brink of breaking. No telling what the guy's next move was going to be, but if it was preceded by breaking Joe's hand, it couldn't be anything good. The baseball bat was hopelessly out of reach; Joe clenched his left hand and brought it back for a roundhouse.

And the guy released him and stepped away, hands open and up. "Well," he said, "I guess I should be going."

"Yeah," Joe said once he could catch his breath. "I guess you should." In the combined relief and pain that rushed over him, he saw that the guy was older than he'd first taken him for, at least his age. He had a tattoo of some kind on his right shoulder, a figure Joe didn't recognize, done in jaundiced ink. Rubbing his right hand with his left, he walked the shirtless man to the front door and out into the parking lot. He wanted to watch this guy get into his vehicle, start it, and drive away from here.

The man took half a dozen steps across the gravel, stopped, and turned. There was a cigarette Joe hadn't seen him roll or light between his lips. "Almost forgot," he said. He reached his left hand behind him. When he brought it around front, it was holding a pistol, a black automatic Joe had failed to notice tucked into the guy's waistline as he trailed him. The man held the gun by the bottom of the grip, dangling it upside down. "Here," he said, holding the weapon out to Joe, "take it."

He couldn't see how a gun in this guy's possession was a good idea. He caught the pistol with his left hand and the man released it. "Two bullets," the guy said, holding up the index and middle fingers of his right hand.

"Two," Joe said. "Why? For what?"

"You'll know."

Joe slid the gun into his jacket. He heard gravel crunching, looked up to the sight of the shirtless man striding out of the parking lot and along the shoulder of the road. Before Joe lost sight of him behind the silhouette of the auto parts place next door, the guy shouted something at him Joe couldn't distinguish. It sounded French; something to do with Carcassonne, maybe.

His right hand hurt for days, to the point he considered a visit to the emergency room. He opted to increase his intake of rye. It didn't help, nor did the painkillers Kelly slipped him. What reduced if not relieved the pain he discovered one night he was playing with a ballpoint pen. Silver, the kind with the button on one end you click to extend and lock the point, and again to release and retract it, it had been left behind by one of the customers. Doubtful the owner was going to return for it, but Joe had it at his place at the front door, just in case. Bones aching, he pressed the button over and over—until, prompted by a sudden and ferocious impulse, he dug the book of French poetry out of his pocket and opened it to the inside back cover. His hand felt as if it was filled with fire. He pressed the tip of the pen to the blank surface, and started to write.

The room wheeled. High overhead, the moon rolled across the sky, crashing through the stars, cracking the firmament. The pen drove across the paper. Cities shuddered, burst, collapsed in glittering ruin. Across a great distance, someone was speaking. Joe leaned forward to hear what was being said.

INUNDATION

There is water coming into the basement.

It's an old basement, fieldstones stacked and mortared together, a dirt floor. Water bubbles up from the dirt, arcs from gaps in the mortar. A trench runs along the periphery of the basement, intended to channel the annual spring seepage to the room's northwest corner, where a sump pump in a round hole waits to push the water through a black plastic pipe out the front of the house, where it will run down the short, step front yard to the street with its deep gutters. But the pump is designed for modest floods, an inch or two at most, not the briny two and a half feet that has accumulated already and shows no signs of diminishing. The pump continues disgorging water outside, but since there is water springing from the front yard, fountaining out of long cracks in the street, transforming the asphalt into a muddy stream, it's fair to say it isn't helping the larger issue. Water pours over the other side of the street, downhill to the house built there, striking its foundation with a dull hiss, churning up its front door. Did the neighbors get out? Their Subaru is parked beside the house, submerged to the bottom of its doors in swirling water. This does not augur well for Lena and Mike and their daughter, Jo. On the other hand, they had a boat, didn't they? a canoe they secured to the roof of the car for weekend excursions, so maybe the three of them piled into that and paddled for higher ground.

Should the waters swallow the neighbors' house, which looks ever more likely, that is the plan for Mick and his husband, Vin, and their son, Edward: use the boat they've improvised outside the garage to float to safety. Already, Edward is on the vessel, surrounded by a barrier of suitcases, knapsacks, and duffel bags, each filled to bursting with as much of the house as they could squeeze into it. Vin continues his last-minute inspection of and adjustments to the boat, checking the cords that lash the heavy plastic barrels to the platform, the seal on the boards of the top deck, the plastic sheeting sandwiched between it and the lower deck. He wanted to add gunnels to it, if only lengths of plywood nailed upright, but there hadn't been time. He settled for a three-foot post at each corner of the platform, clothesline wound around them to form a rope perimeter. Water foams around his shins, sliding in a long sheet down the ridge behind their house. Mick feels a twinge of anxiety that it might lift the boat and sweep Edward away from them, but Vin has employed a pair of thick chains to anchor the vessel to their Jeep on one side and the garage on the other.

From his spot at the side door to the house, Mick can look left to Vin and Edward, right to their neighbors' house (around which the water has risen, finding an entrance to the structure in a window that has collapsed under its pressure), and straight ahead along Main Street—Main Stream, more like. The local radio station's last broadcast included a report of something sighted in that direction, a gray, leathery hump the size of a barn, rising in the vicinity of what had been Sturgeon Pool and then sinking again. For the last three days, similar stories have come from points up and down the eastern US, as the water has erupted. Before they lost wi-fi and cable, there were images, photographs and videos, the majority of them blurred, difficult to distinguish, full of immense shapes and shadows, a few frighteningly clear, a grey fin rising behind a sailboat, something like a hand grabbing the bridge of a trawler. Anecdotal evidence indicates creatures larger still, capsizing Coast Guard vessels, shouldering aside supertankers. Mick finds the prospect of animals of such dimensions terrifying. He remembers a whale watch he and Vin took out of Provincetown, early in their relationship, and the queasy sensation that squeezed his stomach once they found a trio of humpbacks, and he gazed down at them and realized each whale was the length of their ship, and more, the whales were in their native element, whereas he and Vin and the other passengers were intruding. (At the same time, a secret part of him, which continues to delight in old movies about giant monsters wreaking stop-motion mayhem upon major cities, is made giddy by the thought of these things, come alive.)

Vin gives him a thumbs-up, shouts, "Come on!" He hates leaving things to the last minute, while Mick is chronically late. Opposites attract, and all that. Given the situation, it's probably best they do things Vin's way. He turns for a final look into the house, at the area beside the side door that's served as his home office, whose bookcases still have too many volumes on their shelves, and at the long room beyond it, for which they never found a suitable purpose. Edward used it as a play space, carrying his wooden Thomas trains and tracks down from his room and filling the vast carpeted floor with rail lines. How often did Mick put aside whatever article he was supposed to be writing to assist him? It's something his son has always loved to do, gather his toys and arrange them into elaborate scenes, frequently with an accompanying narrative. He's used the back room, the kitchen, the staircase, the upstairs bathroom, his bedroom. His toys have congregated on the stoop outside the side door, in the back seat of the Jeep, in the side yard. What Edward christened his set-ups have occupied him in all manner of weather, from humid summer to frost-bitten winter. Lately, he's been obsessed with water, enlisting Mick and sometimes Vin's help in digging shallow trenches and holes in the yard, at one end of which he tipped a jug full of water, creating a miniature river that swept those toys unfortunate enough to find themselves in its path aside, filled the first hole to overflowing, raced through the channel to the next hole, carrying more hapless toys with it. All the while, Edward voiced the toys' distress, saying, "Oh no!" and, "Aaaah!" and, "Help!" When everything started happening with the water everywhere, Vin asked Mick if he thought Edward's play might have been connected to it, if their son wasn't plugged into it in some way, you know, psychically. Mick told him not to be ridiculous.

The Fracture: that's the name the cable news channels settled on to describe what's continued to happen. A break in the barrier separating their world from another occupying almost the same space. It's a watery place, teeming with all manner of strange fauna. A couple of pundits referred to the other world as Atlantis, but given the steady rise of the waters here, Mick thinks this word might have a better claim to it. No one is certain how long the catastrophe is going to last, how high the waters are going to rise.

The last broadcast to come across the transistor radio advised those who could to head for the Catskills, to higher ground, so that's their plan. If the Catskills go under, then Mick guesses they'll try for the Adirondacks, a considerably further destination. Beyond that, he doesn't want to contemplate.

"Come on!" Vin waves him toward the boat, which shudders as the water begins to lift the barrels. He's right. Mick closes the door on this, the first house they bought, purchased with the help of the first-time-home-owner's tax credit, back when the crash of the housing market was the definition of calamity. He steps from the stoop into the roiling water.

Something slides under his foot, a piece of debris jammed against the base of the stoop by the current. For a moment, Mick is confident he can maintain his balance, and then he's going over, splashing into water that is deeper than he realized, that is already carrying him down the side yard toward the street. He twists onto his belly, grabbing at the ground for purchase it refuses to offer. Salt water slaps his face. The house rises high above him as he drops to the street, under the water streaming there, cracking his chin on the asphalt. Stars flare before his eyes. He pushes to his hands and knees, back into the air, grateful for the road's roughness, giving him a way to brace himself against the flood threatening to continue his journey across the street and down the the neighbor's front lawn. The current is frighteningly strong. He isn't sure how long he can maintain his position. He's on the verge of panic when he sees Vin descending the yard toward him. Due to the rope tied around his waist, and looped over one of the boat's corner posts, he's much steadier on his feet. In short order, he's standing beside Mick, one hand under Mick's right arm, shouting to him to grab hold of the rope, use it to get to the boat, he'll be right behind him.

Relief surges through Mick's chest, tightens his throat. He turns to say, "I love you," to his husband, and catches sight of a figure standing in the middle of the street, maybe a hundred feet from them. It's shaped like a man, albeit, one seven and a half feet tall, heavy with muscle. The skin of its arms and legs is ghost white, the hue of things used to living far from sunlight. Rough bronze armor wraps its torso. A bronze helmet like a cage, like the jaws of some nightmare fish, conceals most of its head, but Mick can pick out great white eyes staring at him and Vin. What could be a sword, four feet of jagged bone and metal braided together, hangs from the figure's right hand. It pays no heed to the water churning at its knees.

INUNDATION

I, for one, welcome our Atlantean overlords. The paraphrase of a line from an old episode of *The Simpsons* occurs to Mick without warning, almost causes him to laugh. There's no guarantee the figure is hostile, right? The armor, the weapon, could be for its protection, scouting an unknown location. Right?

In the middle distance beyond the (*Atlantean*), something large splashes through the water, moving closer. Hand over hand, Mick begins to pull himself up the hillside, towards the boat where his son waits for him. Because what else is there for him to do?

TO SEE, TO BE SEEN

I

Diaz had the guy's story. He always knew the details of whoever's place they were clearing out. How, Carpentier couldn't figure. It wasn't as if Google turned up any information about the people who'd lost their houses (he'd checked). They were part of the ongoing collapse of the housing bubble, the calamity that had pulled the larger economy into a pit that appeared to have no bottom. Most of them had walked away from the lives their over-mortgaged houses represented, taking only what could be carried in overnight bags and suitcases, abandoning the furniture, the appliances, the electronics whose costs crowded the credit cards they had defaulted on. They were a type, but somehow, Diaz was aware of their individual histories. For a time, Carpentier had assumed Ocampo gave Diaz the information, but the boss claimed not to know anything about the former owners of the houses whose contents they removed. The creditors had a guy who called Ocampo, gave him the address, told him where the find the key to the front door, and that was all. Nor did the payment for the completed job come with bonus facts about the men and women whose sofas and refrigerators Ocampo, Diaz, and Carpentier had spent hours relocating. Eventually, Carpentier asked Diaz point-blank where he'd heard these stories he told. Diaz shrugged, looked away, and said, "You know, around," and refused to be drawn any further on the subject. Annoyed, Carpentier decided that what his coworker was telling them was most likely his own invention, fiction.

Except there were enough instances where Diaz's narratives coincided with the contents of the houses with such quirky accuracy that it seemed he had to be in possession of some secret source of information. The third place Carpenter had worked with him, a pale green McMansion in Huguenot whose strip of overgrown lawn was the same size as the front walk, Diaz had predicted they would be done with quickly. "Couple put all their money in the house," he said. "Although there's supposed to be a nice TV in the living room and some top flight Scotch in the liquor cabinet." Which there was—as there was a top flight gas grill on a house in Cold Spring's back deck, and a framed display of vintage baseball cards hung in the study of a place in Rhinebeck. There was never a question of Diaz taking any of the things he described, which, in the case of smaller items like the gold-inlaid music box or the trio of Seiko watches, he could have. Yes, Ocampo had a strict no-stealing policy; even the liquor they found, he did not want them drinking. But he had only ever asked them if their pockets were empty, and that, months ago, when Diaz was new and Carpentier was newer. At this point, it would have been easy enough to remove one or two little things without raising Ocampo's suspicion. But no: all of it, every last bit of property in the houses, they packed or wrapped, loaded onto the truck, and delivered to one of several warehouses down in Westchester.

After he had been working for Ocampo for a couple of months, Carpentier felt sufficiently comfortable to tack on a last-minute addition to their house-clearing routine. Once the truck was full, the rear door lowered and locked, Carpentier returned to the now-empty house. He told Diaz and Ocampo that he was making sure they hadn't forgotten anything, which Ocampo at first believed, crediting Carpentier as a conscientious worker, then grew suspicious of, demanding to know if Carpentier had hidden something, a small valuable he was running back to reclaim. Carpentier wasn't, and turned out his pockets as proof of his honesty. Diaz spoke up on his behalf, told the boss to be calm, the guy was being responsible, Ocampo should be grateful. When the two of them were on their own—walking out to their cars, say—Carpentier expected Diaz to ask what he was up to with his final inspections. He did not.

In fact, Carpentier told him one night, when they stopped at a sports bar near their office in downtown Poughkeepsie prior to heading to their respective homes. He had been debating the matter with himself for several days. Following their toast to another day cleaning up other folks' messes, Carpentier drained half his Heineken and, as the alcohol splashed around his stomach, started to speak. "You, uh, you know how I go through the houses before we leave?"

"Yeah," Diaz said.

"First—you know I'm not stealing anything, right? Hiding stuff and taking it when no one's around?"

"I know it."

"What it is, is there's this feeling I get."

"You get a feeling."

"Yeah."

"What kind of feeling?"

"That's what I'm trying to figure out how to say. Like, nothing."

"You don't feel anything?"

"No," Carpentier said, "I feel *nothing*. It's like… Okay: if we were in a really old place, somewhere people had been living for, you know, generations, it would have a certain kind of…energy. Like all the stuff that happened there, all the history, had left an impression. Or, as if the house was a battery, and it had built up a charge that could be measured, like…like with a voltmeter. That's what I am, the voltmeter. These places we're emptying, though, most of them are too new for any of that kind of stuff—for a charge to have built up. You'd think that would be that. Like you said, there wouldn't be anything to feel. Except there is. There's this space…not inside the house, but this other space, that's waiting for what whoever was living there was supposed to give it. I noticed it a while ago, on the first couple of jobs we did. I wanted to, I don't know, check it out, so that's what I've been doing." Carpentier was suddenly aware that he had been talking for a long time. He looked down, embarrassment coloring his face.

"Man," Diaz said with a grin, "that is some fucked-up shit. Crazy." He drank from his beer, shook his head. "You psychic or something?"

"Nah," Carpentier said. "I don't know. I mean, I've always been aware there was something going on in houses I was in, but I didn't think anything of it. This is the first time I've picked up on this particular feeling."

"Well, that's a relief," Diaz said, "'cause I got shit I do not want you finding out about."

The joke served its purpose, defusing the awkwardness that had gathered around Carpentier's confession. Diaz moved the conversation onto the subject of the latest Prince CD, which Carpentier hadn't heard and Diaz said was some of the singer's best work, ever. "I'll burn you a copy," he said, a gesture Carpentier said wasn't necessary but Diaz insisted was no trouble. "You got to be educated, young man," he said, which Carpentier found funny, because Diaz and he were the same age.

Afterward, once Carpentier was in his room at the boarding house in Hyde Park, he thought that what he'd said to Diaz, the way he'd tried to explain what he experienced in those emptied houses, hadn't been right at all. He hadn't told Diaz how fragile the houses seemed, how flimsy, as if they were stage sets, painted plywood and lighting effects, the theater on the other side of their false walls. And in the seats, watching his progress through the houses...what? What audience regarded his performance? He didn't know.

II

A couple of weeks later, the day's assignment took them north to Wiltwyck, to an address on Montague Street that Carpentier thought looked like a witch's house. Orange with brown trim, it was tall, narrow, the peaked roof overhanging the second storey in a way that made the residence appear to be wearing a giant pointed hat. The place was sided with rows of wooden shingles whose lower ends were curved, which gave the impression it was covered in scales. Its paint was faded, chipped in spots. Situated at the top of a short rise, the house stood at one end of a block whose other dwellings were larger, multi-family structures on whose front steps men of various ages sat alone and in pairs, the hands of more than one clutching bottles wrapped in brown paper bags. To reach the front door, you had to climb six marble stairs set in the ground, then another half dozen wooden steps. It wasn't the worst situation they'd encountered, not by a long shot, but the stairs were the type of extra complication that would grow noticeable as the job progressed. Ocampo parked the truck so the rear door was at the foot of the stairs.

"So," Carpentier said to Diaz as they pulled their work gloves on, hauled blankets out of the back of the truck, "what're we gonna find in here?"

"Seems this guy," Diaz said, "was a movie freak. Collected all kinds of shit: posters, props, some costumes."

"Huh," Ocampo said.

"All right," Carpentier said.

There was more of the movie-related stuff than Carpentier expected. There was more of everything than he expected. Unlike the places they usually cleared, which hadn't been inhabited long enough to fill with many possessions, this house held the detritus of decades. On the first floor, every available foot of wall space was lined with bookcases, their shelves stacked two and in some cases three volumes deep. The kitchen table, a desk in the back room, card tables scattered throughout the rooms held stacks of paper, most of them covered in single-spaced typeprint, with a few photocopies of black and white pictures that hadn't been that clear to begin with. A stale odor of must lay heavy on the air. In the kitchen, beside a toaster oven whose glass door was opaque with baked-on grime, a flat wicker basket held layers of envelopes on whose fronts were printed URGENT and FINAL TERMINATION NOTICE in large red letters. "What do you think happened?" Carpentier asked.

Ocampo shrugged. "Not my problem."

"Home equity loan on an overvalued property," Diaz said. "Has to be."

"Man, you should be in real estate," Ocampo said.

Diaz smiled. "Who says I'm not?"

Ocampo snorted.

The second floor was considerably tidier. A pair of conjoined offices held display cases in which an assortment of small items was arranged on red velvet. A pair of round, tortoiseshell glasses, the right lens cracked, the legs askew, sat next to a nickel-plated revolver, beside which was a faded cream fedora with a blue band. There were no cards next to any of what Carpentier assumed were film props to identify them. Unsurprisingly, Diaz recognized a few. Leaning over a case, he said, "Those are Clark Kent's glasses from *Superman II*. The scene where he gets his ass handed to him in the diner.

311

The gun was held by Sam Spade in *The Maltese Falcon*. The hat…that's Peter Ustinov's hat, isn't it?"

"If you say so," Carpentier said.

"What was the movie? *We're No Angels*? The one with the snake, Adolph? That gets the halo, too, at the end?"

"No idea," Carpentier said.

"Don't you watch any movies?" Diaz said.

"Sure," Carpentier said. "I watch movies."

"Whatever's on HBO, right?"

"Nah, I can't afford that shit. Network."

"Damn."

Despite his coworker's attempt at making him feel ignorant, Carpentier knew the titles on most of the posters framed on the walls. *The Man in the Iron Mask. Citizen Kane. On the Waterfront. Kramer vs. Kramer.* Those hung in what must have been the bedroom were in foreign languages, German and what he was pretty sure was Japanese, but he recognized the word Nosferatu under a line drawing of a bald, white-skinned man with pointed ears and a vampire's fangs. "Hey," he said, "I know this one. It's about a vampire."

"Good for you," Ocampo said from where he was measuring the bed.

"Where's Diaz?"

"I sent him to check the attic."

The stairs to the attic were behind a door in the room next to the bedroom, what might have been a spare bedroom but was now filled with long clothes racks, each dangling clear plastic garment bags in which were zipped suits and dresses new and old, uniforms of armies real and imaginary. A samurai sword and a saber were mounted one under the other on the rear wall. No doubt Diaz could shift through the costumes here and name the actor who wore it, the movie they wore it in, and what they had for breakfast the last time they had it on. He crossed to the stairs.

Unfinished and unfurnished, the attic was an open space dominated by the thick brick chimney rising through its floor up out its ceiling. In front of the chimney, lying on a pair of sawhorses, was what Carpentier took for a coffin: a rectangular box, lidless, behind which Diaz stood with his arms crossed, shaking his head slowly from side to side. "I did not believe it," he said as Carpentier walked toward him. "I knew it was supposed to be here—the information was good—but it seemed so...obvious, you know? Like here, in this place, is where you're gonna find this. Of course you are, right? When we didn't see it on the first floor, or the second, I thought, *I knew it.* Then I climb those stairs, and..." He nodded at the crate. Carpentier was shocked to see the man's eyes bright with tears.

"What is it?"

"Oh," Diaz said, wiping his eyes, "oh, you have no idea. This is a piece of a movie that was made a long time ago. We're talking black and white, silent. *Das Cabinet des Dr. Caligari. The Cabinet of Dr. Caligari.* Ring a bell?"

"No."

"No," Diaz said. "No. It's one of the greats. It's about—there's this guy in it, Dr. Caligari. He's a traveling entertainer, a hypnotist. He has this guy, Cesare, he's kept in a trance forever. Cesare lies in a box—in this box. When Caligari does his shows, he props up the box so the audience can get an eyeful of Cesare—who's dressed all in black, with this creepy-ass white face with big black circles around his eyes. Because he's in a trance, Cesare's supposed to have access to hidden knowledge. The audience can ask him questions about whatever they want. Which isn't to say they like his answers.

"Anyway, after the film was done shooting, most of the props were taken apart, repurposed for other productions. No one knew they'd made a masterpiece, that stuff connected to it would be valuable. This was a movie, cheap entertainment for the masses. Cesare's box, though," Diaz wagged his right index finger at it, "somehow, this survived. Crazy. You would think, if there's one thing you're gonna find a use for, it's a box. Nope. It's a woman who saves it, some Austrian countess who sends her lawyer to make inquiries about the prop and offer a ridiculous sum of money for it. The rich are not like you and me, that's for damn sure. Or maybe not: you ever collect anything? Comic books? Trading cards?"

"*Star Wars* figures," Carpentier said, "when I was a kid."

"There must have been some you really wanted, ones you couldn't find anywhere, no matter where you looked, which if you could've, you would've paid more than what they were worth for."

"I guess, yeah."

"The countess was into mystical shit, had a castle full of all kinds of weird objects: crystal balls, magic mirrors, cursed statues. Half of it sounds like it came from a fairy tale, the other half from a horror movie. Somehow, this lady had gotten it into her head that Cesare's box was one of these items, that the process of shooting the film had changed what was a wooden crate into something else, charged it with supernatural power. It's how magic works, through association, you know? Just to be on the safe side, she carved mystical symbols into the interior. Come here."

Carpentier did. Inside, the crate's plain, unvarnished wood had been incised with hundreds of figures. They ranged in size from a dime to a half-dollar. Some he recognized: a sun wearing a collar of triangular rays, a crescent moon, a ringed planet, a comet whose tail arced behind it. These were interrupted by more elaborate characters, pentagrams ringed by concentric circles, squares containing circles, flocks of circles connected and arranged by sets of parallel lines into strange geometries. Scattered throughout these symbols, Carpentier saw combinations of letters he thought were Greek, as well as a couple of designs he could not place: a circle broken at about the eight o'clock point, a square whose bottom line turned up inside it then continued to turn at ninety-degree angles within it, forming a kind of stylized maze. Although he hadn't set foot in a church since his father's funeral five years ago, Carpentier had the urge to cross himself. He resisted it, opting instead for, "What the fuck?"

"You a Friend of Borges?" Diaz asked.

"Who? Borges? I don't think so. Should I be?"

"It's a group," Diaz said. "They're into puzzles and shit—weird puzzles, I mean. They're named after a guy who wrote stories about that kind of stuff."

"Oh. No, man, I'm not much good at those games."

"It's cool. It's just, if you were, this would be, like, the mother lode."

"Yeah," Carpentier said, "I can see that. So what about the lady who wrote all this? The countess? What happened to her?"

"World War II," Diaz said. "She was a Nazi; didn't work out too well for her. After the war, Cesare's box moved around a lot. Orson Welles had it for a little while. You know who he was?"

"Yeah," Carpentier said. "The *Touch of Evil* guy, right?"

"Nice," Diaz said, nodding. "He was thinking about shooting his own version of *Dr. Caligari*, maybe playing the doctor, himself—which would have been *sick*. He liked the idea of using the prop from the original movie. When his version didn't happen, he sold the box. Eventually, it came to the

US. Went from collector to collector, until it wound up here."

"Huh," Carpentier said. "That's pretty wild. You have to wonder why the guy didn't sell it."

"What do you mean?"

"He was obviously in trouble. What'd you say, bad home equity loan? This thing," Carpentier gestured at the crate, "must be worth a lot. Could've paid off what he owed, maybe. At least got him back on his feet."

"Pretty hard to let go of something like this."

"What about letting go of your house? Not to mention, the box is still here. Wherever the guy went, he didn't take it with him."

"Maybe he was experimenting with it."

"What?"

"Like the countess, trying to tap into its mystical power."

The suggestion was ridiculous, but rather than making him laugh, it made Carpentier's mouth dry. "Sure," he said. "He was talking to the spirits here, in Wiltwyck."

"Why not?" Diaz said. "You think your location would matter to a bunch of ghosts?"

"I guess they don't have bodies, do they?"

"Exactly. You know, this whole area—the Hudson Valley—used to have a reputation for weird shit."

"Like the Headless Horseman?"

"No, I'm talking about legitimately strange goings-on. What my old grandma would have called some serious *brujería*. This was before the Civil War, middle of the nineteenth century. Everyone was into Spiritualism, which was their version of New Age stuff. The mediums who came here said they had visions of supernatural creatures, of passages to the spirit world."

"I thought it didn't matter where you contacted the spirits."

"It doesn't, but that doesn't mean some places won't make it easier."

"Whatever," Carpentier said.

"Hey!" Ocampo shouted from the foot of the attic stairs. "You two find anything up there?"

Had Diaz answered in the negative, Carpentier would not have been surprised. The crate was the single most valuable item they'd come across during any of their jobs; not to mention, Diaz's knowledge of it was even more extensive than usual. Carpentier half-expected his coworker to try to talk him into leaving the prop where it was and returning for it later, with a promise of a generous percentage of the price Diaz received for it. Instead, Diaz called, "Yeah, we got a big-ass crate that's probably worth a lot of money."

"Seriously?"

"It's true," Carpentier called.

"Goddamnit," Ocampo said.

As it turned out, Cesare's box was less difficult to bring down to the truck than Carpentier feared. It was the excess of papers on the first floor that proved to be the job's biggest challenge. Every last sheet had to be collected in reinforced garbage bags, which were to be delivered together with the furniture and film memorabilia. What should have taken three or four hours stretched to six and a half, by the end of which, Carpentier's legs were screaming from he'd-lost-count-of-how-many trips up and down stairs. On Diaz's recommendation, they waited until the truck was almost full to slide Cesare's box, safely blanketed, on top of the bed of filled garbage bags they had prepared for it. By the time Ocampo lowered the rear door and secured it, Carpentier had lost any desire he might have had for his usual last-minute walkthrough. "You sure?" Ocampo said when Carpentier told him just to drive.

"Yeah," Carpentier said. Not only was he exhausted, he was reluctant to feel whatever remained in this house.

III

Later that week, at the end of a long afternoon spent removing heavy wooden furniture from the fifth floor walk-up it was crammed into, Carpentier joined Diaz for a beer at the sports bar. Someone had switched the TV above the bar to one of the cable news channels. The stock market had not reached the end of its decline, while the major banks were teetering like so many shacks in an earthquake. Unemployment was swelling; although the economist the news anchor interviewed insisted that the economy was fundamentally sound and the country was definitely not heading into another depression. One of the other patrons seated at the bear, an overweight woman in a burgundy pantsuit, called to the bartender, "Hey, can you change this shit? I didn't come here to listen to more bad news." The bartender reached for the remote, and a baseball game replaced a story about a family who had lost their health insurance together with the mother's job, and were struggling to cope with the costs of the father's worsening MS.

Carpentier drained his Heineken. "Fuck," he said when he was done. "We are so fucked."

Diaz lifted an eyebrow. "What are you saying?"

"That." Carpentier waved his empty bottle at the TV. "Not the game, what was on before, the news. Fundamentally sound my ass. We're already in a depression, man. They're just playing with the numbers 'cause they don't wanna freak out everyone."

"Sure," Diaz said. "So?"

"'So?' Dude, did you hear a word I said? The economy's a fucking disaster."

"Yeah. It is. And who's got a job?"

"Well—"

"Who's got a job?" Diaz said. "You do. I do."

"But that's only because all these other people got fucked over."

"Maybe," Diaz said. "Nothing I can do about it, is there? Doesn't change the bills I got to pay."

"Man…" Carpentier searched for words, couldn't find any. The bartender noticed his empty bottle, pointed at it, but Carpentier shook his head.

"Never mind this shit," Diaz said. "You up for a drive? There's something I want to show you."

"What?"

"You have to come with me."

"I don't know," Carpentier said. "It's getting late, and I'm pretty exhausted."

"Come on," Diaz said. "It's like five o'clock. This shouldn't take that long. Honest."

"Can't you tell me what it is?"

"Uh-uh. You have to see it."

"Where is it?"

"Five minutes away. Ten, tops."

The trip took closer to twenty-five minutes. Since Diaz knew their destination, they took his dinged Accord. He drove them east, out of Poughkeepsie, past strip malls full of vacant storefronts, houses signposted with the placards of realtors, larger buildings whose parking lots were cracked, full of weeds, all the way to the Taconic, where he steered onto the south bound side. There was a Prince album in the CD player, *1999*. When the title track came on, Carpentier said, "You know what this song is about, right?"

"Nineteen ninety-nine?"

"No. That's a common misperception. It's actually about nuclear war."

"What?"

"It's in the lyrics."

"If you say so."

Diaz signaled, slowed, and turned left onto a crossroad that climbed a short, steep slope. As the road leveled, Carpentier saw houses lining both sides of it. They were large, boxy, their lawns overgrown, their driveways empty, their windows dark. Diaz drove past half a dozen of the dwellings and swung left onto a side street. It was lined with more houses of the same style, the second storeys overhanging the first, as if a child had stacked a larger block on a smaller one. Their roofs slanted to sharp peaks. None of the places on this street appeared inhabited, either, nor did those on the cul-de-sac Diaz made a right onto. The evening light made the houses look curiously flat, as if each had been painted on a huge piece of word and propped up. Diaz drove to the end of the dead-end, straight into the driveway of the house there. Carpentier couldn't see anything especially noteworthy about this residence; although he noticed that it shared its minimal backyard with a house facing the opposite direction, toward the end of another cul-de-sac bordered by more vacant houses. Diaz parked the car and climbed out of it.

"You know what these were priced at?" Diaz said to Carpentier when he shut his door.

"I don't know," Carpentier said. "Three hundred thousand?"

"Not bad," Diaz said. "Four. Too much for most of the locals, but for someone living in Westchester, say, and willing to travel a little bit to get to their job in the City, that's about two hundred less than they might spend. That's pretty good."

"Until it wasn't."

"Until it wasn't. You might have sold a few of them, but all this…"

After a moment, Carpentier said, "So this is what you wanted to show me?"

"Inside."

"In there?" Carpentier nodded at the house, but Diaz was already striding up its front walk. By the time Carpentier reached the door, Diaz had removed and opened the keybox hung from the doorknob and was slotting the key into the lock. "What are you doing?"

Diaz glanced at him. "Seems pretty obvious to me."

Dim, the house's bare rooms echoed with their footsteps. Carpentier accompanied Diaz as he completed a slow circuit of the first floor. Had his coworker brought him along to strip the house of its valuable materials, copper wire and the like? Carpentier couldn't imagine the place held enough copper to be worth the risk of discovery by the cops; although, what was the likelihood of the police devoting much attention to a neighborhood of empty houses? The most they were likely to do was drive up and down the main street and move on. Which meant that, provided Diaz had access to other houses, he could have the run of the development until at least sunrise. Carpentier was brainstorming excuses for why he had to return to his car when Diaz stopped, turned to him, and said, "Well? What do you feel?"

"What do you mean?"

"A few weeks ago, at the bar, you were telling me about the sensation you get walking through these houses after we've cleared them out."

"Yeah?"

"So I'm asking you what you're getting here, now."

"I don't know," Carpentier said. "I haven't been paying attention to it."

"You were worried I drove you to this place to rob it, weren't you?"

"No, that wasn't—"

"It's cool," Diaz said. "I played it pretty mysterious; I don't blame you."

"We drove all the way out here because you wanted to know how it made me feel?"

"Come on, man. What you described was more than that."

"Maybe. But why did we need to come to this spot? I mean, we could've gone to any empty house. Isn't as if there's a shortage of them."

"True," Diaz said. "But this location…if you were to look at a map of this neighborhood, you would see that the house we're in sits at the perihelion of the dead-end. It's back-to-back with the house that occupies the same position the next dead-end over. Imagine a pair of horseshoes placed with the closed sides touching, the legs facing away from one another. It's a spot where certain kinds of energy might converge."

"I'm not sure what you're talking about."

"That group I mentioned? The Friends of Borges? We study stuff like this. We know about these kinds of things. Look," Diaz said, "don't worry about it. Just tell me what you're picking up on here."

"Seriously?"

"Seriously."

The thing was, Carpentier was aware of something, an intensification of his previous sensation. It was as if the walls were great sheets of paper, surrounded by a space from which a sound was audible, a low droning that caused the walls to vibrate—that Carpentier felt in his teeth, his bones, a kind of deep-seated ache. Something about the drone, a peculiarity of the way its single note went on and on, gave an impression of its source, an enormous throat, its gelid sides quivering. "Yeah," Carpentier said, "I'm definitely getting a…vibe off this place. Like the other houses, but *more*, you know?"

"Okay," Diaz said, "good. Come this way."

"Is this gonna take much longer?" Carpentier said. "'Cause the sun's going down, and I don't want to be stumbling around here in the dark."

"Not much longer at all," Diaz said. "Come on."

Carpentier followed him up the stairs to the second floor. A short hall on the left off the main hallway led to an open doorway, which admitted them to a large, L-shaped space: the master bedroom, Carpentier guessed. In the corner to their left, an oblong shape stood propped against the walls. Except for the change of location, Cesare's box appeared unchanged from the attic in Wiltwyck. "Dude," he said to Diaz. "Dude. What the fuck is this?"

"It's all right," Diaz said. "I know what you're thinking, but it's all right."

"Oh really? And exactly what am I thinking?"

"That I stole the box, and I'm trying to make you a part of it. Which," he added, "is not what's going on."

"You just found this here."

"Don't be an asshole. Of course I brought it here. One of the guys I know at the Friends of Borges, he's got some money. Scratch that: he's got a lot of money. After we dropped off the box at the warehouse, I called this guy, told him about it, how much it had to be worth. He made some calls, some bills changed hands, and it was his. All perfectly legal."

"Then why is it here? Is your friend planning to buy this place?"

"I told you: our group, it's interested in weird shit. Like what you experience when you're in one of these places. I had mentioned our conversation to another member of the Friends. She knew about this development, said it might be an idea to bring you here and see what happened. I was planning to do that when we found the prop. I thought maybe it would give you a boost."

"Give me a—you realize how crazy this shit sounds."

"Please. You're already halfway there with your *Psychic Friends* deal."

"Whatever," Carpentier said. "I'm done. I'm out of here." He turned toward the door.

"Thought you might say that," Diaz said. He dug his right hand into the front pocket of his jeans. Carpentier tensed, expecting him to produce a knife, even a gun, but when his hand emerged, it was holding a thick roll of bills wrapped in rubber bands. "Five hundred bucks," he said, tossing the money to Carpentier. "For humoring me."

"How do I know this is five hundred dollars?"

"Jesus Christ," Diaz said, rolling his eyes. "Count it."

Carpentier tugged the rubber bands off the roll, relaxing it into a wave of twenty dollar bills. He thumbed through them, stopping every five or six notes to check for fakes, green paper with green magic-marker on it.

"Satisfied?"

He was holding five hundred dollars in his hand. "You're serious about this?"

"As a motherfucking heart attack," Diaz said. "Do you want the money?"

It wasn't much of a question. Carpentier nodded, removing his wallet and wedging the money into it. He had to force the wallet into his pocket. "Okay. What do you want me to do?"

"Get in the box," Diaz said. "Carefully. The thing's still a priceless piece of film history."

From the outside, Cesare's box appeared narrow, too tight for Carpentier to fit in comfortably. To his surprise, once he leaned back into it, shoulders hunched, arms crossed, there was ample room for him to relax. As he looked out at Diaz, the empty room, he had the momentary impression something was off about them, as if he were seeing them through the thick lens of a friend's glasses. When he focused on anything, though, it appeared fine, undistorted.

Diaz had retrieved a can of spray paint from beside the box and was bent over, marking a large, silver circle around the box. The paint's metallic reek filled the air. "Maybe you don't care, but here's the theory behind what we're doing. In *The Cabinet of Dr. Caligari*, the box is the spot from which Cesare has his visions. As far as that story is concerned, that's its function. 'But wait,' you say, 'that shit was made up.' That's true. Thing is, a whole lot of people saw that piece of make-believe, and they bought it. Not for real, but the way you do when you're watching a movie. That was after all the actors, the director, had done more-or-less the same thing. It was enough; it solidified the role the film had given the box. This is why that countess was so desperate to get her hands on it. The prop was full of all this accumulated energy, energy that kept accumulating every time another audience sat through the movie. The stuff she did to it—the carvings—not to mention, the stuff she did with it, augmented it."

Aware of the wad of money pressing against his ass, Carpentier said, "I'm sorry man, but you're talking shit. That's…magic. That isn't how the world works."

"I guess we'll find out." Diaz was almost finished with his circle. Instead of completing it, however, he left an arc open directly in front of the crate.

"Run out of paint?" Carpentier said.

"Circles keep things out," Diaz said, straightening, "and in. The broken circle helps to channel forces the way you want them to go."

"You really are into this shit. I'm kind of impressed."

"Yeah, well, it's not the kind of thing you talk about over lunch." Diaz set the spray can on the floor. "You ready to give this a try?"

"I suppose. What do you want me to do?"

"Same thing as downstairs."

Carpentier was on the verge of asking Diaz how he suggested he do that crammed into an upright coffin, but the fact was, while the two of them had been talking, he had noticed the return of the sensations he'd experienced on the first floor, only amplified, as if the volume on a radio playing in the background had been dialed from one to five, not enough to distinguish the lyrics of whatever was playing, but more than sufficient to pick out the tune and name the artist. As he concentrated on his impression of the house, it increased again, the volume being spun to ten. He flinched. "Shit, man."

"What is it?" Diaz said. "What's happening? Are you getting anything?"

"Yeah," Carpentier said. "It's pretty strong." He swallowed. "Hate to say it, but you were right. The box is definitely amping things up."

"Good," Diaz said. "Good."

"I don't know." The room's walls were rice-paper thin, vibrating like drum skins with the drone Carpentier had tuned into downstairs, which had escalated to concert-level. The light in the room dimmed, the way it did in a theater before the performance started. Across from Carpentier, the walls glowed with pale luminescence, then faded translucent, transparent. "I'm seeing something."

"What? Can you describe it?"

It was a bare, white floor, surrounded on three sides by darkness. He might have been looking at a stage, or the floor of a cave. At the far end of the space, almost but not quite concealed by the dark, a figure squatted. "It's—there's nothing there. Aside from a floor, I mean. But there's someone on the other side of it."

"Who? What do they look like?"

"No, I can't… Wait. Something's happening." From out of the darkness, a low, heavy fog poured across the floor. In a moment, the surface was gone, hidden beneath roiling vapor. "There's like, fog all over the place now."

"What about the person? What're they doing?"

"Hang on…" The shape rose to its feet. There was something wrong— something profoundly wrong with it. Slowly, it shuffled toward the center of the space. As it drew nearer, his stomach lurched, its contents rushing halfway up his throat. "Aw, no," he said, "aw no, man, come on."

"Talk to me," Diaz said. "Tell me what you're seeing"

How could he? Maybe he could have called the naked figure a man and left it at that. He could have omitted the deathly pallor of the man's flesh, the way it trembled as if not entirely solid anymore. He would have found it more difficult to avoid mentioning the shades of red smeared and crusted around the man's mouth and jaw, his neck and chest, his hands and forearms. He could not have ignored the massive wound that was the man's belly, a bloody space from which the contents had been removed with terrific violence.

"Talk to me," Diaz said.

"It's a guy," Carpentier said, "there's a guy, and he's—his stomach—his intestines—it's all gone, but he's still moving, still walking around."

"Okay," Diaz said, "okay, good. What else do you see?"

Quickly as it had arrived, the fog was departing, sinking to the floor and draining into it. On the way, it revealed a group of people at the disemboweled man's feet: a man and a woman, a girl and a boy. The man and the woman looked mid-to-late thirties, the kids either side of ten. All were dressed well: the adults in a suit and blazer and skirt, the children in new jeans and long-sleeved t-shirts with Pokémon characters on them. The stereotypical white, upper-middle-class American family. Around them, the floor was littered with dozens of nails, each anywhere from six to nine inches long. A few claw hammers were scattered amongst the nails.

"There's a family," Carpentier said, "um, Mom, Dad, couple kids. They're on the ground—lying on the ground. The fog's gone. They're surrounded by hammers and nails. I'm talking big nails. They…oh, hey. Hey, no, don't do that. No. Hey! Hey! Jesus! Fuck!"

The people on the floor were scrambling for the hammers, the nails. The instant each had a hammer and a nail, they twisted to whoever was closest, pressed the point of the nail against their arm, leg, or chest, and brought the hammer down. The nails dove through their clothing. Faces contorted, the family members slapped the ground for a second nail, seizing it and smacking it into the nearest limb. Blood splashed the mother's blazer, the father's slacks, the children's jeans. They hammered nails into one another's calves, shoulders, knees, feet. The nails grew difficult to handle, the hammers slipped from their bloody hands and clattered on the floor. They retrieved the tools and continued their gory work. Ten, twelve nails protruded from each member of the family. Their blood smeared the ground, soaked their clothes. The children joined forces, succeeded in nailing the father's left foot to the floor. In a shower of blood, he tore his foot free, pivoting on his side to set a nail against the mother's thigh.

"What?" Diaz said. "What?"

"They're using them on one another," Carpentier said. Tears were streaming down his cheeks. "The hammers and nails."

"How about the Gullet?"

"What?"

"The other guy—the one with the missing insides."

"He's…" The ravaged figure had lowered to a squat in the midst of the violence. Blood spattered his white flesh. The mother turned her attention from the nail she'd pounded into her daughter's back to raise her cupped left hand to the empty man's mouth. He caught her hand with both of his, steadying it while he brought his lips to it. He slurped its contents, which pattered out of his torn esophagus in red droplets. The boy held up both his hands for the creature to drink from; he did, blood trickling from the wound of his throat onto his ruined pelvis. "He's drinking their blood," Carpentier said. "They're offering it to him, and he's fucking drinking it." The father's benefaction was followed by the daughter's.

"And he's satisfied with it?" Diaz said.

"How the fuck should I know?"

"Okay," Diaz said, "okay. Be cool."

The figure Diaz had called the Gullet stood, allowing the family to devote their full attention to one another. With a shift of the creature's head, Carpentier realized that he had been discovered. For a moment, the Gullet considered him, then began to move in his direction. "Oh shit."

"What is it?"

"He saw me. The guy—the Gullet saw me and he's headed this way." Carpentier shifted side to side, trying to work his way forward out of the crate.

"Hey!" Diaz said. "What're you doing?"

"Did you not hear me? The fucking guy saw me, and he's coming over here. We need to move." Carpentier pushed and pulled, but it was as if the box had shrunk around him. No matter what direction he turned, Cesare's box held him fast. "What is this shit?"

The hiss of spray paint being discharged drew his eyes down. Diaz had grabbed the can of silver paint and was completing the broken circle from outside its circumference. Once that was done, he dropped the can and regarded Carpentier. "This kind of information," he said, "it's hard to come by. Lots of risk. The inhabitants of the Base are unpredictable. Most of the time, they'll leave you alone. Not always, though. It's a shame. I thought we got along okay."

"What are you doing?" Carpentier said. Already, the Gullet was approaching the room's walls.

"The price you pay," Diaz said. "Well, the price you pay for us. Some kind of lesson in economics there, right?"

"Come on," Carpentier said. "Get me out of here, man, come on."

"None of the Friends is sure what the Gullet is, exactly," Diaz said. He was backing towards the doorway. "Some say he's a god, a remnant of one of the old pantheons, the bloody ones. Others say he's a manifestation of the collective psyche—which, to be honest, sounds like the same thing to me. One member says he's an ideation with teeth. I just thought you might want to know, we don't understand him, ourselves. But he does have his uses. And, I'm afraid, his costs."

The Gullet pushed one pale hand through the wall, into the room. The air rippled.

"Please," Carpentier said. "Please man, please."

The empty man slid the rest of his arm out of the wall.

"We'll find someone to replace you," Diaz said, "don't worry." He was standing outside the doorway. "Lot of people looking for work. Looks like there will be, too, for a while. Oh," he added, before he left, "and the box should be fine."

WHAT YOU DO
NOT BRING FORTH

I n the right circumstances, Pete's daughter, Lee, is fond of telling people that her father has at least one knife on him at all times. Since these circumstances tend to arise at larger events—book signings, readings, dinner parties—there is never a shortage of raised eyebrows, furtive glances between guests, murmurs of disbelief. At Lee's prompting, Pete shoves one hand into the front right pocket of his khakis or slacks and retrieves a folding knife whose handle is paneled with dark cherry wood. He opens the knife with his left hand, disclosing a shining blade whose shape resembles a miniature scimitar. He's known for writing novels that feature serial killers, most of whom favor knives, and the audience for his display is unsure whether the weapon is produced ironically, or in earnest. The majority deem it a piece of theater, though a few make reference to the perils of living in the City. None of them could guess the reason for this knife and the one like it Pete keeps in his other pocket. For the matter, neither could his charming daughter.

That reason wears a brown fedora pulled low over his brow and a tan trench coat with the collar tugged up, as if in imitation of every private eye in every *film noir* since the form took shape. Pete has never seen enough of the man's face to be able to describe it to, say, a police sketch artist. Only the eyes, deep set, and the top of the nose, dented above the bridge, as if it had been struck with a blunt instrument, or the edge of a hand, and failed to heal properly. The man's hands have remained hidden from view—at least, Pete thinks they have. He has a confused memory of seeing them in heavy gloves, which he cannot place and therefore does not trust.

It must be noted, Pete carried some form of knife long before his first glimpse of the man he has christened Alan Ladd. It would be more accurate to say that, the moment his gaze settled on the trench coated figure standing at the back of one of his readings, he was overcome by a sensation of such distress, such dread, that he stopped reading. He reached for a cup of water with a hand trembling so severely he spilled the water all over his shirt. Mumbling apologies, he brought the event to an immediate conclusion, retreating to a bathroom in the bookstore's stock room, then slipping out the back door. Half-expecting the man to be waiting for him, he had one knife out and opened, his free hand on the other. The alleyway was empty, but as he hurried to the nearest subway station, he understood that it was for this man he had been arming himself for years, since he was a teen, earlier.

He did not speak to his therapist about Alan Ladd (a name he had selected not for any overwhelming resemblance between this man and the actor, but because Pete's glimpse of him had brought to mind the actor's furtive, hunted air in *This Gun for Hire*). At the time, he and Dr. Mobley were discussing a dream Pete recorded in the dream journal she had instructed him to keep. In this dream, he was trying to climb a step-ladder to reach a cord hanging from a door set in the ceiling of the room he was in—which he had the strong impression was in his aunt and uncle's house outside Chicago. With each step higher he took, the ladder grew less steady, swaying from side to side as if the bolts and screws holding it together were dropping out of it. He knew with absolute certainty that a) he was going to fall and b) the consequence of his fall would be severe, possibly fatal. Despite this foreknowledge, he continued his ascent, gripping metal less and less firm to the touch. When he was almost at the rope handle, the door in the ceiling flapped down, clanging against the step-ladder and releasing a cloud of large, parchment-colored moths into the room. The insects filled the air around him; he swatted at them, lost his balance, and plummeted to what should have been his death, but was instead his awakening in his bed, pulse racing, pajamas soaked in sweat.

While Dr. Mobley would not commit to a definitive interpretation of his dream, it was apparent she saw it as an expression of Pete's anxieties about his continuing success as a writer, of his concern that whatever critical status he had achieved was in danger of slipping away, and suddenly, at that. Given the facts of his life, the analysis was reasonable, even compelling. Yet Pete remained unconvinced by it. Where the doctor focused on the detail of the ladder, he was drawn to the door in the ceiling that had crashed open, the moths whose wings had fluttered against the backs of his hands, his cheeks, his ears. He had been climbing toward something, reaching for admission to whatever lay on the other side of the ceiling. Had that been only the moths? Or was there something beyond them? Each night following that of the dream, he went to bed telling himself that this time, his dreams would return him to the room in (maybe) his aunt and uncle's house, where he would discover what the door in the ceiling concealed. That space, though, remained closed to him.

When he saw Alan Ladd standing at the back of the bookstore, Pete immediately connected him to the dream. It wasn't that he was part of the dream—what was waiting behind the ceiling door—so much as it was that he seemed in some way to *be* the dream, made flesh through a process Pete could not guess and set loose on the world. This was lunacy, of course, but his recognition of the fact did little to alter his sense of the fundamental rightness of his impression. It helped, he fancied, to account for the terror that continued to grasp him each time he spotted the fedora and trench coat toward the rear of whatever space he was delivering his current reading in. After all, dreams were inherently irrational, knots of image and action that stood in for emotions and experiences writhing deep within the brain's folds.

Though he has yet to discuss Alan Ladd with his therapist, Pete has had a brief exchange with his daughter about the man. This took place after they participated in a panel discussion at the CUNY Graduate Center on the one hundred and fifteenth anniversary of the publication of Freud's *Interpretation of Dreams*. Pete talked about the significance of psychoanalysis to the literature of crime and horror in general, and of his novels in particular. Lee compared Freud's ideas concerning the significance of dreams to those of

Jung, about whom she published a well-received popular study. One of the other panelists, a bearded man with glasses of whose credentials Pete was uncertain, pronounced it an essential quality of dreams that they retained a degree of opacity to the dreamer. Even in cases of lucid dreaming, the bearded man went on, he had never encountered an instance in which the dreamer fully understood what was happening. "A dream does not explain itself to you," he said.

"Neither does life," Lee said.

"Life is but a dream," Pete said, adding, "Oh, sorry: Merrily, merrily, merrily, merrily," which drew a laugh from the audience.

Afterwards, before he descended from the stage on which the panel had been seated, Pete saw Alan Ladd lurking at the rear of the auditorium. With as much grace as he could muster on legs gone wobbly, Pete retreated to the table behind which he had spent the past hour and lowered himself onto the chair he had just vacated. Catching sight of him there, Lee ran up the short flight of stairs to the stairs and rushed to his side. "Dad," she said, crouching beside him. "Are you all right?"

"No," he said, too agitated to lie to her.

"What's wrong? Is it your heart?"

"My heart?" he said. "No, my heart's fine. No," he shook his head. How to phrase this to her? "There's a man who's been coming to my events for a little while, now. He wears a hat, a fedora, and a trench coat. He stands at the back of whatever venue I'm at."

"That guy?" Lee said. "I thought he was a fan."

"A fan?"

"Yeah. He dresses like the hero of *The Cellar* does at the climax—what was his name?"

"Baggins, Fred Baggins."

"Remember, he even thinks he looks like something out an old *film noir*? And then he winds up in the cellar of that bar, where he has the showdown with the cop…"

"Pforzheimer."

"Who's wearing a trench coat and fedora, too, right? Jesus, Dad, you wrote it. I saw this guy the first time he showed up at one of your readings. I figured he was playing dress up—cosplay, right?"

"He isn't," Pete said. "He's…dangerous…"

"What do you mean?" His daughter's brow lowered. "Has he threatened you? Is he stalking you?"

"Yes. Not the threatening, but I believe he is stalking me."

"Has he said anything to you?"

"Not one word." Pete waved his hand. The strength had returned to his legs. He stood. "Maybe you're right. It could be—maybe this fellow is a fan, and that's all."

"Don't get me wrong," Lee said, rising, "some of your fans are pretty creepy."

"Never mind," he said. "It's probably all in my head."

As the words left his mouth, Pete could taste their dishonesty. It wasn't so much that he was protecting Lee from a potential threat—she had been taking *krav maga* classes for a couple of years, and had successfully incapacitated a man who had made the mistake of attempting to mug her. Besides, Alan Ladd didn't seem the slightest bit interested in anyone but Pete. No, what he wanted to preserve was his freedom to pursue this matter in whatever way he judged best. His daughter narrowed her eyes, a sure sign she suspected Pete of dissembling to her, but she did not follow her critical look with the usual statement masquerading as a question.

Since that night, every time Alan Ladd has put in an appearance at one of Pete's events, if Lee is present, he has noticed her noticing the man. On a couple of occasions, she has attempted to navigate the room to him, only to have some woman or man stop Lee to talk to her. No matter how short she cuts their conversations, by the time they're done, Alan Ladd has slipped away. Although Pete keeps an eye on her during these moments—one hand in his pocket, knife in his grasp—he has not said anything to his daughter about her efforts to confront Alan Ladd. He isn't sure she is aware he's been watching her. Nor has she raised the matter with him.

If he has preserved his freedom of action in regards to Alan Ladd, Pete has not decided how best to use it. He could hire a private detective to watch for the man at his next reading, tail him when he ducks out, trail him to whatever address he calls home and use that location to unearth information about him. He could talk to Dr. Mobley about the intense dread Alan Ladd's appearance continues to evoke in him, work at digging down to the reasons for this. He could focus on ignoring the man. He could take a break from public life, test whether his absence might cause

Alan Ladd to lose interest in him. Each option has its drawbacks, but this is not what keeps Pete from choosing among them. Rather, it's because he has a sense that, when he arrives at his course of action, he will do so all at once, in the heat of the moment. He will lift the phone and punch in the number of the private detective he Googled. He will lean forward in his chair and say to Dr. Mobley, "I want to talk to you about something." He will avoid looking in Alan Ladd's direction. He will send a group e-mail to every venue at which he is scheduled to speak for the next twelve months, explaining that circumstances beyond his control require that he withdraw from all such things for the foreseeable future. Dr. Mobley has warned him against impulsive behavior, which has not done him any favors in the past, but Pete feels, somewhere below the pit of his stomach, whatever he is to do must be done in this fashion.

That Alan Ladd might escalate their encounters drastically, dramatically, is a possibility Pete entertained a good deal the first times he saw the man but which, as time has slipped by, he has worried about less, on the principle that, if Alan Ladd were going to do anything more, he would have by now. Yet the next time Pete sees the man, this is exactly what he does. This happens in a small theater in Brooklyn, where Pete is part of a discussion of *Spellbound.* For the length of the panel—which includes Lee and a bearded man he recognizes from a previous event—the fedora and trench coat are absent from the audience. Nor does Alan Ladd put in appearance during the question and answer period, which cheers Pete so much he remains in the theater to talk to a pair of young writers who have taken the train from Connecticut to attend the panel. After he has signed the copies of his books they have produced, posed for pictures with them, and sent them on their way, he climbs the stairs to the stage and the table where the panelists were seated, on which, he realized, he left his dream journal. He brought the book because some of its more bizarre imagery made a good fit with the film's famous sets, and while he has come to doubt the therapeutic usefulness of this record of his brain's nighttime activity, he thinks that a few of its scenarios might contain the germs of possible stories, even a short novel. As his fingertips brush the journal's leather cover, he hears footsteps hurrying up one of the theater's aisles. Lee, perhaps, coming to ask him what's taking so long. He turns, a quip at the ready, and sees Alan Ladd striding toward him.

What You Do Not Bring Forth

Pete's response is immediate, automatic. He runs. Journal in one hand, he bolts for the back of the stage, where a red EXIT sign glows over a door. Pete slams into the pressure bar across the door, flinging it wide. He expected to emerge into an alley behind the theater; instead, he's at the top of a flight of wooden stairs. There's no other choice: he races down them. Overhead, the door booms as Alan Ladd heaves it open. At the foot of the stairs, a brick corridor stretches left and right. Pete chooses right, runs along a passageway barely wide enough to admit him, his flight lit by weak light bulbs caged every ten feet or so. Underfoot, the floor angles down. Behind him, Alan Ladd's shoes thwack one-two one-two.

The corridor empties into a large room. Thick brick pillars support a sagging ceiling. Wood crates stacked two and three high line the walls, their sides stenciled with words Pete cannot make out. His eyes dart around the room, searching for another way out of it. He must be under whatever building is next to the theater. (What is that? A bar?)

Coat flapping, Alan Ladd erupts into the room. Too late, Pete thinks that he should have used one of the pillars to conceal himself. He drops the dream journal, fumbles in his pocket for the knife there. Alan Ladd advances. There's something in his right hand. Black, snub-nosed, a pistol. He brings it up as he closes the distance to Pete, who has his knife out and is trying to open it with trembling fingers. The blade sweeps out and clicks into place. Alan Ladd is an arm's length away, pointing the muzzle of the gun at the center of Pete's chest. With a grace of which he would not have believed himself possessed, Pete steps forward and to the right, catching Alan Ladd's wrist with his left hand and sweeping the knife into the man's chest with his right hand. In quick succession, he stabs Alan Ladd half a dozen times, while twisting the man's wrist sharply, causing him to release the gun. Pete lets go of him, and Alan Ladd sits down hard. There is surprisingly little blood on the knife, which Pete holds in front of him as he side-steps to where the pistol lies on the floor. He doesn't want to chance stooping to retrieve it, so he kicks it skittering to the side.

He is exuberant, exalted; he feels as if he could run a hundred miles, a thousand, skip across continents, seas. He should speak, say something to Alan Ladd, who sits hunched over, his head tilted low, dark patches spreading across the breast of his trench coat. Now is the time to demand the man explain himself, account for his relentless presence. But his victory has placed Pete momentarily beyond language.

It is Alan Ladd who breaks the silence between them. In a voice that sits low in his mouth, he says, "I could not bring you forth."

"What?"

"If you cannot bring forth what is inside you," Alan Ladd says, "it will destroy you. So."

His words ring in Pete's head like the tolling of enormous bells, loosening his tongue. "What are you talking about? Who are you? Why have you been following me? What is it you want?"

"How many nights—" The man coughs, spraying blood over his coat. "I've sat in the diner, pen in hand, notebook open, trying the waitresses' patience with my endless cups of coffee."

"I don't—"

"Minotaur," Alan Ladd mumbles. "You were there, hiding between blue lines. I could feel you, roaming the long corridors." He sags forward, vents a liquid breath, and is still.

"Goddamnit," Pete says. Suddenly, he is deflated, exhausted. Nausea tightens his throat. He considers the blade in his hand. No doubt, the police will want it. He crouches, sets the knife on the floor. He looks at Alan Ladd, whose face remains obscured by the fedora. Pete shifts into a half-kneel, reaching his hand to lift the hat's brim.

The instant his fingers brush its edge, the hat bursts into a cloud of fluttering insects, of moths, their furred bodies the color of antique paper. Alan Ladd is gone, the space in which he died full of the moths and their frantic motion. Pete scrambles backward, lurches to his feet, and flees along the passage that brought him here. Moths cling to his shirt, his hair.

VISTA

for Michael Cisco

<Login complete.>

Welcome to College Writing: Special Workshop. The purpose of this special topic section is to allow the instructor to explore a subject of particular interest to them. In this instance, your instructor wishes to consider some of the implications of recent developments in the field of necrolinguistics. In a few minutes, your instructor will read a series of prompts to you. After each, you will have between one and two minutes to respond to it here. Please do so as completely as you can, and please, whatever else you do, *do not stop typing*. Thank you for your participation.

Who are you?

Do you know what a subduction zone is? Do you know anything about geology? How about plate tectonics? Try this: have you seen one of those 3D jigsaw puzzles of the Earth? The kind you fit together into a globe? Reduce the overall number of pieces so that you have seven to join into the model. Another dozen, each smaller, help to fill in any gaps. If you enjoy jigsaw puzzles, if you're up for the challenge of completing them in an extra dimension, it's not a bad way to pass a couple of hours. Do you like jigsaws? (It doesn't matter if you do.)

However, there's a problem with this particular puzzle. The pieces don't fit properly. In some places, the edges don't lock together. In others, there's a gap. A few pieces are too big for their allotted space. It seems the jigsaw is defective, but there's no place for you to return it to. You have to do the best you can, bending one piece in the middle to adjust its size, forcing two pieces against each other, pushing the edge of one under that of its neighbor. Instead of the smooth globe you used to spin in the school library, the result is a rough, wrinkled ball.

Those spots where you jammed one end under another? Those are subduction zones. They're the points of contact between two platforms of rock, each a hundred million tons, each of sufficient area to carry millions of people. Rock faces that would dwarf the Himalayas grind together in a struggle millennia long. Slowly, one side forces the other under it. It's a process measured in inches, but every now and again—geologically speaking—the edges slip, maybe a couple of inches, maybe as much as a foot. The energy released bunches the ocean into tsunamis, raises mountains, shudders cities to rubble.

Call one of those jigsaw pieces the past. Call its opposite the future. How trite, right? Sometimes, I think it's the future being submerged by the past; others, I think it's the past being forced below the future. Does it matter much? Or is it a distinction without a difference? What matters is that I am the place along which one register of experience is struggling against another and losing.

Have we met before?

Before what? This class, which has not started, not really? (Spare me your pedagogic rationalizations. You are here to teach, not to read random questions to us.)

(And no, we haven't met, previously; although I am reasonably sure I've seen you out running. This was last summer. I had a temporary job in a warehouse near the river, which consisted of me filling in wherever was necessary on a particular day. Sometimes this meant folding wee-wee pads and packing them into cardboard boxes. Sometimes it consisted of running the press that sealed the backs on plastic trays of Christmas cookie cutters. Sometimes it was a day of testing a box full of old video game joysticks on an ancient console hooked up to an even older TV. A block over from the warehouse, there was a deli, and for lunch every day I would walk to it, fetch a cream soda from the coolers along the left wall, and order a sandwich [generally turkey and Swiss on a hard roll with a little bit of oil and vinegar]. I would carry my lunch someplace to eat. Usually, this was the park on the riverfront, the one with the view of the bridge, which reminds me of the erector set I wanted as a child, but which my parents never bought me for Christmas or my birthday. The bridge is a network of steel beams. It gives the impression of having been *made*, assembled by teams of workers following detailed schematics. This is unlike many of the other bridges in the city, which evoke an entirely different sensation, of having been strung, like great Aeolian harps, by people unlike us, giants twice, three times our size. This bridge, the erector-set one, looks like something we could have made. I can't remember its name, or the name of the park, but I'm sure you know the place I'm referring to. The river isn't that wide, there. You can look across and see the pilings propping up the other shore, the tall buildings in front of the taller, the much taller buildings. Those tall buildings remind me of doormen, of ushers screening their more grandiose fellows from the rest of us, from our side of the river. Anyway, in the park, which is long, narrow, there's a footpath running beside the river. It's there for exercise. Young mothers jog along it, pushing their children in front of them in strollers fitted with large rubber wheels. Groups of lawyers and accountants, released from their offices for their daily exercise, move in packs, the superficial distinctions among their clothes and running shoes obscured by the ghosts of their price tags, flickering around them. The occasional cyclist, dressed in skintight shirt and shorts and a helmet like a stylized vision of speed, the back tire of the bike a solid black wheel, weighted, zips past.

(And you—as I said, I'm not positive, but there was someone who might have been you, or your double, pounding up the footpath, face flushed, panting. I heard the exhalation first, a gathering susurrus. This was followed by the thud of your feet striking the path, and if I used my index finger to bookmark the page I was reading and looked up, I would see you hurtling toward me. You tended to come from my left, so south, and followed the path's curve to the right, northeast. You wore a gray t-shirt rendered shapeless by washings that had erased whatever logo or image had been stenciled onto it. The frayed legs of your black denim shorts suggested they had been cut from former jeans. Most incredible of all were your black Doc Martens, laced a third of the way up your shins. The boots were what stuck with me, the detail fixing the rest of you, of the park, the bridge, in my memory. How could you run in them? Why did you run in them? Was it the same principal as the cyclist with his heavy back wheel, a way to increase your strength? This didn't seem to be the case—it didn't *feel* like the case. It felt... penitential, or some entry under the masochistic column. Which was it? Why did you run so fast in those weighty boots?)

What is your name?

You have a roster, don't you? Even if you don't, I'm pretty sure you can look it up on the classroom desktop. Our pictures are right beside our names, aren't they? Sadly, I don't look much different now from what I did when I started at this place. I shouldn't be too hard to identify.

Or is this another attempt at a profound question, a provocative one, a variation on "what's in a name?" If that's the case, then how about this: names are the most common kind of fortune telling. Our parents give them to us in the hope—at least partial—of their predicting our future lives. Most of the time, they do so not because of etymology, but due to metonymy, i.e. Mom and Dad associate our names with a specific person—people, even— and they hope the name will carry the person's better qualities with it and transfer them to us. It's a form of sympathetic magic, isn't it? Perhaps that's why, across cultures, there are so many customs and traditions in place to guide the selection of names. You want to make sure proper procedure is followed, because you don't know what you might be risking, otherwise. Case in point, my family. Do you know who I was supposed to be named after, according to the dictates of my heritage? My paternal grandfather, as my younger brother was supposed to receive our maternal grandfather's name. Instead, my parents chose to give me my father's name, and to add to it the then-current Pope's name. In contrast, my brother was named in accordance with tradition. He was valedictorian of his high school class, is studying to be a physician. My life has been a more qualified affair.

What do you want?

Not to die. How's that for cutting to the chase? Sometimes, I think my dread of death lies at the root of all my other anxieties. (Don't ask: it's a long list.) It's as if my life is a group of tiny vessels tethered together, afloat on the surface of a vast, dark ocean. I'd like to attribute my fear to having been raised in a devoutly Roman Catholic household, one in which the existence of Hell, the Devil, and his minions was a given. As with so many (all?) religions, what comes after the grave was often more of a concern than what lies on this side of it. The threat of an eternity of torment is guaranteed to make an impression on the mind of a child, which was reinforced by the multitude of illustrations and dramatizations of Satan and his domain. If I'm being completely honest, I have to admit I'm still haunted by the visions of damnation I was taught in my youth. All it takes is an effective book or movie and the old fear is right there waiting.

Most of the time, though, I'm not troubled by my possible place in Hell. I'm more concerned about an eternity of nothing. Don't get me wrong: once I no longer exist, I understand, I won't be aware of it, as I wasn't conscious of the vast span of time before my life. I guess you might say I wasn't too terribly conscious my first couple of years, until I began to learn how to speak. I'm not acquainted with enough philosophy to be sure whether you can argue that language is consciousness, but the two certainly seem connected, don't they? (Here's where I would place a long digression on the question of whether you can think without language, but I don't want to wander too far away from my main topic.)

(This might also be the place for an observation about the relationship between creation and language at the beginning of the Gospel of John. I can't decide if it would be another digression, or central to what I'm reaching toward here.)

To be more precise, what fills me with nausea deep in the pit of my stomach is the prospect of dying, of feeling myself slipping away, disintegrating into not-being. The image I have of it is sliding in slow-motion over the top of a waterfall at whose bottom is pure emptiness. (Though being jerked out of existence by a stroke or car accident is no more comforting a fate.) The moment of crossing from life to death, from is to isn't, terrifies me.

Silly as it sounds, this was part of my reason for wanting to take this workshop. While I wasn't certain what exactly necrolinguistics was, I had this—call it a fantasy the term had something to do with the connection between language and death, between words and absence. Typing it here makes its folly apparent. Instead of secret revelations concerning the relation between writing and death—writing in death, a kind of composition in decomposition—we're just responding to a series of prompts.

Why did you bring me here?

To teach? the class your name is beside in the course listings? For which, presumably, you're being paid? (Though I hear it isn't much, since you're an adjunct. Sorry about that.)

Or are you trying to evoke the saying, "When the student is ready, the master will appear"? That's a martial arts thing, isn't it? It certainly sounds like something you'd run across in a kung-fu movie, one of those maxims intended to promote internal growth as much as external, so the student has to mature enough to recognize the master who's been in plain view the entire time, sweeping the street or serving soup or some such. I guess there might be a version of it where the master hears about this fabulous student and thinks, *Boy, I have got to teach him (or her)*. Or another in which the student has been under surveillance by the master—who's probably part of a secret group of elite teachers—who reveals him- or herself to the student when the moment is right. Are any of these scenarios applicable? I won't lie: I wouldn't mind being the special student, the one who's drawn you to this drab classroom with its fluorescent lights and plastic desks. But it's as likely the prodigy is one of my fellow classmates, and I'm only a member of the supporting cast, the loyal friend, or the rival who pushes the chosen one to the limit, or the love interest.

Here's a thought: what if it's the room that's brought us both here? I think it's you as teacher, you think it's me as student, but it's actually this space, this white-walled box with its nondescript carpeting, its smart board whose screen shows an ERROR message. This space was sectioned off to be a classroom, to contain an instructor and at least one student. Until teacher and class were present, the room was unfinished. The need for it to be completed drew us to it, you and me and the other students, brought us here to grant the space its apotheosis.

Are you there?

Is this a riff on the Cartesian question? Do I earn extra credit if I answer in Latin? *Cogito ergo sum*. How's that?

Unless the focus of the question isn't on me, but on my presence, on my being present. In which case, I have no idea how to respond. I mean, what we call the present—the place, I suppose, where you might be present—isn't truly a location, is it? It's a confluence, a seam where past and future wash together, where the current of what was and the current of what will be merge in a foaming tumult. The present is a turbulence, full of brief whirlpools that spin you around, suck you down into a momentary recollection or aspiration. You'd do as well to ask, "Are you afloat? Are you swimming?"

Are you ever coming back?

To…? This classroom? I presume I am, unless the class is moved, or canceled, which I don't imagine it would be, at this point, though I've heard rumors of it happening, students showing up for the second, or third, or tenth session to be greeted by a notice taped to the door informing them that their class has been discontinued. From what I understand, if the class has met more than once, there's no refund issued, and the course remains on your transcript with an asterisk for a grade, symbol of something started but never completed. Then again, this may be part of campus folklore, one of those stories like, If your roommate dies during the semester, you receive automatic A's in all your classes, or, If your professor doesn't show up within ten minutes of the start of class, you can leave without it counting as an absence.

Why can't I see you?

Because you aren't looking at me? It's hard to tell, with the glasses you're wearing. The lenses don't seem especially dark; even so, the light in the room is poor enough I'd think they could be a hindrance. When I walked into the room, you had them off—or rather, you had had them off, and were replacing them. You had been talking to that girl—at least, I assume the two of you were talking, though neither of you was speaking as I made my way to the side of the class next to the windows and took the first seat. I went to nod hello to her, but she didn't look well, a little green around the gills. Where did she go? I'd swear I didn't see her leave.

(What's weird is, when I'm not looking directly at you, I'm sure I see someone standing behind you. Not my missing classmate, no. I almost typed "something," because the figure I imagine I see is tall, broad, and impossibly thin, a shadow cast by someone standing near you, an enormous paper doll.)

What are you saying?

I'm saying that I don't see the girl who was here when I entered the classroom and that I didn't notice her exiting the room. Obviously, she did. It's fine.

Isn't it?

(I also mentioned my impression of someone/thing looming over you from behind, which persists but must be some type of perceptual glitch, right?)

What was that again?

It was me clarifying my statement about the girl who (apparently) vanished.

(And the figure that isn't behind you.)

Are you smiling?

One minute, I'm being asked why you can't see me, the next, I'm being asked if I'm smiling? To be fair, sometimes you can hear a person's smile in their words, can't you? The contraction of the facial muscles must cause a detectable shift in the voice. Or is it that a smile is often accompanied by laughter, so what you're picking up on is the hitching of the breath, the tightening of the vocal cords? I'm typing, though. What about the sound of my fingers on the keyboard suggests I'm smiling?

Anyway, what does it matter? Are you one of those people who reads a smile as a challenge, as the prelude to mockery? This isn't how I operate. If I'm preparing to make fun of you, my face will grow still. In part, this is because my blend of humor tends towards the dry, the satiric, and is best delivered with a minimum of expression. This leaves the target of my remarks unprepared for them, ensuring their efficacy. Should you witness me smiling before I say something, laughing, even, you can be reasonably sure whatever follows will be offered with the intent to make both of us laugh.

I wasn't smiling, though. At least, I don't think I was. Funny how your body can do that, betray you, isn't it? When I was a child, every time I would play a sport, I would laugh, especially if I had to interact with someone else. If I was playing soccer, and I was struggling for the ball with a player from the other team—if I was attending my Tae Kwon Do class and

I had to spar with another student—I would erupt in high-pitched giggles. It was embarrassing, of course, but it seems beyond my ability to control. It infuriated my father, who coached my soccer team, and my Tae Kwon Do instructor, who told me I wasn't taking the martial art seriously enough. To both of them, it must have looked as if I were ridiculing the thing they were trying to teach me. I wasn't. It was more a case of, once I felt myself entering into motion with someone else, our feet kicking at the ball, our hands out in a guard, the laughter welled up in me, as if the movement and the laughter were one and the same.

In any event, I wasn't smiling.

Do I have to take these?

Our answers? You don't *have* to do anything, but I would think you'd be at least a little curious to read our responses.

Oh. You meant those. What are they? I mean, I get that they're pills, but those aren't aspirin. Talk about horse pills. Unless—are they candies? They look like jelly beans; although they seem more...oily. I've never cared for the black ones, myself. I've never understood why whoever makes them includes something so bitter, so harsh, together with all the fruity sweet. When we were kids, my brother and sisters and I would sort out the black jelly beans from the rest and give them to our dad, who took and ate them without complaining. He wasn't much for sweet things, so I figured he didn't mind the candies, maybe even liked them. I wonder sometimes if he did, or if he was just eating them for us. What a trope for fatherhood, right?

Those aren't jelly beans, though, are they? I can see the seam around their middles. Plus, you asked about taking them, didn't you? Which is not the verb you use in conjunction with candy. What are they? And what makes you think you have to swallow them? Because your use of the imperative suggests a reluctance to obey it. If I knew what the black pills were, then maybe I could give you a better answer. Don't you know?

(A last thought, too weird not to be enclosed in parentheses. I'm pretty sure I dreamed about those same pills last night. They were on a white saucer, which had been placed at the center of a small, plain table. I was seated on one side of the table. There was a child across from me, an enormous child, one as big as an adult. I couldn't see his face, because I was concentrating on the black ovals on the dish. That isn't right. It was more a case of, I was focusing on the pills with their oily shells so I wouldn't have to look at the man's face. I could see his hands, which he had placed flat on the tabletop, one on either side of the dish. The fingers were long, thick, the knuckles large, almost swollen. The skin was the milky white of a soft cheese. Fine black hairs rose out of it. The wrists emerged from the cuffs of a white sweatshirt, which in turn protruded from the sleeves of a black winter coat. The air was heavy with the smell of spoiled milk. I wanted to reach out and grab one of those hands—those patient hands, was how I thought of them—but I knew if I did, my fingers would sink into the soft flesh, which would part and slide off the bone. Which would be bad, but not as bad as when the hand began to move, sloughing skin as it pulled itself out of my grip. So I kept my hands in my lap and my eyes on the pills.)

Why did you abandon me?

I assume you mean the rest of the class, since I'm the only one sitting here, still answering your questions. I didn't hear any of them leaving, which seems to be the theme of the day. Am I the only one left? It looks that way, doesn't it? Does this mean the class is going to be canceled? Probably, I'm guessing.

For the moment, though, I'm here. Aren't I? (Unless the other students are all in the classroom, typing away, and I'm the one who's gone someplace else. Except, where would that be, exactly? A parallel universe? A pocket dimension? Hell? If any of those is the case, then why does it look as if I've remained in the same, drab, institutional space? Is it a Sartrean, even-Hell-is-banal kind of situation? [Or, to indulge in the truly bizarre: do you remember what I was saying about the room, before? That it was what brought all of us here? Suppose it did so for purposes of nourishment? My fellow students, seemingly departed, were instead digested. I will be, too, once the space's appetite returns. You? You're the lure, the tiny light those deep-sea predators dangle in front of them to draw fish close enough to their fangs.])

What is this?

It's a bottle. Glass, I think. Based on the flattened shape, I'm guessing it holds liquor. It reminds me of a bottle of orange liqueur my father used to keep in the pantry for a glaze he made when we had a whole chicken.

What's in the bottle you're holding looks more milky, like *pastis* (that's a French liqueur). I'm not sure what else to say about it.

Are there side effects?

You can't mean the liquor. Can you?

Or—wait. What did you do with the pills, the ones from before? Did you swallow them? Whatever they contained, they held a lot of it. It it reacts with the liquor, there could be side-effects galore.

Will I get what I want?

What is it you want? If it's some form of inebriation, then yeah, probably. If it's the systematized derangement of the senses, there appears to be a pretty good chance of that, too. Oh, and fired, because I assume that's what happens to you for popping pills and taking pulls from your bottle of whatever during class time. Although, really, it's only me here and I'm not inclined to say anything to anyone. I mean, in all likelihood, the class is going to be canceled (assuming the people who left intend to drop it). There doesn't seem much point in adding insult to injury.

What is going to happen next?

Depending on how potent the contents of that bottle. I expect you will at the very least feel the need to sit down. Should the alcohol interact with the pills, then I'm not sure. Some type of synergy, which will enhance the effects of each. I'm hoping they contained a mild sedative, and not a powerful hallucinogen. I imagine you'll start to feel a little weird.

When will I be released?

Class is over in ten minutes. If the powers-that-be decide to cancel it, I'd expect they'll let you know in the next couple of days. Should the class escape the axe, there's only fifteen more weeks to go.

You don't sound as if you're talking about your teaching contract, though. Is it the drugs? Have they started to kick in? Are you having some kind of prison hallucination? You aren't behind bars. You're an adjunct instructor for the City University. (Same difference, right? Sorry.) Are you religious? Is it a Biblical reference. (Do you know the Kerouac poem, the one about being free of the heaving meatwheel, safe in heaven dead? I'm not a huge

Kerouac fan—nor am I much of a believer—but there are time when those words cut straight to the heart of me, of my life. [And why do you suppose I think your question has nothing to do with the drugs or religion? Why can I almost see the figure standing behind you, one milk-white hand on either of your shoulders?])

I think you need to stay calm. Try to focus on your breathing. You

Have you forgotten your promise?

Who is saying that? WHO THE FUCK IS SAYING THAT?

Oh God. Oh my fucking God.

Be calm. Be calm.

Oh Christ. Oh Jesus Christ help me.

Afraid—so afraid I pissed myself. Sitting in a puddle of my piss because I'm too afraid to move.

Only thing I can do is keep typing. Which is ridiculous. Always laughed at it when I ran across it in fiction, characters who continue to write as their situation turns to shit, monster tromping up the stairs, ghost at their elbow. All I can do, though; all I can do.

Hands on his—on your shoulders. Fingers curling, digging into your shirt, the muscle beneath. Taking hold. The expression on your face. The face of the form behind you. A character. A letter in an alphabet I've never seen. A signifier without a referent.

The hands pull to either side. You tear. As if made of paper. You split, and you come spilling out of the rent. The room is full of you. You as a boy. You as an old man. You as you were two minutes ago. You as you would be two minutes from now. They flutter and twist, papers dolls caught in a hurricane wind. A deep sound, the moan of someone suffering a pain they did not know possible. The yous twirl and dart out of view. (Where?) The figure behind you opens his hands, allowing the halves of you to float to the floor. He steps back to/into the smart board and is gone.

You took the drugs and I had the trip. Can see the pieces of you lying crumpled on the carpet. Empty snakeskin. Abandoned exoskeleton. The pills. They were full of it, weren't they? A language that isn't a language, a language that's undead, a wound in the world. Did the liquor dissolve them, or was it to numb you for what was coming?

Why? Why would you do this? Surely there are easier ways to kill yourself—to destroy yourself. (Was that what happened? What else could it have been?) And why bring us into it? Why—unless—were we part of it? Did you need us for it? Did you need us—me, really, answering those questions in that order? Why? What did my responses do? Did they contribute to this? Facilitate it? How?

What happened to you? What happened to everyone else? Why am I still here? What is it you think I promised you?

What will happen when I stop typing?

SLIPPAGE

B ecause of its size, we had to turn the horn on its side to fit it in the back of my Saturn. There, it coiled upward like a cobra caught rising to strike. The prop was lighter than its dimensions suggested, fashioned from a rubbery material that left a greasy film on my fingers.

"You're sure you're okay with us taking this?" I said to Phil, whose movie the horn had been cast for.

"Of course," he said, although his body language, arms tightly crossed, hinted at a more complicated response. "I don't have any use for it."

"Thanks again," Laird said. "This is gonna look so cool in the front yard. Wait till Jessica sees it."

"What every writer needs, right? A souvenir from the film version of one of their stories."

"I'm happy you can take it," Phil said.

"All right," I said. "We'd better get on the road."

Leaving Providence took longer than I had anticipated. In the time since I had last updated the GPS, there had been a minor construction boom on the route that should have taken us to I-95. As a result, the pleasant woman's voice directing me kept insisting on turns onto streets that were now buildings, or one-way, or looped through blank spaces on the device's screen. "It's like we're in a Goddamned Ligotti story," I muttered. The sole structure untouched by the changes to the area was a modest bar standing in the center of a dirt lot, its green metal siding battered. I nodded at it as we passed it for the third time. "There's a setting."

Laird nodded. "Yeah. You know there are all kinds of things happening in a place like that."

"Clandestine meetings," I said. "Couples who are having affairs. Gamblers slouching in to pay down debts. Desperate men and women looking to hire someone who knows how to use a baseball bat. Or a knife. Or a gun."

"I ever tell you I used to drink in a place like that?" Laird said. "This was when I moved to Seattle. Money was tight, so I found a dive bar for my booze. Full of all kinds of charming characters. Mostly, everyone kept to themselves. Although, sometimes a bunch of frat boys would crowd through the door, there for the cheap pitchers and to snicker at the locals. There was this one old guy, he used to come into the place every day at one, sit at the bar, and spend a couple of hours drinking shot after shot of bourbon. I never learned his name. He was tall, dressed in a black suit with a white shirt and a black string tie no matter the season. Late fifties, early sixties, I would have said. Wore his hair long, only it was fine, so it frizzed out around his head. His face was square, tanned like a piece of leather. Anyway, this one afternoon, an especially large group of frat boys from WA U occupied the bar. I think there was a big football game on, but I'm not sure. Doesn't matter. After they had emptied four or five pitchers of beer, one of these guys walks up next to the man in black and offers to buy him a drink. From the way the kid acted, you could tell he thought he was being funny. The bartender knew what was going on, but he poured another shot. The man in black nodded to the frat boy, and tossed back the liquor. I couldn't hear everything the kid said next, but the gist of it was, now he wanted the old man to pay for his drink. The man in black shook his head, No. Why not? the kid says. He doesn't want to go over his budget, the old guy says. The frat boy makes a big production. Some of his buddies start to move forward to join him. I'm watching all this happen, but I don't have any plans to get involved. If anything goes down, I figure the bartender has an ax handle under the bar. Well. Finally, the man in black nods, holds up his hands, and says okay, he'll buy the kid a drink. He reaches inside his jacket, and removes his wallet. Except, it's more like a purse, or a pencil case, long, made of black material. The old guy unzips it, slips his hand inside, and throws something on the bar. Right away, the frat boy leaps back. His eyes are popping out of his head. He almost trips over his feet. His buddies rush up to him. *What is it, man? Dude, are you okay? It's nothing*, he says, *let's get out of here.* Which they did. It wasn't nothing, though. From where I was sitting, I could see what the man in black had tossed onto the bar: fingers, half a dozen of them. All different lengths. Some smooth, one covered in grey hair. None was what you'd call fresh. A couple looked mummified. One by one, the old man picked them up and returned them to his pouch. As he did, he caught me watching him. *You want me to buy you a drink?* he says. I looked away."

"Jesus," I said.

"Yeah. That was the last time I drank there."

By now, I had found my way out of the city and was heading west toward home. For the first few miles, traffic was heavy, but by the time we crossed into Connecticut, the cars had thinned out, and I sped up. "Did Phil say how the shoot went?"

"Okay, I guess."

"I thought he sounded a little, I don't know, squirrelly. Know what I mean?"

"Kind of. Mostly, I think he's tired. Filming ran way over, and then with what happened to Gage…"

"Exactly what is the story with Gage?"

"Exhaustion, mostly. They had to recast the horns a bunch of times. The things kept breaking. It took him until the shoot was underway to find the right blend of materials, and one of the ingredients he used meant the stuff needed longer to set. Pretty stressful, you can imagine. Once they were on site a few days, he found the skull—you haven't seen that, have you?"

"No."

"Apparently, Gage was out walking in the woods, waiting for the horns to finish drying, and he comes across an animal skull on top of a pile of rocks. Phil sent me a picture of it, said it was exactly what they needed. Looked like a horse skull to me, but massive. We're talking Clydesdale, bigger, even. Plus, there were these…deformities."

"What do you mean?"

"Places where the bone had grown in all kinds of weird ways. When this thing was alive, it must have been hideous.

"Anyway, Gage became obsessed with the skull. There was a particular look he envisioned for it, but he couldn't get it. Eventually, he dragged his hands all over it. Those irregularities in the bone? A lot of them were sharp, almost serrated. Tore his fingers and palms to shit. By the time anyone discovered what he'd been doing, he'd given the skull several coats of his blood. From what Phil told me, Gage said, *The design isn't perfect, but it's the best I could do.*"

"Ouch. Poor Gage."

"Yeah. He'll be okay, but the crew was pretty freaked out. Still used the skull, though."

"I don't know if I think that's messed up, or hardcore. Or both."

"I'm pretty sure it's both."

"What do you think the skull was doing there?"

"You mean on the rock pile?"

"Sounds like an altar, doesn't it?"

"I suppose. Probably just some kids screwing around. Although, the place where they shot, Phil said there had been some cult activity there in the seventies. Not Manson-level stuff, but enough weirdness for the local cops to close the party down."

"Bone wouldn't last that long out in the open," I said. "We're talking forty-plus years of upstate New York winters and summers. And I want to say some rodents will eat bone; I can't remember where I read that. Unless one of the original cultists saved the skull, and went back when the coast was clear."

"Could be."

"Strange about the skull. The deformities, I mean. I've never heard of that happening to a horse."

"Me neither. To tell the truth, it could have come from a horse, but it could have belonged to another animal, too. All I had to go on was a cell phone picture."

"What else could it have been? A moose?"

"No. I've seen moose skulls. This wasn't one of them."

"What did they do with it? I'm surprised Phil didn't offer to let you have that, as well."

"They buried it, near where Gage found it."

"Oh."

SLIPPAGE

"The thing is…" Laird sighed. "When I was driving east to yours and Fiona's, I stopped the first night at a rest area in South Dakota. It was late, one or two in the morning, and I was fighting to keep my eyes open. Athena was in the passenger's seat, and she kept nuzzling me. It was like she knew I needed help staying awake. The rest area was in the middle of nowhere, just a parking lot and a cinderblock building with men's and women's rooms, surrounded by fields rolling into the night. Earlier, it had snowed, and everything was covered in a layer of white. We were the only ones there. I figured I would park for a couple of hours and catch some shuteye. Before I could settle in, though, I had to give Athena a walk, and visit the facilities, myself. It was cold, and there was a wind blowing across the fields that felt as if it had come all the way from Canada. Sliced straight through my jacket. Athena did her business, and I locked her in the truck while I went to the toilets. When I came out, I heard her barking. Even with the wind whistling—that's how loud it was. I couldn't see anything, but I assumed someone had pulled up on the other side of my rig and was trying to get into it, maybe to grab Athena. I ran across the parking lot, almost slipped in the snow. Usually, I would have had a knife on me, but I'd left it in the truck, under the driver's seat. I was hoping the sight of me charging toward them would scare off whoever Athena was barking at. I rounded the front of the truck, expecting to find one or two guys waiting for me. But there was no one there, no vehicle, nothing. I was so relieved, I felt sick. I had gone from zero all the way to a hundred and back to zero again so fast, my system was swimming with adrenaline. I leaned against the door. Athena was still going nuts, barking and snapping at something in front of the truck. I raised my head, and all I saw were empty fields. Spots danced in front of my eyes. My mouth tasted like metal. *Athena*, I said, and then I saw it. Way out at the very limit of where the lights from the rest area reached, something was moving. It was too far away, and the lighting was too poor, for me to see clearly. I thought it was a deer, but it was too big. The proportions were wrong for a moose. It was prancing, kicking up puffs of snow, which reminded me of a horse, but its head was—what I could make out was wrong, misshapen, like a cubist painting brought to life. I watched it dance, and the next I knew, I had the door open and was pushing into the cab, shoving Athena back as she tried to leap out to go after whatever the thing was. I stabbed the key in the ignition, and hauled ass out of there.

Didn't stop until I was clear of South Dakota and the sun was shining."

"Wow," I said. "What do you think it was?"

"Probably a deer. I was super tired, and super stressed. That's a combination that'll make you see all kinds of stuff. I gotta tell you, though, I understand what I saw was something like a waking dream, but it feels as if it was real. When Phil sent me the photo of the skull, it was as if the universe was saying to me, *You didn't imagine that, after all.* Which is bullshit—"

"But still freaky. I hear you."

The GPS had taken us from the interstate onto a series of smaller roads heading north by northwest, away from the coast, into Connecticut's interior. Rows of stores and restaurants, their neon names unfamiliar, passed to either side. "So does Phil have any idea when the movie's gonna be ready?"

"Nah. It sounds like it could take a while. He may have to reshoot several scenes. Some kind of artifacts showed up on onscreen, and he doesn't think he can edit around them."

"Oh, man. I wouldn't have expected that to happen with digital."

"Yeah. Data corruption, I guess."

"Frustrating."

Laird shrugged. "It is what it is."

"Funny," I said after a few minutes, "what happened to you in South Dakota reminds of something Bill at the post office told me. About ten or fifteen years ago, he said, he received an envelope with no return address. Inside was a single Polaroid. It showed him as he'd been in his twenties, sideburns, bell bottoms, the works. He was standing beside a man wearing a butcher's apron and heavy gloves. The guy had one arm around Bill's shoulders; they were both grinning. In his other hand, the guy was holding an enormous cleaver. There was blood everywhere: on the cleaver, the gloves, the apron, all over the man's face and hair, spotted on Bill's shirt and jeans. Bill was holding a glass of something, and there was blood floating in that, too. The thing was, he had no memory at all of what the photo showed. He would have written it off as Photoshopped, a friend playing a strange joke on him, but the picture was a Polaroid, which he didn't think you could manipulate in that way. Or, if you could, he wasn't aware that anyone he knew had the capability. He showed me the photo. He kept it in his desk, because he didn't want his wife seeing it. I understood what he meant. There was something deeply disturbing about it. Like, this wasn't a

Halloween stunt. I'm not much of a judge, but the picture looked authentic to me. *What did you do?* I asked him. *What could I do?* he said. Which was fair enough, I suppose, but…"

"Huh."

"Sometimes, it's like, the world slips, you know?"

"Yeah."

Ahead, the road plunged into a tunnel through the side of a long, low mountain. Orange light strobed the inside of the SUV. The GPS screen contracted to a bright point, went black. "What the hell?" I tapped it. "Can these things blow a fuse?"

"Beats me."

The tunnel opened on a deep valley, its slopes aglow with hundreds of red-orange dots. *Bonfires*, I thought. Overhead, half a shattered moon trailed a tail of yellow fragments after it. I cried out, jerked my head away from the sight. To either side of the road, tall, slender poles arced toward the moon's remains, bent in that direction by the round objects mounted atop them. I took my foot off the gas, but the Saturn carried us forward, anyway. "Laird," I said, "where the hell are we?"

He didn't answer. Behind us, the horn rose spiraling to the roof.

STORY NOTES

I love great big story collections. I can still recall the thrill I felt unwrapping my copy of Stephen King's *Skeleton Crew* on my birthday the year the book was published (1985). There was a heft to the hardcover that promised a host of stories inside, which there was, from the short novel, *The Mist*, which opened the collection and which remains one of my favorite of King's works, to such stories as "Gramma," "The Monkey," and "Word Processor of the Gods" (other favorites).

When I decided to start assembling the stories for my fourth collection, I found I had enough material for such a big book. It was a varied group, its contents including elements of science fiction and fantasy, its diversity appropriate for a large volume. To begin with, I was concerned the book didn't appear to have the same kind of thematic unity as my previous two collections. The majority of the stories had been written in response to invitations to anthologies devoted to a single writer: Lovecraft, in the main, but also Robert Aickman, Robert W. Chambers, and Thomas Ligotti. Even when I hadn't been writing for a tribute anthology, I'd tended to do so with a particular writer in mind as a kind of guiding star. But this, I realized, was what bound the group of stories together: they constituted a (rough, imprecise, incomplete) genealogy.

Think of these story notes as additional observations about the gnarled branches of my family tree. For each story, I've listed the writers (and sometimes filmmakers) who were foremost in my mind as I was writing it. As ever, if such explorations aren't your thing, feel free to skip them.

(And yes, this family tree is pretty white and very male. In part, this is due to the subject matter of the anthologies to which I've been invited to contribute. But it's also true that I haven't done well at exploring the other branches of my literary genealogy. Frankly, I've been blind to those leading to Charlotte Bronte, Emily Bronte, Angela Carter, Willa Cather, Shirley Jackson, Vernon Lee, Flannery O'Connor, Katherine Anne Porter, and Virginia Woolf, to name a few, as well as to Gabriel Garcia Marquez and Salman Rushdie. I'll try to do better, folks; stay tuned.)

"Sweetums" (Robert W. Chambers, David Lynch): Joe Pulver contacted me to ask if I'd be interested in contributing to a pair of anthologies he was editing. The first was an homage to Robert W. Chambers. (This was before the first season of the *True Detective* TV show popularized the author of *The King in Yellow*.) (More on the second below.) Joe had been obsessed with Chambers's work for years, even making a pilgrimage to the author's grave site. Although I knew Chambers's name, I hadn't read him and understood him mainly as a precursor to H. P. Lovecraft. I dug out my copy of *The King in Yellow and Other Horror Stories* and sat down with it. When I was done, I had a better sense of what Joe saw in Chambers. I suppose you might describe him as an American decadent. His weird fiction has a fleshly, sensual quality that distinguishes it from the work of the majority of his contemporaries. In this regard, he seems more to anticipate the work of Clark Ashton Smith and Fritz Leiber; although he employs the same technique of what might be called fragmentary allusion you find in Machen and Lovecraft. His stories return to a few conceits, the best-known of which is probably the sinister drama, *The King in Yellow*, but which also include a kind of alternate history of the US.

I'm not certain how exactly it occurred to me to bring together Chambers's weird fiction with the films of David Lynch. I've loved Lynch since I first saw *Blue Velvet*; though it was the first season of *Twin Peaks* that cemented me as a lifelong fan. I can't think of any other director whose work I find so affecting on a visceral level; I don't know of anyone else who has so consistently inspired such deep unease in me. *Mulholland Drive* is probably my favorite of his movies, but *Inland Empire* has stuck with me in a way I find hard to understand. (And yes, I'm sympathetic to those who can't stand it; YMMV, as the kids say.) In particular, there's a scene of Laura Dern delivering a monologue in the latter film that refuses to leave my memory. For Joe's anthology, I had the idea I might write my own version of the speech and build the rest of the story out from it. I imagined my protagonist wandering through a vast labyrinth of sets drawn from Chambers's work, a kind of spatial realization of the fragmentary nature of much of his fiction. At its end, she would find herself still within the world of Chambers's fiction.

It occurs to me now that this is another way to conceive the stories in this book, as wanderings in the *topoi* of other writers, influence and response presented spatially, geographically. I suppose the collection's subtitle might equally have been, "labyrinths."

"Hyphae" (Edgar Allan Poe, Stephen King): Silvia Moreno-Garcia and Orrin Grey solicited this story for an anthology about fungi, one of the lesser-known but nonetheless interesting subsets of the weird/horror field. There are fungous things in Lovecraft and also William Hope Hodgson's fiction, not to mention, the cult classic film, *Matango*. Oddly, a title came to me first: "Usher's Toadstool," which I thought was going to be a fungus picked up in the Paris catacombs. (Did this draw on details from my father's life, who when I was a child took business trips to Paris for IBM and several of whose toenails had been twisted by some form of fungus? I'm sure it did.) Initially, I imagined an explicit connection between the fungus and Poe's story, but as it turned out, the story turned in an autobiographical direction. The house I grew up in had just such a closet at the foot of the basement stairs, which I used to regard with dread every time I passed it, certain that the space behind its door was vast. (No doubt the subterranean spaces in so many of my stories [not least of them "Children of the Fang"] owe their origins to this place.) Although it wasn't a conscious decision on my part, Stephen King's presence in the story's DNA seems obvious to me now; indeed, I wonder if it's a riff on his early story, "Graveyard Shift."

"Muse" (Stephen Graham Jones): Paul Tremblay approached me and Laird Barron about collaborating with him on a joint appreciation of Stephen Graham Jones's work for a convention booklet. The idea, Paul said, would be for each of us to write something in response to the other, a kind of chain-essay. I turned to the first story of Stephen's I'd read, "Raphael," in *Cemetery Dance* magazine, which had knocked my socks off first in its evocation of a particularly Stephen King-esque experience of adolescence, and then by an astonishing turn into mad, full-tilt supernatural horror. I also had in mind the brief times I'd spent with Stephen (particularly at the 2011 World Horror Convention in Austin). The piece of writing that resulted is story-as-appreciation, a form of which I've become especially fond in recent years. It probably owes something as well to the animated Hellboy film, *Blood and Iron*, whose image of a vampire crawling up a wall I found unexpectedly chilling. I'm sure Stephen would approve.

In the years since I wrote this piece, my esteem for Stephen's work has continued to grow, until he's become one of my favorite contemporary writers, someone whose every story I look forward to eagerly. As of this writing, I'm in the early stages of a new story inspired by his work, a piece whose working title is, "The Last Graduate Student."

(Oh, and in his response to my piece, Paul trashed it. Bastard.)

"Zombies in Marysville" (Stephen King): In 2012, back when blogs were still a big thing, Erin Underwood, one of the principal architects of the annual Boskone convention, asked me if I'd be interested in participating in a multi-author blog event. Over a two-day period, a group of us would, in the spirit of Orson Welles's *War of the Worlds* radio broadcast, write blog entries detailing the outbreak of a zombie plague. By this point, my older son, Nick, had become a police officer with Baltimore city, and he'd supplied me with a vast store of anecdotes, most of them amusing, a few disturbing. One of them involved a guy who had, as a result of a domestic dispute, freaked out and thrown a huge stone planter at the cops who had arrived to address the disturbance. Subsequently, he was taken safely into custody, but I thought the report might serve as the kernel for my blog entry. It allowed me to focus on the early days of the outbreak, which struck me as more interesting and unsettling than the post-apocalyptic aftermath to come. In writing my entry, I reached for the kind of plain storytelling style I associate with Stephen King. My contribution to the event succeeded better than I anticipated: a couple of friends who read my blog entry thought it was true until they reached the banner for the Zombie Apocalypse blog-a-thon at the bottom.

"With Max Barry in the Nearer Precincts" (Mary Rickert, Jeffrey Ford):
Eric Guignard contacted me about writing a story for an anthology concerning various visions of the afterlife. Many times, when an invitation drops into my mailbox, it takes me a while to figure out what my response to it is going to be. Every so often, though, the answer is right at hand. In 2007, I had participated in a Halloween-related event for APR's *Weekend America*. Along with Neil Gaiman and Mary Rickert, I came up with a 30-second horror story to be read Halloween weekend.

(Actually, I submitted three possibilities, of which the following was selected:

The Visitor

I had barely switched off the bedside light and settled down to sleep when I heard my son shuffling down the hall. Since we'd moved, he'd been doing this most nights: leaving his bed in favor of Ann and mine's. It had reached the point, I hardly noticed him climbing into bed with us anymore. We assumed it was a phase he'd grow out of.

He was early tonight. I felt the bed shift as he crawled over Ann, wriggled under the sheets. His breathing was heavy, almost hoarse. I wondered if he were coming down with something.

When I woke a couple of hours later, it was to Ann saying, "That's okay, come into bed with Mommy and Daddy," my son scrambling into the empty space between us.

Although, to be honest, I preferred this one:

The Dead

You have to go for the head. They tell you that in all the literature, the public service announcements, the infomercials. The government video even gives you suggestions for the best spots to aim at: between the eyes, behind the ear. What they don't tell you about— what none of them tell you about is the voices. You think they'll be silent, like in the movies we laughed at when we were kids. Or maybe they'll moan, say, "Braaaaiiiinnnns." You don't expect to hear them out there crying. You don't expect to hear them saying, "Mommy? Mommy, where are you? I can't see so good. What hap-

pened to me? I'm scared. Mommy?" For all the world like they were
your babies again, and you lining up your sights.

(But I digress.) One of Mary's stories employed a striking conceit, reversing the standard advice to the dying to head into the light. No, her piece
said, the light some see at the end of life is in fact an annihilating fire. I
loved the idea of the glowing tunnel being something terrible, and when
Eric's invitation arrived, I reached for it. At the same time, I knew I was
going to write something inspired by Jeffrey Ford's fiction. Ford has had
a place among my writing heroes since I burned through a bunch of his
stories in 2003-2004, when I used to read them in *The Magazine of Fantasy
& Science Fiction* while my then-infant son napped in my arms; one of the
big thrills of my academic career (such as it was) was having Ford as a guest
for the two Fantastic Genres conferences I helped run at SUNY New Paltz
in the mid-2000s. I had been thinking about Ford's fiction a great deal,
particularly the way in which he employed narrative devices from the later
nineteenth century in his stories, as well as the way he drew on a variety of
sources for the material of his fiction. The first sentence of the piece came
to me right away, as did certain of the images, such as the enormous broken
staircase. (I have the sense of having dreamed some of them, particularly
the ancient brick towers Max Barry sees, but I'm not sure about it.) I liked
the idea of a devastated afterlife, which of course raised the question, what
had happened to it? I believe the answer had its roots in a trip to the British
Museum I had taken with my wife and younger son a year or two prior,
where I had been impressed by the exhibits focusing on ancient Assyria.
In revising the story, I was helped by Eric's editorial suggestions, which
brought to the fore its strangeness. It's another piece in which topography
plays an especially important role.

"Into the Darkness, Fearlessly" (Thomas Ligotti): This was the second
part of the invitation I had from Joe Pulver, for a tribute to the work of
Thomas Ligotti. I've been aware of Ligotti's fiction since the mass market
paperback publication of *Songs of a Dead Dreamer* in the early nineties; at
roughly the same time, *Weird Tales* published a special Ligotti issue which
included a far-ranging interview with him. I'd read his second collection,
Grimscribe, and had written and published an essay on the use his story,

"The Last Feast of Harlequin," made of Lovecraft's work. I never felt much direct influence from him on my own writing, but I respected the achievement of his fiction, which seemed to me to build on Lovecraft's in genuinely innovative and intriguing ways. In this regard, it reminds me of both Laird Barron and Caitlin R. Kiernan's achievements. At roughly the same time I was thinking about how best to respond to Joe's invitation, I read Laird's response to Ligotti, "More Dark." A relatively small detail in the story struck me as worth expanding upon, and this developed into my story. Not until I came to write these notes did it occur to me that this story, like the other one I wrote for Joe's invitation, involves a character becoming lost inside a fictional world.

"Children of the Fang" (H.P. Lovecraft, Robert Penn Warren): I guess you could say Ellen Datlow asked for this story, but it might be more accurate to say that I invited myself to write it for her. Laird Barron and I were doing a reading with her at a public library in Mount Vernon; I drove Laird down and we picked up Ellen at the train station there. While on our way over to the library, she told us she was putting together a reprint anthology of stories using Lovecraft's monsters. Did either of us have anything she could use for it? I didn't, but I told her I would write something for her, if she wanted. Was I sure? she asked. The pay wouldn't be much. To be in one of her books, I said, I was sure.

From the beginning, I knew I didn't want to use one of Lovecraft's more popular monsters, the shuggoths or the Mi-Go or some version of Cthulhu. I'm not sure exactly how I hit on the lizard people who figure obliquely in his story, "The Nameless City," but they struck me as sufficiently distinct from the usual, gelatinous entities you associate with Lovecraft to be worth using. (It's possible I was thinking about the serpent people who feature in some of Robert E. Howard's stories and who were illustrated so well by the great John Buscema during his time on the *Conan the Barbarian* and *King Conan* comics.) As I've remarked in other places, for some reason, whenever I have an invitation to contribute to a Lovecraft-themed anthology, I tend to turn in a more domestic, rather than cosmic, direction. I'm not sure why this is. In this case, it led me to bring together the Lovecraftian element with the work of Robert Penn Warren (and probably Faulkner behind him). During my study for my Bachelor's and Master's degrees at SUNY New

Paltz, I did a lot of work on writers of the American South, particularly Warren, on a couple of whose poems I wrote a 130-page Master's thesis. I attended several conferences in Tennessee and Kentucky focused on Warren's work. The landscape of Kentucky made a strong impression on me, from the dome mountains in its east to the rolling flatlands in its west. Together with Scotland, it's one of the few places I've dreamed about repeatedly. In my time reading and writing about Warren's work, and then visiting the place in which he lived his early life, I had been treated to a variety of stories about the people of the region, some of which I decided to incorporate into this narrative. (I also decided a visit from Detective Calasso of the Albany, NY, police department was in order. Previously, he had played a small role in my story, "City of the Dog." I enjoyed having him back, which probably explains why he would return in a short time as the protagonist of my story, "The Communion of Saints," about which, more below.) I structured the narrative largely by instinct; it wasn't until after its publication that the very smart Usman Malik observed the parallel between the human family and the community of lizard people, which I realized was completely accurate and which made me appreciate how much smarter my creativity is than I am. (Which is developing into another theme of these stories; although, to be honest, it could apply to pretty much all my writing.)

(Oh, and Ritchie Tenorio keeps asking for a story about the Hippie War. We'll see.)

"Episode Three: On the Great Plains, in the Snow" (Stephen King): Ellen Datlow asked me if I had anything for a non-themed crowd-funded anthology she was editing. I had the beginning of this story, maybe the first eight or ten pages, which I had written a few years before and then put aside because I didn't know what was responsible for the horrific scene my two ghosts(?) had come across. The protagonist, I sensed, was some version of my father, dead these many years, and as the story progressed, I discovered he shared many of my father's loves and experiences, from the music of Ella Fitzgerald to driving an MG with me in the passenger's seat. As for the beast he and his fellow ghost(?) must confront, it's another effort on my part to fulfill a request made by my older son to me years ago, namely, to write a story about a giant monster. But I realize, too, its origins in an old horror movie I watched while home sick from school, one in which an invisible

Allosaurus terrorizes a mining camp. (I kid you not.) It occurs to me that there are some interesting connections between the vision of the afterlife in this story and that in "With Max Barry in the Nearer Precincts." Both involve posthumous experiences full of monsters and devastated spaces and end with more exploring to be done.

As for the title: one of the first stories I published was called, "Episode Seven: Last Stand Against the Pack in the Kingdom of the Purple Flowers." After I was finished with it, I thought I might have more to say about its protagonists. (I still might.) But as time went by, I also realized I could write other episodes, as it were, in which a couple of characters had to face a seemingly overwhelming threat and find a way to defeat it (or not). This story fit such a description, and thus, Episode Three.

Oh, and Lynch's name is indebted to Tom Lynch, who helped support the fundraising for the book. He's a good guy, with a delightful family.

"Tragōidia" (E.M. Forster): Aaron French solicited this story for a book of stories about satyrs, of all things. I liked the challenge of the subject, and I took the opportunity the story provided to revisit the landscape of Provence, another favorite place. I also indulged an interest which has developed over the last twenty-five years or so, with the figure of Pan in British literature of the late nineteenth and early twentieth centuries. In writing the piece, I think I was drawing on E.M. Forster's portraits of English women and men out of place, sometimes subtly, sometimes obviously, in other cultures.

"Ymir" (Laird Barron): Many years ago, in one of his earliest published stories, "Hallucigenia," Laird Barron made a passing reference to a character named Barret Langan. One of these days, I told him, I was going to write a story about that character. So when Ross Lockhart and Justin Steele asked me if I would be interested in contributing to an anthology of stories about Laird's work, I had a character in hand. He wasn't the protagonist, though: she came from a story Laird and I had discussed writing together. I had been struck by news reports of the truckers who had gone over to post-invasion Iraq to move supplies from one US base to another. The pay was good, the danger considerable. Truckers saw and sometimes did terrible things; some were murdered horribly. I proposed we write a story about a woman who is either on vacation from such a job or done with it entirely and seeking a change of scene in either Greece or Turkey. There, she comes across a well from which a monster, some form of ghoul, emerges and pursues her through a forest. Ultimately, the story wasn't sufficiently compelling for either of us, but I was able to repurpose many of its elements. In the process, the well became vast, containing within itself elements from many of my favorite Barron stories, including "Hallucigenia" and "The Broadsword."

Laird keeps insisting the story isn't canon. Secretly, I think he knows better.

"Irezumi" (H.P. Lovecraft and William Gibson): As I recall, the idea of a volume which would bring together Lovecraftian tropes with those of the cyberpunks came from Brian Sammons. Initially, I have to admit, I was pretty dubious about the proposed combination. Lovecraft's gelatinous monstrosities seemed at a far remove from cyberpunk's gleaming circuitry. What helped me to bridge the gap between the two was an idea I'd been kicking around that at least some of Lovecraft's cosmic entities might find the ruin we've been making of the planet quite to their liking. After all, why put yourself to the trouble of conquering a place when its inhabitants have already customized it to your needs? Of course, not all of Lovecraft's entities might agree with this point of view, which might lead to conflict among those figures. With this underlying framework established, the rest of the story unfolded in a series of linked extrapolations. The result was the most out-and-out science fictional story I've written, many of whose visions remain depressingly possible, even likely. The title is a transliteration of the Japanese word for tattoo: its literal meaning of inserting ink seemed particularly apt to certain of the story's details.

I missed the deadline for Brian's anthology, but Nick Gervers took the story for a double issue of *Postscripts*.

"The Horn of the World's Ending" (H.P. Lovecraft, Robert E. Howard, Fritz Leiber, Michael Moorcock, and Gene Wolfe): Darrell Schweitzer has faithfully invited me to anthology after anthology, most of them inspired in some way by Lovecraft. There isn't one I haven't had an idea for, but I usually wind up missing the deadline by a wide margin. That was not the case with this story. The theme of the anthology was Lovecraftian elements in different historical periods. Given Lovecraft's interest in the classical world—manifest in many ways most succinctly in his famous Roman dream—I knew the plot would involve the famous lost legion, the 9th, also known as the Hispana. The voice for the story came in part from Gene Wolfe's brilliant novel, *Soldier of the Mist*, and its sequels, while many of the elements owe themselves to a melange of the works of Robert E. Howard, Fritz Leiber, and Michael Moorcock. (Indeed, the Atlantean sorcerer-king owes a great deal to Moorcock's Elric. And yes, the lizard people against which he and his kingdom fight are the same ones from "Children of the Fang.") In many ways, this story draws more heavily on the writers I read as a child than any I've written. I'm not certain what happened to the black horn and its self-appointed guardian following this story, but I suspect I'm not done with either.

"The Underground Economy" (Robert Aickman, David Lynch): At the first Necronomicon Providence, Simon Strantzas told me he was contemplating putting together an anthology of Robert Aickman tribute stories in time for the centenary of the writer's birth. He was concerned, though, about news of a similar book already announced. I suggested there were more than enough writers indebted to Aickman to justify Simon's project, and possibly more like it. When Simon went ahead with *Aickman's Heirs*, I was pleased to receive an invitation to it. Robert Aickman is a writer who has come to mean more to me as I've grown older, both for the excellence of his prose and the mysteriousness of his conceits. In important ways, he reminds me of Peter Straub. There were a number of Aickman's stories I considered responding to: "Pages from a Young Girl's Journal" and "The Hospice" at the front of the list. But it was "The Swords" that provoked the most immediate reaction in me; I could hear the voice of its narrator immediately. A number of reviewers of the anthology remarked on the presence of David Lynch's films in a number of the stories, and I suppose that's the case in mine (specifically *Twin Peaks: Fire Walk with Me*). *Aickman's Heirs* deservedly won the Shirley Jackson award, and serves as a fine tribute to the writer's work.

"The Communion of Saints" (Stephen King, Peter Straub, Dario Argento): In my early twenties, I moved to the state capital, Albany. The reason I gave my parents for leaving home was my desire to pursue a Master's degree at SUNY Albany; the truth was more complicated. After four years commuting to SUNY New Paltz, I was desperate to get out from under my parents' roof. My then-girlfriend had already located to Albany to work on her MAT in TESOL (also at SUNYA) and I wanted very much to join her. In addition, Albany was possessed of a certain glamour due to the presence of William Kennedy. In his Pulitzer-Prize-winning *Ironweed*, as well as in the other novels of what was being called the Albany cycle, Kennedy had done for New York's capital what Faulkner had done for Jefferson County, Mississippi, and Stephen King for central Maine. Kennedy was listed as part of the SUNY Albany faculty, and I had the fantasy of studying with him.

This did not happen. In fact, the two years I spent in Albany were something of a disaster. I failed most of the classes I took at SUNYA; I worked a couple of terrible jobs; and my girlfriend quickly finished her degree and returned to Long Island, from which she dumped me for a rich French guy. (Really.) When I limped back to my parents', it was just in time for my father's death. To put it mildly, my feelings about these years and the city in which I spent them are not the happiest. Perhaps for this reason, I've returned to Albany as a location for my fiction on a number of occasions, starting with "City of the Dog" and continuing (briefly) in "The Shallows" and "Children of the Fang." When Ross Lockhart invited me to submit to a tribute anthology to the giallo films of such directors as Mario Bava and Lucio Fulci, Albany volunteered itself as the setting. Perhaps erroneously, I associate giallo with the urban, and while I could have used my local city of Kingston/Wiltwyck, I felt a larger city was required for the story I had in mind. This narrative would revolve around a group of monsters including Freddy Kruegger, Hannibal Lecter, and the Xenomorph from the *Alien* films. I had been thinking of these figures as the successors to the monsters of the earlier part of the twentieth century (i.e. Dracula, Frankenstein, and the Wolf Man). Compared to those older monsters, the newer batch struck me as possessing less depth—maybe because they were largely devoid of the tragic dimension that often attached itself to their predecessors. (Even Lecter, for all his elegance and eloquence, is not as complex a character.) I liked the idea of these second-rate monsters running amok in a city whose best days were behind it. For a protagonist, Detective Calasso of the Albany PD, who had played a supporting role in a couple of my previous stories, stepped forward. It turned out he had his own exhaustions to deal with.

In writing the story, I drew on the stylistic example of Peter Straub's fiction, adding details from Dario Argento's movies. Only when it was done and published did I realize the story's profound debt to Stephen King's *It*; indeed, it's as much a response to the novel as it is to Argento and company. So involved was I with Calasso's interior life that I missed what now seems glaringly obvious.

Nor was this story the end of my involvement with Detective Calasso. Now retired from law enforcement, he's become the proprietor of an antique shop which has featured in a more recent story, "Madame Painte: For Sale." I expect I'll be hearing more from him in the future.

"Aphanisis" (Michael Moorcock): The talented young Scottish writer, Chris Kelso, emailed asking if I'd be interested in writing a story set in his invented world, the Slave State, which features in a number of his novels and stories. It's a strange terrain that owes a debt, variously, to the works of William S. Burroughs, Philip K. Dick, and Alasdair Gray. As the name suggests, it's also a place in whose populace is in various states of bondage. That kind of totalitarian setting always brings out my inner rebel, and I imagined a character whose ultimate act of resistance to this state of affairs would be to remove himself from it, not just physically, but in every way conceivable, to eradicate all there was of him experientially, both consciously and unconsciously, so that every aspect of him would be put beyond the control of the authorities. The resulting story owes itself to my youthful love of Michael Moorcock's Elric of Melniboné stories and novels. I liked the idea of the protagonist fighting increasingly bizarre figures from his unconscious and even preconscious mind. (Any excuse to put a sword in a character's hands, it would seem.) I borrowed the title from psychoanalysis, where it refers to the loss of sexual desire, and also from poststructural theory, which has used it to refer to the disappearance of the self.

"Gripped" (Joe Pulver): After Joe Pulver became quite ill, a group of his friends decided to write a series of stories and poems for him on our blogs as a way to raise his spirits. My contribution imagined the early days of his life as a visionary writer. I enjoyed tying the tradition of cosmic horror together with that of French poets including Rimbaud, Verlaine, and Apollinaire.

"**Inundation**" (Stephen King): Before we bought our first house, my wife and I lived with our son in a large house set on a rather steep hillside. During heavy rains and the spring thaw, the basement would flood, water streaming from the back wall to the front. An especially intense storm would send a sheet of water down our hill and across the street, to wash at the foundation of our neighbor's house. This was in my head when I opened Aaron French's email saying he was guest-editing an Atlantis-themed issue of the *Lovecraft eZine*. Atlantis was part of the popular culture of my youth, whether as the subject of episodes of such pseudo-scientific TV shows as *In Search Of*, or as the home of the titular character of *The Man from Atlantis*. This is not to mention my exposure through comic books to residents of the lost underwater city ranging from Prince Namor, aka the Sub-Mariner, to Arthur Curry, aka Aquaman. Aaron's invitation conjured an image of an Atlantean warrior (I'm pretty sure it was Namor's enemy, Attuma). So many stories of Atlantis touch on the idea of the lost city or some aspect of it rising to the surface; I liked the idea of the watery place rising into our existence from another dimension—which also seemed to give the story a slightly more cosmic dimension, in keeping with its place of publication. As with "Zombies in Marysville," I liked approaching a great catastrophe from the margins.

"**To See, To Be Seen**" (*The Cabinet of Dr. Caligari*, Jorge Luis Borges): When my wife and I decided it was time to start shopping for a house, we looked at one in the city of Kingston that was in many ways the perfect kind of house for a horror writer to live in. It was tall, orange and brown, with a pointy roof like a witch's hat. There wasn't really any land attached to it, though, so we wound up searching elsewhere, until we found the place we're in now. That house, though: I continue to drive past it on a regular basis, and I think, Maybe, someday. It was inevitable it would appear in a story.

The piece in which it finally featured had its beginnings in an email from Joe Pulver, who before his illness wrote asking if I'd be interested in contributing to a book of stories inspired by the great silent film, *The Cabinet of Dr. Caligari*. There was no question I would; the real question was what form my response would take. I kicked around ideas set within the world of the movie, and also of its filming, but what ultimately occurred to me originated in the move Fiona and I made from our last rental to the house we purchased. I should add that we bought during the Great Recession, taking advantage of the substantial first time home owner's tax credit the government offered. We hired a team of movers, one of whom told me a brief story during a break. I can't remember what question of mine prompted it, but he told me that he and his companions were getting more and more calls from banks to go to houses and empty them of their contents. Because of the cratering economy, more and more people were walking away from their over-mortgaged houses and everything in them, leaving it all to be repossessed by the lenders. I knew this was the kernel of a story the moment I heard it. What, I thought, might a crew of movers stumble across in one of these houses? What if it were a prop left over from a famous film, one whose very fame had charged it with a certain...resonance?

This was where the orange and brown house found its way into print, as the location of the prop. I see now that this is very much a story of houses, from this one to the empty neighborhood to which the characters drive later in the piece. (I think it was Des Lewis who recognized its film-set quality in his real-time review of the story; well done, Des.) There's a little bit of Borges here, both in the name of the mysterious and sinister group, the Friends of Borges, and in the presentation of a savage trap. It's a bitter piece, but I like it, because it is bitter, and because it is my story.

"What You Do Not Bring Forth" (Peter Straub): Peter Straub's fiction has continued to mean more to me than the work of any other living writer. I've returned to it on a fairly regular basis: every now and again, I'll decide I should reread something of his, and when I do, I find all manner of new dimensions unfolding within it. There's some longer work of fiction, a novella or novel, waiting to be written based in my response to Peter's work. In the meantime, there's this, which arose from an invitation by S.T. Joshi to contribute to a new anthology on the theme of dreams and dreaming. The only rule was that stories could not be set in Lovecraft's dream world. This possibility hadn't occurred to me; instead, I opted to draw on elements from a number of Peter's novels and stories, including *Shadowland*, *The Throat*, *A Dark Matter*, and "Lapland, or Film Noir." The result was much shorter than I might have predicted, but there's something oddly appealing about the idea of a brief response to such an overwhelming influence.

"Vista" (Michael Cisco): Of the stories gathered here, this one has probably the strangest origin. Joe Pulver had gotten his hands on an early copy of Michael Cisco's brilliant *Unlanguage*, which is a novel told as a workbook for the eponymous (un)tongue. Cisco includes a list of questions typical to Unlanguage; Joe's idea was to put together a book of responses to these questions from an assortment of writers. In taking up this challenge, I was inspired in part by an article Cisco had written about contemporary weird writers, in which he had observed that many of the younger weird writers of today, a list on which I found myself, shy away from the immense vistas of time and space of previous figures such as Lovecraft and Ramsey Campbell. As part of my response to the *Unlanguage* challenge, I decided I would include a number of sweeping vistas. The further I went on, though, the more my own preoccupation with narrative began to assert itself over the evocation of immensities of space, time, and the self, and I wound up with a story, after all.

For perhaps the first time, I completed the story well before the deadline. Ironically, Joe's health problems then put the anthology on hold. I wasn't certain what to do with so idiosyncratic a piece until it came time to assemble this collection, where I realized it could have a home as the original story I like to include with each collection. I contacted Cisco to clear it with him; he gave me the thumbs-up, and here we are.

"Slippage" (Laird Barron): In 2017, my good friend, the Honey Badger, was one of the guests of honor at the 37th annual NeCon. The organizers of the convention emailed me asking if I'd contribute an appreciation of Laird. Once again, I thought that the best way I could express my feelings for my old friend were through a story. A few months before this, Laird and I had driven to Providence to visit Phil Gelatt, who had adapted Laird's story, "-30-," to film as *They Remain*. As we were leaving, Phil gifted Laird with one of the props from the film, a curving sculpture of a great ram's horn. We rode back to Kingston with the prop in the back of my SUV. That trip seemed a perfect event on which to hang an impressionistic tribute to my friend. It occurs to me, now, that the celestial imagery at the end of this final story circles back to the celestial imagery at the end of the collection's first story, which was not planned, but pleases me.

ACKNOWLEDGMENTS

While writing the story notes for this collection, I was reminded of the debt I owe my lovely wife, Fiona. Without her—her love, support, and patience—I don't know what I would do. Thank you, Love; here's a fresh bouquet of dark roses.

My sons, Nick and David, are a continuing source of joy to me. Thanks, guys, for your love and support; I look forward eagerly to the art each of you is making.

Laird Barron and Paul Tremblay remain my dearest friends, the brothers I never knew I had. Their fiction inspires me to try to do better in my own work. Nadia Bulkin, Michael Cisco, Glen Hirshberg, Stephen Graham Jones, Sarah Langan, and S.P. Miskowski are pretty cool, too. Oh, and extra points to Stephen for writing a terrific introduction. (How he knew about my eyes is a mystery to me...)

Many thanks to my agent, the indefatigable Ginger Clark, her assistant, Nicole, and the film and foreign rights folks at Curtis Brown. As the story notes indicate, I owe these pieces to invitations from editors, and I'm grateful for the support Ellen Datlow, Aaron French, Nick Gevers, Orrin Grey and Silvia Moreno-Garcia, Eric Guignard, S. T. Joshi, Chris Kelso, Ross Lockhart, Joe Pulver, Darryl Schweitzer, Justin Steele, Simon Strantzas, and Erin Underwood showed these stories by first publishing them. Thanks, too, to Ross Lockhart and Word Horde for publishing this collection.

Finally, thanks to you, whoever you are, for the gift of your time and attention. You make books such as this one possible, and I'm grateful for that. I'll see you down the road.

PUBLICATION HISTORY

"Sweetums" originally appeared in *A Season in Carcosa*, edited by Joseph Pulver, Sr. (Miskatonic River Press 2012).

"Hyphae" originally appeared in *Fungi*, edited by Orrin Grey and Silvia Moreno-Garcia (Innsmouth Free Press 2012).

"Muse" originally appeared in the *2012 Mile Hi Con Program Book*.

"Zombies in Marysville" originally appeared online at jplangan.livejournal.com on October 8th, 2012.

"With Max Barry in the Nearer Precincts" originally appeared in *After Death*, edited by Eric J. Guignard (Dark Moon Books 2013).

"Into the Darkness, Fearlessly" originally appeared in *The Grimscribe's Puppets*, edited by Joseph Pulver, Sr. (Miskatonic River Press 2013).

"Children of the Fang" originally appeared in *Lovecraft's Monsters*, edited by Ellen Datlow (Tachyon Publications 2014).

"Episode Three: On the Great Plains, in the Snow" originally appeared in *Fearful Symmetries*, edited by Ellen Datlow (ChiZine Press 2014).

"Tragōidia" originally appeared in *Songs of the Satyrs*, edited by Aaron French (Angelic Knight Press 2014).

"Ymir" originally appeared in *The Children of Old Leech*, edited by Ross Lockhart and Justin Steele (Word Horde 2014).

"Irezumi" originally appeared in *Postscripts 32/33 Far Voyager*, edited by Nick Gevers (PS Publishing 2015).

"The Horn of the World's Ending" originally appeared in *That Is Not Dead*, edited by Darrell Schweitzer (PS Publishing 2015).

"The Underground Economy" originally appeared in *Aickman's Heirs*, edited by Simon Strantzas (Undertow Publications 2015).

"The Communion of Saints" originally appeared in *Giallo Fantastique*, edited by Ross E. Lockhart (Word Horde 2015).

"Aphanisis" originally appeared in *Slave Stories: Scenes from the Slave State*, edited by Chris Kelso (Omnium Gathering Publishing 2015).

"Gripped" originally appeared online at johnpaullangan.wordpress.com on April 26, 2016.

"Inundation" originally appeared in *Lovecraft eZine Issue 37*, guest-edited by Aaron French (CreateSpace Independent Publishing 2016).

"To See, To Be Seen" originally appeared in *The Madness of Dr. Caligari*, edited by Joseph Pulver, Sr. (Fedogan & Bremer Publishers 2016).

"What You Do Not Bring Forth" originally appeared in *Nightmare's Realm*, edited by S.T. Joshi (Dark Regions Press 2017).

"Vista" is original to this collection.

"Slippage" originally appeared in the *NeCon 37 Program Book*.

ABOUT THE AUTHOR

John Langan is the author of two novels and four collections of stories. His second novel, *The Fisherman*, won the Bram Stoker and This Is Horror awards. He is one of the founders of the Shirley Jackson Awards, for which he served as a juror during their first three years. He reviews horror and dark fantasy for *Locus* magazine. He lives in New York's Mid-Hudson Valley with his wife and younger son, and is slowly disappearing into an office full of books. And more books.

CPSIA information can be obtained
at www.ICGtesting.com
Printed in the USA
LVHW010326140920
665930LV00003B/181

9 781939 905604